STRANGER IN THE MIRROR

A Novel

Tina Wainscott

Stranger in the Mirror
Copyright© 2019 by Tina Wainscott
(originally published as Shades of Heaven)
ISBN: 9781709470974
www.WrittenMusings.com
www.TinaWainscott.com
Cover Design by AustinWalp.com
U.S.A.

This is a fictional work. All characters and events in this publication, other than those clearly in the public domain, are solely the concepts and products of the author's imagination or are used to create a fictitious story and should not be construed as real. Any resemblance to real persons, living or dead, is purely coincidental.

All rights reserved. No part of this book may be used or reproduced, stored in a retrieval system, or transmitted, in any form by any means, without the prior permission in writing, except in the case of brief quotations, reviews, and articles.

For any other permission, please visit
www.WrittenMusings.com/contact for contact links.

DEDICATION

Dedicated to Billy Dean, country music singer, for inspiring me as Jesse came to life.

PROLOGUE

The carat diamond on her wedding set sparkled as Hallie DiBarto ran her fingers across the black velvet surface of the sofa. Not the appropriate distraction to avoid her husband Jamie's eyes, she realized, and shifted her vision to her silk stockings. She deserved the bitterness those blue depths radiated at her. But if she didn't go through with this, who knew what Mick would do to her. Or to Jamie.

"I want a divorce," she said softly, her words absent of emotion. She would have to put more meaning into them to convince him. If only her migraine would subside enough for her to summon her acting skills.

As it turned out, she didn't need to.

"Absolutely," he told her.

That word sent a chilled rush to her bones in spite of the warm California sun pouring through the windows.

Her voice quivered. "Just like that?"

Jamie sighed, running a hand through his blond hair in frustration. It was a gesture she had seen many times, had *caused* many times, if she was honest with herself.

"What do you want me to do, Hallie, drop down on my knees and beg you to stay, to stop seeing that maniac? No, I'm done. Done with you, this marriage, and the farce it's become."

Pain shot through her skull like an iron lance. She'd had horrible headaches all her life, but this sense of fear enveloping her was new, the pain sharper. She dropped her head into her hands, and her thoughts scattered like ants on a trampled hill. Jamie's words were unintelligible, as if spoken through layers of gauze. Her body convulsed under tremors of cold, and she slid onto the tile floor, unable to stop herself from falling.

"Make it stop. Make it stop!" she cried out through a fog of pain.

The touch of Jamie's hand, tight on her arm, seemed to tingle, then disappear. She tried to move her hand, her arm. In sheer horror, she realized she could not. Black dots clouded her vision, and she heard her heartbeat slowing to nothing as the darkness closed in. She heard a whistling sound, like a faraway train. As the pain lessened, she welcomed the dark cloud of death as it took her away. Anything to make the pain go away.

CHAPTER 1

Hallie DiBarto had come back from the brink of death a changed woman. That in itself was not unusual. Coming back in a different body was.

And not just a different body, but a different life. Someone else's life. Marti, they kept calling her. Who was Marti? Hallie felt the surge of panic that enveloped her every time she realized that *she* was Marti. Before she'd had a chance to ask where Jamie was, or tell them they'd made a mistake in her identity, she realized something was terribly wrong.

She glanced down again at short fingers and stubby nails, at the body of a stranger. She took a deep breath, willing away the panic. How had she ended up in Chattaloo, Florida? In this bruised and aching body? She remembered dying as if it were years ago, remembered jagged pieces of a life in California. During her stay in the hospital, those memories melded together to form a past that did not coincide with what she'd found here.

She had never before been to Florida, been a brunette, or been short. She had never seen the tall man who helped her out of the wheelchair after they went through the hospital doors, watching her with a worried expression. The man who claimed to be her husband, Jesse.

Jesse's thick brown hair lifted in the fat breeze as they bid the doctor farewell and walked into humid sunshine. He was twenty-five years old; she'd seen his date of birth on a form. He studied her openly, and for that she could not blame him. After all, he'd been told that his wife had been assaulted, nearly raped, and hadn't spoken to anyone since the attack. She didn't know how the man with those dark green eyes would take her crazy story: that a tall, blue-eyed, blond stranger lived inside his wife's petite body. Hallie had to cling to the only truth she knew: that woman still existed.

For now, playing the part of silent trauma served her best. She looked to the cloud-riddled sky. *God, I know I've made mistakes. Okay, I was awful, hating myself and taking it out on the people closest to me. Looking back, I see how much anger I held inside me. Lord knows—okay, You know I haven't prayed often. But I guess you gave me this second chance—or is it punishment? I'm not sure yet. Give me a sign, God. Tell me what to do.*

It was not God who spoke, but Jesse.

"I don't know what's going on," he said, softer than she thought a man of his size could speak. He held out a hand to her. "But let me help you."

A sign? His hand remained in mid-air, unwavering as she contemplated. Then, very slowly, she reached a thin arm toward him. Somewhere deep inside her, down where she still existed, a small coal of warmth sparked to life as his fingers wrapped solidly around her own.

"The truck's parked over there."

She nodded, maintaining the silence that had seen her through the ordeal of being questioned by Deputy Thomas, the doctor, and Jesse. It bought her time, if nothing else. She stuck her finger in her mouth to nervously chew on a nail, but found with dismay she had none to chew; they were already clipped short. Jesse helped her climb into a dusty red pickup truck.

"Marti, if you want to talk about"—he glanced uneasily at her, then looked ahead—"what happened, I'm here. Dr. Toby said not to press you, and I won't." He reached over and grazed a spot on her cheek where she knew a violet bruise blossomed. "I want to make it better, but I don't know how. Tell me."

Give me back my body and my life! she wanted to scream out but clamped her lips shut instead. Keeping the panic from her eyes was harder than keeping her mouth shut. Could he see the confusion she saw whenever she looked in the mirror?

Jesse sighed as he turned back to the steering wheel and started the engine.

After spending most of her life nestled between the Pacific Ocean and the mountains of Southern California, the small town of Chattaloo seemed flat, boring. She picked at the lace on her jean shorts. A thin scar edged along the top of one knobby knee. How had that gotten there? She loosened the scarf Jesse had bought to hide the bruises around her neck. The sight of them had aroused a queer sense of fear in her, even though she had not suffered the attack herself.

Trying not to look overly interested, she pulled the worn-out wallet from the vinyl purse lying next to her. Not leather or alligator, but *vinyl*. Even when she was dirt poor, she at least owned leather. Maybe from the thrift store, but still. One library card and a driver's license. The brunette gave the camera a forced smile. Next to the photo read, "Marti Jeane May." Marti was twenty-three years old, four years younger than Hallie. Marti had an identity, a life, a husband. Now Hallie had those, and she didn't want them.

"Is anything missing?" Jesse asked, breaking into her thoughts.

A strangled laugh escaped, which she disguised as a sob. Only her life and identity! At his concerned look, she shook her head, keeping her silence.

The orange groves flanking the two-lane highway grew gradually into downtown Chattaloo. Tiny frame houses were snuggled under oak trees, kids raced each other on bicycles, and groups of teenagers gathered around trucks and Jeeps. Normal life, going on as if the strangest thing in the world hadn't just happened to her.

Jesse turned onto a dirt road. Distant barking materialized into one of the ugliest dogs she had ever seen, speckled, stocky, and, worse yet, large. It ran alongside the truck as they passed under a canopy of oak trees to a house in the middle of the hammock. Its tail was wagging, so that meant it wouldn't eat her ... she hoped.

The dog jumped all over Jesse when he got out of the truck, but he didn't seem to mind the grubby paws. He opened the passenger door and held out his hand, but she didn't move. The dog looked hungrily up at her, flinging its tail, heck, it's whole rear end, from side to side.

"What's wrong?" He followed her stare to the dog. "You're not afraid of ol' Bumpus, are you? You've been living with him for two weeks."

She opened her mouth to say something, then caught herself. Yes, she was afraid of ol' Bumpus. But that ugly dog was the least of her problems, she thought, trying to put him in perspective. Bumpus cocked his head, his wrinkled brow looking thoughtful as he waited for some acknowledgment. Jesse whistled, then gestured. Bumpus moved to where he pointed and sat down with a whine.

"He's just concerned about you, is all."

She took Jesse's outstretched hand and climbed down. He led her up the stone walkway to the small gray house washed pink by the dying sunlight. Bumpus followed, his tail wagging wildly as he sniffed around her ankles. She moved away, but he followed, trying to jump up in front of her.

"Bumpus, what's your problem?" Jesse turned to her. "Maybe he knows you're hurting."

Maybe he does, she thought, eyeing him. And maybe he knew she wasn't Marti.

Inside, the house looked larger than it seemed from the exterior. A ceiling fan whirred above, barely moving the wilted leaves of an ivy. Marti obviously hadn't had much of a chance to feminize the place, and a brief glance at Jesse left Hallie little doubt as to where the bride's time had been going. Probably enjoying marital bliss. He was a kicker, as she used to call the good-looking ones. In a country sort of way.

The blue plaid couch looked lumpy, but it reminded her how little sleep she had gotten last night. Jesse was watching her, perhaps thinking she might faint, cry or worse. She tried to put herself in his place.

His wife is almost raped and nearly strangled. When she wakes at the hospital, she is so traumatized, she appears not to recognize either him or the doctor. And she has not spoken a word since. He might reasonably expect her to fling herself out the nearest window.

"You look tired," he said.

Again, he held out that large strong hand of his. She only hesitated a moment before reaching out and letting him lead her someplace where she could hopefully let sleep wrap her in the comfort of familiarity. Would she dream Hallie dreams or Marti dreams? The thought was disturbing.

He led her to a room that held a king-size bed, one long dresser and not much else. She sat on the edge of the bed while he dug through a disorganized drawer and pulled out a long nightgown splattered with blue flowers. She hadn't worn a nightgown like that since she was five years old, but she wasn't in the mood to be picky.

He stood by the door, shifting from one foot to the other.

"Do you want me to sleep on the couch tonight?"

It took an effort for her jumbled mind to put together what he meant. Well, of course, if he and Marti were married, they slept in that king-size bed together. The thought of his body lying next to her was unsettling. A stranger who might hold her in his arms. He wouldn't expect anything more, not after what she'd been through. Still, she wrapped her arms around herself and nodded.

There was a strange light in his eyes, deep and protective. "If you need anything, anything at all, let me know."

But he didn't leave. "I know you're not in a talkative mood, but can I ask you something? Why haven't you asked about the baby? Even Dr. Toby expected you'd be freaked out, worried."

She could only give him a blank expression. Was there a baby in the house?

His shoulders drooped, and he stepped closer. "Don't you even remember that you're pregnant?"

She slid off the edge and fell into a heap on the dark green carpet. "P ... pregnant?" she croaked out, then realized she'd broken her silence.

Jesse pulled her to her feet and helped her back on the bed. His green eyes held a mixture of confusion and surprise. He still gripped her hands in his, kneeling in front of her.

"Thank God you can still talk." He gently touched the bruises that ringed her neck, causing an aching tingle. "Dr. Toby was worried that your vocal cords were damaged." He removed his hand and looked intently at her. "Did you really forget about the baby?"

Her stomach flip-flopped as she tried her best to compose herself. Could he tell her hands were shaking within the confines of his grasp? She took a deep breath, hoping for some divine intervention in the form of a really good reason his revelation had shocked her into talking. Damn, but this complicated matters, even more than they were!

"The past is muddled right now," she whispered in a hoarse, strange voice. Her hand slipped from his and touched her nearly flat stomach. "Are you sure?"

"I'm sure. You're only two months pregnant. Didn't Dr. Toby tell you that the baby was all right?"

She shrugged. "She might have, I don't know. My head was spinning most of the time." She covered her mouth. "Oh gawd, I'm pregnant."

"Maybe I'd better call Dr.—"

"No," she blurted out. "I ... I'll be fine. Really. Just give me some time."

"Time," he repeated with a nod. "I'll give you time. But this not remembering stuff is scary, Marti. Maybe your brain was deprived of oxygen for too long."

"My brain is fine." It was, wasn't it? She did some math problems in her head. Remembered a joke about a priest and a frog in a bar. Her first kiss in third grade, her self-absorbed mother. She shuddered. She'd sure like to forget that woman.

"Are you sure you're okay?"

He'd been watching her ruminations, no doubt. She nodded, then walked into the adjacent bathroom so he wouldn't see the panic in her eyes. Her heart sank when she saw the stranger in the mirror. She had looked at that reflection a hundred times in the last day and a half, but it was always the same. The swelling was going down, making the purple bruises look more pronounced. There was one bruise, or mark really, that was different from the others. It looked like a sideways V with two little marks below it. The skin was broken where a sharp object had dug in.

Oh, how I wish this were all a nightmare, and if I screamed, I would wake up in my bedroom with pounding heart and realize it was all over. Then I'd just be back to worrying about the obsessive, crazy Mick. But it's not a nightmare, is it? She'd pinched herself so many times red marks lined her arm.

She had to remember a life she had not participated in. Or run like hell from this place. But run where? Home to her husband, Jamie, and tell him that she had somehow gotten herself into the body of another woman, a *pregnant* woman?

She thought of Jamie, her real husband back in her real life. It had been two months since then for him, where she had lived in some abyss. She couldn't dare to hope that he missed her. And she couldn't dare blame him if he didn't.

***

Jesse flipped on the television and settled onto the couch. The room was dark except for the bluish glow from the set. Two weeks ago, he had married a woman he hardly knew because she had manipulated him into getting her pregnant.

He couldn't deny the protective instincts this attack on her aroused, but he didn't much like them. Could she have staged the whole thing to elicit sympathy from him? He shook his head. No, Marti wasn't gutsy enough to pull off something like that.

Through the night, he kept moving, twisting, sighing deeply every time he realized he wasn't asleep. It didn't take much to put him on alert, even the sound of quiet footsteps walking past him and the *snick* of the front door. Had he really heard Marti go outside alone, after what she'd been through?

Swinging to an upright position, he eyed the digital clock: 5:49. He located his jeans and slid into them as he walked toward the window. He spotted her silhouette on one of the swings that hung from the large oak tree out front.

She was slumped over, using her toe in the dirt to move slowly back and forth. He watched her for a while, trying to imagine what it would feel like to be overpowered and attacked in such a vicious way. He couldn't. What he really wanted to do was find the son of a bitch and rip him apart. His hand clenched with the need for that, the fury.

He glanced at the clock again: 6:10. He wasn't going to let her wallow in self-doubt or whatever else she was dealing with any longer. He walked out into the damp foggy morning.

"What the devil are you doing out here by yourself?"

She shrugged, staring down at the toe that kept her swing moving. He dropped down in the swing next to hers. They sat in silence as the early morning glow filtered through the oak trees. She looked at him for a few minutes, studying him. He held her gaze, wishing he could read her eyes. There was something different about her, but of course, there would be, given what she'd gone through.

"Do you believe in God?"

He narrowed his eyes. "Sure, I do. Do you?"

"I do now."

"You think it was God who helped you get away from the ... creep who attacked you?"

"It's a lot more complicated than that."

He wasn't following her, but he wanted her to get out her anxieties. "Sometimes near-death experiences bring people closer to God, or give them religion when they didn't have it before."

She laughed, a strange thick sound. "I'm not talking about a near-death experience." She pressed a clenched fist against her lips. "What do you think happens to people when they die?"

"They go to Heaven. Or hell." He shrugged. "But you didn't die."

"Do you think it's really cut and dried like that? I

mean, is your only choice Heaven or hell, or is there another option?"

He crinkled his eyebrows. "Catholics believe in Purgatory, so I guess that's a possibility."

She studied him again, as if weighing whether to go on. Then she took a deep breath. "What if a person dies, but they don't go to Heaven or hell. They wake up and are alive ... but it isn't their body they're in anymore."

"Marti, you're not making sense."

"Humor me. *If* that happened, what would you think had occurred?"

Something had gotten knocked loose in her brain. "It couldn't happen."

She bit her bottom lip, shaking her head. "I knew you wouldn't understand."

"Marti, what you're saying is crazy. It would be incredible, amazing."

"But God can do anything, right?"

"I guess, sure. But things like that don't happen."

"Yes, they do. Something crazy, incredible, and amazing happened to me. I don't know why, but it did." She took a deep breath, muttering what he thought was, "'Cause I sure didn't deserve it." She spoke louder and enunciated each word, as though he were slow. "I am not Marti. My name is Hallie DiBarto, I'm from California, and I'm married to a man named Jamie."

She might as well have been speaking a foreign language as far as he was concerned. It had to be delirium. Encouraged by his silence, she continued.

"Two months ago, something happened inside my brain, and I died. I think God gave me a second chance here, in this body, this life." She gestured vaguely around her.

There was no hint of craziness about her, no odd light in her eyes, but she was sure talking crazy.

"You've been through a lot. It's just the stress—"

She stood and faced him, taking the chains of his swing in her hands. "It is not stress. I know it sounds crazy, it *is* crazy." Her voice dropped to a whisper. "But it's true."

"Wait a minute, let me understand this." He ran his fingers through disheveled hair, trying to make his brain understand. "You're saying that you're someone totally different in Marti's body?" He was trying to put it together, but it sounded so ... she had the right word: crazy. "That you died and came back in Marti's body?"

"That's what I'm saying."

He stood and paced a few feet before turning to face her. She dropped into her swing again and twisted nervously, watching his reaction.

"If you're really some woman from California, then where's Marti?"

She touched the bruises around her neck. "I don't know. She must be dead."

"Nolen Rivers swore you were dead when he found you by the side of the road, but—no, it's crazy. I'm calling Dr. Toby—"

"No!" she said as loud as her hoarse voice could manage. "There's nothing she can do about it. Do you think I'd make something like this up?"

"The problem is you believe it."

She looked so fragile, sitting on the swing with desperation in her eyes. Like a battered doll. But it couldn't be true. Yet, it could explain why she didn't know she was pregnant. And why she didn't look at him with annoying adoration the way she had before the attack. He shook his head.

She stood and crossed her arms over her chest. "Well, it doesn't matter if you believe me or not, I won't be around much longer anyway."

He realized then that the woman before him was like a stranger. Those were not Marti's words. "What do you mean by that? Where are you going?"

"Probably home to California. I can't stay here. I'm married to someone else, for Pete's sake, and I don't even know you."

Those words made him smile. "You didn't know me before the attack either, doll." The endearment had slipped by.

She relaxed her tensed shoulders. "What do you mean?"

He shrugged. "I hardly knew you before we had sex. It just sorta happened, and you said you were on the pill to make your periods lighter. A month later, you were pregnant. That was two weeks ago."

She seemed to absorb that. "She tricked you into getting her pregnant?"

"*You* tricked me into getting you pregnant. At least you finally admitted it."

She let out a sound of exasperation. "I'm not admitting it. As bad as I was, I would never has used a baby to snag a guy."

"Marti, enough of this bizarre conversation. Let's go inside."

After breakfast, Hallie watched him clear away the dishes. "Tell me about Marti. What was she like?"

He bowed his head. "Marti, this conversation is making me crazy."

She gave him a smile that probably looked macabre

19

rather than persuasive. "Humor me. Please?"

He huffed out a breath. "You work at the Bad Boys Diner with my sister, Caty. She brought you home for dinner at my Ma's a few times. You were quiet, nice enough."

"How'd you, um, get with her?" she asked, interested in knowing everything she could about the girl who used to be Jesse's wife. "I mean, if you didn't know her very well."

Exasperation saturated his expression. "One night after dinner, you looked like you really wanted to talk, and Caty had to take off for class. So, we picked up a six-pack of beer and headed down to the river. You were lonely, weren't making many friends. You got another six-pack, and we kept talking. We were both full-out buzzed when you leaned over and kissed me. That's how it started."

Hallie rolled her eyes. "Sounds romantic."

"Drunk sex is never romantic." He stuck his hands in his jean pockets, tilting his head. "Marti, are you doing this because you want out of the marriage? Because if that's what you're after, you don't have to make up all this—"

"How can I prove to you that it's real?" She was mostly asking herself.

"Why don't you call home, this place in California where you supposedly came from? You've got to have family there, someone who knows you."

Home. What was home to her anyway?

She dropped back onto the chair. "Oh, sure, and say, 'Hey, remember me? I died, but now I'm in some other body in some godforsaken town in Florida.'" She felt a frown stretch her mouth. "Besides, there is no home.

My mom's a bitch; I've never even met my father." Her tears, previously pent-up with disbelief, slipped down her cheeks. "I was a lousy wife." She sat up, facing Jesse. "Look at me. I'm a brunette, shorter ... and pregnant! How can I tell them I'm alive? They'll think I'm crazy."

He raised an eyebrow. "No-o-o, why would they think something like that?"

She snapped her fingers. "Where's the phone? Do I even have one?"

"Yes." Jesse got a phone from the living room and handed it to her. He was waiting for her to make the call. Testing her. If she talked to Jamie, told him who she was, would he believe her or disconnect? Would anyone believe her? Another look at Jesse's smug expression prompted her to start pressing buttons.

First, she called the mansion in California. Solomon, the butler, sleepily informed her that Jamie was at Caterina. Jesse leaned against the doorframe, watching her with curiosity. She punched in the number for Caterina.

"'Mornin', Caterina," a sing-song voice answered.

"Jamie DiBarto's office, please."

"Certainly, one moment."

The accent brought back memories that seemed like days ago.

"Good morning, may I help you?"

Hallie's heart stopped mid-jump when she realized it wasn't Jamie's voice. It was Miguel, Jamie's brother. Her hands didn't stop shaking, however.

"May I speak to Jamie DiBarto, please?" she whispered hoarsely.

"He's out on the boat all day at Stingray Point, heading up one of our excursions. Can I—"

"You have excursions to Stingray Point now? Since when?"

"Since his wife started swimming with the stingrays. She had this great idea to make it one of our excursions. If you're adventurous—"

She choked out the words, "H-his *wife?*" Heat engulfed her face. Holy Toledo, Jamie had already remarried! "Is her name Renee?" *That conniving—*

Miguel barked a laugh. "No, it's Hallie. Who *is* this?"

"*Hallie? Seriously?*" The shock of that walloped her in the gut. How was that *possible?* Hallie regained her composure. "Is H-Hallie there? Right now?"

"No, she's out with Jamie. They always do the tour together." The joviality had left his voice. "Who is this?"

You'd never believe me. Even using two hands to hold the phone, it slipped out of her grasp.

Jesse hung up, giving Hallie a curious look. "You all right? That was an odd conversation."

She swallowed the huge lump in her throat. "Odd's not the half of it. It was...Hallie is *there.*"

"So, this Hallie didn't die which means you can't be her, right?"

She shook her head, taking deep breaths to calm herself. "I did die. I was Hallie. So how is she still alive? How can that be?"

"Same crazy logic that you're here when you supposedly died?"

Her eyes widened. "That's it! Someone got a second chance in my body. With my husband." *And what a mess I left!*

"That's not what I meant."

"But you're right." She pulled her hair away from her

face in a tight ponytail, staring at the blanket. "I'm not the only one. See, there are more of us getting second chances in other people's bodies. It's possible. Does Jamie know?" How had he taken the news?

"Marti, you're talking crazy again. So now you're going to tell me that you're jealous and want your husband back, right?"

She shook her head, reality sinking to the bottom of her soul. "It doesn't matter. I asked him for a divorce right before I died."

"Oh. I'm ... sorry?"

She blew out a long breath. "You don't have to be. I'm sorry enough for both of us."

CHAPTER 2

For the rest of the day, Jesse kept busy around the house, staying close in case Marti needed him. What a heavy story she'd laid on him that morning. Wherever she had called that morning, she'd talked to real people. And knew the numbers by heart. Marti didn't know anyone in California or someplace called Caterina. And she'd been devastated by what she'd found out.

His curiosity got the better of him. He found her phone and redialed the last number.

"'Mornin', Caterina. May I help you?" a woman's rich voice sang out.

"Hey, uh, morning back. Where are you located?"

"We be just east of Jamaica, on da Isle of Constantine."

That threw him. That was nowhere near California. "I see. Can I speak to Hallie DiBarto?"

"Yah, though I'm not sure if she's here at da' moment. I can put you through to her extension to leave a message if you like?"

"Sure, but can I ask you a delicate question first? Did Hallie ... die two months ago? Something to do with her brain?"

"Yes, she be in California when her brain explode, but she come back to life. It was a miracle from God."

So she *was* from California.

"This is going to sound a bit crazy, but since the brain thing, is she different? Because when I talked to her the other day, she was like a whole other person."

"Oh, yah, night and day. She and Jamie have da light of love in 'dere eyes, you know? Hold on, and I put you through to her."

Jesse hung up. Hallie DiBarto did exist, she had suffered some kind of brain thing in California, and she did have a husband named Jamie. Jesse sauntered over to the front window. Marti wasn't sitting on the swing with slouched shoulders anymore. She was ... *swinging*?

Every time she reached the bottom of her arc, her shoulders rose up to give her more height. At first, he was glad to see her doing something besides moping. When the swing went so high that it created slack at her upward reach, a pang of fear shot through him that she might jump.

He strode across the leaf-strewn ground toward the swings, camouflaging his worry with a smile. "What'cha doing?"

Marti grinned. "I haven't done this since grade school."

She appeared to be enjoying herself. On the forward swing, she closed her eyes in the sun; on the backward swing, she got lost in the sun-dappled shade beneath the oak tree's upper branches. He liked watching her hair floating behind her, then washing over her shoulders on the way back.

"Who built these swings?" she asked.

"I put them up for my brother Billy's kids. They haven't gotten much use since his ex-wife, Abbie, took the boys and left town two years ago."

"Why did she leave him?"

"He was a jerk. Spent more time with his fishing buddies than her and the boys. Abbie was going nuts, raising two little hellions by herself, so she dropped 'em off here now and then. Eventually she got a job in Georgia. I get a postcard every month."

"You're a good uncle."

"It's easy with the buggers." He ducked around her and sat on the other swing and soon got in sync with her. "You look like you're feeling better. The swelling in your face is starting to go down, too."

"I feel a little more in control. I've kind of accepted that I'm Marti. That I got a second chance. I'd really messed up my old life. Now I've got to figure out what I'm going to do."

What if she leaves? He would be free again. Not that he'd planned on settling down, but he wouldn't have to wait until the baby came before getting back into racing.

"Do you know what Marti's passwords might be for, say, her bank app and whatever else I might need?" Marti had been a social media hermit, it seemed. Which was helpful actually.

He gave her a chagrinned smile. "It's either my birthday — 1030 — or *ilovejesse1030*."

"Oh. She *was* pushy."

Marti didn't love him anymore. Not that she'd actually loved him; he knew the difference. But this Marti had no feelings for him whatsoever, and it was jarring.

Another surprising thought crept in, too. That was

his baby inside her. His. No matter the inconvenience, that he wasn't ready to be a dad, that baby was his responsibility. No, he couldn't let her leave until she had the baby. Then she could do whatever she wanted, and he'd work the rest out somehow.

Hallie sat on the swinging bench out on the front porch that evening. What *was* she going to do? Getting back to her home turf would help, but she had some planning to do before she could hop on a bus to California. Losing her identity was the hardest part.

She looked down at herself, then held up her cell phone and turned on the selfie camera. Oof, not a good idea with her face all misshapen and purple and green. She scrolled through the pictures and got a better idea of what she'd look like. Well, she had an identity; it just wasn't hers. Since she was stuck with this one, the first step was to make it her own. *I am Marti now. I'm Marti. Marti.* She sang it softly, repeated it like a mantra.

So it was Marti who glanced up as Jesse came out the front door and sat down beside her, making the whole thing creak and swing.

He said, "Chuck called today, wondering when he could expect you back to work. I told him when you were good and ready. Don't let him push you."

Work? She'd heard mention of a job before but couldn't remember what it was. Work meant money, and money meant escape. That was the second step to regaining control over her life. She'd already discovered that Marti had only twenty-nine dollars in her savings account and not even one credit card. Now *that* was crazy.

"Where did Marti work?"

"She — you work at Bad Boys Diner."

She wrinkled her nose. "A diner? Don't tell me I was a cook."

"No, you're a waitress."

"Oh, gawd."

"It was good enough for you before."

"Before was a completely different story. I didn't deliver other people's food and clean up their dirty dishes."

"Well, la tee dah. Maybe you should have picked a princess's body to pop into."

"Like I had a choice. I didn't even know what had happened until I was already here." She narrowed her eyes at him, sitting there in the crook of the swing, a smug grin on his face. She didn't let herself notice the muscles beneath his white T-shirt with his arms crossed in front of him. Okay, she'd noticed, but she wouldn't dwell on it. "I think I'm being tested." She gave him a pointed look. Or punished. Which she totally deserved.

"*You're* being tested?" He gave a hearty laugh, making the swing rock. His expression sobered as he shook his head. "If you hadn't been nearly raped, I'd think this was one of those practical joke shows."

"It's not."

"Okay, miss priss from California. What did you do in this other life? CPA? Attorney?"

"I'm not talking about it." She looked away, concentrating on a squirrel hanging upside down to steal from a bird feeder.

"Ah, you might as well tell me. Maybe you'll have some useful skills."

Her nose wrinkled. She met those green eyes of his and realized he was still having fun on her. "I, well, I went to college. And I modeled."

He raised an eyebrow. "You were a model?"

"Don't look so surprised. I was tall, blond, and I had nice boobs."

Jesse regarded her appraisingly. "Nothing wrong with the way you look."

"But this isn't me. I wasn't petite; I was sexy. I even did ads in major magazines. That's how I met my husband."

Jesse leaned back on the swing and propped his feet up on the porch railing. "This Jamie was a model, too?"

She smiled, remembering the first time she'd seen him. A beautiful redhead was brushing his hair, flirting with him. Jamie's eyes were on Hallie, though.

"Yeah. He was rich, good looking, and fun. We got married soon after we met. About a year later, he bought acreage on an island and turned it into a resort."

"If he was so great, why were you a lousy wife?"

Marti's shoulders tensed before she remembered she'd used those exact words earlier. "I didn't appreciate what I had."

"Sounds like you still have that problem."

She glared at him. "What do you mean by that?"

"Well, if I died and got a second chance, I'd be happy in any type of body, just to see the sunshine and smell the fresh air some more. Playing along with you, it seems you should be damned grateful you got a second chance, no matter where you are or what you look like. But all you keep talking about is how rich and gorgeous you used to be."

She couldn't even argue with him on that, though she wanted to.

"Why were you going to leave your good-looking,

rich husband?"

"You listen too much, you know that?" She stood and leaned against a nearby wooden post. "Like I said, I wasn't smart enough to appreciate what I had when I had it." She sighed. "I wasn't all that smart anyway."

"I thought you went to college."

"I went to three classes, all right? That's when I got into modeling. That seemed a lot more fun than sitting in a classroom. And I made good money at it."

He shook his head almost imperceptibly. She looked away. Why did he put her on edge just sitting there beside her? They remained silent for a while. Her past was nothing to be proud of, and she didn't want to share it with anyone, particularly Jesse.

All the times she and Joya went out dancing, flirting ... *oh, be honest with yourself, picking up men, that's what you were doing.* The day after, on the phone with Joya, talking about how great or how lousy their man had been in bed. Only Hallie had lied most of the time, varying the details so Joya wouldn't pick up on the fiction of her bedroom tales.

Like an addict, she craved the validation men's attention gave her. Having sex was something she couldn't do, so she invariably ended up picking a fight and stalking out in a huff before ever getting to the bedroom.

She let out a soft sigh and sank down on the bench again, focusing on the wood grain on the post. "I can see so much more about myself and my life from a distance. As though Hallie DiBarto is someone else. She tested Jamie. Because she didn't feel she deserved him, or anything nice. She pushed him past his limits so he'd leave her, just like she was sure he was going to eventually."

"Why'd you feel that way?"

"It's how I was raised to see myself. Maybe it was how my mother was raised, too, to put all her value in her looks. When I hit my teens, I suspect she felt threatened by a daughter who got the attention she no longer did. I don't think she did it on purpose, but she made me feel insignificant and ugly ... inside."

Wait. Where had that come from? She'd never had the clarity to see the truth, but now it seemed so obvious. She shot to her feet, her hand over her mouth. "I was becoming like her. Oh, God, I was." She pictured the woman desperately clinging to the only attributes she thought she had — her sexuality. The makeup and skin-tight, low cut clothing ... the same kind of clothes Hallie had worn. "You're right. Dying was probably the best thing to ever happen to me."

Now some other woman was having to deal with her mother. But the new Hallie wouldn't have the childhood scars she had borne, scars that still marked her soul. Or the memories of a mother who negated every compliment Hallie got, even as a child.

That woman's obviously blind. Look at your mess of hair. The only reason he said that is 'cause he wants to get in your pants.

Men'll tell you anything ...

Can't believe a word they say ...

After a while, Hallie started doing what her mother did, eschewing compliments or viewing them with jaded eyes.

She dropped back down to the bench again, realizing she was acting jumpy. "You think I'm crazier by the minute, don't you?"

"Well, we started out pretty high on the scale already."

"I suppose we did." She laughed, trying to see this from his point of view. It was a wonder he hadn't trotted her off to a mental hospital. Yet.

He rocked the bench, assessing her as though he were considering just that. He was actually kind of cute, when he wasn't irritating her.

She decided to change the subject. "I can't believe my name is really Marti May. At first I thought it was some cutesy nickname."

"That's your maiden name. We joked about how funny it was, you going from Marti May to Marti May West."

She raised an eyebrow. "And that makes you Jesse West?"

He bowed. "Jesse James West, if you please. My brother's Billy the kid. And my sister's Calamity Jane West, although my parents didn't want to actually name her Calamity, so they shortened it to Caty."

Marti forced a smile. "Well, it sounds as if your parents had a sense of humor, anyway."

"My pa was obsessed with old westerns. You're not going to want me to call you Hallie now, are you? I couldn't get used to that."

"No, it'll make things easier if I adopt Marti's name." Her breath hitched as she realized what he'd said. "Does that mean you believe me?"

He shrugged. "I won't say that I do, and I won't say I don't. But I do know there's something between here and Heaven."

"Why do you say that?"

"It was a weird thing that happened when I was seventeen. Ah, it was nothing."

Marti leaned closer. "No, tell me. Come on, if anyone'll believe you, it's me."

He chuckled. "You are right about that. It was three in the morning when I woke out of a sound sleep. My granny was standing by my bed. She said, 'I'm going now, but don't worry 'bout me none, you hear? God's going to take good care of me. Your pa's up here. He says you're doing really good in the races, but you pulled too early in the fifth lap last Sunday. You need to get a handle on that. He's proud of you, Jesse.'"

He had a wistful smile. "Then I fell back to sleep. It was true; I did cut too early in the fifth lap. The next morning at breakfast, I told Ma about the weird dream. She got the willies, and a minute later, she got the phone call. My granny had passed away in her sleep, they figured around three." He shrugged. "It's my one claim to fame around the campfire."

"Ooh." Marti rubbed the goosebumps on her arms. "That's spooky."

"I thought that was spooky enough. But then here are you claiming to be some dead woman from California turned up in my wife's body."

"Yeah, I guess that does sound pretty spooky when you put it that way."

He sank into silence, a contemplative expression on his face. His eyes always seemed to be smiling, crinkled at the corners. After a few minutes, he turned to her. "Tell me what dying was like."

Marti pulled up her knees and rested her chin on them. She would make him believe, if it was the last thing she did. "I'd had these terrible migraines all through my teenage years. The doctors couldn't find any cause for them. I was talking to Jamie, and my

33

head felt like it was going to explode. I went cold, and my arm went numb. Then everything went black." She stared off into the bare branches of a nearby oak tree, remembering.

"I didn't wake up until I was in the ambulance. Except it wasn't really waking up. I could see everything, and I could hear the machines beeping. The paramedic said the woman on the stretcher was in a coma; he was moving frantically, giving the woman shots, feeling pulses. Jamie was there, holding this woman's hand. I was mad at first, that he was holding her hand and not mine. Then I realized the woman was me.

"I panicked at first, trying to get Jamie's attention by yelling, but no one could hear or see me. I was floating up by the roof of the ambulance."

She shoved her fingers into her hair, pulling it tight as she plunged back into those moments. "When I realized I was dying, I tried desperately to get back into my body. After the initial panic, I felt this rush of peace and joy. It's hard to describe, but it was overwhelming.

"Then suddenly I was in this dark cave, and someone else was with me. I say someone, because I don't know how else to explain it. I think it was God, but not the old guy with the beard. I felt no sense of whether it was a he or a she. It was more like a presence, a brilliant light, warm and pure. It asked me, but not in a real voice, what I had done with my life. Not in a condemning way, just asking. I'd done nothing, but I felt I must do something. I didn't know what, and I still don't. but I had this strong sense that I needed to make my life matter. Through this strange communication, the presence told me I would get a second chance. That's all I remember. Wherever I was, I was there for two months."

Jesse had been listening intently, no trace of that skepticism. "I'm glad to know there's something out there, beyond death. I believe in Heaven and God, but I've never heard of anyone getting a second chance in someone else's body."

"Me either. But I did."

"Why do you think God gave you a second chance? I mean, did you save someone's life or do something really great?"

"No, I never did anything great." She felt the regret, the waste of her precious years on Earth. "Maybe I got another chance so I *could* do something important." Something that didn't involve other people's hearts because she'd sure made a mess of that. She turned to Jesse. "Have you ever been married before?"

"Nope. Didn't plan on it for a while, if ever. I had other things on my mind."

She found herself curious about the man who was suddenly her husband. "Like what?"

His eyes had a spark that reminded her of a little boy recounting some magical experience. "Stock-car racing. A few months ago, an oil company offered me a ride in the ASA." At her blank expression, he added, "They asked if I was interested in driving their car in the American Sports Association. It's to racing what the minor leagues are to baseball. It wasn't final or anything, but that was before you told me you were pregnant. I couldn't see juggling all the hassles of setting up a house and you having a baby while I was on the road every weekend. You can't have that kind of fuzz on your brain while you're driving a hundred and fifty miles an hour."

"So, you gave that up when Marti got pregnant?"

He held up a finger. "I put it on hold. As soon as the baby comes, and life is settled, I'll get another ride. I turned the oil company onto a friend of mine, Mark Ankins, and now he's driving for them."

Marti could see a hint of resentment in tightness of his mouth, held carefully in check. She wondered if he would have ever forgiven Marti for getting pregnant, probably on purpose. Or would he come to love her instead?

She shook her head at that sentimental thought. "Do you still race?"

"Oh, yeah. We've got a track on the edge of town. It's a good starting point, but I didn't think I'd be back to it so soon." He sighed. "For now, I'll just keep beating the local boys."

"You must be pretty good."

"When it comes to racing, I'm damn good. Cars have been part of my life since I was three years old. Making 'em run and making 'em run fast, that's what I live for."

"Is that how you make your living? Racing cars?"

"I wish. For now" — he shot a meaningful look at her stomach — "I have to keep fixing other people's cars at Harry's Garage."

She glanced at his hands, remembering the black grease encrusted in the ridges of her Porsche mechanic's fingers. Jesse's were spotless.

"Looks like we both got derailed," she said, pulling her gaze from his hands.

"Ain't that the truth?"

Her derailment was good. His, not so much.

Long after the sun went down, she and Jesse walked inside. Gravity dragged her down, making her eyelids feel like concrete. She glanced toward the bedroom, then at Jesse. The couch looked too short for his tall frame. She thought of the bed, warm and comfortable.

"Jesse, why don't you let me sleep on the couch? I don't want to kick you out of your bed again."

He stretched his arms upward, his untucked shirt revealing a slice of tan, flat stomach. "That's awfully nice of you, doll, but I thought we'd both sleep in the bedroom. We're adults, and that's one big bed in there. We can work on putting a bed in the second room for you."

She nodded, not sure how at ease she would be sleeping with a strange man. She wasn't tempted, she assured herself. Jesse was good-looking, strong ... but he wasn't her type. Even if her stomach did tingle every time he called her 'doll'?

"Sounds reasonable."

When Jesse walked out of the bedroom, she slipped into the oversized Garth Brooks T-shirt she'd found earlier. She slid over to one side of the bed and wrapped the sheets around her, facing the dresser.

Everything felt so much more real tonight — the scent of his cologne from the bathroom, the feel of the cotton sheets against her skinny legs. Just as real were her memories of the past, of Jamie. He was a good man, and once, he'd been warm and affectionate. In the last year of their marriage, he'd become cold, withdrawn. Had she caused that?

Yes, she probably had. Love had been hers once, and she'd destroyed it. Would it be any different just because she was in a new body?

You still have the same self-destructive soul. Let's not go destroying anyone else's heart.

It could have only been a few hours after Jesse finally drifted off to sleep when he heard her scream. She was sitting straight up in bed, the sheets pulled up to her chin, her eyes wide. Then he heard Bumpus barking and growling as though he had cornered a demon.

"Somebody's out there!" she whispered.

"It's probably a coon, but stay here just in case."

Jesse was up with his rifle in hand by the time he'd reached the bedroom door. Bumpus raced back and forth in front of the large window in the living room, leaping up on the couch to peer out and snarl.

"Why is he doing that?" she asked behind him.

He whirled around. "Geez, you could get yourself shot sneaking up on a guy with a rifle!"

She looked at the gun, then up at him. "What's going on?"

He leaned forward and opened the door. "Check it out, boy." Bumpus raced out the front, making the sound of eight elephants as he charged across the damp leaves.

Jesse watched the dog race into the darkness, his barks fading. What had he seen? His fingers tensed on the rifle as he fought the urge to walk out there and find out for himself. He didn't want to leave Marti alone in the house. A few minutes later, Bumpus trotted back, his mouth stretched in that funny grimace when he missed his quarry. Usually a lizard or mouse.

Jesse turned around to face her. "Didn't I tell you to stay in bed?"

She put her hands on her hips. "I'm not staying in there by myself when that crazy dog of yours is barking up a storm."

"Come on, let's go back to bed."

She stared out the front window for a second before letting him lead her back to the bedroom. "What did he go after?"

"I don't know. Probably a raccoon." He wasn't so sure. Bumpus never made a fuss about the critters he was used to seeing in the dark.

Jesse didn't want to talk anymore, to let on how fired up the thought of confronting Marti's attacker had him. It had been his first thought. His finger was still crooked, ready to pull the trigger. The rage had him shaking. He had been ready to find someone standing in the hall, waiting to finish what he might have already done: kill Marti.

CHAPTER 3

Marti hadn't gotten much sleep after Bumpus's barking fit. Shadows had her jumping, frightened of some faceless man with his fingers reaching for her.

As soon as Jesse stirred, she sat up and stretched. He turned over on his back, and she found herself grinning at his early morning hairdo. Just as she was about to say something, a strange twinge lighted in her stomach. Hunger? Ooh, the thought of food turned the twinge into a full-blown twist.

"Crackers are in the top drawer over there."

Inside she found half a package of Saltines. She grimaced as another wave of nausea washed over her, then jammed one in her mouth.

"Please don't tell me I have morning sickness," she said through a mouthful of crackers.

"Okay, I won't."

As she swallowed the lump of chewed-up cracker, she held her stomach and ran with as much dignity as she could muster to the bathroom.

"You okay in there?" Jesse called from the other side of the door a few minutes later.

"Fine and dandy," she mumbled into the towel she held over her face as she emerged.

He rolled out of bed and scooped up the jeans he'd deposited on the floor the night before. His briefs were bright white, and why she was watching him pull up his pants baffled her. She looked elsewhere, floor, dresser, jeans pockets, whoops, back to the floor.

"You ready for some breakfast?" he asked as he buttoned his fly.

She shot him a dirty look. "You've got to be joking. I don't feel like eating anything for the next two days."

He leaned close and brushed his hand across her stomach. "I don't think he'd like that too much." With a smile, he disappeared into the hallway and was soon clattering pots and pans.

She called out, "What makes you think it's a boy?"

"That's what I want it to be. And I always get what I want," he called from the kitchen.

She shook her head. Exasperating male, she could already tell.

Jesse poured two glasses of orange juice and put them on the table as she moseyed into the kitchen. She dropped down into the chair and took a sip, testing. After a moment, she dared another sip. So far, so good.

At those words, her gaze drifted to Jesse, cracking eggs one-handed into a pan like he knew what he was doing. She found herself studying his broad shoulders and the faint spray of dark hair that sprouted from the indent in his chest. With every movement, his muscles rippled beneath his tan skin. She used to enjoy watching Jamie swim his laps, marveling at how beautiful the male body could be. Now she marveled at Jesse.

"Do you work out?" she asked.

He gave her an odd look. "I don't lift weights at the gym, if that's what you mean." He flipped the eggs, a perfect toss that landed them back in the pan. "What makes you ask that?"

"Just wondered. You've got a nice build."

He shrugged. "Working on engines and pushing cars into the garage are my weights." He lifted hands cleaner than most of the pampered men she'd known had, though they had their share of calluses. "My boss gives me hell for putting more effort into washing my hands than anything else."

Good grief, let's stop talking about his body, Marti. Food's safer. "You're not making grits, are you?"

"Not unless you want 'em. I hate 'em."

"I thought everybody down South liked grits."

"I guess I'm not everybody then." He leaned on the counter separating the kitchen and eating area. "And speaking of cooking, my gourmet abilities end with breakfast."

"Meaning?"

"I could use your help in the kitchen."

"Well, as far as cooking goes, I'm useless. I forget about boiling water and it all burns out. I can't even get Jell-O to set." She gave him a smile. "We could eat out a lot."

Jesse smirked. "In case you haven't noticed the fine selection of restaurants Chattaloo offers, we have one pizza place, two diners, and a deli. I think we'd get tired of that real quick."

"I'm telling you, I cannot cook."

"We'll have to fix that, won't we?"

She did not want to cook, did not even want to talk about it. Time to change the subject again.

"I want to go back to work," she told him as he set down a plate of toast and jam in front of her, waffles and bacon in front of him.

"Are you sure you're ready?"

"As ready as I'll ever be."

He shrugged. "When? Tomorrow?"

"Yeah. I don't suppose you could give me any training tips on the waitressing part?"

"Oh, that's right. A model from California wouldn't know much about that working-class thing."

As if he really believed her. "My experience ends with a six-month stint at a beachside burger joint, and the customers came to me for the food and threw away the plates and utensils when they were done."

"Being on the receiving end of the restaurant process, I wouldn't be much help. Caty would be your best bet. I could stick to the story I already told them, which is you don't remember much since the assault. I was going to ask if you wanted to have dinner over at Ma's tonight anyway. She and Caty have been asking to see you."

"Might as well get it over with." As if meeting his family wouldn't be hard enough. Now she was facing her first speaking part as Marti May West.

As they drove over to Jesse's mother's that evening, the tension coiled tighter inside Marti. Money, escape. She kept telling herself that she had to go through this process before she could get back to California.

"Does your mother like Marti? She probably hated the woman who trapped her son into marrying her."

He shot her an odd look, then shook his head and concentrated on his driving again. "I don't know. She's definitely not used to the idea of me being married and expecting a kid. Heck, neither am I." His fingers tightened on the steering wheel. "Besides, couldn't prove you got pregnant on purpose."

"Now we'll never know." She turned down the radio. "Can't we listen to something other than country music?"

He turned the volume up again, giving her a stern look. "Never, ever, turn down Kenny Chesney in my truck."

"Well, excuse me. I didn't know the rules."

He gave her a sharp nod. "Now you do."

How was she supposed to discern between Kenny Chesney and all the other crooning country singers? Katy Perry, Adele, Lady Gaga, all artists she could intelligently discuss. She wondered if her fidgeting hands in her lap betrayed her nervousness.

He took the curve rapidly, his hands firmly on the wheel. Strong hands and long fingers. Hardly nothing sexier than strong hands. Except for a guy wearing jeans and nothing else, like he had while making breakfast. She averted her attention to the dirt roads that spread out like fingers to the right. On the left was a golf course.

"I wouldn't expect to see a golf course around here," she said.

"Didn't think country hicks liked golf, did you?"

She shot him a look. "I didn't mean it like that." Well, she had, sort of, but not on purpose.

"Mark, Alan, and I play golf there in the summer, when the snowbirds go back up north."

"You play golf?" She tried to picture Jesse teeing up in yellow pants and a green-checkered shirt and almost laughed.

His tone dropped to a low, Southern drawl. "Yep,

'magine that, a redneck like me playin' that there golfin' game. 'Course, for a while, we thought hittin' a birdie was aimin' fer a blue jay. Poor birds didn't know what hit 'em. H'yuck, h'yuck."

She nudged his arm, trying to keep the smile from her lips. "Yeah, yeah." She still couldn't see him playing golf. Nor could she figure out why her fingers tingled where they'd touched his bare arm.

So not her type.

When he stopped at the one traffic light on the main road, he turned to her. "I've heard of strokes damaging the memory areas of the brain. Do you think that being strangled deprived those parts of your brain of oxygen too long? I'm serious, Marti," he added at her impatient expression.

"Have you ever heard of those people remembering pasts that were not their own? I know you're looking for some logical explanation; I was looking too, that whole time I was in the hospital. But I remember my other life, right up until the time my brain felt like it exploded."

He bit his lower lip, tapping a beat on the top of the steering wheel before shaking his head. "I know a way to tell if you're Marti or not. It's an instinctual kind of thing. If you're game."

"What is it?"

"Uh uh, can't tell you. You'll have to go along with it. That is, if you want me to believe your story."

She narrowed her eyes at him. What could it be? Probably taking her to the place Marti had been attacked to see if she had any reaction.

"Fine, do what you have to."

As she prepared for him to continue driving, he

leaned forward and kissed her, pressing her right against the window. His mouth engulfed hers, his tongue teasing its way inside her mouth. For a moment she felt dizzy, and her stomach did flip-flops. As her mind told her hands to push him away, her mouth responded to him in exactly that instinctual way. A warmth spread where his hand rested on her thigh. Why was he kissing her like this? her mind asked. Who cares? her body answered, drowning in the sensations.

In a second Jesse leaned against his door with a resounding thud.

She didn't wait to catch her breath. "W-why'd you do that?"

He rubbed his fingers across his parted lips, still moist from their kiss. "The test."

She straightened, stiffening her shoulders. "*That* was your test to see if I'm really Marti?"

"I wanted to compare how you kiss now with how you used to kiss."

"So, did I pass?"

He ran his fingers over his lips again. "Inconclusive. It was different, but I have to take the element of surprise into account."

"Don't tell me you have to kiss me again." She hoped he didn't pick up that ridiculous tremor in her voice.

His gaze dropped to her mouth, tightening her stomach. "No, I'd better not. I mean, I don't think it would do much good."

Marti held onto her seat as the truck lurched through the green light. How dare he tell her that kissing her again wouldn't do much good! How dare he kiss her like that in the first place. Who cared if he believed her or not? She crossed her arms over her chest and ignored him ... and the tingling of her mouth.

She studied the scenery as though her life depended on it. The tension inside the cab eased. She studied the houses, most of them small and quaint. One had a swamp buggy named "Troublemaker" out front.

Marti saw the Bad Boys Diner before Jesse pointed it out. It was an old building, and the lines of brick showed through the once-white paint. On the sign that stood high next to the road was a pudgy boy in a cowboy hat with a devilish grin. In a small corral, five mannequins clad in vests and ten-gallon hats were in the middle of an old-fashioned shootout. One had a missing arm, but she doubted it had been shot off by the cowboy holding the six-shooter across from him. She wouldn't have thought about eating at a place like that, much less working there.

"It's been around for as long as I can remember, although Chuck's only owned it for a couple of years now since he moved into town. He bought those cowboys from some barbeque place up north, and he's proud of 'em. When people talk about Bad Boy's waterfront dining, that's because the parking lot gets flooded after a good rain."

Downtown quickly dwindled after the Chattaloo River Hotel. Stands of pine and oak trees with the occasional farm dominated the landscape for a few miles. Jesse pulled onto a dirt road into a quiet area that was less developed than the one in front of his house. Oaks and maples overshadowed the driveway that led to a small, two-story house.

"This is where I grew up," Jesse said as he got out of the truck. As he looked around, he seemed to inhale a hundred childhood memories. From the smile on his face, she could only guess they were happy ones. She envied him that, for she could hardly bring herself to think about her childhood at all.

Two beagles jumped off the front porch and lazily made their way to the truck, barking with tails wagging. Though they were smaller and not ugly like Bumpus, she still moved closer to Jesse.

He crouched down to greet them. "Hey, fellows. Come out to greet your ole' buddy?" Turning to Marti, he said, "This one's Trick, and the smaller one's Treat. Aw, don't look at 'em like that. They're so old, they'd have to take a nap before even chomping at a fly. They used to jump all over me when I'd come home. Now they just bark and wag their tails."

She sensed melancholy in his voice but couldn't imagine why he'd want them jumping on him. Must be something a pet owner would understand.

She followed Jesse into the cozy home, feeling like an outsider. The wooden floors creaked beneath the braided rug inside the front door. A game show blared from the television.

"Hey, Ma," he called out.

"In the kitchen, hon."

He nodded for her to follow. The tall, curvy woman at the sink had to be Helen West. He walked over to her, wrapping his powerful arms around her and resting his chin on her shoulder. Why did that make her heart swell when it didn't even involve her? She bit her lip and stifled a smile.

After a second, his mother patted his arms and pulled out of his embrace to walk toward Marti. Helen was attractive in a way that Hallie's mom hadn't been, her designer jeans and lacy, long-sleeved cotton blouse her only adornments. She needed nothing else, with soft blond hair and round brown eyes.

She took Marti's hands in hers. "I'm so glad you're here, darling. Jesse said you needed some time alone, but it was everything I could do to keep myself from rushing over to check on you."

Marti vaguely remembered seeing her at the hospital when she was fitfully dozing. "I — I appreciate your concern. I'm okay now."

Helen placed a pink, manicured thumb to Marti's cheek. "The bruises are getting better. You poor baby. It's scary, something like this happening here. I've always felt so safe. Are you all right, really?"

Marti nodded, a lie. Helen had her soft, warm hands around Marti's. She wasn't at all what Marti had envisioned when they'd pulled up: a haggard woman with gray hair tied up in a bun and hands shriveled from cleaning.

"Stop it, Billy!" a voice ordered from outside the door.

When it opened, two calm people stepped through. Based on Jesse's descriptions, the man was probably his brother, Billy, and the girl had to be his sister, Caty. She was Marti's height, with a mane of golden curls. Her eyes were seafoam green, bright, and fringed with long golden lashes. She came right over and hugged her hard. Marti hesitantly put her arms around her slender frame.

After a moment, Caty stepped back. "I was so worried about you! Then Jesse wouldn't let us come over" — she shot him a dirty look —"and we thought the worst. But you look okay, considering. It must have been awful. No, don't tell me about it. Unless you want to." Caty's energy spilled over, filling the room.

"There's nothing to say, really. I don't remember a thing."

Caty's hair washed over her shoulders, and coming from it was a skinny, white rope that hung down amongst the curls. Marti was considering asking what it was when the "rope" suddenly moved up to form a mustache above Caty's lips.

Caty laughed, pulling the tail from her upper lip. "Jed, how rude."

Marti was sure her eyes were wide enough to allow aircraft landings. The "rope" disappeared, and from inside Caty's hair appeared a little face with quivering whiskers.

Marti pointed. "Th — there's something in your hair!"

Puzzlement tinged Caty's smile. She reached in and disentangled a furry black and white creature from her hair. "Don't you remember Jed?"

Marti glanced at Jesse, chastising him for not warning her about this — this *thing* she was supposed to remember. He was merely amused, and she turned back to Caty, who was holding it out, its four tiny feet and tail extended in all directions. Marti moved away, hoping Caty wasn't handing it to her.

"She doesn't remember some of her past," Jesse said.

Caty looked confused. "How could you forget this cute guy?" She nuzzled the creature.

"What is it?" Marti asked, trying to keep the disgust from her face.

"Jed's a rat. Not like the ones that live out in the fields or in the attic. He comes from a pet store."

It was then that Marti noticed Billy still standing by

the door. He wasn't as tall as Jesse, and in fact didn't look much like him. He had beady brown eyes, a thin mustache, and long wavy hair that was receding in front.

She turned back to Caty and tried to force a smile. A rat. For a pet. God, get her back to California. Sure, they had pet iguanas out there, but not rats.

Helen stepped in, her hands clasped together. "Put Jed away, dear. It's time to eat."

"Dean's coming over tonight," Caty announced after dinner. She glanced at Marti. "Hope that's okay."

Jesse leaned back in his chair. "Why?"

Billy wiggled his arched eyebrows. "They're gonna neck on the front porch."

"Billy, shut up! He's helping me study for my test next week, as if it was any business of yours."

"What kind of classes are you taking?" Marti asked.

"Don't you remember?" Caty smiled with pride. "I'm getting my Associates degree. Someday I'm going to be a veterinarian."

Marti hoped to have that same look in her eyes when she figured out what she wanted to do.

The sound of the beagles barking outside made Caty jump up and head over to the door. A tall young man with a medium build walked in. He had dark, curly hair and eyes that looked warm and mischievous at once. Dean, Marti surmised.

"Howdy, Caty," he said with a drawl more pronounced than the Wests's. He nodded toward Billy, Jesse, and Helen, but his expression changed when he saw Marti.

He loped over and gave her a hug. "I heard somebody hurt you."

"Uh ... yeah." His forwardness threw her off, but the sincerity in his brown eyes made her feel more comfortable.

Caty strode up next to Dean. "You remember Dean, don't you?" To Dean she said, "She lost some of her memory."

Marti shook her head. "No, I don't. Nice to see you again, though."

"I heard you was attacked," Dean said. "I had an aunt that was attacked, too."

"I'm sorry to hear that," Marti said.

"It was by a herd of bees, though."

Marti's gaze dropped to the floor for a minute to gain composure. "That's ... terrible."

"Yeah, it was. She had stings all over her body, all puffed up and red." Dean demonstrated by puffing out his cheeks.

Jesse interrupted him. "Dean, that's a really interesting story, but I've got to" — he looked around the table, then grabbed a handful of lettuce from the salad bowl — "feed Jed."

Dean scratched his chin. "Is that a herd of bees or a pack?"

Jesse shook his head as he escaped to the living room to drop the lettuce into Jed's cage. His mother's computer, on a desk in the corner, caught his eye. He didn't have much use for surfing the Internet, wasting time sitting on his butt, but now it drew him.

He knew enough to find a search site and type in the names Marti had given him. He tried a couple different spellings before he got what looked to be viable hits.

The most interesting headline was on YouTube, a clip from a show called, "Americans in Trouble

Abroad." He clicked on the link, and the screen popped up.

A thin man in a dress shirt and tie looked incongruent amidst tropical foliage and people in bathing suits lounging around a sparkling pool. "On our story today, Californians Jamie and Hallie DiBarto ran into some serious trouble in paradise last weekend. I'm here on the Isle of Constantine, just east of Jamaica. Fellow Californian Mick Gentry flew to Caterina, the resort the DiBartos own, stalked the couple for several days, then broke in and viciously ripped Mrs. DiBarto from her bed while she slept.

"Gentry slammed Mr. DiBarto over the head with a metal pipe before forcing his wife along this beach and over those rocks where he had a sailboat anchored offshore." The camera followed the route along the beach and over a hill of sharp-edged boulders.

"Barely holding onto consciousness, Mr. DiBarto dragged himself to the raft Gentry was struggling with as Mrs. DiBarto fought him. He managed to knock Gentry unconscious and drag him to shore. The DiBartos, still shaken about the ordeal, agreed to grant us a short interview."

A beautiful blonde sat in one of the swinging chairs that surrounded an outdoor bar. She could definitely be a model, Jesse thought, feeling a strange tightness in his chest. Beside her sat a handsome blond man, everything Jesse pictured when Marti described Jamie.

"Did you know the man who tried to kidnap you, Mrs. DiBarto?"

"Yes. He was ... an old lover from a lifetime ago. He was very jealous when I broke things off. I wanted to leave Mick and that whole life behind me." Hallie looked at her husband with determination, then at the camera. "It's a good warning: always be careful who you let into your life."

"And what about Mick Gentry, you might ask," the reporter said, now standing outside a stucco building amidst a curious crowd of colorfully dressed black people. The camera focused on a hand-painted tin sign swinging in the breeze that read *JAIL*.

"Mick Gentry spent time in this primitive, four-foot-by-four-foot jail cell." As the reporter stepped inside, a thin man in uniform demonstrated incarceration, waving his hands through the bars. "The most serious crime in this village of three hundred is the occasional rum-soaker, as they call the drunks here. Strangely enough, Gentry was released without any further punishment other than being banned from the island forever."

"Dat loony be gone, mon," the man said, coming out to stand beside the reporter, his white teeth in stark contrast to his jet-black skin.

"This is Bailey, the local jail keep. What can you tell us about him?"

"Dey make some deal and send him from our island." He smiled. "But we kept da' sailboat."

"We just wanted him off the island," Hallie said in a clip from the earlier interview. "There's no reason for him to come back."

"And so," the reporter finished, "the DiBartos continue rebuilding their lives, and only time will tell if old wounds heal. Gentry couldn't be reached for comment."

"Wow, the power of obsession," a woman at a round desk said, closing the story. "Check out our other stories on our channel, where two sisters fight pirates..."

Jesse tuned out the rest, stunned. Jamie, Hallie, the island resort. All that craziness Marti had told him, true. It was hard to imagine that the woman in Marti's body had looked like the Hallie on television. No wonder she wanted her old body back. He closed his mouth for the first time since clicking on the link and marched into the kitchen.

"There you are," Helen said. "Would you please start on those dish—"

He took Dean's arm with one hand, and Billy's with the other. "Why don't you two fellows take a walk down by the river? I have something to talk to the girls about, and it's personal."

Billy laughed. "What, you gonna talk about periods or something?"

Jesse didn't answer, just steered the two toward the swinging door. Dean looked apprehensively toward the river, then at Billy.

"He won't throw you in again." Jesse gave his brother a meaningful squeeze on the shoulder. "Will you, Billy?"

"'Course not." He put an arm around Dean, then looked at Jesse. "You girls have a nice talk now."

Jesse turned to find all three women watching him, waiting. "Okay, sit down. I've got something to tell you."

They sat down at the table, still cluttered with serving dishes and crumbs.

"Ma, Caty." Jesse turned to Marti. "I'd like you to meet Hallie DiBarto."

Marti's mouth dropped open. "Jesse."

He put his hand on her arm. "I want to tell them the truth."

And he did, from her inability to recognize him at the hospital, to their conversation on the swings, and when he'd called Caterina. Marti only nodded to this fact or that, probably because he'd taken over. After he'd finished, both Caty and Helen sat back in their chairs with confused expressions on their faces.

"Is this some kind of joke?" Helen asked.

"Would I joke about something like this?"

Helen's and Caty's expressions were mixed now as they looked at her.

"It's true," Marti added.

"The reason I told you is that Marti's going to need help in the next few months, and it'll be easier if you know what's going on. But I don't want anyone else to know, even Billy. No telling who he'll blab to. Caty, I need you to give Marti a quick waitressing lesson tomorrow when she goes back to work. Maybe you can get there early and show her the ropes. Caty?"

Caty snapped out of the stare she was giving Marti. "She's really someone different? It's not just a memory lapse?"

Marti fiddled with a napkin. "I'm really someone else. This is all new to me, the small town, being a waitress." She tried not to wrinkle her nose. "I feel like I'm on a different planet, all alone."

Helen reached over and patted her hand. "You're not alone." She kept looking at Jesse, maybe to make sure it wasn't a joke. Or insanity. "We're just glad you're here, and that both you and the baby are all right."

It was acceptance, tentative, but acceptance all the same. He wasn't sure they completely believed them, and he couldn't blame them. The oddest part, though, was the soft, teary look on Marti's face as she looked at his mom's hand on hers.

Enclosed in the privacy of the truck cab, Marti turned to Jesse. "What possessed you to tell them the truth? And why didn't you warn me?"

Telling her about the news story would only make her worry about that other life, and possibly send her scurrying off to the Isle of Constantine. He didn't want that, not just yet. He settled on the half-truth.

"I was watching you all evening, at dinner and around my family, and I realized that you really aren't Marti. I believe you."

"Was it the kiss?" she asked, her throaty voice sounding odd.

The kiss. He knew what he was trying to prove until his mouth touched hers, and then he forgot how the old Marti even kissed. The way this Marti responded was far different than the way she used to, which lacked anything that would make his heart go as fast as his racecar.

"Forget that," he said, wishing he could. "It was everything."

Her expression grew softer. "You really do believe me?"

"Yes. And once I believed you, the truth burst right out. Now Billy and Dean I wouldn't trust with this crazy secret, but I trust Ma and Caty." Jesse started the truck but turned to her before putting it in gear. "You know, that was almost as hard as the first time, when I told them you were pregnant and we were getting married. I wasn't sure if Ma would throw me outta the house or have the men in the white coats haul me away."

She rolled her eyes. "Too much time spent here, and

the men in the white coats will be hauling *me* away."

While Jesse took a shower, Marti wandered around the living room and scanned the photos on one wall. She stopped at a picture of Jesse standing next to a black Nova with a yellow thirteen on the side. He held up a trophy, his white smile triumphant. A black and white picture showed the front of a car, parked in a garage with the hood up. Sticking out of the roomy engine compartment was an older man with Billy's beady eyes and same silly grin.

"That's my dad," Jesse's voice said from behind her.

"Geez!" She spun to face him, her hand on her heart. "And you yelled at me for sneaking up on you the other night."

He shrugged, looking boyish with his towel-ruffled hair. "You're not carrying a rifle."

She narrowed her eyes at him. "I wish I was." Turning back to the engine picture, she said, "What happened to him? You said something about your grandmother seeing him in Heaven."

"It was a freak accident during the grand finale of the stock-car season—demolition derby. A guy from Arcadia hit Dad's car, and his gas tank exploded. There was nothing they could do for him." His mouth tightened as he stared at his father's picture.

"And yet you still race?"

"I couldn't not race. It's my life. I made my car look like his, so in a way, he's there racing with me."

She looked at him; saw the burning determination in his eyes. "You must have been mad at Marti for getting pregnant."

He shrugged, then leaped over the side of the couch to land in a sitting position. She walked around front, seeing nothing in his closed expression.

"Jesse, it's normal to feel anger at something that takes your dream away."

"That's the way life is," he said, each word a block of ice.

She sat down next to him, wishing he would open up. Since the couch sagged in the middle, she found herself leaning against his bare arm. Why the feel of his skin bothered her, she didn't know, and the scent of clean male and deodorant scrambled her thoughts. She made a casual movement out of scooting away from him.

When he stretched, he seemed like a lion, strong and intense. His arms reached up over his head, leaving her to stare at the depth of his chest, the rib bones that dropped off to a flat stomach. Her gaze traveled lower where blue jeans encased his hips; the contours of his thigh muscles showed even through the thick denim.

She forced her thoughts and gaze toward the television. *None of those thoughts for you. Haven't you learned that you do nothing but destroy anyone who loves you? Not that Jesse would ever love you. And what are you going to do, my precocious libido? Lure me into lust with him so it's harder to leave? No way, I'm smarter than that now. Yessiree, much smarter.* Strangely, the biggest urge she had at the moment was to crawl into his arms and ask him to hold her tight. Just hold her.

"Who's Mick Gentry?"

She hoped he didn't hear her sharp intake of breath at the unexpected question. "Where did you hear his name?" She wanted to buy a few seconds to think his question through.

He shrugged, pretending a casualness she knew wasn't wholly there. "You said the name in your sleep."

"Oh. What else did I say?"

"Nothing I could understand, only his name. So, who is he?"

She pulled a throw pillow onto her lap, fiddling with the edge of braided rope. "He was ... a mistake. A man I met in California, the wrong kind of friend to make."

"Was that all he was, a friend?"

Marti looked Jesse in the eye, straightening her shoulders. "He was the best part of dying. And so you don't think all I ever did was blow my life on mistakes, I'll leave it at that."

He shrugged again but kept studying her in that thoughtful way of his. "Do you ever think about him?"

What was he talking about? "Not at all. I don't know what the woman who took my place is like, but she's obviously smart enough to figure out who the right man in her life is. Mick's probably in France sulking. Why do you ask?"

"Just wondering."

CHAPTER 4

It was still dark when Jesse led Marti out to the truck the next morning. He told her he was driving her to work until he'd had a look at her car. It only needed gas, but he wanted to have some control over her movements for a while. Bumpus followed them out, wagging his tail. Jesse glanced at Marti's uncomfortable expression, then back at Bumpus, who was used to accompanying Jesse to work at the garage.

"Another time, boy."

It was odd, but she didn't look right in the dress with the Bad Boy on the apron anymore. He knew she hated it, a California model in a polyester waitress uniform, but he'd reminded her how lucky she was to even wear the thing.

He reached over and touched her chin, lifting it to face him. "Cheer up, doll."

Something warm lit in her brown eyes, and she smiled. He didn't know why he was calling her that now. The word seemed to slip out of his mouth. He removed his hand, suddenly feeling too intimate with her.

She tugged down the skirt, which came to mid-thigh.

"I'll be okay. Once I get used to it."

"You'll be fine."

A few minutes later, he pulled into the dusty parking lot of Bad Boys Diner. As promised, Caty had shown up early to show Marti the ropes.

"Take good care of her," he said to Caty. "She's feeling queasy this morning." He gestured to his stomach and made a rolling motion with his hand.

"I won't work her too hard."

Marti nodded. "I'll do the best I can. As soon as I learn what I need to do." She looked around, scanning the long countertop, the tables that seemed to number in the hundreds.

Jesse touched her arm. "Good luck. See you at lunch."

He walked away, feeling almost like a father might after taking his daughter to her first day of school. Ah, she'd be fine.

With Caty's good grace, and a smaller than usual section, Marti made it through the breakfast crowd. By ten, only a few people lingered, reading the paper and drinking coffee, only requiring the occasional fill-up.

Caty looked at the clock, her curly ponytail swinging over her shoulder. "The owner should be here any minute. Chuck usually gets here after the breakfast crowd."

As if on cue, a short, skinny man in his thirties nearly crashed through the door. He surveyed the few people in the diner and headed right to Caty.

"How was the breakfast crowd? Better than this, I hope."

"Chuck, you ask me that every morning. Why don't you come in earlier so you can see for yourself?"

"Yeah, yeah." Chuck stopped when he looked at

Marti. "Gawd, you look awful. Do you want to scare the customers away with those bruises?"

With that, he walked back into the kitchen.

Marti frowned.

Caty waved him off. "Sensitivity isn't his strong point. Before the hour is up, he'll be asking you, in his gruff way, how you're feeling."

Marti glanced at Chuck, now wearing a white baseball cap and moving purposefully around the kitchen as he talked to the cook. "I hope he doesn't say anything to me at all."

Fifty-two minutes later, Chuck walked over to where Marti was wiping down the counter. "D'ya know who did it?"

She shook her head, wishing he would go away. "No, I don't remember anything about it."

"Probably better."

"Yeah, probably."

He looked at her for several seconds past the comfortable range. "Do you think you'll ever remember?"

"I don't think so."

He shrugged. "Sick son of a bitch outta pay for what he did. Well, I'm glad you're back. That table over there needs clearing." With that, he walked back to the kitchen.

When she relayed the strange conversation, Caty didn't think it sounded out of the ordinary for Chuck. Marti wondered. He did seem concerned about her remembering her attacker. Would it be his face Marti would remember? He was watching her again when she glanced toward the kitchen.

A while later, a woman walked in and sat down at the counter. She had a barrel-body, with short, almost-white blond hair, and a phony smile. Marti glanced at Caty, who sidled over.

"That's Donna Hislope. She's a gossip and general bitch. A while back, she had a thing for Jesse, and he pretty much gave her the brush off. Definitely not his type. Anyway, that's the history. Go see what kind of small prey she wants."

"Goody." Marti sauntered over. "So, Donna, what can I get for you?"

She picked up the menu and looked it over. "Um, diet soda — no, make that a chocolate shake. That's all. Gotta watch my figure."

"Uh, yeah." Marti set down the shake a few minutes later. "Here you go." As she was about to make an escape, Donna spoke to her.

"You look pretty good. I mean, considering what happened to you."

Marti turned around, forcing a smile. "Why, thank you."

"It must have been awful."

"I don't remember anything about it."

Donna's mouth twitched. "I bet they don't catch him. He was probably just passing through. Do you think he was a drifter? Probably, huh?"

Why was it her place to assure the woman? Wasn't it supposed to be the other way around? "It could be anyone. Even someone you see every day."

Marti walked back to the other side of the counter, pretending to clean a dirty spot. That was the scary truth: it could be someone in town. She was fairly certain it wasn't Jesse, not with the tenderness he'd shown. It probably wasn't Dean; he looked too innocent. Only two people stood out as strange so far —

Chuck and Billy.

As the clock ticked toward eleven, people trickled in for lunch. Caty made a point to clean something nearby and whisper each new person's identity, as she had that morning. Three young men walked in, shoving one another jovially as they dropped down into a booth in Marti's section.

Caty scooted over to Marti. "The plumpish redhead wearing overalls littered with pieces of dried grass? That's Josh. He's probably been mowing lawns. Skip is the skinny blond with the blue and white hanky around his neck."

"Looks like a German Shepherd I saw once. Who's the other guy?" He was dark-haired, tall, and nicely built, wearing dress pants and a crisp white shirt.

"That's Paul Paton, the sheriff's son. This week he's selling insurance. Be careful around him. He and Jesse are like two fighting tomcats; you never know what Paul will do just to piss him off. In fact, don't get friendly with any of them. They're all jerks."

Marti smoothed her skirt, pulling out her pad and pen. "Why do Jesse and Paul fight?"

"There's bad blood between them, starting in grade school. Some backstabbing, fights over girls, that sort of thing."

Marti walked over with pad in hand. "What can I get you to drink?"

Paul's green eyes were as penetrating as Jesse's could be. "How are you doing, Marti? I heard about" — he glanced uneasily at the two men opposite him — "what happened."

"I'm fine, thanks. Drinks?"

They spoke on top of each other, giving her their

meal choices as well. As she turned to leave, Paul's pendant, an eagle with wings spread in flight, caught her eye. Something about it bothered her, or intrigued her. Without thinking, she leaned down and took it in her fingers.

"Wow, that's some pendant," she said, avoiding Paul's eyes now that she realized how close she was to him.

"Haven't you noticed it before? My dad gave it to me last year."

Her fingers traced the edges of the wings before she abruptly let go and straightened. "Guess I never really saw it." She retreated to clip their order on the chrome carousel. No computer system in this joint.

Caty reached up to clip her own order. In a low voice, she said, "You'd better watch that flirting. You're a married woman, and pregnant no less."

Marti caught the glint of jest in Caty's eyes, but the warning came through all the same. She started filling a glass with Coke. "I wasn't flirting. Have you seen that pendant of Paul's? It's beautiful."

"Oh, yeah, he's shown it off plenty of times. It's the only thing his father's ever given him."

Marti returned with the drinks, careful now to avoid Paul's eyes. She didn't want to give him the wrong idea. "Here you go. Your order should be up in a few minutes."

"You sound kinda sexy, with your voice low and husky like that," Josh said.

She looked him in the eye. "It's from being strangled." She turned her back on the three and strutted to the counter, her gait stiff with outrage. Out of the corner of her eye, she watched them.

Josh leaned in. "She doesn't look all that upset considering what happened to her. Maybe she liked it."

It was all she could do not to stalk back over and punch him. *Stay cool. Listen.*

Skip said, "Maybe she did, but she says she don't remember anything."

Josh snorted. "How can a woman forget something like that? No, I think she liked it so much, she doesn't want to put the guy away." He licked his lips. "Maybe she wants him to come back, and —"

"Shut up," Paul whispered vehemently, getting up and walking away from the table.

After taking another order, Marti turned to find Paul sitting at the counter behind her.

"Maybe I shouldn't have asked you in front of them, but I really wanted to know how you were. You seem so, well, different."

She glanced away for a second. "Yeah, something like that can change a person." Now that was an understatement.

"We've all heard — I've heard things, but you know how facts can get blown out of proportion."

She pressed her hands flat on the counter, facing him. "I'm surprised your father didn't tell you all the gory details." Maybe he'd share some.

A bitter laugh escaped Paul's lips. "He doesn't tell me anything about his job since I told him I didn't want to become a cop. I wouldn't even ask him."

Chuck slammed the bell down twice to indicate her order was up. She loaded the food onto a tray, glad to see Paul rejoining his friends. With only a few items on her tray at a time, Paul's table took two trips. She was glad when they were taken care of.

As though he'd materialized like a ghost, she turned

to find Jesse sitting at the counter, wearing a surly expression directed at Paul. Despite that, she was glad to see a familiar face.

"Hi, stranger," she said in her whispery voice.

He tore his gaze from Paul and his buddies. "What did he want?"

"Who?"

"Paul. I saw him talking to you."

She was surprised to see so much malice in the usually easy-going green of his eyes. "Fine, and how's your day going, dear?"

He caught himself, then smiled briefly. "Sorry. How's it going?"

"I hate it. I already smell like a French fry, and I've dropped two glasses so far, making me glad they use plastic here. I would trade government secrets to hear one, just one, song by Lady Gaga. And I have a tremendous respect for servers now. Now ... he was asking how I was doing. Probably more to pump me for information to feed the gossips around here."

Jesse leaned forward. "Don't tell him anything, understand? Especially about you being—"

She put a finger against his lips. "Are you kidding? I'm not telling anyone anything." His mouth was warm and soft, and she jerked her finger back as though he'd singed her.

Curiosity flared in his eyes, but he picked up the menu. "I'll have a hamburger with pickles and ketchup and a sweet tea. Dear," he added with a smile that was more like his usual self.

Her cheeks warmed, even though he was reflecting her use of the word. She hurried to get his tea, then took another order. As she passed the large refrigerator, she paused to peer at her reflection. Yep, she looked awful. Not the tall blonde she kept imagining, but the short, thin girl with the bruised face.

By noon, the place was crazy-busy. Paul and his friends lingered, but Jesse apologetically said he couldn't stay long. He squeezed her hand before leaving, and she wished he would have pulled her out of the chaos. She was working for her escape, she reminded herself. Thoughts of carefree, windblown days full of sun and fun made her homesick. She sighed, bringing her focus back to the diner and the cacophony of voices and laughter.

Harry, Jesse's boss, asked how she felt. Billy sat at the end of the counter and gave her a faint smile. Most people were friendly, inquiring about her well-being, *tsking* at how something so terrible could happen in Chattaloo.

"That's Carl, the sheriff," Caty murmured as she passed by. "The guy with him is Lyle, his deputy."

Carl approached with that confident air of the law. Only a few strands of gray glistened in his black hair, and except for a small paunch, he was in good shape. He walked up to the counter while Lyle found a table.

"How are you doing, young lady?"

"I'm okay, Sheriff. Any leads?"

Carl let out a long sigh. "I think it was a transient passing through, probably long gone by now." He rubbed his fingers down his mustache. "Have you remembered anything yet?"

"Not a glimmer."

"That's a shame. Be nice to throw the bastard in jail and keep him there a long time. Might even have an accident, slip and hit his head." He shrugged. "Happens sometimes."

She shivered, hoping she never ended up in jail.

But it was more than the thought of vigilante justice that raised a slew of chill bumps on her arms. Wherever she looked, people watched her, speculating or with concern. Being in the spotlight was one thing. This kind of attention was something entirely different.

The man watched Marti clear a table with deliberation, as though she'd never waited tables before. In the din of lunchtime activity, he could observe all he wanted without seeming overly interested. Every once in a while, her gaze would sweep the restaurant, passing over him as casually as it did anyone else.

She'd looked right at him, not a hint of recognition. He chewed his food but didn't taste it. He had fought those erotic, demanding impulses for so long. He'd had the best intentions when he'd pulled over to help Marti. She'd been wearing those cut-offs and a tank top that accentuated small, firm breasts. Something about her helplessness summoned those old urges back from the tomb he'd buried them in.

With an embarrassed smile, she'd told him she was out of gas, but he could feel her hesitancy around him. It was the same way his true love, the blood of his heart, had acted after she'd broken off their affair. Marti acting the same way had set something off inside him with that spark of distrust in her eyes and the way she stepped away as he moved closer. He'd grown hot, throbbing, and that dizziness overcame his senses. He lunged for her, and her scream of surprise stirred him more.

With his hand over her mouth, he'd dragged her into the woods that bordered the highway. She struggled so hard that he had to pin her beneath his body, his weight on her stomach and hips. She was crying, "Please don't! I'm pregnant, don't hurt my baby."

He'd looked down at her flat stomach, but he'd heard that she was pregnant, with Jesse's baby, no less. He'd smiled. And she fought even harder.

He'd been surprised at the petite girl's strength and desperation. He'd wanted to be gentle, but the harder she fought, the harder he had to pin her down. He ripped off her top — he remembered liking that part the first time he'd raped a woman. The power of control, the shame, and fear in her eyes ... intoxicating.

He'd shifted his weight down her thighs so he could unsnap her jeans and tear open the zipper. She'd lunged up at him, scratching, pulling out his hair. He fell on top of her, pressing himself hard against the length of her.

His hands had crept around her throat before he realized it. She kept kicking. He wanted her to stop fighting so he could show her how gentle he could be. But he kept pressing harder, squeezing until her eyes widened in shock when she couldn't breathe.

He'd let go, but too late; her limp body lay sprawled on the mat of leaves, finally complacent. He'd killed her, or thought he'd killed her. Panicked, he'd stumbled like a coward to his car.

He couldn't understand his violent streak. It hadn't been that way when he'd been with the blood of his heart. She'd calmed him. When she left — rejected him, damn it — and gone back to her husband, the cobra of violence had reared its head within him. He'd taken a woman against her will. Not that she would ever talk; he threatened her into silence, and she left town. He'd held the cobra back since then, but Marti had weakened him.

Noise penetrated his thoughts. Absently, his fingers moved down his chest where beneath his shirt he bore the gouges her fingernails left behind. He watched her, wondering if she would ever remember; wondering what he should do to make sure she didn't.

Marti expelled a deep breath at two o'clock when the last customer left, and Caty locked the door behind him. "I couldn't have survived without you."

Caty dropped down into the chair she'd just wiped clean. "I don't mind helping out. And the extra money doesn't hurt. But if I keep up like this, I'll be too exhausted to enjoy it."

Marti picked up the wet rag Caty had tossed onto the table and continued cleaning up. "Don't worry, I plan to take my share as soon as I get a handle on this waitressing thing. Besides, I need the money myself."

Caty eyed her curiously. "What do you need the money for?"

Marti sat down. "I'm going home to California as soon as I can. Nothing against good old Chattaloo, but it's not my style."

"Does Jesse know you're leaving?"

"I'm not sure."

"You'd better tell him. Marti, it's probably none of my business, but you are carrying my nephew or niece in there, which happens to be my beloved brother's baby. I'd hate to see you do something that might hurt either one. Or yourself."

Marti stood and continued wiping down the last tables. "It's not something I'll decide lightly. And I will tell Jesse. Soon."

A few minutes later, Caty turned off most of the

lights and grabbed both their purses. "I'll drop you by the garage."

They drove a few blocks, then turned left. A large, hand-painted sign showed a car with a happy face beneath the words *HARRY'S GARAGE*.

Caty got out and headed into one of the open bays. "Here's your wife, safe and sound," she said to the car in the back.

As Marti approached, she saw Jesse peer around the front of the open hood. He had a black smudge across his cheek. "How was work?"

Caty snapped her gum. "Marti did pretty good, but she definitely ain't made to waitress."

Marti leaned against the car. "Aw, come on, I wasn't that bad." After a pause, she added, "Was I?"

Caty made a so-so sign, then smiled. "You'll get better. You've never worked that hard before, have you?"

Marti's shoulders drooped. "Guess I've had it pretty easy."

Jesse put an arm around Caty, keeping his blackened hand from her sleeve. "Thanks for showing her the ropes, kiddo." To Marti, he said, "I'll wash up and be right out."

A few minutes later, he helped Marti climb into the red truck, then slid behind the wheel. They waved goodbye to Caty, and he started in the other direction toward home. Home, Marti thought wryly. For how long?

They pulled in the driveway to the tune of Bumpus's barking. After Jesse helped her out of the truck, he didn't let go of her hand. "Come walk with me."

"Where?"

"To the river. Come on, I won't throw you in."

She allowed him to pull her a few steps. "My feet hurt so bad. Can't we sit down here and talk?"

Without a word, he swooped her up into his arms. He carried her behind the house, through a thicket of pine trees to the same river that ran behind his mother's house. Bumpus followed noisily behind, his tail pointing to the sky. She felt weightless in Jesse's arms, her white shoes bouncing along as they walked.

Her hero, her heart sang.

Stop thinking stuff like that.

The sun cast dancing shadows on the water's surface as it filtered through the tangle of oak leaves. He set her on her feet, stripped off his button-down shirt, and laid it on the ground for her to sit on. Southern gentleman, she thought with a smile she hid from him.

He dropped down on the layer of dead leaves beside her and looked out over the river that flowed lazily by. His air of hesitancy suddenly made her wary. Was he going to ask her to leave?

He took a rock and threw it across the expanse of the river, skipping it three times. "My friends and I used to have contests about who could get their rock to skip the farthest."

He was beating around the bush, moving in for the kill. She was too crazy, too different ... too whatever. He was going to tell her to move out. Where would she go? She felt a twinge of anxiety. With twenty-nine bucks, plus money she'd gotten in tips, she wasn't likely to get far. She decided to tell him about her plans before he could say whatever he had to say.

"Jesse —" All the words jumbled forward, then disappeared like a puddle illusion on the highway when you got close. "I can't stay here. I mean, I can't stay long."

"What are you talking about?"

"I don't belong here. I don't even belong in this body, but I haven't much choice about that. I can get used to that part, but not this town, this life. It's not me, and inside I'm still Hallie DiBarto. I have to get back to California."

"I thought you had no one to go back to."

She swallowed hard. "I don't. My friends — they weren't really friends." She couldn't stop thinking about how empty her life had been. She'd been too busy partying to notice. Too busy trying to fill the hole in her soul.

"Then what are you going back for?"

"I don't know. All I know is I have to get out of here."

He drummed long fingers on the mat of leaves, looking out over the water before returning determined eyes back to her. "What I brought you out here to talk about was ... what I wanted to say was that I want you to stay and have the baby."

"Jesse, that's nice of you, but I can't."

His lips thinned. "I'm not being nice." He placed his palm on her still-flat stomach. "This little guy is mine, my responsibility, my blood. I can't let you take off, never knowing what happened to him. I figured you'd go back where you came from, after the baby is born. Until then, I want you here with me."

He wanted her there. *But not you, really. The baby.* "I'm not going to do anything with the baby. Once I'm settled, I'll let you know where I am. When the baby comes, I'll call you."

She didn't want to look at him, because she could see his expression of disbelief from the corner of her eye.

"Marti, how are you going to get out of here without

money? How are you going to support yourself?"

"I'm going to work hard for a few months, save up, and drive my car out there."

He turned her chin so that she had to face him. "Why can't you stay here so we can take care of you, and be with you when you have the baby? What's so bad about this place?"

Face to face with those green eyes, she groped. "I was attacked here. How do I know that the attacker was just passing through? Maybe he's still here, lurking. I had a creepy feeling today, when the restaurant was packed. Like he was watching me. I know, everyone was watching me, waiting for me to crack or something. But this felt different. Evil."

His reaction surprised her. He got up on his knees leaning over her, taking her face in his hands. His eyes burned with a mixture of anger and determination. "No one will ever hurt you again, Marti." His voice dropped to a whisper. "I won't let it happen."

She felt a strange squeezing in her heart as his fingers stroked her cheeks. At the same time, an alarm went off somewhere inside her. *I'd be the one to hurt you, Jesse. I can't stay here, not a minute longer than I have to. Please stop touching me.* Yet she didn't move away, couldn't take her eyes from his.

She found her voice. "Marti's attack wasn't your fault."

He sat back. "Yes, it was. I should have made sure you had gas in your car. I should have made you carry a weapon of some kind, I should have —" He punched at the ground. "I should have done something. It's all I can do to keep from tearing up the entire town to find the son of a bitch who did this."

"Jesse, stop blaming yourself. You weren't responsible for the attack, and you're not responsible for avenging it. I'm sure the sheriff and Lyle are doing the best they can to find out who did it, but —"

"I'm not letting you leave until you have the baby."

She drew her knees up and wrapped her arms around them. "You can't make me stay. What are you going to do, tie me up?"

His expression was dead serious. "If I have to."

She remembered something he had said earlier. "I thought there was something mechanically wrong with my car. That's why you didn't want me to drive it this morning."

He avoided her gaze. "I'm not sure it was just lack of gas. I'll look at it this weekend."

She knew he was lying. He didn't want her to drive, maybe because he was afraid she'd take off. Well, she wasn't an accountant, but she wasn't going to get far on fifty bucks. Her goal was to save enough to get out to California and have a little to get started until she found a job. She didn't want to think about her chances of getting a job with a protruding belly. In California, anything was possible.

"I'll be here for a few months."

"Why can't you wait a few more months?"

"Because I don't want to stay here any longer than I have to."

Jesse picked up another stone and made it skip across the water to the other side. "What's so bad about this place, anyway? Or is it me?"

She raised a hand to his cheek, then pulled it away when she caught herself. "It's not you, and it's not the town really. It's me. I'm out of my element."

He smirked. "Sounds like that's a good thing, from what you've said."

"I wasn't that bad. And I'm not going back to that kind of life. I desperately need something familiar." She heard her emotion leaking into her voice. Even imagining being at one of her favorite beaches filled her with longing.

Jesse reclined on the grass, his arms behind his head. Contemplating his next strategy, no doubt. Or maybe considering his threat of tying her up. She had to think he wouldn't do such a thing. If she stayed until the baby was born, she might lose the courage to leave. She'd be stuck in Chattaloo forever. Stuck. It gave her the shivers.

While Marti was deep in her thoughts, Jesse reached out and pulled her down beside him. She allowed him to draw her closer, wondering if he would try to kiss her again, like that test of his. Wondering if she would let him.

He lay on his side facing her. "We made a baby together. Doesn't that mean anything to you?"

She fiddled with a piece of grass. "*We* didn't make a baby; you and Marti had all the fun."

He smiled, a devilish light in his eyes. "Fun, huh?"

She blushed. "Well, I'm only guessing it was fun." She looked away before returning her gaze to him. "Was it?"

"I guess. To be honest, we were both sloshed and didn't remember too much of it."

Marti steeled her courage, unable to keep from asking the questions that bugged her. "Was it ... fun later?"

He looked at a cardinal fluttering from one branch to another, chirping intermittently. "We never slept together after the first time. She told me it would hurt the baby, something about my" — he glanced downward — "hitting the baby's head. Dr. Toby said that was impossible, but I wasn't going to force her, wife or no. I didn't even want to."

Warmth crept up to her cheeks. Still, she had to know one more thing. "Did you love her, Jesse?"

He moved closer, dropping his head just over her upturned face. "My Pa always told me I'd know it when I loved a woman. He said, 'It's a clenched gut, drop-down-to-your-knees-and-die-for-her feeling, and you ain't in love till you feel it.' Racing's the only thing that makes me feel that way, and I didn't want anything to get in the way of that. No, I didn't love her, and I didn't want to." Anger sparked in his eyes, but he banked it and sighed. "But I didn't want her to die, that's for sure."

"Me either. Nor did I want to die, but sometimes we don't have a choice." She reclined on her side. "So, were you never going to get married, content to be a lone racecar driver?"

Jesse smiled faintly, looking at the blade of grass he was twisting between his fingers. "My first ambition was, and is, getting to NASCAR. That kind of life doesn't lend itself to the quaint family picture most women have. Marti figured she'd have me settled down once the baby came, but it wasn't going to be that way. Nothing is going to get in the way of making it."

He paused, then glanced at her and continued, "And no one. Ma and Caty have already volunteered to watch the baby while I race. But between races, I'll be the best dad I can be. And when the baby is old enough, he'll be part of it all. Aside from that, I don't have any intention of getting messed up with a woman who'll fuss and be jealous because I spend more time with my racecar than with her."

"I see." She did see the truth of that in his eyes. She felt a funny pang as she pictured Jesse letting his son pretend to drive his car. On the other hand, she understood his point about a woman getting jealous of his racing pursuits. "Love stinks."

He tossed the mangled piece of grass away and plucked another one. "Did you love Jamie?"

She looked past him, unable to think about Jamie while looking at Jesse. "Yes. I think I loved him, anyway. I'm not even sure I know what love is." She returned her gaze to Jesse. "I seemed to screw it up a lot. I had my chance, and I blew it."

"You'll have another chance."

She shook her head. "I don't deserve another chance. Life is enough, love is too much, too difficult to manage."

"Who says you have to manage it? It should flow, like this ole' river."

She watched the leaves drift past, floating on top of the brown water. "I wish it were that easy. It's hard to think of it like a lazy river when your life has always been the rapids."

They sat in contemplative silence, facing each other. Her thoughts turned outward as she realized with chagrin that Jesse went around without his shirt much too often.

She wondered if the first Marti had been in love with Jesse, whether she'd been fascinated by the subtle way he smiled, by the deliberate way he spoke. Had Jesse's wife ever run her fingers across the expanse of his chest, trailed the edge of her fingernail down the indent in the middle? They had had sex once, enough to make the baby inside her body. Maybe she'd been afraid of failing in bed, of not living up to expectations.

Her gaze traveled down her own thin, tan arms, skinny legs with knobby knees. No big promises here, she thought, sighing inwardly. On the other hand, nothing to live up to either. In her old body, she had been sexy since she was fifteen. Now she felt like she did at thirteen, before her chest had blossomed and her hips had grown curvy. Before her first kiss. Awkward and unsteady. Would she ever feel comfortable in this body?

"Marti?"

Jesse's low voice drew her from her disturbing thoughts. "Yes?"

"You have to promise me something."

She wanted to back away from a forced promise, but she didn't. "What is it?"

"That you won't hurt that baby inside you. That no matter what happens between you and me, you won't do anything to hurt him, or have an abortion. Promise me."

"I promise." That was easy, she thought, releasing her breath. She put her hand on her belly, imagining the fetus she saw on anti-abortion billboards. "I would never hurt him."

He released a breath, too. "You're off on Sundays, so we'll get you a bed."

He stood, stretching out his large hand for her to take. There was something secure about his fingers closing around hers. A mental picture flashed into her mind, Jesse with his brawn and muscles holding a fragile baby. She found herself smiling at the thought and wiped the grin away. Still, the picture remained, along with the feeling of security that went with it that cloaked her in a warmth she hadn't felt in many years.

For all his gestures of warmth and security, though, Jesse James West wasn't letting anyone into his heart except his family. He'd probably go to any length to protect her, but he wouldn't let himself fall in love with her. Not that she wanted that, she reminded herself. That was some other woman's loss.

CHAPTER 5

"**H**ave you ever seen Paul's eagle pendant?" Marti asked around a forkful of pancake the next morning.

Jesse's eyes narrowed across the Formica table at the Someplace Else Cafe. "I meant it when I told you not to talk to him again. He's trouble."

Her shoulders stiffened in response. "Keep your rifle in your jeans, cowboy. Husband or not, you can't tell me who I'm allowed to talk to. The only reason I brought him up was because … oh, it's probably nothing. Never mind."

"What? What were you going to tell me?"

"Have you noticed his pendant? Really noticed it?"

"Sure. He showed it off to everyone when he got it. Why?"

"It caught my attention for some reason. Last night, when I saw the scratch on my chest, I realized why. It looks like the kind of object that could make that scratch."

Fire lit Jesse's eyes as he leaned closer. "What scratch?"

"I have a scratch, though it's almost healed now. You

didn't know?"

"I want to see it." Apparently not.

She glanced around at the busy diner. "Not here. It's too low." She pointed to where it was, at the upper curve of her breast.

He pushed his plate away. "Come on, let's get out of here."

After they pulled out of the parking lot, he turned onto the first street they came across and found a vacant lot. Dust surrounded the truck as he screeched to an abrupt stop.

He cut the engine and faced her. "Show me."

His intensity made her nervous. She tried to make a funny to ease the tension. "Don't you want to flirt a little first?"

"Marti, this isn't the time to joke around."

"Sorry, nervous humor." She erased her smile and stretched her shirt down.

He studied the scratch, pressing his finger on it. "You're right, it's almost gone." He leaned back. "Dr. Toby took pictures to document the assault."

Jesse started the truck and slammed it into reverse. She grabbed onto the strap to keep from flying around.

"You really hate that guy, don't you?" she asked.

"I hate the guy who did this to you. If it was Paul, he's dead."

She shivered at the vehemence in his voice. Jesse came off easy-going, but inside he carried a lot of heat.

At the hospital, Dr. Toby explained that she had turned over all the photos to the sheriff. She pulled up the report she'd made and read her brief description of the scratch. "The picture will be much clearer," she said.

Jesse was just as intent on getting to the sheriff's office, and Marti became very friendly with that strap.

The sheriff's office looked more like a storefront, with reflective windows that mirrored the main street from the outside and a brick façade. Lyle was sitting at the front desk in the small office, reading through the pile of mail. He looked up, then squinted as the morning sun reflected off the glass door. The blinds on the front windows left the office with a subdued feeling.

"Hey, Jesse. Marti. How are you two doing?"

Jesse leaned on the desk. "We might be doing really well if you can help us. I've got to see the pictures Dr. Toby took of Marti."

"You'll have to talk to Carl."

"Why? You were the investigating officer."

"I know, but Carl took over the case." Lyle sniffed at the air. "He wanted to investigate the biggest case we've had since Mr. Peekin's poodles were kidnapped for those dog fights. I guess he didn't think I could handle it. I could've, you know."

"I'm sure you could have, Lyle," Jesse pressed. "As good a job as anyone. We just want to see those pictures for a minute."

"A quick peek, in and out," Marti added.

Lyle shook his head. "You'll have to talk to Carl, and he's not in. I can radio him if you got a lead."

"No, don't radio him." Jesse clamped his hand on Marti's shoulder. "It's her body; let us look at the pictures. No one will know. We'll give you the credit if what I want to look at does turn into something."

"What do you have?"

"I'll tell you when I have more to go on. The photos?"

Lyle hedged, looking out the door behind Jesse. "One

quick peek."

Both Jesse and Marti breathed a sigh of relief as Lyle went searching through the drawers of the spotless desk in back with Carl's name and title spelled out prominently on a nameplate. He brought a large white envelope and pulled out a stack of photos. Marti took them before Jesse could grab hold.

"I'll show you the ones I want you to see." She flipped through them, the images clenching her stomach even though she'd seen the injuries in person. "There are none of my chest."

Lyle took the stack and went through them. "Every injury is supposed to be documented. Where is it?"

He went to another computer. After a few minutes of tapping keys and squinting at the monitor, he said, "Nothing in here either. Maybe Dr. Toby missed it."

"She didn't miss it," Jesse said. "Maybe someone deleted the picture."

"No, we're very careful about that."

"Come on." Jesse tugged Marti out the door.

"Do you think they did it on purpose?" she asked as they got into the truck.

"I don't know. Carl might be protecting his son, if he connected that scratch like you did."

"I can draw what it looked like. Will that help?"

"It'll help, but it won't be proof."

After stopping at a furniture store, Jesse carried in the bed frame and mattress with Marti guiding him verbally to avoid walls and obstructions. With the bed positioned, Jesse dropped down onto it, arms outstretched. He stared at the ceiling, and she stared at him. Catching herself, she checked out the room that was to be hers for a while.

It was smaller than Jesse's room, with dark blue walls. The lone bare window would allow anyone to look in at night. The closet was an indent, not even big enough to stand in. Jesse still looked a thousand miles away, and she searched the room for something to break the silence.

She saw the packages of sheets on top of the dresser and grasped at the opportunity to bring him back. "What are these for?"

He looked at the packages she held up, his eyes still tinged with some distant anger. "Marti bought those. We couldn't afford the fancy curtains on the JC Penny website, so she was going to make curtains out of those sheets. This is going to be the nursery."

Marti looked at the tiny white lambs on a mint green background and imagined them as ornate curtains for the bare window. She lacked in the creativity department, but maybe she could do something nice with them.

When she looked at Jesse again, he was staring out the window. His thoughts were miles away again, obviously some unpleasant place by his expression. The curves of his mouth that usually tilted up in a smile, even when he wasn't smiling, were straight.

He stood suddenly. "I've got to go out for a little while."

Something in his expression tightened her heart "Where?"

He swiped something off the dining table. "To see an old buddy of mine. I'll be back."

She watched him walk determinedly to his truck, realizing that the dark fire in his eyes had been there ever since she'd told him about the pendant that morning. The sketches of the pendant and her scratch were gone.

What if Jesse killed Paul? What if they arrested Jesse? The questions numbed her mind. After pacing in front of the living room window for a few minutes, she turned back to her new bedroom and put her nervous energy to work.

Jesse had finally maxed out his self-control. From the moment Marti had mentioned the pendant, he'd wanted to confront Paul — hell, he wanted to beat the crap out of him. Even the irony of bed shopping with Marti hadn't distracted him. Now he couldn't hold it back anymore. Not that he would start pummeling Paul's face and ask questions later. He couldn't do that until he had more evidence. But maybe he could gently persuade Paul to admit he'd attacked Marti. Yeah, gently persuade him.

Paul's fancy new truck, black with neon ribbons trailing across the sides, sat outside. The house was partially hidden by a large banyan tree, roots dripping down from the branches to find a hold. Two stories of brick house stood a short distance away.

Jesse headed right for Paul's truck. He wasn't sure what he was looking for, but he started digging through the piles of receipts, papers and cigarette packages anyway.

"I don't believe there was a for sale sign on my truck, so would you mind telling me what you're doing snooping around in it?"

Jesse swung on Paul so fast, Paul was pinned against the cab of the truck before he could think of fighting back. Jesse had more important things to do before beating him senseless. He grabbed at the pendant and pressed it against the inside of his wrist.

"What the hell are you doing?" Paul jerked out of his grasp before Jesse could get an imprint.

The rage twisted up in Jesse's throat, and his voice came out strangled. "You son of a bitch, you attacked my wife. You kill — tried to kill her."

Paul's chest heaved as he tried to gain his composure. "I didn't touch your wife!" He shook himself free, his blindingly white teeth gritted together.

"Don't think I believe that for a minute. Your daddy might tamper with the evidence that proved your eagle scratched Marti's chest, but I'll find another way to nail you."

Paul's eyes narrowed. "What are you talking about? What evidence?"

"Why don't you ask your daddy? He'll tell you about the missing pictures, the one with the imprint particularly. The imprint that matches your pendant. I will prove it, and you will pay. Not even your daddy will be able to save you when I'm through with you."

Paul crept around the truck and toward the house. "Isn't it a little late to go around protecting your wife? Now that it's over, you want to be the big avenger. Why don't you spend your energies making sure your wife has enough gas in her car? Oh, and Jesse? You ever try something like this again, and you'll be the one to pay. I promise you that."

"You'd better be as ready to back up your promises as I am," Jesse shouted.

He watched Paul head back into the house, then studied the faint imprint of the pendant on his arm. Close, real close. Unfortunately, it would be faded by the time he got home. He'd been so mad that he'd forgotten to bring his phone. He needed to always take it with him, in case she needed him.

Ever since they were kids, Paul had a snake-edged tongue, always slicing through where Jesse was most tender. But he felt in every cell of his body that Paul was the one who attacked Marti. Not that he had much proof, but he could take a smidgen of hope and turn it into something tangible, like he'd done with racing. He would do it here, too.

Chuck was kind enough to close Bad Boys for Thanksgiving. Then Marti learned that it wasn't so much out of kindness, because most of Chattaloo's businesses were closed for the holiday.

She searched for large pans and serving dishes in Jesse's cabinets, stacking them up on the table for transport to Helen's at two o'clock. When Jesse walked into the kitchen wearing a maroon dress shirt and black pants, she just stared at him. Not only because he looked so formal and handsome and — she clamped her mouth shut. "I thought we were eating at your mom's house."

"We are. Why?"

"You look ... nice." She resisted the temptation to say, *Boy, you sure clean up nice.*

He shrugged. "We always dress up for holiday dinners." He looked down at himself and grinned. "Then we crowd into the kitchen and sweat and get food all over our nice clothes before dinner even begins. It always did seem silly to me, but Ma insists."

Marti dropped a large, plastic spoon into the stacked metal bowls. She felt an expression of controlled panic seize her face. They all worked together in the kitchen? Doing what? Talking about what?

Jesse's grin disappeared. "What's the matter?"

"I don't do family get-togethers. Traditional dinners were usually my mother's latest lover trying to impress us by taking us to some fancy restaurant. Big dinners with everyone cooking together, chatting about what a wonderful year it's been, that's the stuff of commercials."

He took her hands in his. She tried to avoid his gaze by staring at the hollow of his throat, but something made her meet his eyes.

"As long as you're my wife, you are part of my family. There's nothing to be afraid of, and believe me, it's never as picture-perfect as a commercial. We usually have as much fun making the meal as we do eating it. You'll be fine."

She nodded, but inside was sure she'd fail at her part of the preparation and lively conversation.

Her mother's voice echoed in her head: *You'll never be good at anything, Hallie. You think being a sexy, pretty young thing will be enough for someone qualified to love you? Maybe for a time or two in the sack, but that's it.*

She wasn't sexy or pretty anymore.

She remembered their dinner last week, the lighthearted conversation and smiles. That was an ordinary meal, though, and this was Thanksgiving.

The former Marti had few nice dresses. Still, she wanted to wear something special, so she slipped into a pink dress plastered with white tulips. She brushed her hair, surveying her reflection. Pretty enough, she supposed.

Hearing Jesse's voice outside, she put on white sandals and headed toward the door. He was playing Frisbee with Bumpus. She watched as he reared back, then threw the disk to the dog that was crouched and ready to start the chase. Jesse's hair was still wet; combed back, it looked slick with styling gel. He had nice hair, thick and wavy, and did little more than brush it.

He headed toward the truck, disk in hand. Bumpus watched intently, waiting for a signal.

"I hope you don't mind if he comes along. He'd be heartbroken if I left him behind."

Picturing him riding in the back of the truck, she said, "Well, I certainly don't want to break his heart."

Jesse helped her in the truck, then gave the signal Bumpus waited for: a wave of the disk. Bumpus took a running leap, lunging at the Frisbee. With it in his mouth, he landed on the seat next to her, upsetting the pile of cookware in her lap. She scrunched toward the door.

"Jesse, he's in the truck! Get him out of here."

Instead of telling the dog to get out, Jesse slid in next to him. "He always rides in the cab."

"Can't he ride in the back? I've seen dogs do that before."

"Not mine. You don't let your dog ride in back when you see a truck's brakes slam and watch the dog in back fly through the air and into traffic. Luckily, he was able to limp away before he got run over."

"What if I gave you an ultimatum? It's either the dog or me."

He grinned. "I'd say, hope it's not too breezy for you in the back. And don't open your mouth or you might eat a bug."

She crossed her arms in front of her. "Humph."

No point in arguing, obviously. She stayed flat against the door. Bumpus turned toward her, sending a drop of drool hurtling through the air. She leaned to the side, and it barely missed her. *Augh*.

As Jesse headed down the road, she opened the glove box and found a package of tissues. She pulled out five and balled them up. Every time she saw the saliva forming on Bumpus's lips, she swabbed it. He was too busy enjoying the ride to pay much attention.

"What are you doing to my dog?" Jesse asked, obviously more attentive.

"I'm mopping him up. He's drooling all over."

Jesse shook his head and returned his attention to the road. His light expression of earlier darkened. "I take care of my own. I'd never do anything to endanger my people, and Bumpus is my people, too."

"I get it. I wouldn't want him to get thrown out."

"I wouldn't make you ride back there either. Just so you know." He flicked her a smile, the shadow on his face gone.

"Makes me feel all warm and fuzzy inside." She kept swabbing Bumpus's chin.

As soon as they turned on the road leading to Helen's, Bumpus stood. His tail thumped Marti's shoulder, his gaze going back and forth, making it harder to jab the tissues at his drooling mouth. When they turned onto Helen's driveway, he went berserk, whining and dancing a jig on the front seat.

"Does he have to go to the bathroom?" she asked, ready to grab more tissues.

"No, he always goes nuts when he realizes we're visiting grandma," Jesse said.

"Ah. And how does Helen feel about being this ... thing's grandmother?"

He shrugged. "She doesn't mind. What with Dad and

his dogs, and Billy and me catching every kind of critter you could imagine, including baby raccoons and squirrels, she gave up being squeamish. Even now, Billy's got a pet possum, and Caty's got her rat. Ma's easy going."

"I can't imagine getting used to those kinds of animals in the house."

He cut the engine and turned to her. "You never had critters when you were a kid, did you?"

"No. My mother wasn't into animals, or really anything that required work." Including having a kid.

He nodded, as though that explained everything. "Animals teach you unconditional love, if you'll just let yourself learn to accept it. Give them food, water, and some attention, and they love you. Simple as that. You don't have to look pretty or have a college education or money or anything else that people think gives them value." He rubbed Bumpus's head. The dog licked Jesse's hand and actually seemed to smile. Then, as though he were full of love, he turned and licked her hand, too.

She pulled it back with a grimace. "How can you learn to be loved? I don't even get that. I thought it came naturally, or maybe from growing up in a loving family. And is that the same as being lovable? I mean being loved for who you are, not what you are?" She shifted back a few inches when Bumpus tried to lick at her face. "By people. I think it's something that gets turned on when you're young ... or not."

Jesse took her in for a moment, probably trying to make sense of everything she'd bombarded him with. Finally, he said, "Start with the dog."

She blinked. "What?"

"Just let him love on you. Stop being so, *'Oh, it's gross!'*" He'd mimicked a high-pitched voice on those words. Her voice, no doubt.

She gave him a *You've got to be kidding* look. "You want me to let a dog lick me to learn about being loved. Really?"

Jesse leaned forward, so close that she thought he was going to kiss her. He stopped an inch in front of her. "Yeah, really. 'Cause here's the thing: you gotta love yourself before you can expect anyone else to. See, to Bumpus, you're not pretty or ugly, important or insignificant. You're one of his people, and that makes you significant. Start with that."

He pushed open the door behind her. Bumpus jumped out and she heard dogs sniffing and scrabbling around in the dirt behind her. She was still looking at Jesse, who hadn't moved back yet. Who, in fact, remained close enough that she felt the soft exhale of his breath on her chin.

She yearned to be significant to him, to hear that from him. A different kind of yearning had her wanting to touch her mouth to his, to *feel* her significance to him. Whoa. Wasn't that her problem, needing to feel important to someone other than herself? Validation.

She cleared her throat and nodded. "Start with the dog."

His gaze slid to her mouth. "The dog."

She backed away, nearly falling off the edge of the seat.

He grabbed her arms and jerked her forward, right into him. "You okay?"

She'd gripped his shoulders, her cheek brushing his. "I've got my balance now." *You need to keep your balance, which means backing away from this very close position with Jesse ... who smells so good, I want to eat him up.*

She backed away at that crazy thought, her heart tripping. "We should go in, I suppose."

"Yeah. I suppose." Did he look a little shell-shocked, or was it her imagination? Probably the latter.

She followed him into the house, ducking under pilgrim and pumpkin decorations hanging over the door. A fat pumpkin squatted on the coffee table, surrounded by a variety of smaller squashes in wacky shapes. A football game blared on the television, and the aroma of roasting turkey filled the room. Marti couldn't help but smile, feeling her anxiety slip away.

"Hi, Ma!" Jesse hollered.

"Hi, hon, Marti! Happy Thanksgiving!" Helen called from the kitchen. She appeared in the kitchen doorway. "Marti, why don't you come in and help me get the feast process started? Caty's helping Dr. Hislope with one of Nolen's cows. Bessie Blue's having a hard time calving, and Donna's nowhere to be found."

"I'd love to help. I will warn you, though, that I can't cook."

Jesse picked up one of the strangely shaped gourds and regarded it curiously. "Mom, give her a few lessons, will you? I can't cook all the meals now, can I?"

Helen cocked her head at him. "Aw, that would be awful, wouldn't it?"

He raised his hands in surrender. "I know when to exit gracefully. I'm going to see if Billy needs any help fishing. We'll be in shortly to give you a hand."

Helen headed back into the kitchen. "I didn't raise my boys to depend on a woman to eat and have clean clothes." She handed Marti a peeler and several potatoes and set her up in front of the sink.

"Jesse's one of the neatest men I've ever met," Marti

said. "Most bachelor pads are pretty disgusting, but not his place. Not that I've seen a lot of bachelor pads," she felt inclined to add.

"He's always been that way. I hardly ever had to tell him to wash his hands before dinner either. Billy, unfortunately, was always a slob." Helen whispered, "I even put him over my knee and spanked him once after he said it was a woman's place to cook and clean. He was twenty-three years old."

"That must have been a sight."

Helen's brown eyes twinkled with mischief. "It was. He never said anything like that again, at least in my presence."

"I guess not. Well, it's a good thing you taught Jesse to be independent, being that he's not the marrying type."

Helen's laugh was more of a sputter. "What do you mean? He *is* married."

"Yeah, but against his will. And I'll be heading back to California soon, so he'll be single again. According to him, he'll be that way for a long time so he can concentrate on his racing."

"Don't let him send you away, hon. A good woman can bring happiness to a man whether he wants it or not. And vice-versa."

"Oh, he's not sending me away. I feel the same. We're a perfect match, in that respect."

Helen gave her an odd look, but Marti's attention had been snagged by the scene outside the window: Jesse stealthily approached Billy from behind, then tossed a small rock into the water. The resulting splash made Billy perk up, then quickly reel in the lure and cast it in the area of the splash. After the third time, Billy turned around and pointed at Jesse with a menacing finger. The two wrestled for a few minutes. Oh, to have that kind of sibling camaraderie.

"Are they goofing around again?" Helen asked, basting the turkey with an oversized syringe.

"They were wrestling, but now they're starting a game of horseshoes."

"They never grow up. And frankly, I don't want them to. They're still my little boys when they wrestle and tease each other." She smiled wistfully. "These are the times I miss Bernie the most. When you love someone, it doesn't go away."

Marti felt a twinge in her heart. She would probably never love someone like that. She'd end up hurting them, no doubt. "Doesn't that make you wish you'd never felt that love if it hurts so much to lose it."

Helen tilted her head, giving Marti a sad look. "Haven't you ever loved someone fiercely?"

"I've been in love, and I thought I loved someone, but turned out it wasn't the real thing. I've never hurt the way you're obviously hurting, so maybe that's a good thing."

Helen put her hand on Marti's arm. "Surely you've heard the phrase, 'It's better to have loved and lost than to never have loved at all'?"

"Yeah, but I figured it's just a way to make yourself feel better, like sour grapes and all."

Helen smiled, soft and sweet and a little sad. "To feel the real thing, whether it's family love or friendship love or romantic is worth every bit of heartache when it's gone." She fisted her hand at her chest. "Because it's always here. It touches you and changes you, probably for the better. And it never goes away." She sighed, bringing herself back to the task at hand. "Once we get the potatoes going, we'll start the green beans and sweet potatoes. This kind of dinner is like orchestrating a production."

Glad to be focusing on something other than love, Marti shook her head as she took in the steaming pots and piles of beans. "I could never do this. Cooking's not in my genes."

"Nothing to do with genes, hon. It's a matter of learning. It's a labor of love, an adventure."

Marti watched as Helen deftly shaved the carrots clean. "Maybe if my mother had taught me how to cook. She was more of the Hamburger Helper type." Even in a lacy apron, Helen didn't visually fit in a kitchen. Yet, she worked like a pro. "Where are you from? Not here, right?"

Helen gave her a sheepish grin. "I'm still not Chattaloo'd, am I?"

"Well, I can tell you weren't born in any small Southern town."

"I was born in a prestigious Connecticut community. I went to private schools, attended the dances and all that social poopoo. I had fun, but it wasn't me."

Marti raised her eyebrows. "You look like you'd fit into that kind of world. I mean, you're so pretty and classy."

Helen curtsied, never missing a beat with her carrot peeling. "Why, thank you. Everybody thought I'd marry the senator's son and have three bright, beautiful children, and live in a big white house. I did, too. But there was something inside me that was still searching. After I graduated from college, I drove down to the Keys by myself."

Finished, she moved onto the bowl of dough. "My

Jaguar broke down here in Chattaloo. I thought I was going to get ripped, a young woman alone in a small town. Bernie gave me a reasonable estimate, and his Southern drawl made me melt. He had to order the part from the dealer, and it was going to take a day or two. He took care of me, making me dinner at his house, taking me horseback riding. When my car was ready to go, I wasn't."

Marti was trying to pay attention to how Helen was kneading the biscuit dough, but she was too entranced by her story. "It sounds so romantic."

A melancholy haze fell upon her face. "It was, but it wasn't perfect. I had hoped once Billy was born that Bernie would stop racing so much, but he didn't. We had problems, and I made mistakes. By the time Jesse was born, we'd come to an understanding about the racing. And I'd learned an important lesson about the value of love."

Marti blew out a long breath. "I know about making mistakes. I made a lot of them in my marriage to Jamie. I sure learned my lesson about love: I'm not good at it, and I don't want to try anymore."

Helen turned to her. "Surely you don't mean that."

"I do. I had my chance, and I blew it. If I couldn't find love with Jamie, who was loving and tender, how can I find it with anyone else?"

"Oh, I think you'll find it again. Or more likely, it will find you. Probably in the most unexpected place."

Billy and Jesse busted through the door then, panting and slick with sweat. Billy stripped off his T-shirt, baring a tattoo of an eagle stretching from one shoulder to the other on his back.

"Billy, get your half-naked sweatiness out of here,

wash up, and get back in here to help," Helen said.

Jesse grabbed two bottles of beer from the fridge, pressed one to his flushed forehead, and walked out to hand one to Billy. He stood in the living room, his shirt stripped off, wide shoulders tapering to his waist and narrow hips. The black pants shaped his tight butt nicely. His damp hairs brushed the base of his neck as he moved. When her eyes felt locked to him, he turned and caught her staring. She couldn't tear her gaze away, and a warm fire burned in her stomach.

"Green beans are easy. You just cut the ends off and put them in the steamer." Helen's voice broke Marti out of her spell.

"Hm?"

"Uh oh, having a hot flash?"

The warmth of Marti's cheeks flamed hotter. "H-hot flash?"

"Pregnant women sometimes have them. Hormones. Your face is all red."

Marti waved her hand in front of her face. "It's the first time it's ever happened to me. That's probably what it is." She flicked a glance to Jesse. *Be much safer to believe that.*

Dean stopped by, and after a quick perusal of the surroundings, pushed out his lower lip. "Caty's not here?"

"She's out birthing a cow," Helen said. "Come on, wash up and I'll put you to work."

They kept everything waiting for Caty until Helen decided the turkey would be dried out if it stayed in the oven any longer.

When Jesse set the turkey platter on the table, Dean said, "At least we're not having beef for dinner. Katie would probably be a little upset after helping that baby cow into the world."

Jesse leaned over and whispered in Marti's ear, "Just ignore him. Everyone else does."

Before a single green bean could be dropped onto a plate, they all joined hands for prayer. Jesse's hand enveloped hers on one side, and Helen took her other one. Billy passed the duty of the "head of the household" onto Jesse, who easily took charge.

"Dear Jesus, thank you for bringing us here together, our health and sanity intact, Billy notwithstanding. We thank you that Caty is absent from our table only because she's helping a living thing come into the world." Marti felt him squeeze her hand as he continued. "We thank you for bringing Marti to us and for giving the tiny baby inside her health as he grows. Amen."

Everyone repeated the Amen, and for a moment, four sets of smiling eyes settled upon her. Uncomfortable under their gazes, she reached over to stab a piece of turkey meat.

CHAPTER 6

The following Monday was another long struggle of balancing trays. Marti saw a lot of the same people she had seen on Saturday.

"Don't these people have anyplace else to eat?" she'd whispered to Caty during the afternoon rush. "The same people keep coming in, day after day, meal after meal."

"There's only two other places in town to eat lunch besides us. At least we offer more variety than Pie in The Sky."

"Yeah, well, I guess you can only eat so much pizza."

Marti caught Chuck watching her again. Often, he seemed to be studying her from his steamy place in the kitchen. Was he just curious about the changes in her work habits? Sometimes she'd look back at him, and he'd grin at her, then resume whatever he'd been doing.

Jesse was always a welcome visitor, even though he could only order a couple of sandwiches to go today. He sat at the counter and watched her shoulder a tray of meatloaf specials.

"How's it going, doll? Any better than your first day?"

Whenever he called her 'doll,' her legs got all jiggly.

Which was not good when shouldering a tray of food. Why he could say it so casually and make her go silly boggled her mind. *Romantic. And you don't want it that way, do you?* Her self didn't answer, but she was sure she didn't.

She tried to remember his question. "Uh, it's okay. I don't think I'll ever get used to this kind of work."

"Wish I could stay for a while, but it's busy today at the garage. I'll see you after work."

As he grabbed his white bag, his smile promised more than his words. She was imagining it, of course. That lazy smile, the way he held her hand and called her 'doll,' he probably did that to all his women friends. There were, no doubt, a lot of them, a whole lot of them. She tried to push away the fuzzies dancing in her stomach with reality. And they could have him, because she would be leaving soon.

Once she and Caty cleaned up everything, they locked up the diner and got into Caty's compact. She didn't mind riding with Caty, but Marti resolved to start driving the Accord on her next workday. Jesse's tinkering with the engine was probably a farce to keep her with someone at all times. A little independence sounded good, and she had the can of tear gas to protect her now, courtesy of Jesse.

Caty swerved into Harry's parking lot like a speedster, pulling the compact car up short just before they would hit the building.

"Do you race cars, too?" Marti asked, prying her fingers off the dash.

Caty's eyes sparkled. "Jesse lets me drive his stockcar sometimes. Well, I gotta get ready for a test tonight in class. See you tomorrow."

"Yeah, tomorrow. Thanks for the ride."

Marti walked into the open bay, but didn't see Jesse at first. He was talking, his voice muffled. She approached a red Chevy facing the back wall with the hood up. The engine revved, but no one sat in the driver's seat. When she walked around the hood, she was taken off guard to find a woman leaning on the car peering down into the engine. A tall, lean woman with short brown hair and dark eyes.

She turned and said, "Hey, Marti. How are you feeling?"

Before Marti could answer, she heard a scooting noise, and Jesse rolled out from beneath the car. "Desiree stopped in to see how you were doing." His subtle way of letting her know the woman's name. But who was the beauty wearing a black tank top and jeans?

Marti shrugged. "I'm doing pretty good. Considering."

Desiree walked around the car and leaned against the side near Marti. "What an awful thing to happen, especially around here. You grow up feeling safe and secure and then something like this happens to rock your boots. Your voice still sounds hoarse, but you look good."

Jesse grinned. "She sounds like Demi Moore. I like it, kinda soft and sexy."

Marti turned to look at some tools hanging on the pegboard, hoping to hide her uneasiness. "I want my old voice back." Hallie's voice.

"I agree with Jesse. It probably sounds worse to you."

Something about Desiree bothered her, but she couldn't pinpoint it. Maybe the way she moved, confident, hips swaying as she walked toward the bay door.

That's what it was. Desiree reminded her of Hallie, seductive, with a full mouth and soulful eyes.

Marti watched Jesse's reaction around Desiree. For some reason, she was curious about his feelings toward her. Why did it make her feel good that he was busy putting his tools away and not watching Desiree's exit?

"See you both later," Desiree said as she walked toward a shiny black Jeep. Her snakeskin cowboy boots kicked up puffs of dust.

"Who is she?" The strain in her voice was *not* jealousy. Couldn't be. Jesse wasn't even her type.

"She's a friend," he said, glancing up to see her Jeep pull away. "Let me wash up and I'll be ready to go."

Marti wandered around the shop, kicking at a tire, feeling grungy and small compared to Desiree. A spotty mirror concluded what she didn't want to know: she was absolutely no match for someone like Desiree, someone like Hallie used to be. The part of her so concerned with appearance still lived inside her. She wished it didn't. Desiree and Jesse looked good together, both tall, Southern. They both fit in here. She certainly didn't. It bothered her far too much for her comfort.

His voice broke her out of her thoughts. "Ready?" He came up behind her, smelling of industrial-grade soap. "What's wrong? You've been quiet since you got here."

"Long day. Let's go."

What was wrong? she wondered as they drove home. She had been in a good mood until she'd gotten to the garage. Now she was eager to leave, get her new life started.

When they pulled into the driveway, Bumpus ran out to greet them, barking happily. Strangely enough, his loud happiness at their arrival seemed comforting in that familiar kind of way. Jesse greeted him by grabbing his snout and growling, riling him up even more. Bumpus ran over to Marti and barked, bowing. Yeah, *bowing*.

"That's dog language for 'play with me,'" Jesse said.

Start with the dog. She picked up a nearby rubber bone and tossed it for Bumpus to fetch. She was getting too comfortable here, so much so that Desiree's presence threatened her on a deep, territorial level. She didn't even have a territory. No, she had to do something about this comfort level.

"Jesse, I want to leave in one month."

He stopped trying to tug the bone out of Bumpus's mouth. "What are you talking about?" He looked surprised.

"You knew I wasn't going to stay."

"Yeah, but I thought you'd stay until you had the baby."

"That's seven months away. Here, I have to play the part of Marti. It's hard to fit into someone else's life. I'll come back before the due date."

Jesse strode back to the truck and pulled a manila folder from beneath the seat. "Let's go inside and talk."

She steeled herself to defend her reasons for leaving.

Jesse sat down at the table. He looked business-like, sifting through papers with a somber expression. She joined him.

He pulled out a piece of paper, unfolding it carefully. "I talked to the doctor's office and the insurance company. If the pregnancy is normal, no complications, this is what our bill will be. My bill. The loan officer at the bank said I could qualify for this much money. That leaves a balance of $8,752. I'll give you the rest if you stay."

"You're buying me off. That's ridiculous."

"What are you going to do, drive that piece of junk of a car out to California with a couple hundred bucks in your pocket? You've never lived on your own, have you? I mean really on your own."

"No, but I can take care of myself."

"That's not the point. By the time you get there, you're going to be broke. Where are you going to live, in a homeless shelter? You're not going to have any money to get your new life started. No money for food, rent, or doctor visits. What if you go into labor early? You want to get out of here so bad, you're not being realistic."

He was right, of course. She hated thinking about reality. In her mind, she was going to make it, no matter what. But she had to deal with reality now. He was being fair. After all, she needed money to get a new start, and that was more than she'd ever be able to save working at the diner.

"But you'll be in debt," she said.

"That's my problem. What do you say?"

She looked at the list of numbers, the calculations on that folded piece of paper. "As soon as I'm released from the hospital, the money's mine, and I'm free to go?"

Jesse's expression hardened. "You can leave and never look back."

"You won't try to convince me to stay and play mommy?"

He leaned back in the chair and crossed his arms over his chest. "Nope."

"Promise me you won't put a guilt trip on me for leaving. Because this baby wasn't my decision. I didn't ask for this."

"I promise."

Then she had a heart-clenching thought: maybe he didn't want her in his and the baby's lives. *Gawd, you're insane.*

She put her hand on her stomach, the baby's presence still unnoticeable. "Okay, I'll stay."

Marti breathed in deeply. "I love the smell of clothing stores. Seems like forever since I've been shopping."

Caty eyed her. "I don't think I've ever seen anyone get so excited about shopping. You buy clothes, you wear them. Sometimes you even have to try them on." She wrinkled her nose at that.

"I've never met a woman who didn't love shopping. It's an *experience*. The excitement of finding a dress that fits perfectly, spotting something outrageously cool that nobody else has. Even better if it's marked down. It's absolutely excellent!"

Marti had talked Caty into going to the Ft. Myers mall that evening. She needed decent clothes. Lugging twenty bags of clothing and merchandise finally satiated her need. She glanced at Caty, who was carrying some of the bags over her shoulder, and grinned. Caty was the first woman friend she'd ever had who hadn't made her feel competitive. Caty was just as attractive as she was, more so. Yet she wasn't concerned with one-upping her or pretending to be something she wasn't. It was a new experience, a true friend.

Without thinking, she leaned over and gave Caty a sideways hug. "Thanks for keeping me company. Shopping alone isn't the same."

Caty smiled wearily. "No problem. It was different. I'm not sure I'm going to get used to that hair, though."

Marti touched the blond curls, her most impulsive

purchase. The hairstylist had done wonders with the straight brown hair using dye that wouldn't harm the baby. "I thought it would make me feel more like my old self."

"Does it?"

She shook her head. "Not really. But I like it. You don't though."

Caty forced a smile. "Ah, it's okay. It's a pretty color."

That was another thing; Caty meant what she said. There wasn't the second-guessing Marti had with Joya.

Feeling warm and thankful, Marti spotted a shirt she thought would look great on Jesse. "What do you think about this for your brother?" she asked, holding up the purple, teal, and maroon shirt with the swirly design.

Caty cocked her head. "Hm, I don't know. It's not him."

Marti took it to the counter. "It'll do him some good to get out of character once in a while. Look what it's doing for me."

"Well, you're really out of character. Or out of body."

Marti blew out a breath. "Ain't that the truth."

Caty gave her a wry grin. "He's going to have enough of a time getting used to that hair of yours."

"You don't think he'll like it?" she asked, handing the clerk her debit card.

"You'll have to find out for yourself."

"I'm staying, you know," she said, signing the receipt and cramming the bag in with the rest of her bags.

"You are? Does Jesse know?"

"Of course. He's the one who proposed the deal."

"'The deal'?"

"He's going to take out a loan to pay the hospital bills and give me the balance."

Caty processed the information, and suddenly her opinion was important.

Marti turned to her, pausing in the middle of the mall. "Am I a terrible person for taking his offer? For not wanting to stay in the first place? Tell me."

She shrugged. "I'm not in the habit of judging people. Everyone has their motives and values. I couldn't begin to imagine what it's like being in your shoes. I think I would have stayed to have the baby without the bribe."

Guilt weighing her down, Marti found a nearby bench and sat down. "But you have a family, people who love you and whom you can depend on. It's different for me."

"I know it is. You asked my opinion, and I gave it to you. As long as *you* feel it's the right thing to do, then it is. You have to trust your gut."

That was the problem. Her feelings weren't particularly thrilled about the deal, and buying a silly shirt wasn't going to allay the guilt for putting him in debt. *But I'm staying here, putting my life on hold for seven months for him. He proposed the deal, so he must think it's okay.*

"We went to the doctor this morning, Jesse and I." Marti wanted to change the subject.

Caty's smile returned. "Jesse went, too?"

"He insisted."

"He's going to make a great father."

"We heard the baby's heartbeat. It sounded so fast and loud, kind of like panting." Marti grinned, then leaned closer to Caty. "You should have seen Jesse's face. He was like a little kid who just found out he's getting a pony for his birthday."

"Aw, that's sweet. What did the doctor say?"

"Well, I'm eleven weeks pregnant, due June twenty-second. Everything's fine. I think he took half my blood for all these tests. He prescribed prenatal vitamins and recommended vitamin B for nausea." She put her hand on her stomach. "Caty, I'm scared. This baby is going to go through so many changes. Things could go wrong."

Caty patted Marti's leg. "Everything will be fine, you'll see. And Jesse will be there with you. We all will."

Wow, the thought of having people to depend on. *It's only because of the baby. For Jesse.*

"Dr. Diehl isn't going to charge us for his services. He said he owed Jesse a lot because he saved his daughter's life. Desiree's life." She'd been dying to know more but hadn't felt comfortable enough to ask Jesse at the time.

"Well, that's more money for you then," Caty said in a tight voice.

"I told Jesse to put the amount he allotted for the doctor back on the loan. I don't want it. What I do want to know is what he did to save her life. And who is she? To Jesse, I mean."

Caty leaned back, a contemplative look on her face. "And you want to know because ..."

"Just curious."

"Sure." Caty nodded. "Jesse and Desiree started dating back when he was in high school. I think part of it was the older woman allure. They were pretty hot and heavy. It wasn't love so much as lust. That part fizzled out, but they remained friends.

"About six months later, she up and married some guy who'd just moved into town. Desiree's new husband wasn't only crazy about her, he was insane. He beat her up. She tried to hide it, but Jesse saw through that and when he couldn't talk her into leaving him, he did some checking on the guy. Turns out he was wanted in Kansas for nearly killing his last wife. Desiree didn't even know he *was* married before. Jesse notified the police, and they arrested the bastard. Jesse made sure the guy knew he'd better never come back.

"It took a while for Desiree to get back on her feet, self-esteem-wise, but Jesse stood by her and talked her into getting counseling. He doesn't think he did anything special, but I believe he saved her life."

Caty's story made Marti feel many different things, some of them she couldn't explain. Her mind threw her a picture of Jesse and Desiree in a hot clinch. Then she saw him befriending her, standing by her. He might have been hurt himself if her husband had caught him talking to Desiree. Now they had a special bond. She pushed the pictures from her mind. *Not bothered.*

Just like you weren't bothered seeing them together.

Yeah, exactly.

Jesse fixed himself some spaghetti, knowing Marti wouldn't be home until well after nine o'clock. He thought he'd enjoy having the evening to himself, but long before nine, he was already bored and restless. He wandered down by the river, watching the moonlight ripple along the currents. His thoughts were far from the sound of the frogs singing in different pitches, far from the shadows of the trees as they swayed in the cool evening breeze.

He shook his head, remembering Marti stretching up to push the box of old clothes into the cavernous hole of the Goodwill box, eager to get rid of them. He had offered to pitch the box in, but she wanted to do it herself. So, he'd wrapped his arms around her and hoisted her up. She had waved goodbye to the bags and boxes, giggling, but he'd been caught up in how small she felt in his arms. Inside that delicate body, his baby was growing, a reality that had overwhelmed him. He'd set her down slowly so he could savor the feelings that coursed through him.

Thinking back on it, he realized her laugh was different. So was her smile. Before, she only smiled tentatively, as if she was breaking some rule and someone might catch her. She put her hand in front of her mouth to hide it. The only time he'd really seen her smile was when she told him she was pregnant. *He* certainly hadn't been smiling then.

Now she was smiling again, a new woman inside. When he'd asked her why she was so happy at giving the clothes away, she'd said she felt in control again. His heart chugged like a train racing down the tracks, then and now. For the first time, his wife made him feel something.

And she was leaving.

Headlights slashed across the oak trunks, and Bumpus raced toward the house barking. Jesse headed toward the commotion of Caty's voice greeting the dog and the crinkling of bags.

At first, he didn't see Marti, only Caty and a blonde. Bumpus recognized Marti before he did. Jesse stared at the woman who had left a straight-haired brunette several hours earlier.

Caty watched the two stare at each other for a moment, then asked, "Well, what do you think, big brother?"

He walked closer, touching her hair to make sure it wasn't a wig. "You dyed your hair?"

Marti smiled. "Yep. This is sort of how my hair was

before. Do you like it?"

"Well, 'like' wouldn't be the word for it. Aw, I don't know. I liked it well enough before. Why'd you change it?"

Marti tossed her hair and stalked toward the house. Caty gave him a sheepish grin.

He asked, "Well, what do *you* think about it? You were a party to the deed."

Caty raised her arms. "Not me, no sirree. You think I could've told her otherwise? Nope. I didn't like it at first, but I'm getting used to it. However, I don't have to live with her, so you'd better march your butt in there and tell her you like it."

Jesse ran his fingers through his hair. "I never tell a woman something I don't mean. That policy has kept me out of trouble more times than it's gotten me into it."

Caty brushed a lock of hair from his face and said with a sigh, "You sure do have a lot to learn about women."

CHAPTER 7

After he'd seen Caty off, Jesse wandered back inside and peered into Marti's room. She sat on the edge of her bed, staring at her reflection in the mirror over the dresser.

"Hey," he said as a greeting, leaning against the doorframe. "I ... I really like ... ." He glanced at the window and stepped inside to get a closer look. "I like what you've done with the sheets." Now wasn't the time to change his honesty policy.

Her dark expression lifted when she saw his genuine appraisal. "Do you? I had to do something with that window. It was giving me the creeps."

He looked behind the curtains to see how she'd made the top angular and puffy. She'd cut the curtains at angles, making them drape in the middle.

"This looks like something out of those custom sections."

She beamed. "It's amazing what you can do with a couple of wire hangers and a sewing kit. I poked so many holes in my fingers, I thought I'd leak when I drank something."

He couldn't help smiling at her. Her pride shone, and

she was as adorable as a puppy the way she was looking for the pinpricks in her fingertips. White, pink, and blue bags of every size covered with the floor. Marti dropped back on the bed, stifling a yawn. He looked at her stomach, now rounded a tad. The reality of the baby hadn't hit until he'd heard its heartbeat. It was a thundering realization that his baby, a real human being, lived inside her. He sat down on the bed next to her, imagining his hand splayed out over her midsection, his thumb nestled in the hollow between her breasts.

"You know," she said dreamily. "I had some ideas about the curtains in the living room. Something masculine, but new and different. Would you let me redecorate a little?"

Only when she looked at him did he snap out of his trance. "Sure, do anything you like."

"What about your room? It's kind of dull in there. Can I ..." She hesitated when he leaned closer. "Can I do something in there, too? It's actually exciting, getting ideas about redecorating this place. Oh!" She sat up and started rifling through her bags. "I bought something for you."

When she pulled out the swirly, multi-colored shirt and held it up, he could only stare at it.

"You bought that? For me?" He forced a smile.

Her grin soured. "You don't like this either. Caty said it wasn't your style, but I knew it would look great on you. Try it on."

"I didn't say I didn't like it. Give me a moment to absorb it." Jesse stripped off his shirt. Her eyes were on him the whole time as he tossed his shirt on the floor and donned the new one. He leaned over and looked in the mirror. "I could get used to it." He met her gaze in the mirror. "And your hair, too. You're throwing a lot of new stuff at me at once. I'm too laid back to accept changes easily, and one of those changes is a whopper."

"You've been great about that. If you can handle that one, the small ones should be easy." She bit her bottom lip, letting her gaze travel over the shirt. "It looks absolutely excellent on you."

He leaned close and tucked a blond curl behind her ear. "Thanks." He gestured to the bags. "I can't believe you thought about me while you were doing all the girly shopping stuff."

"It's hard not to think about you." She looked away. "I mean, being with your sister and all, talking about the baby."

"You talked about the baby?" Was she accepting her pregnant body?

"The doctor's appointment and the heartbeat."

"Marti, can I ask you for something?"

Several expressions crossed her face, none he could identify. "Sure."

"I want to touch the baby. Through your stomach, I mean."

She met his gaze and whatever she saw there had her swallowing loudly. She nodded.

He sat down beside her and placed his hand on the outside of her shirt. After a moment, she peeled back her shirt to expose her bare stomach. He pressed his hand against the skin, watching her reaction. Her face flushed pink. Not wanting to embarrass her, he pulled his hand away.

"Sometimes, when Abbie was pregnant with Turk and Clint, I felt the baby move. It was something special, to feel that little flutter. I want to feel my boy's movements, knowing I made him."

"This baby means a lot to you, doesn't it?"

He nodded. "When I first heard I was going to be a father, I couldn't accept it. Once I could, I realized what it all meant. Heck, I wasn't sure what would happen between Marti and me once the baby was born, but I was going to give the family thing a try." He laughed. "I'd do anything for this kid, and he's not even born yet."

"You're going to spoil him rotten."

Jesse's smile faded. "I'm going to have to. I'm all he's got."

Marti tightened her lips. "Jesse, you promised you wouldn't put the guilt trip on me."

He stood. "I already told you how I feel about emotional attachments to women interfering with my racing. And you've told me you want to go back to California. I have no intention of trying to get you to stay after you've had the baby. We're going to get along just fine on that score."

A shadow of disappointment flitted over her face, though he hoped it was only his imagination. That look hardened.

"Absolutely. I don't belong here with you, in this town, and especially with a baby."

He agreed with the words, but for some reason they sounded hollow to him.

The man stood outside Marti's window. He couldn't see inside since she'd hung up that silly curtain, but he could see silhouettes. Bits and pieces of their conversation drifted through the fabric and glass. She and Jesse weren't sharing a bedroom anymore. Interesting.

The wind scattered dead oak leaves across the cool earth, but he stood perfectly still. As long as that damn dog didn't start barking again, he was safe.

Was he safe from the burning truth? From what he'd done, or almost done, to Marti? She had been dead when he'd left her at the side of the road, but she came back. How? At first, he thought maybe she didn't remember anything about his attacking her. Now he wasn't so sure. He'd heard that she and Jesse had stormed into the sheriff's office and demanded to see the photos. What exactly had they seen? What could they tell from them? He'd seen Jesse go into two jewelry stores the other day but couldn't subtly extract from the salespeople what he'd been looking for.

She was remembering, he was sure of it. Damaged memories could come back, and what then? *Think, man, think.* Even if she did remember, it would be her word against his. Her damaged memories. Didn't matter, though. Once she pointed the finger, everyone would be looking at him, wondering. That was the best-case scenario. Worst case: going to prison. He clenched his fists. No, he couldn't do that. He needed to shut her up, permanently this time. Sometime soon she would be alone.

The following week, Caty and Marti were sweeping up after the last customer finally lifted himself off the seat and sauntered out. Caty was right behind him, turning the deadbolt on the door.

Marti blew out a loud breath. "Damn, people are slow here in the South. I thought that lazy pace was exaggerated on television."

Caty laughed. "Well, we don't run around like a bunch of chickens in the butcher yard like you Californians probably do, that's for sure. How was your first day pulling your share of the tables?"

Marti put her hands over her breasts and grimaced. "It wouldn't have been so bad if I didn't feel like the girls were going to explode with every step. Some guy jostled me, and I about screamed."

"Yeah, I know at least a bit of what you mean. Mine get tender when my aunt flow starts planning her visit."

"You have an aunt who makes your boobs sore?" Caty chuckled. "My period."

"Oh, gotcha. Well, this is *nothing* like that kind of pain, let me tell you. They even hurt when I breathe." Marti leaned on the broom handle. "Do you think Marti got pregnant on purpose to trap Jesse?"

"Yes," Katie answered without hesitation. "I was mad at her, but if you knew Marti, it was hard to stay mad at her. She seemed so pitiful. Needy. And we could never prove it anyway."

"Sometimes I think about her, about what she was like. I took her life, and yet I know hardly anything about her. She only has your family's and her doctor's numbers in her phone, no social media accounts. Her life seemed pretty sad and lonely."

Caty scooted an army of ketchup bottles toward her as she sat down. "I didn't know much about her. She came into town, rented a room, and got a job here. I didn't think she was hiding from anyone, but it did seem like she was running away. Whenever I asked about her family, she changed the subject. The only thing she ever said was that they didn't get along and never would. It's hard for me to imagine being separated from my family like that."

Marti stared off for a moment, thinking of her own father whom she'd never met, of her mother. "Sometimes it's better to be separated from them. Believe

121

me."

On the way home, Marti drove to the grocery store to get a ready-cooked chicken for dinner. It was as she suspected: Marti had trapped Jesse into a marriage he wasn't ready for. Maybe she'd known how family-oriented and responsible he was. Still, it wasn't fair. She would return to California with stretch marks and extra weight, and Jesse would be a single dad.

Marti already knew that some of that extra weight she would carry back to California would be guilt. It inched up on her every time she thought about leaving. Which was ridiculous, since Jesse didn't want her to stay anyway.

She glanced down at her gas gauge, now very conscious of running out. It had crept down to a quarter of a tank. Did she dare take a chance that the gauge was accurate? One of the things she had promised Jesse was that she wouldn't stop to get gas by herself. She certainly didn't want to relive Marti's terror. But the first gas station on the edge of town was right up ahead, and it was the middle of the afternoon. What harm could come of it? She pulled in and got out to pump. The modern pumps looked out of place in front of the 1940's-style wooden building.

"Marti, you should have waited another minute. I could've done that for you."

She whirled around to find Paul dressed in green overalls, leaning against the farthest pump. With a casual stride, he walked over and propped himself up against her car.

"I thought you sold insurance," she blurted out, unnerved.

"I do, but business is slow, so I'm earning some extra

cash to put neon lighting underneath my truck. What do you think? Blue?"

There was something beneath the green of his eyes that made her think he didn't much care about her opinion.

"Blue's cool." She watched the numbers on the gas pump, waiting to hit the twenty-dollar mark so she could leave.

He reached out and touched her hair with blackened fingers. "I like this. Sexy, different. Taking a walk on the wild side?"

"No, just wanted a change." She moved away and found herself tucking her hair behind her right ear. Irritated at herself and Jesse for a second, she yanked it back out again.

"Your husband thinks I was the one who attacked you. You know that's not true."

She avoided his penetrating gaze. "I don't know who did it."

He touched her arm, and she flinched. "It wasn't me. Don't you see Jesse's trying to make you distrust me? Hate me? He knows I liked you before he got you pregnant, and he doesn't want anything to flare up between us."

She moved away as far as she could. "I didn't know there was anything to flare up."

"There wasn't. Yet." His fingers loosened their grip on her arm, and he leaned against her car. His smile was pure, unadulterated charm. "Marti, I know that inside is a wild woman clawing to get out. Am I right?"

Her eyes widened. Could he know? "What do you mean?"

"I mean, you don't belong in a pregnant body waiting

on Jesse and pumping out babies." He lifted his hand to graze her cheek. "We could have a lot of fun together. You can have babies when you're older and more settled."

She turned off the pump and closed the gas door. "Are you suggesting I have an abortion so I can romp with you?"

He cocked his head at her directness. "I'd make it worth it."

"No, you couldn't."

She started to get in the car, planning to toss out the money and screech away.

His voice stopped her. "You're carrying a criminal's child."

"What are you talking about?"

"Jesse is a criminal. You're living with a car thief."

"You're lying. Jesse wouldn't steal a car."

Paul crossed his arms and leaned back on his heels. "Oh, but he did. And he was convicted, too. Think about that as you lie next to him at night." Then his smile curved up wickedly. "But you're not sharing a bed with him, are you?"

"How would you know something like that?" She felt confused and violated.

"Someone saw you bed shopping a few Sundays ago. Something like that can mean only one thing—trouble at home."

"It's for the baby." She closed the door and handed him a twenty.

He didn't take it. "Babies don't sleep in regular beds."

Screeching tires drew her attention away from Paul's leer to a face of barely controlled anger: Jesse. His truck pulled to a stop inches away from Paul and her car.

He jumped out and stalked toward Paul. Before he said anything to him, Jesse turned to her. "Go home. Now."

"Jesse, I —"

"Now." The low timbre might as well have been as loud as thunder, the power it contained.

She tossed the twenty out and slammed the car into gear. Damn men. All she wanted was gas. In the rearview mirror, Jesse made pointed gestures while Paul stood back, unaffected. Arrogant even. Still, he'd imparted some unpleasant news, if it was true. A convicted car thief? Couldn't be.

Jesse arrived home five minutes after she did. She steeled herself for his anger. Who was he, anyway, to tell her what to do?

Anger reddened his face. "Damn it, Marti, what did I tell you about getting gas alone?"

"I didn't want to run out."

"You shouldn't let it get that low."

"I can't hide away because someone tried to attack me."

"So, you position yourself alone with the man who probably killed Marti? You're a damn fool."

She felt warmth rising to heat her cheeks. "I am not a fool. It was broad daylight. By a busy road."

He leaned into her face, his voice sarcastic. "And what time of the day was Marti attacked? And by what busy road?"

Her face paled. He was right on that score. "Well, I was handling it just fine, about to leave when you stormed in like the Army."

"He was probably planning on puncturing your tire. Geez, you don't know what he might have done."

"You're only speculating it was Paul because you

hate him. You don't have proof, except for a similarity in his pendant and my scratch."

Jesse sat down, breathless. "No, I don't have proof. But it just so happens that Paul was off the afternoon Marti was killed."

She dropped down on the couch a few feet away from him. "How do you know?"

"Because my friend Alan is dating the secretary at the insurance company. She checked the sign-in sheets; he left at noon for the day."

CHAPTER 8

Marti was having trouble conjuring up the Christmas spirit, even though it was only a week away. It was even harder to drum up excitement for Harry's holiday bar-b-que. She'd laid three different outfits on the bed trying to figure out what to wear, wondering why it even mattered. It was unbearably warm for December, not at all suitable for the season. At least it got cold in southern California, even if they didn't have white Christmases.

Finally, she chose a teal top that laced up the front and took advantage of her swelling chest. White, low-waisted jean shorts went well with that. She pulled her blond curls into a ponytail and tied a ribbon around it. No pearls, lace, or sequins for this party. An outside bar-b-que with a roasted hog and a bunch of burping, dirty-joke-telling, country-music-listening hicks. She stared grimly into the mirror and set her mouth in a straight line. Worst of all, she couldn't even get drunk to numb the situation. The baby was more important than her temporary comfort. Besides, Jesse would never allow it, not even a sip.

Her bottom lip puckered at the thought of Jesse. He

had forced her into this. This hadn't been the first party they'd been invited to, and every time he brought one up, she told him to go without her. But he didn't want to leave her alone, not with Bumpus's barking fits in the middle of the night and no raccoons to be found as the cause. So, he had declined them, never citing her as the reason. He wasn't so obliging with Harry's shindig. It was his boss, and the biggest event of the year, besides the one Harry gave after the Fourth of July parade. Jesse called her selfish, and for some reason it bothered her when he called her that more than when anyone else had. The selfless bastard.

When she opened her bedroom door, the country music seeping under her door in polite volumes now pounded against her. With her hands over her ears, she went in search of the stereo controls. Jesse found her first. He appeared out of nowhere, pulled her into his arms, and danced her across the living room.

"Yeah-eee!" he hollered with a twang.

"Jesse!" she exclaimed, but to no avail.

The room spun around her as his arms held her tight. She could only see Jesse's face, lit with a two-thousand-watt smile. On his head was a black cowboy hat tilting low over his forehead. When the heel-kicking song ended, he slowed his pace to match the slower melody. He also pulled her close against his body, and she could feel the heat of his heartbeat against her cheek.

"Jesse," she murmured against the texture of his shirt.

"Shh, I like this song."

A man's voice sang out that he was born to love her, and the warmth froze over in her blood. Of course, Jesse didn't mean anything by it, she told herself. Still, she moved out of his arms and turned down the stereo. His dismayed expression only held her attention for a minute before her gaze drifted down over his bolo tie, white shirt with cowboy stitching, black leather belt, and indigo jeans. And black leather cowboy boots.

"I've never seen you dressed like this before," she said, a grin creeping over her face.

He tilted his head and smiled, those indents in his cheeks not quite full-fledged dimples. "I don't put on the dog very often. Just when I'm in the mood."

"Your cowboy mood, huh?"

He turned the stereo back up and pulled her close again. "Yep, my cowboy mood. Are you afraid to dance with me?"

She stiffened. "No. Why would I be?"

He started slowly moving her around, swaying to the music. "I don't know. Why would you be?"

"I just don't ... like this kind of music."

His hips pressed against hers. Suddenly he dipped her, poised above her.

"Say you like it, or I'll drop you," he taunted.

"Like what? Dancing with you or country music?"

He grinned. "Both." He dropped her a little lower. "Say it."

"Jesse ... ." His warm breath pulsed against her throat. "Okay, I like it. Now let me go."

He yanked her up and twirled around the room. "Why would I do that? You just said you liked dancing with me."

"Under duress!"

He was having too much fun at her expense. Even in his getup, he looked devastatingly sexy. But only in an objective sense. When he loosened his grip, she slipped out and sat down on the couch. He did a little wiggle of his derriere, ending with a slap to the bottom of his boot. Finally, he turned down the stereo. With a flushed face, he leaned down over her and tucked her hair behind her ears.

"You gotta learn to loosen up and have some fun."

She untucked her hair. "When I did that, I got into trouble. Besides, I don't want to have fun."

"Why not?"

"Because ... ." *I'm leaving in six months. Because you're making me feel very funny inside leaning so close to me like this.*

"Well?"

She slid around him and walked to the other side of the room. "Don't we have to go soon?"

He ran his fingers through his waves, shaking his head. "I thought you didn't want to go. Now you can't wait to get out of the house." He rested his chin on the back of the couch facing her. "Why is that?"

"I just want to get it over with." She reached for her new leather purse.

With a quick leap, he was over the couch and sauntering near her. "I know what it is," he said in a teasing voice. His woodsy cologne wafted over before he got close. Too close.

She backed away, her eyes narrowed. "And what is it, mister know-it-all?"

He took a step closer. "I think you've always had a secret cowboy fetish. Oh, you never admitted it to anyone, but down deep inside ... ." He pressed a finger to the middle of her chest and traced a circle. "It's there."

She batted his finger away. "Don't be silly. I've never had a thing for cowboys. I go for the slick California types, blondes with surfboards attached to the roofs of their cars. You're too arrogant for your own good, Jesse James."

His smile reeked of confidence. "Maybe. But you sure don't trust yourself to get too close to me, now do you? You've moved away from me twenty times."

"Your cologne's too strong."

"Come on, Mrs. Marti May West," he said with a roll of his eyes, holding out his arm. "Be my wife for an afternoon."

Bumpus crawled out of the bushes and followed them as soon as they walked toward the truck. When Jesse opened the door for her, she saw the roll of paper towels on the seat.

"See, I didn't forget about you. And you don't have to ride in the back either."

She slugged him in the arm and climbed up. Did he actually think she was attracted to him because he was wearing cowboy clothing? Or for any other reason? Maybe he was just flirting, part of his cowboy mood. That sounded better.

Bumpus settled in between them and seemed to give her an expectant look. *Good dog, sitting between us.*

He kept looking at her as though he'd understood Jesse's words about starting with the dog. She reached over and pet the top of his head. He licked her, and she pulled back and wiped her hand on the seat. *Yuck.*

Harry's place was farther west than Helen's, down a long dirt road. Anxiety set in at the sight of the cars and trucks scattered along the side of the road and packed into the front driveway. All these people. She was going to have a miserable time.

The house was a new two-story with gray wood siding. The commotion was around the back beneath a strange structure with a roof made of dead palm fronds. Country music blared, people laughed, and Marti grimaced.

Jesse stopped before they reached the house. "Stay nearby so I can help you out with anyone you don't know that you should." He tilted his head, a gleam in his eyes. "That is, if you can handle being close to me."

She slugged him in the arm again, ignoring the pain at contacting hard flesh.

All the hoopla Jesse received when they arrived at Harry's proved that he really didn't dress up like that very often. It sounded more like a construction site with all the wolf whistles and cowboy calls. He took it in stride, even bowing. She couldn't help smiling.

Harry was in his forties with a bulbous nose and an even more bulbous belly. He teetered over to greet them, already intoxicated.

"Jesse, Marti! Glad you could come. Keg's over there, sodas are in the big red cooler, and hog's on the fire. He'll be ready to come to supper about five. Help yourselves."

Marti looked at a primitive brick structure with a whole pig on it: hooves, head, and tail. She wrinkled her nose, wondering if her appetite would ever forgive her for this one.

"What would you like to drink?" Jesse asked.

"A glass of Chardonnay? Martini? Guess I'll have to settle for a Coke, and I'd pay you a hundred bucks if you'll slip something in it."

"Gotcha," he said and walked toward the coolers.

Most of the people sitting at picnic tables and playing horseshoes she'd seen at Bad Boys at one time or another. She saw Skip and Josh, but luckily Paul was nowhere in sight. While talking to some guy, Desiree gave Jesse a cutesy wave.

"Here you go," Jesse said, handing her a cup with a peach hibiscus flower in it.

She frowned at the flower in it.

"Well, you said you wanted something in it. And you don't even have to give me a hundred bucks. Maybe it'll look better here." He tucked her hair behind one ear and slipped the flower in, looking pleased with the result.

His fingers brushed her temple, and she got caught up in his eyes for a moment. He cleared his throat and dropped his hand. "Perfect."

She gave him a weak smile and turned before she stared into his eyes too long.

Dean and Caty showed up a little later. Marti was glad to see a face she knew and liked, but Caty was busy telling everyone about the cow she'd calved and visited earlier.

Dean watched her flit from one group of people to another, longing clear in his eyes.

Hm, hadn't you just looked like that?

No!

Marti moved up beside him. "She's quite the social butterfly, isn't she?"

"Hey," he said, his smile almost too wide. "Where's Jesse?"

"I released him, told him to wander around to his heart's content. I'm not in a party mood."

Dean glanced uneasily down at his beer. "Me neither. Hey, I like that flower. My Aunt Flo used to eat flowers. She'd dip them in batter and deep fry 'em."

Marti's eyes widened. "You're not talking about your ... oh, you really have an Aunt Flo." He was looking at her as strangely as she sometimes looked at him. "Never mind. Did fried hibiscus taste good?"

"They weren't bad if you sprinkled on powdered sugar." His gaze drifted beyond her. "That girl's gonna wear herself out." He wandered off to follow Caty around like a puppy.

Jesse took up a game of horseshoes, he and Billy creaming two other guys. Josh, wearing dingy overalls again but minus the dried grass, moseyed over and planted himself next to her on the bench. His red hair stuck out as though he'd just woken up.

"Like a beer?" He held up his half-empty cup as if to offer her the rest.

"No, thanks. I'm pregnant."

"Oh, that's right. You going to dance later?" He pointed to a cleared area strung with lights.

"Not likely."

Josh made her increasingly uncomfortable as he stayed too close for too long. The smell of his sweat was making her feel nauseated.

"Do you really think Paul was the one who attacked you?" he asked at last.

She eyed him. "Why, have someone else in mind?"

"Could be lots of guys." His glassy eyes leered. "Could've even been me."

She lifted her chin. "Was it?"

"It was if you enjoyed it. Did you?"

She stood up and made a beeline toward the house. Josh walked next to her, more like a bulldog than a puppy. He appeared to be casually walking her to the house, but his voice sounded sinister.

"You better tell your husband he's asking for trouble if he keeps tryin' to pin the attack on Paul. He didn't do it, but people are starting to wonder, the way Jesse keeps sniffing 'round like a hound dog, checking the jewelry stores and Paul's work records. He happens to be a good friend of mine, and it's bugging him. You tell Jesse to lay off."

She turned around before reaching the door. "Why don't you tell him yourself? He's right behind you." When Josh looked to where she pointed, she ducked inside and hid in the bathroom for a while. She wished Jesse *had* been standing right behind him. Only when the third voice outside the door lamented at waiting to pee, did she finally flush the toilet and walk back outside.

Jesse was sitting where she had been earlier. "You all right? You were gone for a while."

"I'm fine. I needed to get away from annoying company." She decided not to get Jesse's ire up over Josh's warning.

"They're about to serve dinner. Are you hungry? Boy, you're going to love roasted hog, smoking all day long in the pit."

With great ceremony, four men pushed aside palm fronds from the pit. They lifted the black mass out and set it up to start slicing away at the carcass. Marti decided to wait at the table for Jesse and let the whole process remain a mystery.

After dinner, everyone sat around and talked about how wonderful the hog was. Burping was the next order of business, compliments to the chef all around. Thankfully, Jesse abstained from that, although he did laugh at some of the more creative efforts, like the guy who burped the alphabet. The next round of conversation was how many men had noticed that the ice cubes were in the shape of women's boobs. She glanced at her glass, realizing she hadn't noticed and not feeling all that amused.

Deep in her thoughts, she drifted off to one of Theresa's parties in California. Her mother-in-law knew how to put on a shindig, waiters making the rounds with trays of champagne, bars scattered around the huge lawn behind the mansion. No boob cubes or burping. She pictured her old self, drinking too much champagne, dressed in black velvet and diamonds.

"Wheeehooo!" Billy hollered, bringing her back to the dreadful present. She turned to see someone's white derriere glaring from atop one of the tables. She didn't bother to see whose behind it was before looking back at Jesse. Her mood was deteriorating rapidly.

"Lighten up," Jesse said goodheartedly. "It's only fun and games. We gotta stay for some dancing, at least."

"You can be so optimistic," she said below her breath. "You're half sloshed."

His smile disappeared. "No, I'm not. Maybe a quarter sloshed, but not nearly half." He reached over and tucked her hair behind the other ear. "Don't be mad. Have fun."

She forced a wide smile. "Oh, Jesse, I'm having a great time. The company is terrific, the hog body gourmet, and the music enchanting. See, I'm getting into it." Her good humor slipped away. With the twangiest voice she could muster, she started singing. "My wife left me for my best girlfriend, my hound dog died on the front porch, and the bank repo'd my land, so I can't even bury him. Woe, woe, woe is me!"

Then she started laughing, howling even. Did she ever think she would be at a party where burping was considered good-hearted fun? Where they had boob-cubes, and you were a boob if you didn't notice your cubes had titties?

Doubled over with tears streaming down her cheeks, her stomach hurt, she was laughing so hard. *Have fun.* Whoo boy, she was having fun now. She tumbled off the bench and onto the grass, and finally gained some control over herself after catching her breath. When she peered up over the edge of the table, everyone in the vicinity was watching her. And they weren't laughing.

Even Jesse looked serious. "You have a strange way of having fun," he stated flatly.

That started her giggling again. "*I* have a strange way. At least I'm not trying to top the biggest, most disgusting belch!"

The others' attention faded away to their individual conversations, but Jesse's gaze remained on her.

"What's the matter?" she asked, getting to her feet.

"At least our way of having fun isn't making fun of others' ways. And others' music."

She sat down on the bench, taking a last deep breath. "So, sue me. At least I can say I had a little fun."

He pointed to her, his finger slipping between the lace of her top. "For that outburst, you owe me a dance tonight. A slow one."

"I don't want to. You know I don't like this music."

"If these people are going to think you were kidding, you'd better get that sweet little butt of yours out there with me. Then we can leave."

She looked to the patch of ground reserved for dancing. The lights defined the square, and inside, several couples were dancing and moving in a circle as they did so. The people who weren't under the tent mingled outside the dance area watching.

"Well?" Jesse said.

"Then we can leave? You promise?"

"Yes, I promise."

She grimaced but stood anyway. He took her hand and led her toward the dreaded square. At his request, a slow song started, and he walked her out to the far edge. The square quickly filled with couples, making her feel less self-conscious. And more conscious of being in Jesse's arms again.

He still wore the black cowboy hat, which cast a shadow across his cheeks and nose. A cowboy fetish indeed. The hat made him seem taller and gave him a sort of refined roughness. His collar points, tipped in silver, caught the light as they swayed to the rhythm. And those boots made him taller yet. She stared down, watching them move in rhythm.

The singer likened his love to Reno, Nevada, cold, heartless, and playing with his affections. Some men may have perceived Hallie of the past that way. She'd held the deepest, most vulnerable part of herself back.

She pictured the scene earlier in Jesse's living room, him moving close, her stepping away. Might he think she was still like that? No, that was uneasiness. Just like the hot flash at Helen's house, she could explain that away, too. She'd think of something, if she gave it a minute.

Jesse lifted her chin so she was looking up to him. His soft smile was subtler than earlier.

"You don't have to watch our feet," he said. "You're doing fine."

She realized then that she had been staring at his boots while lost in thought. Better to let him think she was unsure of her footing than her heart. He tucked her hair behind her ears. The flower was smashed in the grass where she'd fallen off the bench.

"Why do you keep tucking my hair behind my ears?" she asked, loosening it again.

He shrugged. "Just seems like it should be."

"Did you do that with" — she glanced around — "the other Marti?" She wasn't even sure why she wanted to know.

"No. It was different with her."

"How?" She wanted to pull back the question.

He tucked her hair again. "Well, for one thing, there's something different about your eyes. I don't see neediness there, but there's still a wanting. Like you're searching for something, but you don't know what it is."

She glanced away, wondering how he could see something she didn't even know was there. But she was searching, for a new life. A new identity.

"I'm not looking for love, I know that." It sounded hollow, but she believed in those words more than anything else.

Warmth burned in his green eyes as he let go of her hand and trailed his finger up the length of her throat to rest under her chin. "It'll find you someday, you just wait." *But not with me.*

Marti could hear the unspoken addition as clearly as if he had spoken them aloud. She searched for words to respond but couldn't get past the disappointment. Why was she feeling that way, silly fool?

"The song's over," she said, finding it hard to swallow

with his finger still touching her.

His hand slipped from her waist and took hold of her hand as he walked off the dance area. They wound around others who were line dancing to the jaunty tune.

Oh, God, we've been slow dancing through part of a fast song. With half the town watching. They'll think ... . The words dropped down on her head. *They'll think you're in love, too distracted to realize the slow dance was over.* She shook her head, ignoring Jesse's glance at her movement.

Jesse pulled her around to various groups to say goodbye, then to thank Harry for his hospitality, burping, and boob cubes excepted. Good humor replaced the speculation at her earlier outburst. Hopefully they thought she was drunk. Or just stupid. Hopefully they didn't think she was in love with her husband.

Bumpus, like a child having fun, was reluctant to leave his canine pals. Still, when Jesse gave the word, he tromped over to them. All three walked down the driveway in silence, except for Bumpus's occasional slurping noises. When they reached the truck, she armed herself with the paper towels before she got in next to Jesse. With a tiny groan, the dog twirled around and settled down on the seat, nestling his head on her thigh.

Jesse tilted his head at the cozy scene. "I don't understand it, but that dog sure does like you."

She crossed her arms, careful not to disturb Bumpus. "What's not to understand?" A warm feeling curled inside her as she looked at the dog, already half asleep.

He shook his head as he put the truck into gear and pulled onto the dirt road. "You're ornery, snobby, and you can't cook worth a damn. I'm gonna have a talk with that dog. Maybe he can enlighten me."

She shot him a look then rested her hand on the dog's head, feeling a sudden kinship with him. After all, it was safer to be around the dog than it was to be with Jesse James West, the outlaw cowboy.

Florida's weather at least had the decency to get nippy two days before Christmas. When Marti thought the diner might be slower, it got busier. All the usual patrons came in with visiting relatives and introduced them to Caty and Marti like they were family, too. Even her own family hadn't been that friendly.

Tinsel and garland draped all over the walls enhanced the warm, country theme inside the diner. Chuck didn't much want to perpetuate the Santa Claus myth, being much more religious than he let on. A manger with Mary, Joseph, and baby Jesus sat in the corner, displacing one of the tables. Chuck's usual sullen expression had lifted some; maybe he thought he was safe from her memory of the attack ... if he had something to worry about. She hated thinking that way, but the fear lingered at the back of her mind.

Ten minutes after closing time, Jesse knocked on the glass door. Marti felt greasy and shabby and didn't want to see him until she'd washed up. She caught herself starting to smooth her hair back and stopped. It was just vanity, not any special desire to impress Jesse.

She'd forgotten how cool it was outside. And overcast. Puffs of fog appeared when Jesse talked. He looked like a boy anxiously awaiting Santa's visit.

"Let's go Christmas tree shopping, doll."

She glanced at Caty. "I can't. Caty and I are going Christmas shopping when we're done. I'm going to shower and change at your mom's on the way to Ft. Myers." When his smile disappeared, she added, "We can go later tonight."

His smile revived. "Caty, want to come along? You and Mom need a tree, too."

"Nah, she wants to put up that fake thing again. You know, she complains about the needles and everything."

His eyes lit with mischief. "We'll get her one anyway." He looked at Marti, still standing in front of him. "See you at home then." He clicked his tongue and winked, then walked back outside and jumped into his truck.

"He's like a little boy," Marti said with a smile.

"This year, he is."

Marti ignored Caty's wistful smile.

Marti didn't get home until six. She sneaked into the house with her packages and put them in the closet. She was enjoying Christmas more than usual, too. Family celebrations were something she could become accustomed to, although she wouldn't. Couldn't. Still, she'd remember these days with a fondness that was lacking in her past holiday memories.

"What'd you get, what'd you get?" Jesse whispered from the other side of the door.

"Don't you dare come in here!" she said, shoving the closet door shut.

"Does that mean there's something in there for me?"

She threw a shoe at the door. "Only coal."

He was standing at the front door when she emerged. Wearing a white T-shirt and black jeans, his expression radiated joy. She couldn't help but smile. Jamie had enjoyed Christmas, but not as enthusiastically as Jesse seemed to. Maybe that had been because of her, she thought with dismay. Hopefully he was having a wonderful Christmas with his new wife.

"Hey, hey, what's the frown for?"

She pushed Jamie from her memory. "Nothing. I'm ready."

"Good." He took her hand but blocked the front door when they reached it. "Close your eyes."

She eyed him suspiciously. "Why?"

"Come on, trust me."

"Humph."

When she started to close them, she felt him move up behind her and clamp his palms over her eyes. He guided her out the front door and into the crisp air tinged with the smell of chimney smoke. Christmas music wafted over from the vicinity of his truck. He turned her around, and she thought she faced the house again.

"Ready?" he asked.

"Yes."

Still, he waited, pressed up behind her with his hands firmly planted over her eyes.

"What are we waiting for?"

"I don't know. I kind of like standing here like this."

She nudged him, and he removed his hands. The house twinkled every color of the rainbow, vivid against the night air. The lights on the roof spelled out, "Merry Christmas!" The bushes were sprinkled with tinsel, which sparkled as Bumpus rustled through them. A big plastic angel poised above the front door, holding a star in her hands. Marti caught her breath, taken in by the magic of the lights.

"Oh, Jesse, it's beautiful! Like a fairytale."

He wrapped his arms around her, resting his chin on her shoulder. "Just for you."

She turned, suddenly finding it hard to breathe. "Don't say that. You do this every year."

The boyishness of earlier was gone, replaced by a masculine softness. "No, I don't. I wanted to make this a special Christmas for you. I wanted to give you a good memory to think about next year."

She swallowed, feeling overcome by a barrage of emotions. At the moment, with the music and warmth welling up inside her, she couldn't dredge up a foul, underhanded reason for his doing all this. He wasn't trying to get her to stay.

Her voice nearly failed her. "I won't forget you."

The lights twinkled in his eyes as they mesmerized her.

He brushed her chin, then tucked her hair behind her ears. "Let's get our tree, doll."

They stopped at the first lot filled with Christmas trees. There were still plenty to choose from under the yellow-and-white striped tent surrounded by bare light bulbs. Jolly music filtered through the air as they searched for the two most perfect trees left. The ones in the front were either crooked or had massive bare spots.

"There're more out back," the young salesman told them. "It's kinda dark back there, so watch for holes where the trees have been."

Beyond the last line of trees, the empty lot continued before turning into woods. The music was only faint, and she felt lost in a magical forest. One of the trees moved, and before she could mention it to Jesse, a man jumped out and threw a rope of some kind over

Jesse's head, pulling him back. A hand clamped over her mouth and a familiar voice whispered, "Don't say a word, or your husband gets it worse."

Paul suddenly stepped out of the darkness to stand in front of Jesse, who was whipping his fists wildly at the man holding him from behind. Since the man, who she realized was Skip, was shorter, he had Jesse bent backward at an awkward angle. Paul slammed a fist into Jesse's stomach, and he groaned before kicking. His foot connected with Paul's knee, making him groan in pain. With more anger than before, Paul kicked Jesse in the gut, dropping him to his knees. Marti struggled, but Josh pinched her hands tighter behind her back.

"Stop! Stop hurting him!" She felt every punch, every kick Jesse suffered.

"I'm tired of you trying to pin Marti's assault on me," Paul growled. "Mack told me you were checking out my tee times at the golf course. People are starting to wonder what you've got on me, and you got nothing. I was at the course when she was attacked."

Paul slugged Jesse in his face. Marti bit Josh's hand. He let go with a curse, and she spun away and screamed.

Skip dropped Jesse, and both he and Josh tore off into the dark. Paul took a step back, looking down at Jesse. "Leave it alone. Consider this your final warning." With that he was gone, seconds before the tree salesman came rushing over.

She ran to Jesse, who was getting to his feet between violent coughing spasms. When she saw that he was going to chase after them, she pulled his arm back.

"Jesse, no! There are three of them, and one of you. That didn't work well the first time."

"Geez, are you two all right?" The young man's face

contorted with shock. "I know it's dark back here, but I never figured it'd be dangerous criminally. Tell you what, I'll let you have whatever tree you want, for your trouble. No charge."

Jesse started to say something, but she interrupted. "Thank you, that's awfully nice. We'll take this one here, and we also want that one, for his mother. She's going to be so upset when she hears about this." She added in a whisper, "She's very fragile these days."

The salesman watched with growing concern. "Aw, you can have that one, too. I don't want his mama bent out of shape. It is Christmas."

When the trees were loaded into the back of the truck, and the salesman had apologized for the fifteenth time and left, Marti reached up and dabbed at Jesse's lip with a paper towel.

He flinched. "You going to swab me like you do Bumpus?"

"Stop moving. You're bleeding all over."

"Sons of bitches ambushed me. What kind of slime ambushes a guy when he's *Christmas tree shopping*?"

The true amazement in his expression made her laugh before she had the sense to bite her lip. "So, you've been doing some snooping, huh?" She remembered Josh's remarks at Harry's but decided not to share them with Jesse right then. "Do you think he really did it?"

"I — ouch. I don't know. He left work at noon. Apparently, he called the course and arranged a tee time of twelve-thirty. Nolen said he found you at around one o'clock, and ... ." He stared into the distance for a second before looking back at her. "Marti was already dead. But she hadn't been dead for long, so that means the assault happened just before one. Paul checked in at twelve-twenty, but Mack didn't see Paul and those two boneheads start the first hole until about twelve-forty-five. That leaves Paul twenty minutes to drive down the road and find poor Marti stuck. It doesn't exactly prove he's the murderer, but it doesn't clear him either. Apparently that dumb-ass Mack mentioned my inquiries to Paul, who had to get his buddies to help him out." Jesse placed his palm on his flat stomach and grimaced.

"Are you all right? God, I was so scared."

His expression was dark. "So was I. For you." He took her face in his hand. "Marti, I wouldn't have let them hurt you. I can take my punches, but if they'd tried to hurt you, they would have been dead."

"I know," she whispered. Somehow, she did, and she knew how important it was for him to protect his own.

"I've got to find out who did this to you. To Marti. I don't want them to hurt you again."

"How can you hide your anger and determination so well? Like with the racing. And that Sunday when I told you about the indent and Paul's pendant; you just went about the rest of the day like normal, then you confronted Paul."

He looked off into the distance again. "When my pa died, I wanted to scream and yell and never stop crying. He was everything to me, my whole world. Billy withdrew, and Mom had so much to deal with, I couldn't dump her with that burden, too. So, I put it aside until after the funeral, when I could deal with it alone. I do it when I have to."

She put her hand on his arm. "Please don't get crazy. I know you're mad, but remember, he might be a killer." She smiled, trying to make light of what she was about to say. "What would I do without you? I can't have this baby alone. He needs a father."

And a mother.

She pushed that errant thought away.

He turned and started the truck. "I'm not going to do anything stupid." Then he laughed. "My 'fragile' mother?"

She shrugged. "Got us another tree, didn't it?"

"You are one clever girl, you know that?"

She couldn't help but beam at his compliment.

They dropped one of the trees off at Helen's. She was more annoyed at Jesse's bloody lip than she was at having the live tree forced on her. When Jesse and Marti pulled back into their drive, her heart tightened at the lights. Caty had confirmed what Marti didn't want to know: Jesse had never decorated his house full tilt before. Just a paper Santa on the door and a few strings of lights. She bit her lip. How could his decorating touch her more than a long-ago gift of a red Porsche? He was so sweet.

Damn him.

CHAPTER 9

During the entire Christmas Eve day, Marti was surrounded by a flurry of activity. First work, where Chuck gave them fifty-dollar bonuses and let them go home early. He'd actually smiled.

After cleaning up, Jesse locked himself in his bedroom while he wrapped packages. Dressed in a red and black flannel shirt, he looked like a misplaced lumberjack. Handsome, but misplaced.

"I won't tell Caty what you got her," she'd teased.

He had pinched her chin. "But you'll tell Marti what I got her, so scoot."

She had turned crimson, realizing for the first time that Jesse had actually bought her something for Christmas. It was the perfect time to wrap her own presents, and she scrounged up a pair of children's scissors with green plastic handles and some tape. For once, the country music took a backseat to traditional Christmas music by Bing Crosby and Johnny Mathis. It filled the house with the sweet warmth of anticipation.

All those empty Christmases with her mother slipped away with every song, with every package she wrapped in red and gold foil. This year she would spend the most special day of the year with a real family. As Jesse had said, she would treasure the memory when she was alone in California. She shook her head, flinging the lonely thought from her mind.

Marti saved Jesse's presents for last. They were more expensive than the other gifts put together, but it would be worth it to see his face when he opened the box and pulled out the gray ostrich-skin boots. The other box contained a gray cowboy hat with a matching ostrich band. She'd known the moment she saw them in the window that Jesse must have them.

Later in the day, Caty, Helen, and Billy showed up to decorate the tree. Marti felt like a kid, stringing fresh popcorn and twirling it around the tree. Dinner was eggnog, tarts and fried cheese. Helen snapped a picture of Jesse wrapping his arms around Marti's waist and lifting her up high to put the angel atop the tree.

Bumpus even got into the act, fetching the red velvet balls that got knocked off the tree and rolled away. Marti tied a red ribbon around his neck, although it dangled upside down beneath his chin most of the time. And hell's bells, they even had country Christmas music, but she could live with that. Nothing was going to spoil her evening.

Except Billy. Melancholy tinged his smiles, and sometimes she caught him staring off. She remembered his boys, celebrating Christmas without their father. He had made mistakes, but he still deserved his kids for the holidays. Marti involuntarily put her hand on the small mound of her stomach. This baby, she knew, would never be without his father.

She found Billy standing in the kitchen alone, looking out the window. His wispy hair stuck out in places, reaching way past his collar. He was always either quiet or making jokes, and those wild, beady eyes of his fit both personas. She had all but ruled him out as her attacker.

Marti had never quite connected with him, as she had with the other Wests. Most of the time, she wasn't bothered, but watching him standing there like a lost boy made her approach him. The part of her that said *go back to the fun and forget about his problems* lost out to this new side of her.

"Billy?" she said softly.

He turned. "Nice night out, huh?"

"I'm sure they miss you as much as you miss them."

He rubbed his nose, looking away. "I wasn't ... ." Then he met her eyes and shrugged. "I hope so. How'd you know I was thinking 'bout my boys?"

She put her hand to her belly. "Woman's intuition. We've got a box of tinsel out there that we could sure use your help with."

Jesse's expression was one of curiosity when she and Billy walked out of the kitchen together, sharing a private smile. Let him wonder, she thought with a grin.

After every inch of Jesse and Marti's tree was duly covered with ornaments, everyone packed up the food and eggnog and drove over to Billy's to decorate his tiny tree (because Jesse insisted that he have one), and then to Helen and Caty's house. Even though it wasn't exactly frosty outside, Jesse lit the fireplace. Billy lifted Caty up to top the tree with a sparkling star. By the time their tree looked as merry as everyone else's had, exhaustion claimed Marti. She glanced at the clock: nearly midnight. Almost Christmas.

Billy settled in for a night on the recliner. Jesse was

sprawled out on the couch, his bare feet resting on the arm at one end. Helen had retired some time ago. Christmas music floated faintly on the air. After throwing scraps of wrapping paper away, Marti sat down on the floor in front of Jesse. He looked like a sleepy-eyed boy with his head resting on his hand.

"Did you have fun?" he whispered, trying not to wake the others.

Marti didn't have to worry about whispering. Her voice was still soft and raspy. "Yes, I did."

He glanced toward the tree where Caty shifted in her sleep in front of the fireplace. "When we were kids, we used to sleep under the tree every Christmas Eve. Even after we knew there wasn't a Santy Claus (that's what we used to call him) and Mom and Dad put the presents underneath early, we still spent the night there."

His eyes sparkled with the reflection of the flames. "Pa used to try to talk us into going to bed 'or else Santy Claus won't come for you' he'd say. That's when we believed. The three of us would conspire to go to bed, then get up and meet under the tree. And we did, although one time Caty fell asleep and didn't come down. She was mad because we didn't come get her, but we didn't want Pa catching us."

Marti watched the amber glow of the fire dance across his features. "Did Santy come?"

"Yes, he did. We were usually asleep when Santy Pa did his thing. One time we stayed up late, and you know what? My pa actually dressed up in his Santy costume before he came downstairs. Billy and I had already figured out by then that Santy was pa, but we didn't want to spoil it for Caty. She was so cute; her eyes were this big." He gestured with his finger and thumb, then glanced Caty's way again. "I'd feel silly sleeping under the Christmas tree now, and so would Billy, I'm sure. But Caty looks just right down there, like she did when she was six. Hey, what's wrong?"

Marti snapped out of the mental pictures she'd conjured of the Wests' Christmases. She didn't even realize tears had been slipping down her cheeks until Jesse reached out and wiped one away with his thumb.

"I wish you could give me your memories for Christmas. They sound so wonderful."

He pulled her close. "I can share mine with you."

"You are," she said, her voice a squeaky whisper.

What is wrong with me? she thought as they drove back home. This was Christmas Eve, and thousands of lights cheerily lit the town. She stared out the window and hoped he couldn't see the silly tears that continued to flow. But she knew what was wrong. Christmases without Santy Clauses and family and lots of presents were normal for her. Then, when she got older, watching people trying to outdo one another with the most expensive presents.

Everything she'd been told 'was just on the television' had really been happening at Jesse's house. The warmth and love and sharing — it had been going on without her.

When they got home, she went in ahead of Jessie, and by the time he got inside, she was standing by the Christmas tree, a pillow in each hand, blanket on the floor.

"Will you sleep with me under the tree?" Her nose all stuffed up, she sounded like the little girl she wished she was.

He took the pillows from her, laying them down side

by side. After stripping off his shirt, he took her hand and pulled her down. He tucked her hair behind her ears, his gaze never leaving hers. That made her stomach tickle, so she lay on her back, looking up at the glittering tree. Her pulse started racing when he leaned down over her.

"Why are you still crying?" he asked in a soft voice.

She shook her head. "I don't know. For everything, for nothing."

He looked at her for a few moments. "What can I do to make them go away?"

Her lips twitched. *Tell him, Marti.*

No.

Tell him. "Hold me."

Without hesitation, he pulled her into his arms. She nestled her mouth on his bare shoulder, her arms slipping around him as if they belonged there. She realized that she'd wanted this for a long time. Her hands were splayed against his back, and she fought an urge to run her fingers through his hair.

After a moment, he pulled back a few inches and looked at her. His finger trailed down the tracks her tears were leaving.

"You're still crying."

She managed a laugh. "Happy tears."

Jesse leaned close and kissed the tears from her cheeks. He looked angelic, with the colored lights setting off his hair and the planes of his face. Her heart pounded, in fear and excitement.

He seemed to watch her warring emotions. His broad shoulders looked strong, and at the same time soft and creamy in the blinking ambers, blues, and greens. She remembered, for a dreamy moment, what his mouth tasted like, wondered what his body might feel like lying next to hers naked, holding her close through the night. All that warmth and affection in him might pour into her, and fill her with it.

Was it a dream, his lips grazing hers and then capturing her mouth? No, wonderfully, deliciously real. She drowned, lost in the swirl of lights and the dazzling brilliance of his kisses.

She backed up and sucked in a deep breath, meeting his gaze. "Is that your cure for crying? To kiss a girl senseless?"

One side of his mouth quirked up. "It worked, didn't it?"

"Like a charm."

She dropped back down on the blanket. She remembered his earlier words and tried to lighten the mood that threatened to crush her under its weight. "Do you feel silly, sleeping under the tree?"

The grin she hoped would materialize didn't. "Silly isn't quite the word I would use."

What then? Disappointment? Uneasiness? Her heart raced as his gaze stayed locked to hers.

"Do you want to leave?" she asked.

"No."

She smiled, snuggling under the blanket. *Leave it at that.*

"Merry Christmas, Marti," he said, pulling the blanket over his shoulder and closing his eyes.

Great. She didn't want to cry anymore. Now she wanted to jump him. "Merry Christmas, Jesse."

The crinkling sound of Bumpus sniffing around the presents under the tree woke Jesse. He glanced at the clock: almost seven-thirty Christmas morning. He rolled over to see if Marti was awake. She wasn't. Her left hand was tucked beneath her pillow, and her right hand rested between them, as though she'd tried to reach out for him in her sleep.

The wan glow of the lights barely reflected on Marti's skin. He watched her for a few minutes, wondering about the woman who sometimes seemed like a little girl. Now he understood better what her past was like and how it differed from his. Her loss touched him.

That wasn't why he'd kissed away her tears. Not pity, but out of a deep desire to take away her pain. He didn't even want to think about why he'd kissed her mouth, why he'd kept on kissing her. It hadn't been the same as that night when the first Marti had leaned over and kissed him, and they'd made love because he'd felt sorry for her. Still, he was going to make sure he didn't confuse what was obviously a big brother feeling for anything more than that.

Her eyes fluttered open, and she looked at him, then around her in confusion. She smiled when she saw the tree. "It's Christmas."

As though she suddenly remembered their kiss, her gaze shifted away and her cheeks flushed. He threw off the blanket and stretched, aware of the thousand goosebumps that rose on his bare chest when the chilly air hit.

She wrapped the blanket around her shoulders and sat looking up at the tree. "It's so beautiful," she said, an almost reverent smile on her face.

"Haven't you had a Christmas tree before?"

"Yes, but not a real one. My mother had an old silver tree, made from tinsel. She only put red and green balls on it, nothing else. Especially not pretty ones like you have, with the trim and beads and bits of jewelry."

He looked at the pile of presents. "I've always packed up all the gifts and taken them over to my mom's. What do you want to do?"

She shrugged. "Let's keep with tradition."

They both took showers and bundled the packages in the back of Jesse's truck. The sun was shining, and the chill in the air was giving way to a comfortable warmth.

The Christmas music blared from Helen's white house when they pulled up, and even Bumpus hesitated before approaching. Trick and Treat quickly persuaded him to start trotting toward the back of the house.

"Hey, Bumpus," Jesse called out. "Merry Christmas."

He handed the dog a bone-shaped present, which he quickly ripped open. Trick and Treat each got one, too. Within a few minutes, all three dogs had decided they wanted the other's bone and were chasing each other around the yard. He was surprised to see Marti pull out a little bag of beefy bits, open it, and give one to Bumpus. Of course, the other two raced over.

She gave him a funny smile. "I'm starting with the dog. Sort of." She kept her fingers far from the slobbering dog mouths waiting for the next treat she pulled from the bag.

He laughed and shook his head, wondering again exactly who this woman was as he opened the front door with the three fingers he had available. Both he and Marti were loaded down with bags. The warm air, mixed with the aroma of baking ham, made his mouth water. Marti stepped inside, and as soon as Jesse followed, Caty's holler stopped them.

"Wait a minute," she said, holding her hand out like a

crossing guard. Then she pointed up, an impish grin on her face. "Mistletoe."

Caty skipped into the kitchen, leaving Marti to awkwardly turn to Jesse.

He shrugged one shoulder. "You heard her."

Marti stepped a few inches forward, and he leaned across the bags. When their lips touched, a spark of static electricity popped, and they jerked apart again.

He glanced up at the mistletoe. "Wow, did you feel that?"

She nodded, fingers over her lips. "What was that?"

"Static electricity. Or ..." Something more?

"I'm sure that's all it was."

"Yeah."

"Definitely." She followed behind, hidden behind the big paper bag she carried.

Billy was still in the recliner. Jesse doubted he'd moved all night.

"Merry Christmas, Billy. Did you call the boys yet?"

Billy wiped his hand down his face, scratching his nose in the process. "Wasn't sure they'd be up yet."

"Of course, they'll be up. They're kids, aren't they?"

Jesse set the recliner straight with his foot, throwing Billy forward. "Call 'em now."

Helen emerged from the kitchen. "Merry Christmas, you two!"

Marti gave Helen a sincere hug, closing her eyes as though she were savoring it. His mother seemed particularly sentimental this year. Boy, holidays sure did strange things to women.

"Let's open presents!" Caty shouted.

In West tradition, Caty passed out presents Santy Claus style, giving each of hers a little shake. Nobody opened their presents until the last one was given out. Marti seemed to get redder and redder every time Caty handed her a present. Had she realized there wasn't one under there from him?

She seemed more preoccupied with the presents she'd given than the ones piled in front of her. Helen opened up a box filled with sheets and material.

Marti said, "You asked me to redecorate your windows like I did with the baby's room. I thought the pink and beige material would go great in here, and we could do your bedroom in the teal and maroon. The sheets are for your bed." When Caty opened up a veterinarian reference book from Marti, she explained, "I thought that would help with college. And Billy, I thought you could use a new set of horseshoes. If you look on each one, they engraved 'Billy the Kidd West' on top."

Billy's expression was a mixture of confusion and guilt. In his usual show of thoughtfulness, he'd given everybody an assortment of sausage and cheese from the mail order catalog.

Jesse saved opening the presents from Marti for last. By the time he turned to the two medium boxes wrapped in red and gold paper, everybody was throwing their scraps of paper in one of the empty boxes.

"Open that one first," she said, a glow on her features.

He unwrapped a pair of the most beautiful boots he had ever seen. Made from ostrich skin, they were a rich gray color covered in bumps. What was she thinking, spending her California money on him?

"Wow, they're terrific."

Her smile lit up her face. "Open the other box now."

Inside was a felt gray hat with a matching ostrich skin band.

"For your next cowboy mood," she said, but her smile wilted. "You don't like them, do you?"

"I love them, thank you." It made him feel funny that she'd obviously gone to a lot of thought and expense on his behalf. He pointed to the box brimming with scraps of wrapping paper and shipping popcorn. "See that big box there."

Her eyebrows furrowed. "The garbage box?"

"Yep. Your present is in there."

Everyone smiled, but she was still confused. "But that was Caty's box."

"I put something in there for you, too."

She gave him an indignant look. "You mean I have to dig for it?"

Everyone nodded, holding back their laughter. Marti must have figured out he wasn't kidding. With a resigned huff, she crawled over to the box and started digging through the wads of paper. When she gave Jesse a look of exasperation, he nodded.

"It's in there, I promise."

"We do this to someone every year," Caty said. "You're the victim this year."

Marti smiled wistfully at those words. With more vigor, she jammed her hands deep down and retrieved a small box wrapped in purple paper.

She opened it slowly and pulled out the gold chain and looked at the heart that dangled at the bottom. It rested in her palm as she read the name 'Marti' spelled out in raised letters in the middle of the heart. Before she had a chance to look at him, he said, "Read the back."

In tiny writing he'd had the jeweler inscribe, 'Love from your West family — J, C, H, B, and B."

She closed it tightly in her palm, then looked at him. "Who's the last B?"

"Baby. If it's a girl, I'll name her Annabelle. If it's a boy, Eli. I just decided to keep it simple on the heart."

"Thank you, Jesse. It's beautiful."

Beautiful like you, he wanted to say. *Sitting there with your face aglow because everybody loved your gifts.* She looked like an angel, next to the tree with the colored lights setting off her blond hair. For the second time in a month, their gazes locked, and the room and everybody in it fell away to leave only them. There were so many sides to the woman who carried his child: insecure, child-like, sad, confident, sassy, and sometimes selfish. And when she was gone, he would look at their baby and wonder where she was and how she was doing. Even though it was better for both of them that she was leaving, he would miss her, he realized.

Then the dogs started barking, breaking the trance. Dean knocked on the door and brought in new presents for everyone, getting a few of his own to open. Jesse saw his kid sister blush for the first time when she opened the small box containing an emerald ring, her birthstone. She stammered a thank you and didn't meet anyone's eyes. Jesse knew she didn't want to encounter *hmm* expressions on his and Billy's faces.

Helen clapped her hands. "Gentlemen, why don't you set the table? Ladies, I could use your help in the kitchen. The men can clean up afterward."

All three men made a great deal of fuss, but Jesse knew better than to seriously complain. After all, he'd seen his mother put Billy over her knee not all that long ago.

Marti followed Caty and Helen into the kitchen, letting the swinging door close behind her. She grabbed for the bags of green beans that Helen pulled out of the refrigerator; she knew how to do those. Caty settled at the cutting board piled with red apples.

"What nice gifts you two got." Helen's smile reeked of innuendo.

"It doesn't mean anything," Caty retorted. "It's my birthstone."

"I don't know," Marti said. "A ring is, well, pretty serious."

Caty was positively red-faced. "I don't see what the big fuss is about. It's not an engagement ring. And what about you, Marti? A gold heart pendant isn't exactly a box of candy, especially for someone who's leaving town in six months. Anything we should know about?"

Marti thought about the words inscribed on the back. "It's a goodbye gift."

"Humph. That didn't look like a 'goodbye' look you two were giving each other back there in the living room."

"Goodness, Caty, you're acting like a cornered animal. I think you both have a light in your eyes, whether you want it to be there or not," Helen said.

Caty and Marti glared at each other before turning back to what they were cutting.

Forty-five minutes later, with most of the preparation done, all they had to do was wait for everything to get ready.

As Caty washed her hands, she watched the guys playing horseshoes from the kitchen window. "I'm going to teach those guys how to play. Want to come, Marti?"

"No, that's okay. Helen and I will sit in here and talk

about you."

Caty made a face before walking outside. Helen set the packages of fabric on the coffee table. Marti sat in the recliner Billy had spent the night in, feeling ready to take a snooze herself.

"I can't wait to see what you're going to do with this," Helen said, looking at the front windows. I love what you did with the baby's room."

"I just hope it wasn't a fluke."

"No way. You're very talented. The best part is you're doing it on a budget. That's an attractive marketing angle."

"Marketing? You mean selling my curtains to people? For money?"

"Sure, why not? You go in, measure, ask what they what. They can have something as nice as a decorator could do at, say, half the cost."

"I'm not even sure I can do it again. But I've got some neat ideas for those two windows, if it works the way I'm imagining." She cleared her throat. "I don't want you to get the wrong idea. There's nothing between Jesse and me. Nothing romantic."

Helen shrugged. "Maybe I'm seeing what I want to see. For Caty, too."

"Do you think I'm a terrible person, for wanting to leave when the baby comes?"

"If you're really someone else, you didn't make this baby, and you didn't want it. You can't help the way you feel. I know you'll do what you think is best for yourself, the baby, and Jesse."

Marti blew out a breath. "Believe me, leaving is the best thing I could do for them. As a mother and a wife."

"Why are you so sure you'll disappoint them?"

"All my life I've disappointed people, especially the ones closest to me. When I ... died, I saw all those things I did to screw up my marriage. I can't do that to anyone, and I wouldn't want to have a baby involved when I destroyed my second marriage."

"You're so sure you'll destroy it. Jesse's tough, you know. Sometimes I wonder if he wouldn't be willing to give it a try."

"Are you talking about that light again?"

"Mm-hm," she said with a demure smile.

"Okay, I admit there's a light there. But it's not what you think."

"Lust?"

Marti dropped her head, shaking it. "I can't believe I'm talking to his mother about him like this."

"Then think of me as a girlfriend, who's a bit older. I know I've got a good-looking son, who's as stubborn as that river that runs behind the house. So, it's only lust?"

Marti shrugged. "It doesn't matter. He wants me to leave, I want to leave, and we're two totally different people. We have this ... current between us sometimes." She thought of the kiss under the mistletoe. "But it doesn't mean anything, not really."

"If you say so. But you've got a few months before you leave. Think you can hold out?"

"Yes," she answered too fast. "Look at me, getting bigger every day. He's not going to even want to look at me before long."

Helen smiled in an irritatingly knowing way. "I doubt that, sweetheart. I doubt that."

Marti sighed, wanting to change the subject. "I wish I had a mother like you. Maybe I wouldn't have screwed up so much."

Helen tilted her head. "You do. Now."

How those words warmed her and thickened her throat. How different would her life have been if she'd had a mother who cared?

"I wish I could believe in myself the way you do, but I can't. I'm just screwed up. Maybe I am attracted to Jesse. I mean, he is kind of sexy. And, as you pointed out, good-looking."

Helen smiled. "Yes, he is. More so on the inside."

Marti blew out a breath. "That's the point. He's too good for me. He's had this perfect mother as a role model. How can any woman compete, much less me?"

"Don't say that. I'm not perfect."

"But you wouldn't do the things I've done in my life. You're too good of a person."

"Everybody makes mistakes. You're a different person now, in a new life. You can put those mistakes behind you."

"No, I can't. Because deep inside, I have the same soul. That's been the problem all along."

CHAPTER 10

Most of the town's Christmas decorations were gone by the second week of January. The lunch crowd had dispersed at Bad Boys, leaving Marti time to count her tips and wonder how she was ever going to pay that awful department store bill from her two shopping sprees. Still, she was glad she'd spent the money. It was the most peculiar phenomenon, but buying gifts for other people was more fun than buying stuff for herself.

She looked up when the door opened. Carl stepped inside, smoothing his hair back. He settled onto a stool in Marti's section. It was unusual that he was without Lyle for lunch.

"How are you doing, young lady?" he asked, green eyes sparkling.

"Fine, thank you."

"I understand you were in the office looking at the photos of yourself."

"I didn't think it would be a big deal to look at photos of my body," she stated, ready to defend her actions.

"Well, it is official property now." He smiled graciously. "But it's okay. Lyle seemed to think you and

Jesse were onto something. An idea, maybe. Care to let me in on it, considering I'm the investigating officer?"

She shrugged. "It's only a theory. We'll let you know if it pans out."

His smile disappeared. "You think Paul has something to do with it, don't you?"

Of course, Paul's father would be aware that they had checked into his son's whereabouts on the day of the attack. Even as recently as last week, she overheard Jesse discussing it with someone on the phone. "Maybe. It might be, well, hard, to investigate your own son."

Carl's eyes narrowed, all traces of friendliness gone. "You think I wouldn't nail that good-for-nothing son of mine if I thought he'd done that to you?"

She stepped back, the anger in his eyes steaming like the coffee in his untouched cup.

"I—I don't know."

Just as suddenly, the anger was gone. "Marti, my son didn't attack you. I know he didn't. Don't you think a father could tell?"

"Maybe, and maybe not. Your son and his friends attacked Jesse right before Christmas. I bet you didn't know about that, did you?"

Carl's fist tightened. "No, he didn't. Damn kid's got a rocket up his ass." He looked up. "He's reckless, but he doesn't go around attacking women. You two don't have a thing on him, do you?" She didn't answer, and he nodded. "That's what I figured. You know, he and Jesse have always had this feuding blood between them, and Jesse took your attack personally. Now he wants to pin it on his best enemy. You're a smart girl. Can't you see that?"

She shrugged. "I don't know. But your son was in

the area at the time of my assault. And the scratch on my chest could have matched the kind Paul's pendant might make. And isn't it strange how the photos of that scratch are gone?"

Carl stood, jamming his newspaper beneath his arm. "Both your imaginations are running wild. The guy who did that to you is probably long gone, but if he isn't, I'll find him. Leave the investigating to the police." Just as he was about to walk away, he turned around again. "Don't forget that Jesse is a criminal himself. He doesn't have a lot of right to be pointing fingers."

After work that day, Marti drove by Harry's Garage to ask Jesse if he wanted to go to the mall with her to shop for larger sized pants. Ugh. She was solidly in that awkward not pregnant-looking but heavy phase. Caty couldn't go, and Marti hated to shop alone.

Marti had distanced herself a bit from Jesse since Christmas, for his own protection as well as hers. She noticed that he had done the same. Those moments under the tree on Christmas Eve still held her in a spell when she allowed herself to daydream about them. That kind of thing couldn't happen again. Shopping should be safe enough.

When she pulled into the dirt parking lot, her heart sank. Desiree's black Jeep sat out front. Marti chewed her lip. Well, she certainly wasn't going to ask Jesse to go shopping for larger clothes when Desiree was there. Pride, yes. And a smidgeon of jealousy, if she were being honest. She backed out of the parking lot and headed for the mall.

It was nearly six when she returned home. Jesse's truck was out front, and Bumpus was keeping watch from his usual vantage point in the bushes. With tail wagging, he stepped out to greet her.

Her instinct was to back away as he approached, mouth agape in what looked like a smile. She forced herself to stay put and smiled back. Did dogs recognize a smile?

"Hi, Bumpus." She patted his head. "Do you like me?"

He tilted his head and whined.

"This is just silly." With her one bag, she had no trouble opening the front door.

Jesse launched off the couch and, instead of any kind of greeting, boomed, "Where the hell have you been?"

She blinked, still paused in the doorway. "Shopping."

She started to walk by him, but he grabbed her arm and swung her around to face him.

His eyes flared. "I have been looking all over for you. Calling, texting. Nothing!"

She dug her phone out of her purse and discovered it was dead. That was bad. He'd be just as angry over her allowing that to happen than her not answering.

He jabbed his finger at her. "Do you know what I thought? That he got you this time. I hunted down Paul and drove all over this damn town looking for cars pulled off the road."

She groped for something to say in the face of his anger. "Your baby's fine, Jesse."

When she started to walk to her bedroom, he jerked her back, almost slamming her into his chest. His fingers held her chin.

"I wasn't just worried about the baby. Did it ever occur to you that I might be worried about you?"

"I'm not sure who you really care about," she said, and annoyingly enough, Desiree popped into her mind.

His voice softened in anger, but not in intensity. "I care about you *and* the baby, not you *because* of the baby. Don't take off without telling me. I about went out of my mind tonight."

She moved out of his grasp but remained in front of him. "I was going to ask you to come along, but you were busy."

He appeared to wait for more explanation. "Busy? With what?"

"Actually, the question should be, with whom."

He gave it some thought before the light dawned. "Don't tell me you saw Desiree's Jeep and took off." He waited for her denial, which didn't come. "You thought she was at the garage and went off without telling me?" His expression was one of disbelief.

"Thought she was there? She wasn't?"

"No, her car was making clanking noises, and she dropped it off this afternoon so I could look at it first thing in the morning."

He leaned against the back of the sofa, his arms crossed over his chest.

She realized she'd admitted in so many words that she'd been jealous.

"I figured you were busy, whether she was there or not, so I left. That's all. It was a stupid thing to do, and I'm sorry."

He shook his head. "Marti, I can't figure you out."

"Don't try."

"You were jealous, weren't you?"

She moved away, desperate to put some distance between them. "I was not jealous. I have no right to be jealous. I thought you were busy, that's all."

"Then why did you mention Desiree's car? *With*

whom?" he imitated in her haughty tone. "I'll be darned."

"Well, then I guess you'll have to be darned, because I wasn't jealous." Damn him and his arrogant attitude. And her heated cheeks. "Why would I be jealous over a ... convict?"

His amusement disappeared. "What are you talking about?"

"You're a car thief, convicted even."

"Who told you about that?"

So, it was true. Her admiration for him fell into a heap, where it felt much more comfortable. "Paul told me, that day at the gas station."

Instead of getting defensive, he shrugged. "I was nineteen. Big deal."

"*Big deal?* I'm living with a common criminal! You're pointing at Paul, and you've probably got more of a police record than he does."

Jesse's expression became rigid. "You know why I do? Because Paul's daddy got him off. I'll bet Paul didn't tell you he was the one driving the car, did he? The car was his aunt's, up in Sarasota. He got pissed because we didn't want to joyride it down to the Keys, so he ran away. Alan, Mark, and I got busted because we were the ones returning the car. Marti, I already stood before the judge on this one. You going to try me again?"

Every ounce of fight drained from her. Before she could say anything resembling an apology, he scooped up his keys from the end table.

"I need some fresh air. See if you can keep yourself from wandering off while I'm gone."

He didn't quite slam the door, but she felt its firm impact all the same. She walked to her room and dropped down on the bed, feeling as small as a bug.

See, I let myself have a few interesting thoughts about Jesse, then I screw it up with my insecurity. By the time I have this baby, he'll be glad to see me go.

The quiet of the house lulled her into a light daydream before dropping her into the abyss of sleep. She didn't remember dreaming about anything when the noise woke her. In the dark, her eyes adjusted to the familiar shadows of her closet and dresser. At first, she listened for the sound of Jesse's keys, of any sign that he was home. The house was still, except for the peeping of a frog outside her window. She let out a long, soft breath and started to let her eyes drift closed again.

A shadow moved. Her eyes flew open, wide and scanning.

A distinct shape evolved from the blankness in front of her, moving closer to her bed. Her lungs were frozen — she couldn't scream, couldn't breathe. It wasn't Jesse; somehow she knew that. A dead weight pressed down on her.

Fingers slid around her throat. Her arms couldn't move to push them away. Panic seized her. She was going to die, right here in her bed! The fingers tightened. Her breath came in jagged gasps. Then she could scream, and the terror frozen inside her let loose like a wail from beyond the grave. She blinked as she realized the lights were on, had been on. Her bedroom door flew open, and a rumpled Jesse barged in.

All she could do was breathe, finally, pulling in one deep breath after another.

He took a quick inventory of the room and her before visibly relaxing. "What happened?"

She found a laugh in a tiny place the fear had not

filled. "You look as scared as I feel."

"When I hear a blood-curdling scream like that, you better believe I'm scared. Are you all right?"

She shivered, wrapping her arms around herself. The laugh was gone. "I had a nightmare. He was back."

"He? The man who killed Marti?"

She nodded. "I saw him standing right there in the shadows. He started strangling me. I felt his fingers around my throat, and I couldn't move." She buried her face in her hands, afraid of the images she was dredging up.

The bed dipped when Jesse sat down beside her. "You want to sleep in my room? I mean, we've done it before."

She looked around the room, weighing the sanity of that move. "No, I'll be all right. I'm going to leave the light on, though."

He ran his fingers through his wild waves of brown hair. "If you change your mind, don't be afraid to slip in."

"Thanks."

"Well, good night then. Sweet dreams this time, okay?"

She smiled. "You better believe it."

The man stepped out of the shadows again, standing just outside the glow of light from Marti's window. That scream sounded like the one she'd uttered when he'd wrapped his fingers around her neck. Her eyes bulged with fear and then her scream became a gurgle. She'd forced him to do it, by resisting, by kicking him.

Now she was forcing him to linger in the shadows, wondering when her nightmares would show her that he was the one who had pinned her down. How long could he go on like this, a coward hiding in the dark, once again letting a woman rule his fate? If she and Jesse got the slightest bit closer to him, he would have to ensure her silence.

You weren't a coward that day, now, were you? You took the situation in hand. You took action. He felt a surge of power and confidence.

Except she didn't die.

The other voice, the snide, cruel one.

No, somehow she survived. But she wouldn't be alive for much longer if she and Jesse didn't drop their investigation. They were getting too damned close.

"The last time you wanted to talk to me like this, you told me Marti was pregnant. What's bugging you, sweetheart?"

Jesse looked up at Desiree from where he was sprawled out on the ground with his head on her thighs. He'd taken the morning off to clear his head of the thoughts making him pretty much useless all morning. He wished he could toss his aggravations into the Chattaloo River, flowing only five feet from them, but he couldn't. Desiree owed him a few hours of listening time, he figured. He was cashing in.

"Marti's driving me crazy. She keeps throwing things at me to keep the distance between us. Last night, it was the fact that I stole a car when I was nineteen. Paul kindly supplied the information without telling her all the details."

"Wait a minute. She wants to put distance between you and her? Is this the same girl who followed you around with goo-goo eyes a few months ago?"

"No. She's completely different since the attack." True enough. No need to tell anyone else the bizarre truth. "She's leaving for California after the baby's born. Alone."

"Leaving? She's the one who got pregnant!"

"With a little help from me, if you'll remember."

"Yes, but she manipulated you into making love with her that night and lied about being on the pill."

"No matter. I was the idiot who gave in."

Desiree shook her head. "So, she's dumping you with the baby?"

"It's still my baby, no matter how it came to be mine. What else can I do?"

She smoothed some hair off his forehead. "You, Jesse, could do nothing else. You're just built that way." Her voice became soft, nostalgic. "Why couldn't we have made it? We were so good together."

He laughed. "We would have driven each other mad."

She laughed. "Probably." The humor wilted. "Are you afraid, Jesse?" she asked softly.

He shrugged; that question wasn't easy to answer. "Most of the time I'm fine with it. There are those times, though where it scares the hell out of me."

"You won't have any trouble finding a woman to help."

"I don't want a wife. Women are nothing but trouble."

"I beg your pardon."

"You know exactly what I mean."

"There are plenty of women who would be glad to help you out, babysitting and stuff like that. Heck, I'd even do that, and I don't do kids."

"Yeah, but I want … ." the words dropped away.

"Marti?" Desiree supplied.

"No. I don't know."

It seemed strange that he was the confused one, and Desiree was playing counselor. For so long, it was the other way around. She'd sneak away from her abusive husband, and they'd sit by the river, with her head on his lap, her tears dampening his jeans. The turnabout bothered him.

"You said she's different. How?"

"Well, she used to be quiet, clingy, afraid to speak up, or do anything on her own. Now she's feisty, hates living here, listens to dance music. Heck, she even threw out all her old clothes, bought new stuff, and dyed her hair blond."

"And how do you feel about her now?"

"Fascinated," his mouth blurted out without checking with his mind first. "I mean, because she's so different. She laughs different, smiles different. She's started redecorating the house, and she's sweet the way she beams with pride. One time I caught her dancing in her room, swaying to the beat with her eyes closed."

Desiree studied him, but he couldn't identify the expression on her face.

"What?" he asked.

"Your eyes sparkle when you talk about her. I think you're in love with her."

He sat up. "I'm not in love with her." Yeah, way to *not* sound defensive. He softened his tone. "I'm fascinated with her. Heck, she's carrying my baby; I should feel something. Sometimes it's just plain irritation."

She narrowed her eyes. "I'm telling you, you're in love with her, Jesse James West."

Desiree's observation sent him atilt. What was she seeing that made her think such an impossible thing?

He put a skeptical expression on his face and settled

back on her thighs again. "Even *if* I felt that way, it wouldn't matter. She's leaving for California soon."

She flicked him on the nose. "Well, get her to stay."

He grabbed her hand. "I can't. I promised I wouldn't talk her into staying after the baby's born. I can't go back on a promise, you know that."

She leaned over him, a devilish glint in her eyes. "I didn't say anything about *talking*."

Marti pulled up beside Jesse's truck and barely made it into the bathroom in time. She didn't know why her stomach was rebelling in the middle of the day, but every smell in the diner seemed magnified ... and gross. For Caty's sake, she held out until Priscilla arrived.

After her retching session, she cleaned up and wandered through the house looking for Jesse. She didn't know why she'd been so hard on him about that convict thing.

You're looking for reasons to push him away. Admit it, you're happy to find a flaw in the perfect guy.

She had sure fired him up. All she wanted to do was lie down, but first she wanted to let him know she was home. Maybe he'd see her wan expression and put his anger aside. He'd hardly even looked at her that morning.

After searching through the house, she walked outside. A rustle in the bushes stopped her cold. At first, she didn't see anything, then the leaves started quaking. Two light brown paws inched forward under the hedges, and Bumpus's nose peered out and rested on them. His tail thumped against the side of the house.

"You!" she said, then cracked a tiny smile. He almost looked cute snuggled in amongst the bushes. Almost.

As soon as she headed toward the river, she could

hear the dog disengage from the bushes and follow her. She had to admit she felt safer knowing he was back there.

Seeing Jesse and Desiree felt like walking into a block of ice. His head was on her thighs, and she was resting against a tree. They seemed in deep discussion when Desiree reached down and flicked Jesse's nose. Even worse, he held onto her hand.

An uncomfortable tightness in her chest made it hard to breathe. The man could at least wait for her to leave before reigniting old flames. Or maybe the flame had never gone out. She stalked back to the house.

Why are you so mad? her inner voice asked her.

Because ... because he's my husband! He should behave while he's married to me. When I'm out of here and starting my life in California, he can do whatever he pleases.

But it's more than that, the voice taunted. Isn't it?

No, it's not! He's not my type. What would I do with a man like that? Break his heart, that's what.

She slammed the door behind her, slipped the "Phantom of the Opera" CD in the stereo, and headed to her bedroom. The soprano's voice filled the air. She stripped off her uniform, slipped her long T-shirt over her head, and pulled out her Hairlady. She turned it on and started running the rotating blades over her legs.

"Ouch, ouch, ouch!"

Hallie had never shaved her long legs. She had always waxed them to avoid stubble. The former Marti had shaved, but it wasn't too late to get rid of the short, stubby hairs. After a few minutes, the music volume lowered.

"Marti?"

She jumped at Jesse's voice suddenly in her room, but

didn't take her eyes off the buzzing plastic machine. "I'm *fine*. Go back to whatever you were doing."

She could see him advance closer. "What are you doing home so early?"

"I didn't feel well so I came home. Ouch."

"And what you're doing is making you feel better? What *are* you doing?" he asked over the racket.

She finally turned it off. "I'm shaving my legs, in a matter of speaking. These wheel thingies spin, grab the hairs, and pull them out. Then the hairs don't grow back stubbly and stiff." She started the machine again.

Jesse shivered. "So, is it making you feel better?"

"Yes." Because seeing the two of them together like that hurt worse than getting her leg hairs pulled out.

"What are you listening to out there? It sounded like people screaming."

"It's opera. I was the only one who liked it in my previous life, too."

He knelt by the bed and took the machine out of her hand, turning it off. "Why are you upset?"

How could she tell him what she didn't want to admit herself? After all, it was crazy to be jealous.

She still didn't meet his eyes, even though he was looking right at her. "I'm just tired of feeling nauseated all the time. Now I'm getting sick in the afternoons."

"Is that what's really bothering you?"

She finally met his gaze, though she couldn't keep the harshness from her voice. "What else would it be?"

"I don't know. The nausea will be over soon, and so will the fatigue. Hang in there, doll."

His smile zapped her anger, and she sagged down on the bed. "I'll try."

"Good. Listen, I've got to take Desiree home. Then I'll

be back if you need anything."

So, he wasn't going to hide her presence. "Desiree's here?" she asked in a voice that desperately tried not to sound jealous. Because she wasn't.

"Yeah. She came over so I could bend her ear. My head was too clogged to even work on cars. Want me to pick up anything while I'm gone?" She shook her head, and he patted the bed. "Okay, be back in a few."

Minutes later, she heard their voices outside, and she walked to the front window. Desiree threw the Frisbee to Bumpus, who caught it and brought it back to her. She opened her door and held the disk up like Jesse had, giving the signal that sent the dog jumping into the truck. So, she didn't mind riding with a dog. Well, good. All three of them could live happily together when she was gone. Meanwhile, she had made a fool out of herself in front of Jesse *again* and only hoped he didn't think it was because she'd known Desiree was there.

After a moment, Jesse gestured for Bumpus to jump down and go to the house. To protect her. It gave her a brief smile, but her mind went back to her previous thoughts.

Failure. The word loomed in her mind, pushing itself forward with every ounce of self-pity that dropped onto her heart. With her past, Jesse was better off with Desiree. Much better off.

As true as that was, why did it hurt so much?

CHAPTER 11

It seemed to Marti that Jesse had been awfully quiet in the last week and a half since she'd come home to find him and Desiree cozied up by the river. Marti settled on the bench swing with a sigh, wondering if she would have found Desiree's Jeep parked outside the garage had she driven by. Wondering if he was really working on his stock-car on a Sunday morning. He told her he had to get it ready for the point races and something about a transmission.

As soon as he left, she'd gone to work on the living room curtains, pulling down the old ones and installing crisp linen and blue ones. She hoped he would like the new look; she needed a victory to counteract her string of recent failures.

She tried to ignore the bumpy, jumpy feeling in her heart when Jesse's truck barreled down the driveway. When she stood, she pulled her top down to cover her growing tummy.

He jumped down from the truck. "Hey. Hope I didn't wake you this morning."

"Nope. I was already up."

He walked by her and into the house. She wondered

if by leaving the front door open he was inviting her to follow. He paused in front of the curtains, she was sure of it. Then he returned with an icy beer and a small carton of orange juice for her, a towel draped over his shoulder.

"I like the curtains. Please tell me you did that this morning. I'd hate to think they've been up all week and I just now noticed."

She smiled. "No, that's what I started doing as soon as you left."

"Mom's been telling everyone what a great job you did with her living room and bedroom. You might have something with this budget redecorating."

"Nah." She saw no teasing in his eyes. "You think so?"

"Sure. You could do anything you set your mind to, Marti."

Everything that didn't involve other human beings, she thought. Especially their hearts.

"Come on down to the river with me," he said, stepping off the front porch.

She hesitated. Was he going to tell her that Desiree was moving in? The thought made her feel panicky, and her hand involuntarily went to her stomach. When he paused and looked back, she hurried to catch up.

Once they reached the river, she sat down on the grass. "I can't believe it's so warm. It's January! I — what are you doing?"

Jesse peeled off his shirt, then started unsnapping his jeans. "I'm going for a swim to cool off. Come on in."

She didn't like the glint in his green eyes. Well, part of her did, because it tickled right down to her tummy. She shifted her gaze to the brown water. "I'm not getting into that nasty, muddy water."

He shrugged his bare, broad shoulders. "Suit yourself."

She watched his muscles flex as he kicked off his jeans. When he looked at her and grinned, she covered her eyes.

"How can you prance around in your underwear like that?"

"I'm not 'prancing.' Besides, there's no one around for a mile."

How prude, Marti. Criticizing him for being in his underwear, around his wife no less.

He grabbed onto the rope that hung from a branch and swung into the water, letting a call trail after him. "Yeah--eee!" She shook her head, but found herself smiling as he curled into a cannonball and sent a spray of shimmering water everywhere.

At first, she didn't see anything but the ripples he caused. Just when anxiety started creeping in, his head popped out of the water. He flung his hair out of his eyes, sending a spray behind him.

"Whooee, it's nice in here."

She ignored the trickle of sweat dripping down the side of her face. "Good for you."

"Could be good for you, too."

"What if there are sharks in there?"

His laugh was more like a bark. "There aren't sharks in freshwater rivers."

Marti walked to the edge of the bank, hoping she could sit and dip her toes in the water. The bank was too steep.

"What about alligators?"

"Never seen one yet. Not around this part, anyway. I've seen them farther down."

He reminded her of a kid, diving down, holding his breath for an awfully long time, springing up with a gasp. He was younger than Jamie at the same age, mentally anyway. Jamie was too serious at times. Someone like Jesse could generate some childlike fun. *But you're leaving, so don't get attached to him.*

She found a large leaf and fanned herself with it. The water glistened on Jesse's tan skin.

"Is it deep?" she asked.

"In places. It's shallow right here. See, I'm standing."

Marti frowned. She used to be taller. The top of her head would have reached his nose. Now it only reached his shoulders, she thought, remembering their dance together.

"Are you coming in?" he asked. "You know you want to."

"Don't tell me what I know. Or what I want."

He raised his arms in surrender. "You're too good for swimming in a dirty ole' river, right? You're used to those aqua oceans you see in ads for the Virgin Islands."

"I am not."

"I'll bet your ex-husband carried you in."

She pursed her lips. "No, he didn't. And he's not my ex-husband. I'm still married to him."

"No, you're not. You're married to me. I have the certificate to prove it."

She stood and turned away.

"Why don't you just give up that high and mighty attitude and come in the water?"

"I don't have a bathing suit with me."

"Neither did I."

No, indeed. The water did look good. So did Jesse, which made going in more dangerous, alligators be damned. She stripped off her top and shorts, leaving only her bra and underwear. She frowned at the tiny pooch that was her stomach. He was looking at that same stomach with a soft smile. Sitting on the bank and leaning her legs in, she was able to touch the water. The initial feel was cold but refreshing. She advanced farther.

"Oh, no you don't. You gotta come in the Southern way." Jesse nodded toward the rope.

"You've got to be kidding."

"I never kid about anything as serious as this."

She crossed her arms over her chest. "Then I won't come in."

"Suit yourself. I think you're afraid."

"Afraid of what?"

"Plunging in. Maybe being in the water with me."

"Why would I be afraid of being in the water with you?"

He shrugged, a mischievous light in his eyes. "Maybe you don't trust yourself around me."

She made an exasperated noise. "You're impossible."

"Am I?"

She looked at him with his head cocked, waiting for an answer. "Yes. No. Sometimes."

She dropped her arms to her side and stalked to the rope. Trying to remember how he had done it, she grabbed high on the rough rope, jumped up, and let the swing take her over the water. With a small yelp, she let go and plunged into the brown water. She was sure he had looked more graceful. When she came up for air, he was standing next to her.

"That wasn't so bad, now was it?"

She glared at him. "Don't intimidate me into doing

things, Jesse."

He smiled. "It worked, didn't it?"

She started to head toward the bank, but he grabbed her arm and pulled her back. "Come on, it's not a big deal. Don't you feel great now?"

"Only if I don't think about the creatures that might be swimming right next to me. Hopefully they'll bite you instead." She gave him an impish smile. "Maybe they'd nip that arrogance right in the bud."

He made a motion beneath the water she guessed was covering his, er, bud. "You leave my bud out of this."

She laughed, but thinking about his *bud* did strange things to her body, so she changed the subject. "Did you really like what I did with the living room or were you humoring me?"

"I don't lie, even if I should. Remember that if you're going to ask me whether something makes your butt look big. I like it. The curtains, not your butt. Well, your butt's just fine, tight and curvy, and ..." He cleared his throat. "We're talking about the curtains. I was afraid you'd put something frilly in there. That was great what you did with the material above the window, twisting it like that."

She beamed, though she couldn't imagine why his praise pleased her so. "It came to me, while I was looking at the fabric and trying to figure out what to do with it. I was thinking, maybe I could do something with the kitchen. Something small, to add the ... ."

"Woman's touch," Jesse supplied, moving closer.

She looked up at him, wondering why her legs felt so wobbly. Probably the mud beneath her feet. "You need a woman's touch."

"Yeah, I do."

She cleared her throat. "We're talking about the curtains."

His gaze dropped to her mouth, making her heart tighten. "Maybe."

"Jesse ... ."

He took her face in his hands and pressed his mouth against hers. His eyes remained open, looking straight into hers. She had no idea what he saw there. She tried to force away the fear that surely lingered, wanting to replace it with a *No* signal.

His mouth captured hers again, this time more intensely. He tucked her hair behind her ears, then closed his eyes and leaned down once again. Wherever his fingers touched her, the skin tingled.

Her heart thudded around her ribs like a racquetball shot into an indoor court. She couldn't catch her breath between kisses, couldn't swallow. He parted her lips with his, then ran his tongue along her front teeth. Her mind warred with her senses, and her senses quickly gained ground. That feeling of refreshment evaporated into steam, and even the current seemed to pick up, forcing her to lean closer to him.

Her body kicked into second gear without her consent, and she joined the kiss. He deepened it, and ah, what a kisser he was. His tongue stroked hers slowly, enticingly. A kiss with him was better than the whole shebang with other guys. She touched his arms with her fingertips, feeling the silky, fine hairs and firm muscles beneath. That slow seduction of her mouth had other parts of her body all hot and bothered, reminding her how bloody long it had been.

Standing there nearly bare, she imagined them completely naked, pressed together with only droplets of water between them. And if they made love, what then?

You'd be in big trouble.

At first her senses bemoaned the intrusion of consequential thought. Yep, trouble, and they were only kissing. Her heart seemed ready to burst, not a good sign for one planning to leave in a few months. With a groan, she shook her head and backed away.

"Jesse, what are you doing?" Her voice sounded hoarse and raw. "What are we doing?"

"It's called kissing down here. What do they call it in California?"

She moved toward the bank, desperately trying to get away from him.

He came up behind her, pulling her against him and leaning down next to her ear. "It was only a kiss."

His words, his breath on her ear, shuddered through her. She squeezed her eyes shut, trying to block out the feel of his strong arms holding her against his chest. *Only a kiss? Maybe to you, mister, but not to me.* Or was he just toying with her? Only a kiss.

His body gave away that it was more than a kiss to him, though. She felt the hard ridge of him pressed against her back.

She turned to him. "I'm not interested."

"Sure as shooting didn't seem like it to me."

"Instinct, nothing more."

"You'd melt into any guy's arms if he kissed you, is that what you're saying?"

"I wasn't melting into your arms," she said a little too vehemently. "I was being pushed into you by the current."

"Is that why your mouth joined right in?"

"Stop."

She turned and started climbing up the bank again. Her knees felt weak as she stumbled to get her balance.

"Why are you getting so worked up over a kiss?" he asked from behind her.

"Because that kind of kiss leads to something more. Why start something that will have to end soon?"

He didn't want her to stay. He'd said that more than once. And she didn't want to stay either, she reminded herself.

"Ah, so it was more than just instinct that got you worked up."

She dropped down to a grassy area, surprised to find him right behind her. He'd gotten worked up, too. She shifted her gaze away, but the sight of his erection tingled through her. He wanted her, pregnant, homely, however she felt about her new body, he wanted her.

He sat beside her, propping his elbow on his bent knee. "What are you so afraid of?"

"I'm not afraid. I just don't want to start anything I can't finish."

He moved closer, dropping his gaze to her mouth again. Panic raced through her veins, and she backed away.

"Don't tell me you're not afraid. Every time I come near you, I can see it in your eyes, the way you move away."

She turned away. "Jesse, please don't."

"Fine. If you're afraid to even tell me about it …."

"Don't bait me. I don't want to get *involved* with you."

He leaned forward, his face only inches from hers. "Even in some highly exhausting, unemotional lovemaking?"

She pushed him back, her hand flat on the hard curve of his pecs. "Especially in some hi — that way." Certain parts of her body disagreed with that notion. Those parts made it hard for her to pull her hand away from his cool, wet skin.

"What would be so terrible about us doing the dirty? We are married, after all."

"I would be terrible. In bed."

She had to hide the smile of satisfaction at his shocked expression. That shock turned to outrage.

"Did that Jamie guy tell you that?"

"No, he was too nice to say anything like that. But it's true."

"Don't you want another opinion?"

"You'll have to take my word for it."

Water droplets slid down his body to drip on the towel beneath them. She suddenly felt self-conscious in her underthings next to Jesse who looked all kinds of interesting in his briefs.

"You got all kinds of excuses, doll, but *that kind of kiss* only happens when there's something hot between two people." He wagged his finger to indicate him and her, but let that finger touch her stomach. He traced a droplet across the curve over her belly button. She shuddered, but his gaze remained on his ministrations.

"You can stay here if you want. I mean live here, after the baby is born and all." Only then did he meet her eyes.

All she could do was look at him for a second before realizing he wasn't kidding. He was inviting her to stay after telling her that he didn't want any woman in his life to tangle him up. "Oh? Just like that?"

He shrugged, looking more casual than she thought he should. "I'm just saying, consider it an option. What do you have in California, anyway? Why not stay here where you've got a home, a kind of family, and the baby?"

She noted that he hadn't mentioned a husband in there anywhere. This wasn't a proposal. "I thought you didn't want me to stay."

"I never said I didn't want you to stay. I just promised, at your demand, that I wouldn't try to convince you. And I'm not. I want you to know you're welcome to stay."

Why did his words leave her heart aching for something more? Foolishness.

"A marriage of convenience, is that what you're proposing?"

He started to negate that, then shrugged. "I hadn't thought of it that way, but yeah, you could live here with us. No romantic attachments, just two friends living together."

She gave him a dumbfounded look. "Then what was that you just did in the river? You don't call smooching romantic?"

He ducked his head, giving her an innocent grin. "Aw, that was just for fun."

She wanted to smack him, but she didn't dare let on how mad she was. Just for fun, when her heart had been hammering in her throat. Only a kiss, that's what he'd told her. Why couldn't he tell her that he wanted her to stay, that he cared about her?

"Thank you for your *concern*, Jesse, but I'll pass on playing housemother to two kids."

He gave her an insulted look. "What was that comment for? I offered you a home."

"Well, I'm declining, thank you." She got to her feet with amazing grace and started toward the house as she slipped her shirt on. "Besides, I'm sure it was *only* an offer."

Jesse had given much thought to the conversation he and Marti had had two weeks earlier. In fact, bits of it kept creeping into his thoughts at the oddest moments, like in the middle of giving Mr. Glaser's old Mercury an oil change.

A crisp Saturday morning, he couldn't go back to sleep after he'd heard Marti leave for work. Now he walked along the riverbank wondering why his mind and heart weren't coordinating. He thought about their swim and rolled his eyes at his stupidity. Telling her the kiss was just for fun — geez, what was he thinking?

He *wanted* it to be for fun. But even he couldn't deny it was more than that, not if he was going to be the tiniest bit honest. He didn't know why he'd even kissed her to begin with, though the idea was becoming a preoccupation.

The asking her to stay part was the only planned action he'd taken. He still didn't want to get emotionally involved with her, despite what Desiree had said the other day. Racing was more important than that mushy stuff. He wasn't *in love* with Marti, probably just horny.

He enjoyed having her around, and it seemed logical for her to stay on after the baby was born. He still couldn't figure out her hostility about the offer.

The sound of a car pulling into the drive drew his attention as Bumpus tore across the dried leaves. He didn't recognize the car, but he knew the two boys who jumped out and fussed over the dog: Turk and Clint, Abbie's kids. The tall, slim brunette stepped out of the car, and he hardly recognized her.

"Wow, look at you," he said, his attention on Abbie even as the boys jumped into his arms. "You look great. And you two, look how you've grown." The boys looked more like their dad than ever, but he wasn't going to tell Abbie that.

After a few minutes of greetings, Abbie said, "Turk, why don't you take your little brother down by the river?"

"Aw, Mom, I wanna see Uncle Jesse. We just got here!"

"You can go swimming," she said with a lift in her voice. "And we can spend more time with Jesse tonight, if he doesn't mind."

Turk trained his hazel eyes on his mother, then shifted them to Jesse. "'Sat okay with you, Uncle Jesse?"

Jesse mussed the boy's hair. "Surefire, it is."

"Okay. C'mon, Clint," the seven-year-old said, taking his little brother's hand. "See you later, Uncle Jess."

He waved to the boys, who were grumbling about being sent away, then gave Abbie a hug. "I can't believe what I see. You back, after two years. And looking like this. A business suit, hair all done up."

She looked down demurely. "Well, you know I can't do a thing with this hair. I gave up perming it and let it grow straight. Some things you just can't fight, know what I mean?"

Why did Marti come to mind on that statement?

Abbie's fine dark hair, parted down the middle, framed her broad, pale face. He sensed an uneasiness beneath her confident poise as she leaned against the car.

"I got tired of the city, so I packed the boys in the car and headed down. I had an interview today for a position at a bank branch in Ft. Myers." She twisted her mauve lips and narrowed her eyes. "Jesse, you didn't tell me you were married when we spoke at Christmas."

He shrugged. "You didn't ask. I didn't feel like saying anything to the boys, and everybody was there."

"Well, I was ... sort of hoping that we might be able to stay with you for a few days, until I find a place to live. I remembered that you had a second bedroom."

"I'd love to let you use it, but Marti's in there." At her raised eyebrow, he went on. "We have separate bedrooms."

Strangely enough, her expression lightened at his admission. "I'm sorry to hear things aren't working out between you."

"It's not as simple as that. She's leaving after the baby's born."

Abbie's eyes widened at that one. "Leaving? With the baby?"

"No. The baby's staying with me. It's a long story, but I'm okay with it."

"Really?"

Eager to change the subject, he asked, "Have you seen Billy yet?"

"No. I didn't come back to see him. I came back to see you." She laughed nervously. "For two years, I've had this fantasy about you. I'd come back, and you'd fall in love with me. Crazy, huh?" She didn't give him time to answer. "But I couldn't stop thinking about you, especially after we talked at Christmas. So I came down. Your wife didn't quite fit into the fantasy and neither did a baby. Don't laugh at me, Jesse. I've been awfully lonely, and I always had this thing for you, even when I was mar —"

Jesse put his finger over her lips. "Abbie, if you're serious, I'm flattered."

"But," she said with a certain finality. "I know you don't feel the same about me."

"It's not even that. You were married to my *brother*."

She laughed bitterly. "Billy never loved me. I was pregnant with Turk, so he did the required thing. You know as well as I that I, or our sons, don't mean much to him. The four of us were more of a family, even back then." She gestured to him. "I wanted to see if, with Billy long out of my life, there was anything there for us. But I chickened out when I got here and went to see your mom first, to test the waters."

"What did she tell you?"

"Nothing more than you were married and expecting a baby. Of course, she filled me in on Billy's life, as if I care. Maybe she figured I came back to reunite with him. I know it would make her happy, but it would be hell for me. I told her not to count on that."

Jesse was trying to assimilate what she was saying. The boys' laughter, drifting on the wind, interfered with his thought process. "So, what are your plans?"

She took his hands in hers, swinging them nervously. "Well, that depends on you, I guess. They've changed a little since I got here. But I still have a proposition for you."

"A proposition, huh?" He was trying to lighten the conversation, but her expression was intense. "Okay, shoot."

"I want you to think about your baby and my boys. Why don't we get married?"

CHAPTER 12

Even before Marti pulled in to find the strange car sitting in the driveway, she sensed the intrusion into her territory. Strewn along the path to the front door were children's toys: a red-spotted ball, a plastic baseball bat, and a spongy baseball. Even the absence of Bumpus's sloppy greeting felt amiss.

The noise she expected to hear when she walked inside made the silence even more profound.

"Jesse? Bumpus?"

Nothing. She changed out of her greasy uniform and slipped into jean shorts and a white shirt. As soon as she walked out back, a high-pitched child's squeal pierced the air. She followed it down to the river.

The disquiet that had settled under her skin sunk deeper when she saw a woman sitting next to Jesse on the bank. They were laughing at something in the water. Whoever she was, she felt relaxed around him, touching his shoulder as she giggled. She was wearing crisp white pants and a blue dress shirt, and beneath her was a towel Jesse had thoughtfully placed to keep those pants clean.

Bumpus's greeting barks made the pair turn around.

Jesse got to his feet and walked toward her with an easy smile. She wished she could look that easy-going. He put his arm around her and steered her toward the woman.

"Hey, doll, I want you to meet someone." The woman stood and extended her manicured hand. "This is Abbie, Billy's ex-wife. And those rugrats in the river are her boys, Turk and Clint."

Abbie squeezed Marti's hand, giving her a warm smile. The boys perfunctorily waved and went back to splashing each other. Marti found it hard to imagine this attractive woman married to Billy.

"It's nice to meet you, Marti. I've heard a lot about you."

Marti forced a smile. "Nothing bad, I hope."

"No, of course not." He gave her a slight shake of his head; he hadn't told this woman the truth.

Jesse gave Abbie a sideways hug. "When this lady left, she was running around barefoot in cut-off jeans." He gave her an appraising look. "Then she shows up in a business suit, a sophisticated banker from the big city."

Marti felt grubby all of a sudden. If she'd known the visitor was a woman, she would have dressed nicer.

Abbie smiled modestly. "I've been working my way up. I manage the loan department at one of the largest banks in Atlanta."

Marti forced a smile. "That's great. And you're down for... a vacation?"

She gave Jesse a look that smacked of intimacy. "It depends. I've interviewed at a bank in Ft. Myers for the management position."

"Marti's been working on redecorating the house. I keep telling her she should start advertising. She's good."

She beamed at his compliment, glad he didn't mention the waitress part. The boys climbed up on the bank and flopped their wet bodies on the dirt and leaves. They were cute, with brown hair and hazel eyes rimmed with long, wet eyelashes. Both studied her with Billy's scrutinizing eyes.

That black feeling gnawed at her stomach, the same way it had the day she'd seen Desiree with Jesse at this same spot. Abbie wasn't sexy like Desiree, but a look of sensibility that came from accomplishment and confidence accented her bland beauty.

"Abbie's going to stay with Ma until she decides what she's going to do. I invited her to stay for dinner; hope that's all right with you."

Before Marti could even shrug a vague confirmation, Abbie said, "Hey, I can make my famous Turk casserole. I used to make it all the time when I was pregnant with my first, so I named it after him."

"Uh, I've already got something planned for dinner," Marti blurted out before she even realized it. Jesse gave her a surprised look, and she smiled. "I thought about it today at work."

"Okay. What are you going to make?"

She went blank, making it up as she went. "Spaghetti. I have an authentic Italian recipe for the sauce. You'll like it, I think."

"Sounds fine to me," Jesse said.

"I'm looking forward to it," Abbie said with a gracious smile. "The boys love spaghetti." They nodded without a great deal of enthusiasm.

Then Marti realized she'd have to go to the grocery store to get the ingredients she remembered Jamie putting into the sauce. That meant leaving them alone for a while longer. But what could happen with the boys there? And why should she worry about it anyway?

Dinner was a minimal success, even though the sauce hadn't simmered long enough and the noodles were sticky. Nobody mentioned it, and the boys were too busy sucking each long piece into their mouths to notice. They reminded her how little she related to children. Every time she said something to them, her voice sounded phony. Her inner voice rated every sentence: too cutesy, too adult. Her inner voice was becoming a real pain. She'd never heard it before her life-after-death experience.

When Marti started carting the dishes into the kitchen, Jesse started helping.

Abbie stood, too. "Let me do that. I'm sure the boys would love to spend some time with you."

"Yeah!" cried Turk. "Will you twirl us around again like a helicopter? Please, please?"

Marti noticed how easily he left her to Abbie's company and went outside with a squealing boy under each arm.

Abbie had a soft smile on her face as she watched him go outside. "He's good with kids, isn't he?"

"I think he's good with everybody."

"He sure is. He would have made a good preacher."

Marti's eyes widened. "Jesse, a preacher?" She couldn't help but remember him in his briefs, kissing her in the river. It made her feel better that Abbie didn't know him quite so well.

"Sure. He has a warmth that reaches out and touches people. They're drawn to him." She turned on the faucet and started rinsing dishes. "How old are you,

Marti?"

"Twenty ... three." Twenty-seven, she'd almost said.

"So young. You're going to have your first about the same age I had Turk. You're not really a blonde, are you?"

Marti stiffened, then wondered if her roots needed to be done already. "I'm a brunette. Is it obvious?"

"No, but your coloring is more suited for dark hair." She leaned back against the counter with her arms crossed loosely in front of her. "Jesse says you're leaving after the baby's born."

"Yes," she said firmly, more for her own benefit than Abbie's. "I'm going to California."

"Wow, that's far away."

"It's where I'm from."

"You're about five months along, aren't you?"

Marti glanced down at her belly. "Nineteen weeks last Wednesday."

"Have you felt the baby move yet?"

"The doctor says any day now."

Abbie put her hand to her heart. "That's the most exciting moment, when you *know* there's a little human inside you. You're still so tiny. I was *huge* by five months, and I just kept getting bigger."

Marti cringed. "I already feel like a duck, and I'm not even waddling yet."

"Does Jesse touch your stomach a lot?"

"Sometimes."

"He used to put his hand on my stomach all the time when I was pregnant."

Abbie's smile was free from an obvious intent to make Marti jealous. Still, her fingers tightened on the plate she put in the dishwasher.

A peal of laughter drew their attention to the large window facing out back. Jesse jogged slowly by with Clint on his shoulders, making horse sounds and pretending to buck. Marti found herself smiling wistfully.

"He's going to make a great father." Abbie pulled her gaze, seemingly in reluctance, from the scene. "Are you worried about Jesse having to take care of a baby by himself?"

"A little. Not worried that he's incapable of doing it, just that it'll be so overwhelming."

"Then what I'm going to tell you should allay that concern and maybe take away any guilt you might be feeling: I proposed to your husband."

Marti stood there with a dumbfounded expression on her face. She ignored the empty space her heart had occupied before dropping down to her toes. After closing her mouth, she asked, "Proposed what?"

Abbie laughed. "Marriage, of course. It makes sense, don't you think? You're leaving. He's going to be alone with a baby. I'm alone with two boys who adore him more than they do their own father. It's a perfect solution, a marriage of convenience."

Marriage of convenience? The relief that Abbie obviously expected didn't appear on Marti's face. Marti closed the dishwasher door with a little more zest than necessary.

"Oh, maybe I shouldn't have said anything. I just thought that since you were leaving anyway, you might feel better knowing."

Marti swallowed hard, trying to put on a casual mask. "I — I do, really. I just wasn't expecting ... you proposed to him?" And then what she really wanted to know: "What was his answer?"

"He said he had to think about it, that he still had a couple of things on his agenda before he could consider my proposal."

Marti's eyes widened. *A couple of things on his agenda? What agenda?* "I see."

"Being a reasonable and, I'm sure, compassionate woman, I know you'll see it's the best thing for that baby and for Jesse."

"Yes, the best thing," Marti said softly as the boys raced through the front door, followed by a breathless Jesse. He collapsed on the couch, and the boys snuggled on each side of him. "The best thing," she repeated, knowing she should see it that way. After all, it was exactly what he'd just proposed to her.

Jesse never mentioned Abbie's proposal, and Marti didn't tell him that she knew about it. In the five days since her surprise visit, Abbie had only been over twice, and that was to drop off the boys. As Marti and Jesse sat across the table from each other after dinner, she couldn't keep away the picture of Jesse and Abbie and the family eating there. In her picture, Jesse was laughing with the boys, not somber and thoughtful as he was now.

The rain outside made a pitter-patter sound on the roof, and the sky outside was a pasty gray. She crossed her arms in front of her, resting them on her belly. Why couldn't she get the thought of Jesse and Abbie out of her mind? In the cozy picture her mind tauntingly created, he leaned over and kissed her. Marti wrinkled her nose at that.

"What's wrong?" Jesse asked, pulling her from her self-torture.

"Why didn't you tell me my hair looked terrible?"

He raised his eyebrows. "It doesn't look terrible. I thought you liked it."

"I do. But my coloring's wrong." It was. She had studied her reflection and realized Abbie was right. Damn her, the woman was just too sensible.

He shrugged. "I never liked it all that much to begin with, but who am I to say anything? I'm just your husband."

His words bit into her heart. A lock of hair hung down over his forehead, making him look like the boys he loved so much. She caught herself remembering how soft his hair was as it had brushed her hands while they danced. To distract herself, she picked up her fork and poked at the elbow noodles on her plate.

"You've been awfully quiet lately," he said. "It doesn't bother you, the boys being around, does it?"

She noticed he hadn't mentioned Abbie being around. "No, they don't —" Her eyes widened, and the fork dropped from her hand.

He was out of his seat and at her side in seconds. "What's wrong?"

A chill washed over her when she realized what happened. "I felt the baby kick," she whispered, a smile stretching her mouth. "There it goes again." She took his hand and placed it under her loose shirt at the spot where the baby had last kicked. While they waited, the skin beneath his palm grew warm and moist. Crouched beside her, his expectant expression never wavered. Finally, the baby kicked again.

Awe lit his face, making him look breathtakingly gorgeous. "My son did that."

"There's a *baby* in there," she said softly, pulling up her shirt. Her belly looked naked and vulnerable compared to his strong, capable hand. "Abbie was right. She said it would feel more real when the baby started moving."

His expression didn't change, even when he shifted his gaze to her.

Her throat tightened, and she pushed out the words, "I hope it's a boy, Jesse."

"Well, that's up to the Big Guy upstairs. I wouldn't mind a girl, though."

"Do you think you'll be all right, raising the baby alone?"

He gave her an odd look, and she tried to make her expression light. He reached up and touched her cheek, then tucked her hair behind her ear. She didn't untuck it.

"Don't worry about us, doll. We'll be okay. Course, you can always stick around and find out for yourself."

She shook her head. "It seems you have a better offer."

It took him a second to realize what she meant. "Abbie told you?"

Marti nodded. "She figured I would feel better knowing, so I wouldn't worry."

He got to his feet. "I'm glad she offered."

Her chest tightened. "You are?"

"Yeah, it answered a question I'd had on my mind."

"What question?"

Just as he seemed like he was going to answer, he shook his head. "It's not important."

"Are you going to marry her, Jesse?"

He leaned against the wall. "Would it make you feel better if you knew I had a wife when our divorce is final?"

"No, I ... yes." She was screaming inside. It was ridiculous, and yes, selfish of her to not want him to marry Abbie. But how could she explain that to him? *I don't want you to marry her, because ...* She didn't even know why.

Jesse's eyes hardened. "Maybe I will, Marti. Maybe I will."

Time passed faster than Marti cared to think about. She should be happy that her pregnancy was coming closer to an end. It was the beginning of March, the middle of her twenty-fourth week. The baby was happily kicking away a dozen times a day. Still, whenever Jesse saw her expression change, he rushed over and asked where the kick spot was, as he called it.

Abbie had accepted the bank manager's position and moved into an apartment a few miles away. She had gracefully backed away from Jesse, but Marti knew the woman was biding her time. The boys were a constant reminder of her proposal: a family, a marriage of convenience. Maybe a kiss in the river, and then more.

If I stay ...

What bothered Marti most was the realization that Abbie could offer Jesse so much more than she could.

The sound of a truck door slamming and Bumpus's barking drew her to the front window. Jesse was walking up with three fishing rods over his shoulder. She opened the door so the dog could see the intruder was his master.

"Hey," he said, leaning the poles against the wall by the door. "I always like to hear him barking when I come up. Makes me feel safer about leaving you here alone, especially at night."

"I have to admit, he makes me feel safer, too. But

about that barking..."

Jesse was already nodding. "I know, I know. He hears something out there, but I don't know what it is."

"For the last three nights in a row?"

For a crazy moment, as he walked toward her, she thought he was going to kiss her. Instead, he leaned over and patted her belly. "Hi, Eli. Kick for me, little guy." Something in his voice made the baby move, and Jesse grinned. "He likes me already. I can tell." He sank down on the sofa with a sigh. "Those kids sure wipe me out. They're into everything, more interested in exploring around the lake than fishing in it. I ended up having to carry them in when I dropped them off."

Marti stiffened. "So, how is Abbie?"

He shrugged, obviously not hearing the crisp tone in her voice. "All right, I guess."

"No proposals tonight?"

He gave her a curious look. "No. Why, you got one for me?"

She turned away. "You have too many women for my taste."

"What are you talking about?"

"Abbie, Desiree. Is there anyone else out there with their fangs out that I should be aware of? All I ask is that you wait until I leave before you send out the invitations."

"Whoa. Where is this coming from?"

Anger heated her face. "I feel like there are predators anxiously waiting to take my place." She couldn't find the right words to convey what she was feeling: threatened? Left out?

"Abbie's not a predator." He actually laughed at that. "She's just offering to fill a hole you're going to leave.

Desiree and I are friends, nothing more. If there was something between us, we'd have hooked up a long time ago." He released a quick breath. "Talk to me, Marti. What do you want from me?"

She couldn't help it. Her gaze drifted down over his body, solid, sexy. She wanted *him*. "It's hormones, that's all." Hormones that were unleashing jealousy, making her want to cry. "I'm going to lay down for a bit."

Dammit, she wanted to believe that's all it was. Because if what she was feeling wasn't due to them, she was in a big mess.

Marti moved around in her bed for more than two hours before she finally stilled. He had been waiting impatiently for her to go to sleep. Was she dreaming about the attack?

For a while he'd convinced himself that her amnesia was permanent. The anvil-hanging-over-his-head feeling, though, pressed on.

He'd gone to her window at night again, hoping she'd moved on. That she was still not sleeping with her husband meant the trauma continued to plague her. She never seemed to sleep well. Inevitably, her memories would return, and once she saw his face, the anvil would drop.

Three nights after he'd decided to kill her, he was still standing outside her window. But tonight, the dog wasn't roaming the house. He'd seen Jesse lock him in his bedroom. They were stupid enough to think the dog was barking for nothing. Their mistake.

The only sound he could hear were the frogs, celebrating the return of warmth. His feet were bare, better to walk quietly on the wet leaves. He would climb in through the window, strangle her in her sleep, and slip away. It would be morning before Jesse knew she was dead. He would investigate, but without Marti's memory, it would lead to a dead end.

He slipped the glasscutter out of his pocket and cut a half-moon over the window latch. With a suction cup, he pulled the piece toward him, cringing at the soft crunch of the glass parting.

Marti rolled onto her back, and he waited until he was sure she hadn't woken. Then he reached inside and switched the lever.

With the suction cup, he managed to raise the window a half-inch, enough to get his gloved finger in the crevice and lift it all the way.

Crawling in would be the hard part. He crawled halfway in before losing his balance. With the sill at his stomach, he teetered back and forth, his breath caught in his chest. If she woke now, it would be all over. He couldn't have that. Once he had her neck clutched in his grip, she wouldn't be able to scream.

He was able to reach the dresser and regain his balance, but the makeshift hood he wore fell off and landed on the floor. Steadying himself, he awkwardly climbed down from the window. His heart pounded like a cissy boy's. *Man up.*

After feeling around on the floor, he found the hood and slipped it back over his head.

The glow of the nightlight lit the bed. The only part of her body that showed from beneath the crumpled sheets and blanket was her face. Her rounded forehead creased with worry. Not because he was standing next to her, but from the dream that clutched her in its grasp.

The thought of his task pumped adrenaline through

him. He didn't want to kill her; he had to. No choice. He couldn't fail this time. Last time he had threatened his rape victim into silence. She'd had no one to protect her or back her up. Marti did. He rubbed his hands together and reached down to her neck, barely visible. As soon as fingers circled her throat, her eyes opened. But she didn't scream. She tried to move her arm, but it was encased in the sheets. He pressed tighter, anxious to have it done with before she realized she wasn't dreaming.

Her foot escaped the blanket and slammed him in the groin. She pushed back the sheets and shoved at his chest. Then her scream tore loose, filling the room with the hoarse sound of terror. A violent fit of coughing ensued. He grasped his injured balls before realizing he had to get out of there.

"Jesse!" she managed through her coughs.

Working with his survival instinct, he locked the bedroom door just as Jesse slammed into it from the other side. Shoving Marti aside, he dove for the window, scratching his back as he slid through and fell to the ground. The crack of the wood around the door echoed in the night as he tore through the woods to the river. He heard small footsteps and dared a glance behind him. The snarling dog was racing up, as if released from the gates of hell.

His shallow dive landed him a good distance from the bank. He saw the dog jumping into the river several yards behind him. The current ran swiftly, dragging him in its cold wet grasp farther and farther away. The dog disappeared in the darkness.

He reached the shore and stumbled through the woods to where he'd left the truck. He had parked it far from Jesse's house, but it was closer to where he now was. And he could navigate those woods like a sailor on a lake. He found the truck and started it before he'd even closed the door. He tried to shake away the trembling in his hands as he pulled into his drive and turned off the engine. His heart threatened to burst.

He'd almost killed her, twice. It was an omen that she'd survived. An omen that she belonged to him.

He had lost the chance to raise his baby. The woman he'd loved, the woman he would have laid down his life for, had denied that it was his. She'd cruelly taken his child away from him.

Marti was pregnant, as his love had been, carrying high and remaining small. Yes, she was meant to be his.

Holy hell, he'd almost lost the chance to regain what he'd lost. He raised his face skyward and thanked God for sparing her and giving him this message.

Now his only choice was to get rid of Jesse.

CHAPTER 13

Marti wailed and trembled violently in Jesse's arms. He held her so tight his muscles ached, but he managed to stroke her hair and whisper calming words against the top of her head. His eyes never left the open window, his emotions warring between staying with her and going after the son of a bitch with a rifle. Marti's grip was too tight to even think about leaving her.

"Tell me what happened. Can you do that for me, doll?"

Her cheeks were wet with tears streaming down her face. She was still sucking in deep breaths, but she nodded. He tucked the strands of hair that stuck to her face behind her ears.

"I thought ... dream ... not a dream ... standing there ... came at me."

He pulled her close again. "Doll, I can't understand what you're saying. Come on, walk with me to the kitchen. I'm going to call the sheriff's office, then get you something to drink."

He helped her to unsteady feet, then guided her into the kitchen where he poured her a shot of whiskey.

Damn, she wasn't supposed to have alcohol. He tossed it down his throat instead and poured her a water. She gulped it, then coughed and sputtered.

He put his hands on her arms, facing her. "Marti, did you see him?"

"He was black." She shook her head. "No, that's not right. He had a KKK-type hood, only it was black. He was tall, not heavy, not skinny." She was trembling so hard that her teeth were chattering.

"Think. Could it have been Paul?"

She bit her bottom lip, obviously trying to conjure up a painful memory. "It could have been, but I don't know. I just don't know. It was dark, and he ... he ..."

"It's okay, doll." He rubbed her arms, pulled her close, and called the emergency number.

Lyle answered. "'lo?" Then he cleared his voice and seemed to come awake. "Deputy Thomas here."

"This is Jesse West. Somebody just broke in and tried to kill Marti. Get over here right away."

"Ohmigosh! Should I call an ambulance?"

Marti was already shaking her head, clutching tighter to him. "No, I don't think that's necessary. She's just shaken up."

"Okay, let me call Carl, and we'll be right over." To his wife's urgent inquiries, he answered, "Marti just got attacked."

Jesse knew Eileen would be on the phone until sunrise telling everyone about it. No matter; it would get around anyway.

Jesse called Helen to tell her what happened and warn her that he was bringing Marti over after the questioning. Then he took Marti's hand and squeezed it. "I'm going to get you some clothes."

She nodded, but her grip didn't lessen, so they both went into her room. He picked out some clothes and led her to his bedroom. "I want you to stay right here, lock the door behind me, and get dressed."

Her eyes filled with panic. "Where are you going?"

"Outside to take a look around."

"I'm going with you." She ripped off her nightshirt and changed while he turned away to give her privacy.

He grabbed his rifle, took his fishing flashlight out of the closet, and led her by the hand outside. He found the half-moon shaped glass on the ground outside Marti's window but saw no footprints in the mat of oak leaves.

The sound of flapping ears preceded Bumpus, who appeared out of the blackness, glistening with water.

"The son of a bitch went to the river." Which would end tracking completely.

"What's that?" she asked, pointing to something on the ground up ahead.

A single blue glove lay on the damp leaves. He didn't touch it but trained the flashlight on it as he crouched down closer. "It's a golf glove." His eyes narrowed as he tried to remember if he'd ever seen it before. Who noticed golf gloves, anyway? But he did know one thing: Paul played golf.

His anger boiled as he imagined Paul running through the woods. Jesse stood when he heard sirens wailing in the distance.

Carl was the first to show up, and Jesse clenched his fists as he walked outside. Carl was as put-together as he always was, even at 1:15 in the morning. Still, his face was stiff with tension.

"What the hell happened? Lyle told me someone

broke in and tried to kill Marti."

"What happened is that the bastard who's been running around since November is still trying to kill my wife. Where's Paul?"

"Paul's asleep on the couch. I saw him when I left. Did she see the man?"

"No, he wore a hood over his head. There's a golf glove out back. Come on, I'll show you."

Lyle's car slammed into the driveway, lights flashing in silence. He jumped out and met the two men near the front door.

Carl took charge. "Jesse, show Lyle where Marti was sleeping. Lyle, interview her, find out if she can identify the man who broke in. I'll take a look outside and go over the window for prints and anything else I can find."

Jesse didn't want Carl to walk around back alone, where he could do away with any evidence that could convict his son. But he didn't want to leave Marti alone either. Damn, but things were complicated.

Before Carl reached the corner of the house, Jesse said, "Sheriff, don't lose the evidence this time."

Carl turned around in a bull-charging stance, fingers curled like claws at his sides. "What's that supposed to mean?"

"You know exactly what it means. I think you'll do whatever it takes to protect that good-for-nothing son of yours."

"Paul had nothing to do with this. If I thought he did, I'd throw his butt in jail as fast as I'd throw yours in." He pointed to Jesse. "And I'd watch what I'd say if I were you, or I'll do just that."

With every passing second, Jesse was surer that it

was Paul. He led Lyle to Marti's bedroom, then took her aside.

"I'm going to keep an eye on Carl."

Her eyes widened. "You really think it was Paul, don't you?"

He put his hand on his stomach. "Right here in my gut, I do. Carl would be a fool to get rid of the glove, because he knows I've seen it. But there might be something else I missed. I'll be right outside if you need me."

"I need you now," she whispered, then said, "No, go. It's important."

With a last look at her, he went outside to monitor Carl. The blue glove was in a plastic bag on the ground. Carl was dusting the window with one hand, holding a flashlight with the other. He gave Jesse a sidelong glance before returning to his task.

"I don't see any prints on the outside. We might find some inside. There probably won't be any on the glove, but I'm going to check to see where it was bought."

Jesse watched him work without comment. After they'd dusted the bedroom, Carl and Lyle packed up. Marti had stayed in the living room, huddled in a blanket.

"Lyle," Carl said. "Why don't you go on home? I'll take this stuff in and go over it tonight. It seems that I'll have to find this guy so Mr. West here won't think I'm covering up for my son."

"That's the only way I'll believe Paul's innocent," Jesse said, Carl's comment grating on him.

When the sheriff and deputy left, Jesse packed up a few things and reached down to take Marti's hand. "We're going to Ma's for the night. Tomorrow, I'll fix that window, but you're sleeping with me from now on."

She nodded instead of giving him the protest he expected. Probably tomorrow he'd hear one, but she wasn't going to win that argument. If she'd been sleeping next to him tonight, the bastard would be dead.

Once at Helen's house, she led them up to Jesse's old room and settled Marti into bed with a cup of chamomile tea. Bumpus curled up at the foot of the bed.

Caty sat next to Marti. "The tea will help you sleep."

Marti shivered. "I don't want to sleep. I keep seeing floating eyes."

Jesse rubbed her shoulder. "Floating eyes?"

"That's the first thing I thought when I saw him. All I could see were his eyes and, in the dark, they appeared to be floating."

"You didn't notice anything about them? Like their shape or color?"

"No, it wasn't light enough to see color, and the shape ... I don't know."

She drank the rest of the cup, then snuggled under the blankets.

Helen looked expectantly at Jesse as he moved closer to the door. "And where are you sleeping?"

"Right here. When I get back."

Both women looked at him with worry in their eyes.

Marti sat up. "Where are you going?"

He tried to keep the hatred from showing in his eyes. "I've got some checking to do."

"Jesse ..." Helen warned.

"I'll be back shortly."

"I'll stay here until you get back," Caty said, giving him a knowing look. "Be careful."

Helen followed down the stairs. "Whatever you're

thinking, it's trouble."

"It's trouble all right, but not for me. For the guy who tried to kill my wife. And my baby."

"Jesse, don't —"

"I have to. I can't let him get away with this. He's going to keep trying until he succeeds. Again."

Her look of worry gnawed at him as he drove. The anger gnawed harder, right down to the bone. All his life, Paul had tried to invade Jesse's life: sports when they were kids, racing and golf, and even Desiree, although that hadn't succeeded. Now he was trying to destroy his future. Jesse was going to invade his life back.

There were no lights on outside the brick colonial and only Paul's black truck parked in the drive. Jesse felt the hood: cold. Maybe enough time had elapsed for the engine to cool down, so inconclusive. The doors were locked, and it was too dark inside to see anything out of the ordinary.

He pounded on the front door until a disoriented Paul opened it. He blinked twice, as if he couldn't believe who he saw. Before he could react, Jesse shoved him inside and slammed a punch to his jaw. Paul went down instantly, almost too easily.

No wonder. The smell of liquor permeated Paul's skin and breath.

Jesse picked him up and shoved him against the wall. "You son of a bitch, that's the last time you ever touch her." He drove a fist into Paul's stomach. "You got drunk and did it. What'd you do, sit there drinking and thinking that she might remember you were the psycho who tried to rape and kill her by the side of the road? Did it get to you?"

Paul was more cognizant now, standing on his own. "I didn't do anything to Marti. I had too much happy hour and came home. I don't even remember lying down on the couch."

"Where's your golf glove?"

He gave Jesse a confused look. "My golf glove? It's at the club with my irons. What does that have to do with anything?"

"What color's your glove?"

He seemed to search his muddled brain. "Gray and white. I just bought it last week. You can go down and check if you want."

Jesse leaned back on his heels, daunted only for a second. "What about your old one?"

"Uh, blue, I think. Light blue."

"It's your glove, isn't it? You left it in your hurry to get out of there before I got hold of you. But you're not safe yet, Paul. Not by a long shot. We have some things to discuss..."

Marti woke the next morning, her head still fuzzy from sleep. She sat up suddenly as the room came into view. White walls, dark blue curtains covering two windows facing the rising sun. A queen bed and white ceiling fan overhead. Not her bedroom. Caty sat up and yawned, sprawled out at an angle on the bed next to her. Then everything came back, the horrifying nightmare that was real.

"Where's Jesse?" she asked, searching everywhere.

Caty searched, too. "Maybe he's already up. I hope he's up, that he's—"

"All right," both said at the same time, scrambling out of bed.

Marti was already grabbing her clothes. "He'd be in

here, if he'd come home. He would have let us know what happened."

"I can't believe I fell asleep." Caty flew out the door.

Helen was on the phone when Marti raced into the living room, kneading her blond hair with nervous fingers, pacing frantically.

"How much? ... Sheriff, that's ridiculous. I get that, but surely you can understand what he's been through. ... Fine." She slammed the phone down, startled to see Marti standing there.

"Something happened to Jesse?"

Caty came downstairs, half-dressed, her face pale. "They arrested him, didn't they?"

"Oh, my God," Marti muttered, falling back onto the couch. "He killed Paul."

"No, but he nearly did. Paul's at the hospital now. If his ribs are broken, it could be a felony. Jesse's been in jail since four this morning, but Carl didn't want to wake me up any earlier than now to tell me." Her mouth tightened into a furious line. "He's so thoughtful, that one. Jesse is scheduled for his twenty-four-hour hearing at ten-thirty. Bond will be set then. Carl's going to press for seven thousand dollars if it's a felony."

"*What?*" Marti stood and curled her hands into fists. "That jerk deserves everything he got, even if he wasn't the one who broke in last night. Jesse didn't want you to know so you wouldn't worry, but Paul and his two fiendish friends jumped him the night we were Christmas tree shopping. They hurt him pretty bad."

Caty started heading upstairs. "That's it. I'm calling into work and going down there myself. I'll show that sheriff—"

"Oh no, you're not," Helen said. "You go into work.

I don't need two of my kids in jail, with Billy sure to jump into the fray. Lord knows he's been in the tank enough times already. Marti and I will head down and straighten this whole thing out. If we need your help, we'll call."

"But —"

"Go to work."

Caty sputtered before stomping back upstairs. Helen sat in silence for a minute, weighing the situation. Marti wanted to join Caty's army and head to jail to raise some hell, but something in Helen's quiet deliberation showed more strength. She only wished she had that strength.

Helen brushed her hair from her face. "I'm going to get dressed. Get some food in your stomach so that babe doesn't think the whole world is coming to an end. Last night was enough of a scare. Then we'll go down and see what we're in for. After that, I can talk to the lawyer I work for and see how we're going to get out of it."

Helen calmly went to her room, and Marti walked into the kitchen. She put her hand on her belly.

"I didn't even think about how all this affected you. It's not that I don't care, but I think you're in this little cocoon all sheltered and snug. We'll go see Dr. Diehl tomorrow, just to make sure. It's okay, though. Your daddy's going to take care of us at night from now on. Well, after he gets out of jail."

She buttered a piece of bread and forced it down. She thought of those strong arms wrapped around her while she slept, his bare chest pressed against her back. Then she thought about him spending the morning in jail on an old, stained mattress without a pillow. She could have died last night, and the last conversation between them was about Abbie. Why did the thought of his marrying Abbie after Marti was gone drive her mad? How could she explain that she was jealous? He would ask, *What does it matter, if you're leaving?* What else could she tell him but the truth: *I don't know, but it does, dammit. It does.*

"Are you ready?"

Marti jumped at Helen's voice, then turned to see her standing in the kitchen doorway dressed in a coral suit. Marti felt like a ragamuffin in her jeans and long-sleeved top.

Caty came sliding down the wooden banister. "You have to let me know the second you find out anything. I'll go nuts wondering."

"We will."

Helen and Marti followed Caty down the road until she turned off at Bad Boys Diner. Marti knew Caty was using her utmost self-control to keep from heading to the jail.

"Helen, how do I become like you, so strong and calm?"

Her coral-painted lips softened into a smile. "Practice and determination. Every time you resist doing the wrong thing, you become stronger. It keeps building on itself. When you do the wrong thing, you fall down a notch. Then you pick yourself up and keep striving."

"What if you're not good at resisting temptation? What if you have nothing to build on?"

"You have to start somewhere. Something small, like not eating the doughnut when you want it. Then you keep growing, taking on bigger challenges."

"Oh, how I wish you'd been there to teach me this stuff when I was growing up. All I keep thinking about are the mistakes I've made, over and over again. Weakness is like strength, too. It keeps building, small things at first, then larger and larger."

Helen's smile became wistful. "I always think about what I have to lose by acting on my impulses. Flab, hurting someone's feelings, or breaking someone's heart. I weigh whether the desire is worth the price."

They pulled into the parking lot next to the sheriff's office. Marti took a deep breath.

"I wish I could be so confident. I want to scream and kick something. You look completely in control."

"I want to scream, too. You're stronger than you think. You're holding it in just as I am."

The sheriff's office smelled piney, as if the cleaning service had recently vacated the premises. While Helen talked to Lyle, Marti walked to the door behind him, hoping to glimpse Jesse. All she could see was a hallway off to the side of the back room and a hint of bars.

"Jesse," she whispered.

"Sorry, Marti, but you can't go back there." Lyle turned back to Helen. "As I was saying, I can't let you see him until we're through processing him."

"Processing him? He's been here for hours."

He shrugged, avoiding her eyes. "Well, Sheriff Paton has his ways. If it makes you feel any better, Paul doesn't have any broken ribs. He'll be on his way down to sign the papers, but all Jesse will get is battery. A couple hundred bucks'll do it for bail, probably." Lyle sat back in his chair, clearly enjoying his official duty.

Helen crossed her arms in front of her chest. "I don't

suppose it matters that Paul and his friends ambushed my son at Christmas."

"Not if he didn't report it. Why didn't he do that, you think?"

"He's not built that way," Marti said.

When the women walked outside, Helen said, "Self-control is slipping fast. When I can't see my own son, I start panicking. Something's not right."

"What do you mean? Like he's hurt and they don't want us to know yet?"

Helen shook her head. "No, I don't want to think about that. Let's go down to Bad Boys and let Caty know what's going on."

Marti stopped before opening the car door. "Can you do me a favor? Drop me off at the hairdresser's down the street. I'm going to undo one of my earlier impulses."

At ten o'clock, Helen and Marti showed up at the sheriff's office. This time they were prepared to bulldoze any roadblock they had to, even one named Lyle.

As it turned out, they didn't have to. Carl walked out from the back room as they stepped inside. His expression was grim, his lips pulled into a tight red line.

"We're filling out the paperwork now. Then you can get him the hell out of here."

Helen flinched from the tone of his voice. "I don't understand."

"There is no bail. If it were up to me, I'd keep Jesse in jail until I finish this investigation. But it isn't up to me. Paul isn't pressing charges. The kid wimped out on me again."

He went into the back, leaving Helen to shake her head. "I don't understand why Paul isn't pressing charges."

"Maybe he wants Jesse to lay off his case, so he's being nice."

Carl appeared in the doorway, and Jesse walked through behind him. He had a black eye, his brown hair disheveled. A dull look replaced the sparkle that usually lit his eyes. Marti rushed into his arms. Even in his surprise to her reaction, he pulled her close, kissing the top of her head.

She had dreamed about being right there all morning. He had been sitting in a cold jail cell locked away from her. Now he was here, and she squeezed back the tears of relief. Drowning in the feel of him, seeking the strength he freely offered her, the warmth and affection he gave, his arms around her, she realized it was more than relief she was feeling: she was in love with him.

No, she couldn't drown. She cleared her throat and moved away, hoping he didn't see the film of moisture on her eyes. "I, er, missed you."

Helen moved up to hug him. "Let's get out of this dump," she whispered, loud enough for Carl to hear it.

"Jesse, you're looking for clues in clear water," he said in a stiff voice. "There's nothing to see."

Jesse met his angry gaze. "That's what you want me to think. But the truth will come out."

Marti took hold of his arm once they were outside, slowing him down. "What happened? Did they beat you?" She gestured to his eye.

"I didn't go quietly." He seemed to take her in, his expression softening as he brushed a lock of hair from her face. "I'm okay. Don't look so worried."

She let out a long breath. "I'll try."

They stopped at Bad Boys on the way home. Caty squealed and rushed into his arms. The small midmorning crowd turned to look, then whispered speculatively. Marti was sure they already knew about the attack and Jesse's arrest.

"I heard you broke two of Paul's ribs. Good for you, big brother."

"Caty," Helen admonished. "He didn't break anything."

Caty lowered her voice as she took in his black eye, but before she could say anything, he shook his head. "It's no big deal."

"What did they set your bail at?"

"No bail," Marti said. "Paul didn't press charges. Odd, huh?"

"Very odd."

Jesse was quiet, and Marti hoped he was just tired. Helen held up the conversation for the ride back to her house. When they reached home, Helen checked in at the office and found she was needed for a case.

"I'm only part-time, but they get to choose which part. Relax here."

Jesse took Marti's hand and led her up the stairs. It gave her a funny feeling, him leading her up to his old bedroom. Not that she expected anything to happen, not as tired as he must be. And it wouldn't happen anyway, she added tersely.

The bed was still rumpled. Sunlight filtered through the curtains, softly lighting the room. He stripped off his shirt and lay down, pulling her down beside him. His eyes were sleepy, yet something kept them from slipping closed.

He smiled, reaching for a strand of hair. "You dyed your hair back."

She nervously tucked her hair behind her ear before

realizing what she was doing. "Argh. Now you've got me doing it. Yeah, I dyed it back. Easier to take care of."

His smile faded, replaced by that faraway look. He still held her hand, moving and bending it, studying it.

"Jesse, what's wrong? You don't feel bad for what you did to Paul, do you?"

"No, I feel bad for what I did to you."

"To me?" There was a strange pounding in her heart, put there by the way he touched her hand, the way he looked at her with quiet agony in his eyes.

"I let you down. My anger got the best of me and got me put in jail. I promised to take care of you, and it's damned hard to do that locked up. All I kept thinking about was what if something happened to you. If he knew I'd been arrested, he'd know I wasn't there watching over you." He squeezed her hand, finally meeting her eyes. "You're my life right now. I can't let my emotions override your safety. Never again, Marti."

She found it difficult to breathe when he said, *You're my life right now.* What to say to him after he'd said that? How to take away the self-crimination in his eyes?

"You didn't let me down, Jesse. I know you were trying to put an end to this. I was safe here. You knew I'd be okay."

He looked at her for the longest moment, weighing her words perhaps. She tried to catch her breath without letting him know he'd taken it from her. Before she could accomplish it, he leaned over and kissed her. Like under the tree last Christmas Eve, he pressed his mouth to hers, not in passion but in tenderness. Passion she could fight. Maybe. But how could she fight tenderness?

He kissed her again, closing his eyes as if savoring the

feel. Or deciding whether to kiss her some more. She was poised at the edge, hoping he wouldn't, wishing he would.

He didn't. Without opening his eyes again, he laid back, pulling her along with him. Her head nestled against his shoulder, and she could feel his breath on top of her head. His heart beat beneath her ear, lulling her into a dreamy state. His hand still held hers, although his grip loosened as fell asleep.

It hit her again, that scary revelation of earlier. Could she stand a lifetime of this? Of simply being loved?

One of their earlier conversations echoed in her mind:

No proposals tonight? she'd said in a snippy tone after he'd seen Abbie.

No. Why, you got one for me?

Which made it sound like he'd be open for one. From her. He'd asked her to stay, or at least suggested it.

Stay, Marti. Don't lose him.

She couldn't help, though, consider the source of her snippiness: Abbie. Abbie, who could no doubt offer him much more than she could. Who knew about raising kids. Who wasn't so messed up. Who had two boys who idolized Jesse and needed a good father.

I'm trying to be a better person. Jesse's helping me to be better, nicer, to forgive myself, love myself.

Ah, hell. That was the irony of it: by wanting Jesse, she was being selfish once again.

CHAPTER 14

Donna Hislope walked into the diner, flashing Caty and Marti a phony smile before prissily sitting at the counter. She licked her finger and ran it down the hair that tapered to a point at her temple.

"She either wants to know something, or wants us to know something," Caty whispered before slowly making her way over. "Hi, Donna. How's your dad?"

"Oh, the usual. And speaking of that, can I have my usual?"

"Chocolate milkshake," Caty said with a nod, turning to prepare it.

"Oh, you're funny. No, a glass of tomato juice. Got to watch my figure." She leaned against the counter.

"Marti, how are you doing? I heard about the break-in last week. The creep broke into *your* bedroom, I understand. Too bad he picked the time you and Jesse are, uh, having problems."

Either the sheriff or the deputy had a big mouth, Marti thought, cursing the gossips of the small town. She smiled. "Yeah, well, backache or no, *our* bed will have to do until the baby's born."

Donna showed her large, flat teeth in a lascivious smile. "If I had a husband like him, I wouldn't let him sleep alone for a minute. Speaking of that, guess who asked me for a date next Friday? Paul Paton."

Caty's eyes widened. "I hope you didn't accept it."

Donna pulled at her polyester mini-skirt, shifting around on the stool. "Oh, come on. You don't really believe he's after Marti, do you? He's too good-looking to go around attacking women. And he's a lot hotter than the other guy who's been flirting with me lately."

Donna examined her fingernails, forcing Caty to ask, "And who's that?"

"Dean Seeber."

Marti saw Caty's spine stiffen. "Dean asked you out?" Caty asked in a thin voice.

"Well, not directly. Yet. But he sent me flowers today. I have to call and thank him, I suppose, but that's all he gets. I wouldn't be caught dead with him."

Caty's face flushed, a mixture of disbelief and betrayal in her eyes. Marti spoke up before Caty could give away the affection for Dean she always hid, even from herself.

"What's so bad about him?"

"He's just weird, that's all. Not bad looking or anything, just too strange for me." She took a sip of her tomato juice, left some money on the counter, and stood. "Nice chatting with you, girls."

"Be careful on that date, Donna," Marti said.

She held out her arm and dropped her wrist. "Oh, pooh. I think you two aren't getting enough. You're too uptight."

Marti shook her head as the glass door swung shut. "I'm uptight not because I was almost killed last week, but because I haven't had enough sex lately. There's logic for you."

Caty stared out the window with narrowed eyes, watching Donna get into her new sports car. "Do you think Dean really sent her flowers?"

"There's one way to find out: ask him. Um, your concern wouldn't be anything other than friendly, would it?"

Caty met her eyes. "Of course not. But I'd break his nose if he went out with her."

Later that evening, Marti sat across the table from Jesse, watching him pick at his food. Mostly he was stirring it around, and she couldn't take blame for lousy cooking; the peas were canned and the roasted chicken came from the grocery store.

With her toe, she tapped his leg. "What'cha thinking about?"

"A lot of things. I've asked Paul twice why he didn't press charges. He doesn't even meet my eyes, just shrugs and turns away. That isn't like him. It's not that he's even acting guilty, just preoccupied. He knows I'm still determined to prove his guilt. I don't get it."

"Maybe Paul isn't the one. I mean, whenever I've seen him, in the diner, he never acts like he'd murder me if he had the chance."

"Don't be fooled. Paul has always been superb at masking his emotions. But I'm going to have all day Sunday to watch him. You're coming with me, aren't you?"

"To where?"

"Racing."

She shifted in her seat. "I don't know. I'm not really into that racing stuff, the noise and crowds and all."

His flash of disappointment turned smug. "That's okay. I'm sure I'll have a couple of women in the stands to cheer me on."

She stood and threw her napkin across the table at him. "Desiree and Abbie can wear cheerleading outfits and wave pompons for all I care." At his grin, she added, "I didn't say I wasn't going, just that I wasn't sure. And don't use your *women* to manipulate me into doing things, Jesse James."

He shook his head slowly. "You're something else, you know that? I was referring to Caty and Ma."

She threw a bun at him, smearing his nose with butter when he didn't duck in time. "I know exactly who you were referring to, and it was not them."

When she grabbed her plate and glass and headed into the kitchen, he came up behind her and leaned down next to her ear. "Anyway, I have to get you there. I don't want you here by yourself while I'm at the race. Besides, I want to keep an eye on Paul's reactions to you all day."

"Sure, use me." She turned on the water.

Sliding his arms around her belly, he whispered, "Don't tempt me, Marti. Don't tempt me."

It seemed like hours before Marti drifted off to sleep. Jesse had shifted and moved for a while, but she lay silent and still, not wanting him to know she was awake. There was something intimate about sharing a midnight conversation in bed in the dark.

Now she was awake again, and it was still dark. She wasn't worried about finding somebody standing over her bed, not with Jesse beside her. Something woke her, and then she realized what it was. She felt his warm hand on her bare belly. The blankets covered her waist, but her shirt had bunched up. Her eyes adjusted to the ghostly light streaming through the curtains. She turned her head toward him, finding him lying on his side facing her.

She couldn't see his eyes, only shadows. "Jesse? Are you awake?"

"I couldn't sleep," he whispered, his voice velvety in the darkness. "I felt the baby move, and I started thinking about him in there."

She felt a shifting in her stomach and smiled. "What were you thinking about?"

He trailed his fingers lightly over her belly, and in the moonlight, she could see the smile on his face. "What his life is like, what he feels. Is he happy, or does he know what happiness is about yet? Could he feel your terror last week? Can he feel when you're happy?"

She remembered his kiss in his old bedroom, and her heartbeat quickened. Did the baby feel that, too? Part of her wanted to feel Jesse's mouth on hers again, desperate to experience that new sensation of tenderness and masculine sensuality. Part of her wanted to pack up that very moment and run to California as fast as she could because it hurt too damned much.

He reached up and touched her cheek. "You are so beautiful."

"Jesse..."

His finger grazed her lips, skin rougher than his lips would have been. "You are."

"I feel like a duck," she murmured against his finger. "I look like I swallowed a bowling ball."

"You have a glow that's like gold, and your eyes sparkle. Your belly is one of the most beautiful parts of your body."

The glow, the sparkle, they were from the baby. Only from the baby. Her dry throat, the warm flush on her face, that was all from the pregnancy, too. He touched her chin, drawing her closer for another devastating kiss that would rock her insides and her resistance. She squeezed her eyes shut as he moved closer.

"Don't kiss me."

"Why not? I like kissing you."

"I can't handle it."

Well, at least she was being honest. He had kissed her four times, and each time she had felt it farther down in her heart, pushing away reason, lulling her into a false confidence that she could deserve a man like Jesse.

"What's there to handle? I kiss you, you kiss me back. Are you afraid I'm going to jump you?"

She found herself adopting that awful habit Jesse had started, tucking her hair behind her ears. "No, actually, I'm afraid I'll jump *you*. You know, pregnant women, hormones, all that."

He leaned closer again. "I can deal with that risk." His mouth grazed hers before she backed away.

"Jesse, I don't want to ... I mean, I *want* to, but I can't. Physically I want to, but emotionally I can't. Do you understand what I'm trying to say?"

"You don't want to make love with me because you're afraid it might be so wonderful, you couldn't leave."

"No." Yes.

When he touched her mouth with his, she didn't back off. "Who said that if I kissed you, we'd have to make love?"

"Well, we are in bed. It always seems that men can't kiss or hold a woman without expecting more. To men, kissing means sex —"

He was kissing her then, and more than kissing, teasing her lips with his tongue. Her heart tightened, wanting to resist, unable to. Her mouth opened at his invitation, against her will. Without hesitation, his warm tongue moved along her teeth, tickling the roof of her mouth, all in an agonizingly slow, lazy way.

After ravishing her mouth, he kissed across her chin and down her throat. She was caught breathless, drowning again ... not thinking about the consequences for once.

"What if," he murmured against her skin, "I didn't expect to make love to you, but I wanted to pleasure you in other ways?"

His hand drifted down across her belly to beneath the blankets. He slid his fingers over her underwear, making her legs tense in reaction. Even tensed, they moved easily apart for him.

"Jesse ..." she managed until his hand cupped her pubic area.

"Relax, doll. Go with it."

He rubbed back and forth, creating a warmth that spread through her whole body. Damn, it felt good, heat spreading through her body. She didn't relax, exactly. No, she moved into his hand, her pelvis sliding against him. He kneaded her, his fingers reaching all the way down to her opening.

She let out a soft murmur which he took as consent to run his finger under the edge of her panties. She gave him more consent, shifting so his fingers touched more of her. He moved over her folds, sliding through her wetness, then dipping his finger into the well of it and bringing that slick essence to her sensitive nub.

Her body ached with readiness. It had been so long, too long, and all those times she'd seen Jesse in his briefs or hell, even with clothes on, God, she'd been tempted.

She trembled, toes flexed, fingers curled into the sheets. The orgasm claimed her, and she arched her back, her breaths coming hard and fast, a sound like agonized relief coming from deep in her chest.

Finally, finally ...

Jesse settled his hand on her belly afterward, his face close to hers. "Glad you gave in?"

"Yes." No. Now she wanted him more than ever. If he even suggested making love now, she *would* jump him. Drowning. She was on the edge of drowning in him already.

But he didn't. Instead, he pulled her into his arms, forming himself to her back and holding her close. He was rigid, pressing into her, but not insistently.

"Jesse, have you ... made love to anyone since I got here?"

He shook his head, which made his hair brush her neck. "Doesn't seem right to go with some other woman when I'm married. This is a small town. You scratch an itch and everyone knows about it. Besides, I haven't really wanted to be with anyone." *But you.* Did she "hear" those unspoken words or was it her imagination?

She turned her head. "You haven't scratched your itch?"

"Well, there is more than one way to skin a cat." He shrugged. "What worked when I was thirteen still works in my twenties."

He'd stayed faithful, for her. So people wouldn't talk

about Marti's husband straying. She moved her hips, pressing her butt against his erection. His fingers tightened on her hips.

"Marti, are you trying to drive me crazy?"

She turned her face so their cheeks brushed. "Relax. Go with it. There's another way to skin a cat."

He let out a low groan as she gyrated against him, pulling her even closer, moving with her. She could feel all of him pressed up against her back, but mostly she felt that tempting erection. And minutes later, she felt his body jerk, his hands tighten, and his breath catch. He flopped onto his back, breathing heavily, and threw off the sheet.

She could see him in the dim light, wearing nothing but shorts, his hand on his stomach. She wanted to touch him, to run her hands across his chest, link her fingers with his.

"Thank you," she whispered, holding back the rest of what she wanted to do. "For kind of forcing me. It was wonderful."

"My pleasure. Thank you." After a moment, he brushed his fingers over her stomach. "Do you think the baby felt it when you came?"

She giggled. "I'm sure he did. I just hope he didn't know what it was."

Marti and Jesse drove into the speedway mid-afternoon, the truck straining under the weight of pulling number thirteen. If anything had changed between them as a result of last night, she couldn't tell. Except that they regarded each other with a measure of shyness that didn't exist before.

Billy was there, talking to one of the other racers. They parked in the pit area in the middle of the track, a large circular area covered in dirt and tire tracks. There were several other trailers loaded with racecars of every type, including Chevys, Buicks, and even tiny little cars that hardly seemed big enough to accommodate a grown man.

"Those are the midgets," Jesse explained when she asked. "They're the special feature tonight."

"What is your kind of car called?"

"I'm in the late models."

Jesse hopped out of the truck, then held his hand out so she could slide along the seat and get out on his side. She wondered if Billy could tell something had happened last night. Nah, she decided.

"Hey, little brother. Marti. You ready to get the beast going? Steven's got a new Mustang, says it'll beat anything."

"It doesn't look new to me," Marti said after glancing at the car.

"New to the racing circuit," Billy corrected. "You gonna race in the Lady Road Warriors?"

"Me? You mean women race these cars?"

"Yep. 'Course, I don't think they'll let a pregnant woman do it."

"Shucks."

In a weird way, the idea intrigued her.

Jesse shook his head at the bantering as he removed some metal ties and lifted the entire hood off the car. He pulled out a toolbox and started fiddling with the massive engine. A young man with a battered face in dingy jeans and a faded T-shirt that read *I'm not arrogant, just better than you* sauntered over.

"Well, Jesse James, didn't think you'd be back with us so soon. Maybe a sponsor'll spot me as his driver this time."

Marti could see Jesse's expression harden. Without looking up at him, Jesse said, "Sponsors aren't looking for a pretty face, Dwayne. You actually have to know how to drive."

"We'll see 'bout that, West. I think they outta send you back to the dirt tracks." When Jesse didn't take his bait, he walked back to his Camaro a little faster than he'd walked over.

"You probably hate coming back here, don't you?" she asked quietly.

He stopped and looked at her. "Ah, the guys around here will jab at you for anything, but it's all head games." He glanced at the track. "I'll beat these guys to stay in shape. Dwayne knows I can beat his tail end on the dirt, too. That's what this track was before they decided to become a real racetrack and pave it. Asphalt racing is one thing, but racing in dirt is a thrill all its own. You can't imagine the feeling when you're charging down the straightaway, jumping into the left turn. You can feel your backend sliding around, then the car's sliding sideways, and just when you think 'aw, heck, this is it,' you jerk the wheel the other way and straighten the beast out again.

"Or when you're really feeling your Wheaties and end up sliding around a turn on three wheels, and everybody tells you later that you were kicking dirt twenty feet in the air, but you didn't have time to enjoy it because you were too busy making sure the fourth wheel stayed on the ground." He smiled at her. "Nothing like it. Better than sex, or at least any I've had."

Marti shook her head, imagining the scary scenario as he spoke. "You must be trying to kill yourself, Jesse."

"I'm having too much fun to have a death wish. I want to be the best someday, Marti. Right up there with Richard Petty and A.J. Foyt. My dad knew what he was doing when he built my first racecar when I was a kid. It only had a lawnmower engine, but it was a start."

He went back to his work, but she wasn't fooled. Jesse hated being there. Why wouldn't he let his anger show? If only he would share it with her.

"Yee-haw!" a guy yelled out of a stripped Yellow cab, complete with the light on top. She recognized Alan beneath his black cowboy hat as he pulled his car off the trailer and up alongside Jesse's. He nearly lost his balance climbing out of the window but quickly regained his composure.

"Hey, Jesse, Marti. Billy, that you under there?" Billy belched in response. "Nice to see you, too." Alan took his hat off and wiped the sweat from his brow with his shirtsleeve. His blond hair was matted in a ring where the hat had been sitting. "Hey, well I'll be. Another one of our prodigies come back to their old stomping grounds."

A long-legged man about Jesse's age with brown hair and brown eyes sauntered over to the car. Jesse walked over and shook his hand.

"Damn, Mark, what brings you around here? Why aren't you racing?"

Mark? The guy Jesse gave his ASA spot to when he found out Marti was pregnant?

"Serious car trouble, that's what." He shrugged, looking around the track. "Since we were down this way, I thought I'd stop by to see you. Figured you'd be around here."

Jesse leaned on the roof of his car. "How is it driving

in the ASA? Last time I talked to you, it was your third race."

Mark laughed. "It's cool, Jesse. I feel like I'm on my way. You'll get there too, bud."

"Damned straight, I will," Jesse said with fiery conviction.

"Maybe sooner than you think," Mark said meaningfully.

That got Jesse's attention. "What do you mean?"

Marti sat on the back bumper of the car, feeling as good as invisible. No wonder Jesse didn't want to be involved with anyone while he made his way up in the racing world. He was much too focused to pay attention to any attention-needing female.

"Minski's going to build another car. He wants you to drive it."

There was no hesitation. "I'm there. When's he going to have it ready?"

"A few months. How long has Marti got?"

When she looked at them at the mention of her name, she saw that same fierce determination in Mark's eyes that she saw in Jesse's when it came to racing.

"A few months," Jesse answered. "I've got to wait until she has the baby. Then I'm free."

Mark gave Jesse a strange look but didn't delve further. "I'll let Minski know. What if he wants you to start racing before the baby comes?"

"He'll have to wait. I can't leave Marti for days at a time, and she'll be too big to come along."

Mark nodded. "It'll be good driving together again, Jess."

"Yeah," Jesse said, drawing the word out. "It sure will."

Billy crawled out from beneath the car and leaned in to start it. The roar of the engine was deafening. Mark braced his hands on the side of the engine and asked Billy something about the engine. Jesse walked to the back of the car.

"Did you hear that? Minski's going to build a second car. I could have another ride."

"I heard." She smiled, knowing how much it meant to him. "I'm thrilled for you."

"It's what I want most in the world."

She wondered where she fit into his list of wants in the world. If she fit there at all. Feeling crummy, she changed the subject.

"Why doesn't Billy have his own car?" she asked over the noise.

"Billy swore he'd never race again after Dad died, but he's determined to make sure the same thing doesn't happen to me, so he's my mechanic on race day. Listen, doll, we're going to start qualifying soon. It will get crowded around here, and you're not going to want to hear their trashy language, so it'd probably be a good idea for you to sit up in the stands." He flashed a grin and pointed to one particular area. "That's my cheering section. Ma and Caty should be here anytime." His smile disappeared. "Stay away from Paul when he gets here. I mean it."

"You don't have to tell me. You think I want to see you in jail again? No way. Good luck."

He grimaced. "Don't wish a racecar driver good luck. It's bad luck."

She gave him a confused look then rolled her eyes. "Break a leg. A tire. How about 'win, dammit.'"

He laughed. "That'll do."

On her way out, she glanced back at Jesse. In tight, faded jeans and a cropped T-shirt, he cut an impressive picture. He crouched down to commiserate with Billy and Mark.

"Hey, little lady," a heavy man she'd never seen before called. "You want to be my pit crew? My old lady hit the road last night."

He was leaning over his engine, sweaty and red-faced. She tried not to notice the two-inch butt crack showing above his faded jeans.

"How can I be your pit crew if I'm rooting for another driver?" She flashed her wedding ring. "My husband."

"Oh. Who's that?"

"Jesse James West," she said, pride stealing into her voice.

"Hell, forget I asked."

"Forgotten."

She had only been sitting in the sparsely filled stands for a few minutes when she spotted Paul's black truck pulling in with a trailer. Jesse was aware of him, too, but didn't approach him. In fact, Paul chose a spot at the far end when he saw Jesse set up in the front section. Even from a distance, and a week later, Paul's faced looked bruised. She wished she could be as sure as Jesse was that he committed the assault on her. The two had a history that obviously tainted Jesse's objectivity.

Her insides jumped when Paul glanced in her direction, but she couldn't tell whether he was looking at her or somewhere near her. Just as quickly, he turned and went to work on his car, soon joined by Josh and Skip. Josh said something, and all three glanced up at her. She shifted uncomfortably under their interest.

A short while later, she watched Abbie walk through

the gate and across the track to Jesse's car, boys in tow. Billy stayed beneath the car, although he motioned for the boys to crawl under with him. Abbie held onto her floppy yellow hat as the breeze picked up.

The pit was now packed with cars and people busily making last-minute adjustments. Marti concentrated on everyone else but Jesse for a long time, and when she looked back, Abbie wasn't there. Only the boys were.

Abbie picked her way through the bleachers toward her, wearing a deep blue shirt and white jeans. She had a slight flush on her face, and Marti had a feeling it wasn't from the trek up the stairs. She sat down next to Marti, then turned and asked, "Is it all right if I sit here? The boys are going to stay down there with their father."

Marti shrugged, giving more attention to what was going on down below than to Abbie. Jesse illustrated how the four-point harness worked on Clint. Jesse's blue-jeaned derriere stuck out in their direction when he leaned in the car and pulled out his helmet, settling it on Turk's head.

Abbie sighed happily, leaning back against the seats behind her. "It seems like forever since I've been here, watching Jesse race. It's a shame, about ASA and all." She glanced subtly at Marti's belly. "But he told me the sponsor is building a second car so he has another chance. I'm so happy for him. It must be hard to come back to this after getting so far."

"He doesn't seem to mind that much," Marti said, trying to keep the defensiveness out of her voice. Hell, she wasn't even the one who'd gotten pregnant and stolen his chance away.

"I think he does."

"I know he does," Marti said, refusing to have Abbie

know more about Jesse than she did.

Abbie watched Jesse with a wistful expression. "He could do anything well. I told him I could watch the baby while he traveled the ASA circuit, and eventually NASCAR. The kids and I could even travel with him sometimes. The boys would love it, and—"

"Don't you know you'd only be second?"

Abbie's smile disappeared when she pulled her gaze from Jesse and her sons, torn from her happy reverie. "What do you mean?"

"Nothing is going to mean as much to him as racing. Especially since the setback. He's not going to let anyone stand in his way of his dream. Not his baby, and not you. You'll always be second best."

Abbie smiled. "A good wife doesn't stand in the way of her man going after his dreams. If that means being second, that's all right by me."

A good wife ... her man. Abbie's proposal wasn't just a marriage of convenience on her part; she was in love with Jesse. Marti watched him joking around with a group of men.

"You're in love with him, aren't you?"

She was startled to hear Abbie voice her own thoughts. "What makes you say that?"

"I'm sorry, I should have realized it when we talked in the kitchen that first night. But I didn't see it then, the way your eyes follow his every move, the way they drink him in. I wonder if you even see it yourself."

Marti shifted uncomfortably on the hard bench. Of course, she saw it; that didn't mean she was going to admit it. And she didn't want to explore it much, in any case.

"You think because I appreciate him physically that

I'm in love with him?"

"All I know is that you walk in, screw up his life by getting pregnant, and now you want to leave. I'm not condemning you. It's just that, any other woman in that position would be feeling some amount of guilt. So when someone like me comes along and offers him his dreams again, you should feel relieved. But you obviously don't, and there's a reason. Or maybe you're not planning to leave anymore."

Marti felt trapped, searching for an answer to give Abbie — and herself. When she looked up to see Helen, Caty, and Dean walking toward them, she stood and waved, effectively ending their conversation. Then she further insured it wouldn't start again by directing Caty and Dean to sit between her and Abbie.

"Why don't you race, Dean?" Marti asked once everyone was settled.

"I do."

She waited for him to explain why he wasn't out there, but he seemed content with his answer.

"So-o-o, why aren't you racing today then?"

"Oh, I don't race cars. I race frogs. Big, warty ones. They don't give you warts, you know." He nodded knowingly. "It's all a myth."

Marti started laughing, but Dean obviously didn't realize the depth of his humor. Or even that it was humor.

When Dean was involved in a conversation, of sorts, with Abbie, Marti leaned over to Caty and whispered, "So, did you ask him about the flowers?"

"Yes. He said he did it because she looked depressed the day before when he took his hounds in for their shots. I guess I don't have any reason to get mad at him. I don't own him or anything. Not that it matters, really."

"But it does," Marti finished and turned to Helen, saving Caty from having to deny it. "This is probably a pretty familiar place to you."

"Oh, yes. I try to come whenever I can. Still, it's hard sometimes."

Marti grew silent for a moment, realizing that Helen lost her husband to this sport. "Was it here that Bernie died?"

"No, this track didn't even exist then. He traveled all over the state. I couldn't go with him, not with three kids to raise."

Marti wanted to tell Helen that was Abbie's plan, but she kept quiet about it. She wondered if Helen knew about the proposal. That probably depended on how seriously Jesse was considering it.

Then the other woman plaguing Marti these days showed up: Desiree. Wearing her standard boots, jeans, and tank top, she settled in two rows behind them. Marti bit her lip, trying not to let her presence bother her.

Caty leaned over. "Don't worry. She always comes to cheer Jesse on, always has. Even when she's seeing one of the other racers."

"I'm not worried about it," Marti said, almost too fast.

"But you are," Caty quipped, turning to intently watch something in the pit and ignoring Marti's glare. *Damn, she got me the same as I got her.*

When Jesse climbed in the car through the window, she realized that there wasn't any outside hardware on his car or any other racecar. Door handles, hubcaps, and trim were all missing. The doors were welded shut.

Even the headlights were gone. Some of the cars were like Jesse's, shiny and nice-looking, with only a few dents. Others looked like inner-city victims, stripped for parts and left for dead. They were all covered with sponsor names, mostly body shops and mechanics. One had *T&A Racing* painted on it; another had *Crash and Burn Racing*, which fit the dented car well.

The menagerie of old cars assembled on the track and, before long, the qualifying was underway. After a while, when her butt was half-numb from sitting, and her hearing half-gone from the announcer's speaker above them, the first race began.

Jesse nearly went into one of those spins he had told her about, and she found herself clenching her fists. Paul's gold car purposely bumped him in the third turn, and Jesse's backend slipped before he got it under control.

He retaliated by passing him on the next lap. She spent most of the time tensed up watching the cars all clustered together on the turns. One car went into a spin, hitting another and sending it toward the wall. The man who did his flag dance in the box way up high jumped up and down with the yellow flag.

Could she be one of the wives vehemently cheering on their spouse, chasing the stray baby, attending every race? Or would she get bored, become a straying wife? If only she could be sure that things would be different with Jesse.

With Jamie, she had been swept away by his good looks, money, everything. Jesse was good looking in a different way, not glamorous, but strong, warm, and carefree. He hadn't meant for her to fall in love with him; it had just happened. Thinking back, she realized it was inevitable.

That was Jesse, a cowboy, willing to do anything for the woman he allowed himself to love. Not that he loved her, she thought, startled by the direction of her daydreams. Leading her down the path of the brokenhearted.

She couldn't bear to see a betrayed look on his face, like the one that day when she was talking to Paul at the gas station. Her heart would shrivel up and wither if she caused Jesse real pain. And she would; it was as inevitable as falling in love with him had been.

CHAPTER 15

The drone of the engines continued throughout the evening, and heat off the racetrack made Marti think about the day she had gone swimming in the cool river with Jesse. She was now more relaxed, more confident in his driving abilities. He was just finishing his feature race, and he'd be done for the night.

Only the very close calls made her tense and grimace. With Paul out of the race, after his car started making guttural noises, she relaxed even more. The first group of four cars raced around for the last lap, and Jesse roared beneath the checkered flag first. Their whole section, and a lot of other people, stood and cheered.

Bugs swarmed around them, dive-bombing the bright lights above. The smells of French fries and onion rings permeated the air.

"I'm going down to get a soda. Anyone want anything?" Marti asked, standing and stretching. Really, she just wanted to walk around.

After getting everybody's orders, she carefully walked down the steps to the concession stand near the entrance. Before the girl loaded six cups into a carryout container, Marti wolfed down a greasy, forbidden hot dog. Then she balanced the drinks with four more hot dogs for the others. When she turned around, she nearly dropped everything. Paul stood there, his face ashen, not a trace of his usual arrogance.

"Can I talk to you a minute?" he asked.

"We shouldn't be talking at all."

"Marti, I did not break into your house last week, nor did I attack you the first time. I wish to hell I knew who did. And if Jesse wants to keep investigating, fine, I hope he finds the guy. But it isn't me. How can I get you to believe that?"

"I can't talk to you," she said, hurrying away with her load.

Helen wouldn't have talked to him in the same situation, and Marti wouldn't either. As she walked up the stairs, she realized she was doing that more often lately: asking whether Helen would do this or that in the same situation. Her own mother's antics seemed like some long-ago movie now. California, beaches, Jamie—all a dream. She made a mental reminder to get some travel literature on California to remind her of her destination.

At the end of the day, the races ended amid cheers and drunken catcalls. One heavy woman ran down the stands to a middle-aged man wearing a holy T-shirt and a cap. When Marti expected her to run into his arms and congratulate him for coming in second, she smacked his shoulder.

"You idiot! What were you doing down there? My heart stopped! I made a fool out of myself!"

With all the racing done, they opened the gate to the pit area again. Marti headed down with the rest of

Jesse's cheering section to congratulate him. She had to admit that he didn't look all that thrilled and realized he had probably won many, many times. She reached up on her tiptoes and kissed him on the cheek, a gesture that raised Caty's eyebrow. Well, Caty probably kissed Dean's cheek when his warty frog won.

After the ruckus was over and the cars were all loaded up, Marti and Jesse walked out to his truck. She shivered in the cool evening air, after getting too much sun during the day. He walked behind her and rubbed her arms, giving her more goosebumps than warming her.

"I don't think I could handle watching you race all the time. It's too nerve-wracking."

He stopped, leaning down to look at her. "Are you thinking about staying?"

She realized what she'd said. "No, no. Just talking theoretically. I don't know how those women do it, watching their men in dangerous situations all day every week." She tried hard to look neutral. "How would these guys feel if their wives raced in the Lady Warriors?"

"I don't know about the rest of 'em, but I'd find the best damned car we could get and cheer you on louder than anyone else."

He's way too good for you.

But from somewhere deep inside, a tiny voice asked, *But can you live without him?*

The following Saturday, Jesse was at the garage working on his car. Only with Bumpus's protection and her promise to use the shotgun was she able to stay at the house alone. A small ad in the local newspaper gleaned three new decorating jobs. She had given two of Helen's friends' estimates, and one had called this morning telling her to get started. The idea was taking shape in her mind, a budget decorating service.

Bumpus, sprawled out beside her, rolled onto his side. He often stayed close, making her feel safe.

"Here, boy."

He lurched up into a sitting position, looking at her expectantly.

He'd grown on her over these months. She'd never quite gotten used to the drool, but she wasn't all *that's so gross* about it anymore.

She patted her knees, and he jumped up and planted his paws on them. She leaned over and hugged him. He licked her cheek.

"Do you like me?"

He licked her again, and she didn't jerk back or even grimace. Much.

"You do, don't you? And I'm not the one who feeds you or anything. You like me because I'm ... me."

His tail wagged, and he gave her an adoring look.

Jesse was right. Having a creature love you just as you were was special. Accepting love was, too.

"You always liked me, even when I didn't much like you. I hope you sensed something good in me. Because I'm beginning to feel like there *is* something good in me." She rubbed his head and kissed the top of his nose where it wasn't wet.

Over the *Phantom of the Opera* music that poured through the rooms, she heard the front door close. Bumpus tore out of the room, barking. She grabbed the shotgun, trying to remember all the things Jesse had taught her, and walked into the living room.

She saw his truck parked outside and heard the

bedroom door close. A few seconds later, the shower kicked on. She went back to her sewing machine but found her concentration lost now.

She looked into the mirror opposite her, tilting her head. The brown hair did suit her better. This was who she was now, not Marti, not Hallie either. Thank God. She was somebody new and surprisingly strong.

Whenever the Phantom hit a low note, the baby kicked. She put her hand where his foot had been, wondering how big he was. Would he look like Jesse, or more like Marti?

"What is going on around here?"

Jesse's voice jerked her out of her thoughts. His hair was wet, and he was wearing nothing but a dark blue towel wrapped around his waist.

"What do you mean?"

"This ... *music* blaring again. It's awful."

"Well, now you know how I feel about your country music. And anyway, your son sure likes it. He's been kicking up a storm."

Jesse sat down on the bed beside her after moving the sewing cart aside. "He's protesting." He put his hand over her belly, and when the bass sounded again, the baby kicked. "He's going to make a great dancer."

"You're thinking of the two-step, maybe?"

"Well, you can't dance to *this* stuff. Can you?"

Jesse got up and tried to fit country dancing to "Masquerade." Giving up on that, he acted out the trill voices in a parody of the opera. Marti busted out laughing, making the baby kick more. Jesse stopped and looked at her. They stayed that way for a long minute, she swallowing hard beneath his gaze. He held his hand out and she took it, wondering if he was going to ask her to dance. Instead, he turned her around to face the mirror. The glow from her laughter still showed on her face, and she smiled at his reflection.

His intense green eyes met hers in the mirror. "You are so beautiful."

Her heart tightened, and her face flushed. "Jesse, I'm not." *You're the beautiful one.*

"Yes, you are."

She looked at her reflection. She was amazed to see something she had probably never seen on her face before: contentment. The thought scared her, and she turned away.

"Jesse ..." she started again, but he leaned down and held her face in his hands, forcing her to look at him.

"Why are you so blasted sure you can't be happy here?"

She wasn't going to tell him what he wanted to hear, because then he'd know how much she'd fallen in love with him. He only wanted her to stay for practical reasons, not reasons of the heart.

She left him standing in the bedroom and walked as fast as she could to get away from him, from his words. She stood in the living room, fighting the tears and feelings that threatened to flood her. Her stomach tumbled, but she told herself it was only the baby moving. The baby he wanted a mother for. That was the only reason he wanted her to stay.

But he can have a mother for his child. Abbie is more than willing. He wants you, fool. Can't you see that?

"No," she answered aloud, startling herself with the voracity of her words. He didn't want her. He'd never said that, never. She couldn't stay.

Why not?

"Because I want to go back home, to California."

Home is here.

She put her hands over her ears, as if that would stifle the inner voice that had taken Jesse's side. But it was his voice she heard, right behind her.

"What would be the worst thing that could happen if you stayed? Would you at least tell me that?"

"It's not an option," she said through tightened lips. "You promised you wouldn't try to talk me into staying."

"I'm just asking a question. Answer, and I won't bring it up again." He moved to encircle her in his arms. "Tell me you'd be miserable here, that you don't feel a thing for that baby inside you. Tell me that you honestly believe you'll be happier alone in California than here. Tell me," he asked softly, looking directly into her eyes. "And I'll believe you."

She dropped her head, because she couldn't meet his eyes. "I — I'd be happier in Califor —" The sobs tore through her, and she pushed him away.

He pulled her close again. "You can't even say it, can you?"

Holding her face again, he rubbed away her tears with his fingers. Then he leaned close to kiss her, and the passion he kept under control broke through as he claimed her mouth with ferocity. The world spun around her as she was swept into a whirlpool of emotions. At the end, her barest self was left, only needing him and what he offered at that moment.

He kissed her endlessly, his fingers entwined in her hair. She held onto him, clutched his shoulders, afraid to let go lest she drown. His hands trailed beneath her shirt, over her belly to her breasts. He caressed gently, though she knew he had the power inside him to crush her. She wanted him to crush her.

Beneath his towel, she could feel his erection pressing against her, hard and ready. Her hands moved down over his tight rear end covered in soft terry cloth. A tiny growl emanated from somewhere inside him as she squeezed and caressed. He smelled of soap and male and aftershave, deliciously Jesse.

"Marti," he whispered. "If you don't stop me now, I'm going to want all of you. I'm not strong enough to stop this myself."

She could stop this, she thought. No, she couldn't. She wanted this more than anything, even if she regretted it later. Even if they both regretted it. She found the knot where the towel fastened together and wrestled it free. The towel slid down to the floor, skimming her legs. She wanted to touch him, feel his smooth skin beneath her fingertips, and brought her hands around his hips to encircle his erection.

The second she touched him, he groaned louder, closing his eyes. She ran her fingers up and down the length of him, rubbing the velvety tip. She took him in, every glorious naked inch of him as she stroked. With her other hand, she touched his chest, trailed her fingers down his stomach. He was the beautiful one, golden from the sun, strong from work and play.

He swept her up into his arms where he carried her to the bedroom, and the crescendo of the music built with the anticipation. As he stripped off her clothes, he admired her body with his eyes, his hands. What she found bulging and unattractive, he seemed to find beautiful, miraculous. Beneath his gaze she transformed into a swan.

She had thought lovemaking would be awkward with her belly, but it didn't bother her. The feelings that rushed in like a foamy wave crashed over her, receding gently, crashing forward again. His kisses made her ears roar and swept her away beyond all thought and reason.

Her hands were everywhere on him, sliding down his back, over his smooth buttocks, then around to the ridges of his flat stomach. She wanted all of him, wanted to touch and experience every inch of his body. He was hers, for that precious time, even his heart. She saw that in his eyes, eyes that seemed open to his soul.

Her breath came in shallow gasps, between kisses and sighs. His fingers were in her hair, tracing around her ears, her chin. He murmured her name, then captured her mouth again. She felt the tip of his penis prodding, exploring. Then slowly, he moved inside her. Her breath hitched, and when he was fully in, she forgot how to breathe. He watched her expression as he became one with her, hesitated at her sharp intake of breath until she squeezed his shoulders, urging him on.

"Jesse, Jesse, Jesse," she murmured as the wave built to enormous heights, towering over her. "Jesse."

He touched, caressed as he moved inside her, fought his climax, and continued on to satisfy her.

The feelings inside her rose to envelop her in a rush of warm water. She allowed herself to drown in him, in the feelings that made every nerve ending come alive. She didn't have to fight off thoughts and inner voices; she thought nothing. Her senses needed nothing but to simply enjoy what was happening to her body. She felt high, giddy, entranced. Then the wave crashed down, filling her with such elation, she was sure her insides would explode.

She gasped for air as he shuddered, and he captured her mouth as vibrations encompassed her body. Finally, he collapsed beside her, taking her hand with him and pressing it to his chest.

They laid in silence for several minutes, breathing heavily. When he caught his breath, he reached out and caressed her cheek.

Marti moved her cheek into his palm. She still tingled inside, from her toes all the way to her heart. Their gaze held for several long seconds, and she wondered if he could see the question in her eyes. His eyes only reflected dreamy satisfaction.

She was far from satisfied. Physically, yes. But something inside her wanted more, and the fact that it wanted more from Jesse scared the hell out of her. The words slipped away from her like goldfish in a pond. "This shouldn't have happened."

He rolled onto his side, facing her. "I didn't plan on it happening. But I'm glad it did."

She forced out the words, "What are we doing here? Is this just satiating our sexual needs?"

"No, it's ... damn, Marti, living with you, watching you grow more confident and beautiful — on the inside — I can't help but want you."

The words warmed her, but they weren't the ones she needed to hear. "That could have been you visiting Mark at the track, talking about having dinner with one of the NASCAR sponsors about future possibilities."

His voice came out low and flat. "Do you really think you have to remind me that I could have been the one on my way to NASCAR? What's your point?"

"Why do you want me to stay? So, I can take care of

house and baby, cheer you on at the track, and be okay with you caring more about racing than me? I told you I wasn't good at relationships, and I'm still not. Because I can't be that good kind of wife. Yes, I'm selfish. I want more."

He rolled off the bed and slid into his jeans. "If you think I'm going to lose my head and give up racing because we had a good time in bed, you're way off track," he said without looking at her. "No pun intended." He ruffled his fingers through his hair in an attempt to straighten it, then stalked to the door.

"What you need is a woman who will take care of the baby and be okay with being second best. Abbie is so crazy in love with you that she'll settle for that. There was a time where I would have been okay with that, too, because I didn't feel like I deserved to be important to someone, didn't deserve that kind of love."

She fisted her hand at her chest. "But I do. I started with the dog, Jesse, just like you suggested. For the first time in my life, I feel valuable. Worthwhile. That's because of you, because of your family, and that damned dog of yours. But I don't want to fall in love with you knowing I'll never be the kind of wife you need. And you, Jesse, can't be the kind of husband I need. Which leaves us back to square one: you've got racing and I've got California."

His mouth tightened. "You've always had your head in California, and your heart with that perfect, rich husband of yours. I'm just a hick from the sticks. What I need to feel worthwhile is to make something of myself. So, you go on back to where you came from once the baby's born. Don't let the door hit you in the ass on the way out."

She was so angry she wanted to throw something at him. Because she *had* fallen in love with him, and she'd wanted to hear that he had fallen for her, too. She didn't expect him to give up his dream; she just wanted to be as important to him as that dream. "I wasn't the one who started this!" She wildly gestured to the rumpled sheets.

His expression shuttered. "Taking care of my baby, cheering me on, that's not why I asked you to stay."

"Then why?"

She wanted to hear him say that she meant something to him.

"Right now, I can't imagine why." He walked out the door to leave her wondering the same thing.

Over the next three weeks, Jesse was more irritable than ever. He concentrated on rulebooks for racing, car mags, and pointedly shut her out. He slept on the edge of the bed and hardly even grunted at her in the mornings.

Marti understood it, and even dredged up a similar attitude in return. Still, she'd never wanted a man so much, never lusted with her body, soul, and heart as she did Jesse. She could not get their lovemaking out of her mind, though sometimes it was hard to imagine the grumpbag being so tender, so passionate and concerned with her pleasure. If he'd felt anything for her, and she wasn't sure that he had, he had squelched it completely. It was for the best, she told herself. It just didn't feel that way at the moment.

He had revealed, though, his own struggle with self-worth, his need to make something of himself. She couldn't give him that; all she could do, in his mind, was take it away.

That morning, both in bed and awake but pretending to be asleep, the doorbell saved them from stiffness that had nothing to do with Jesse's morning wood. He was up and into his jeans before she could even get out of bed.

"I'll get it," he said, grabbing that ever-present shotgun.

Marti followed, throwing on her robe.

Caty pushed her way in, motioning them to sit on the couch. "Donna Hislope was raped."

"What?" Marti couldn't stop the frantic beating of her heart.

"When?" Jesse asked, his muscles tensing.

"They've kept it under wraps, but Dr. Hislope had to ask for my help because she's too upset to work. He tried to say it was something else, but he's not a good liar. Finally, he broke down and told me. It happened last Friday night."

Marti's eyes widened. "Last Friday? After her date with...."

"You got it. She doesn't want to report it, because she's terrified of anyone finding out."

"After her date with who?" Jesse asked.

"Paul Paton," both women answered simultaneously.

"Jesse, calm down. Dr. Hislope said she doesn't know who it was."

He paced, glancing at his shotgun. "She was out on a damned date with the guy. Who else would have done it? I need to talk to her, find out what she knows."

Caty shook her head. "You can't do that. You're not even supposed to know about it."

"I'll talk to her," Marti said calmly, remembering

Helen's poise in such situations. "After all, I've been in the same situation, or so she thinks. I won't tell her who told me."

Caty threw her hands up in the air. "Great! She'll think everybody knows."

"What if her dad asked me to talk to her? Because I would understand? We could clear it through him first."

"I don't know. Let me talk to him about it."

After Caty left, Marti walked to the window and wrapped her arms around herself. She thought of the man who had tried to strangle her — twice. He was still on the loose, and no one would be safe until someone caught him.

The following Wednesday Caty finally talked Dr. Hislope into letting Marti see his daughter. Jesse drove her over to Dr. Hislope's house. Marti mulled over what she wanted to say as the truck rumbled to a stop beneath a shade tree on the other side of the road.

"I'll wait for you here. Take all the time you need."

Jesse had taken the day off, insisting on going with her because Dr. Hislope's house was near Carl's.

"Hello, Marti," Dr. Hislope said without much of a smile when he opened the front door. "I hope this is a good idea. Maybe you can bring her out again. She hardly eats, doesn't talk to anyone, not even me. Don't be surprised if she won't talk to you either."

"She doesn't have to talk." *At least at first.*

Despite the wooden floors and white walls, the house seemed dim. Outside, birds sang and butterflies danced on the wind, and a breeze rustled through the flowers. Inside, the air was quiet and musty. She followed him down a hallway to the room at the end. He tapped on the door.

"Donna? Marti's here."

The room looked like something out of *Seventeen* magazine, with a lace canopy bed and frilly curtains. Donna sat in the window seat, her knees pulled up to her chin. She kept staring ahead into nothingness. When Dr. Hislope started to say something again, Marti held her hand out to silence him.

He hesitated, then backed out and closed the door. Marti stood there for a few minutes, hoping for some kind of invitation to step closer. She thought then about leaving, but remembered Jesse waiting across the street, desperate for answers. Answers she could get from Donna. Marti spotted a wicker chair and pulled it to within a few feet of Donna's still form. Again, she waited for some acknowledgment, but it didn't come.

"Donna? It's Marti. Do you want me to leave?"

No response. Donna kept looking out the window at nothing. Nothing because the curtains were closed. She didn't have any bruises around her neck.

"I'm not going to ask you how you're doing, because I know you're feeling pretty awful right now. I thought you might want someone to talk to, someone who's been there. Almost."

Marti tried to imagine how being raped might feel. She could easily imagine the fear of being attacked, though. She waited for some kind of reaction, but none came.

"Well, I just wanted to let you know I'm here if you need to talk."

Marti started to get up when Donna spoke in a deadpan voice.

"Everyone knows, don't they? They're all talking

about it, saying how stupid I was."

Marti drifted back down into the chair. "Nobody knows. I haven't heard anything about it and remember, I work at Gossip Gourmet. And you're not stupid. You thought you were safe with Paul." She was fishing for a reaction, but none came. Marti waited. Finally, she asked the question she most wanted to know. "Donna, do you have a weird scratch, right here?"

Without looking to see where she was pointing, Donna rested her palm over her left breast. Finding a small pad and pen, Marti drew the indents she remembered. She walked over to Donna and held it in front of her.

"Does it look like this?" she asked quietly.

Donna squeezed her eyes shut, and a tear slid down her broad cheek. Marti pulled the pad away and set it on the desk.

"I'm going now. Call me if you need anything. I'd like to come back again. Shake your head if you don't want that." No reaction. "Okay, I'll be back."

Marti visited Donna twice a week over the following two weeks, keeping her visits short, learning little with each one. Donna now seemed to expect her and even acknowledged her presence, but barely more than that. Marti was always disappointed that Donna wouldn't share anything or even point out Paul as her rapist. The cut, if it had existed, was now long healed.

Marti arrived later than usual that afternoon, after running some errands when she got off work. Marsala, the Hislope's housekeeper, opened the door, an expectant look on her face.

"Oh, I thought you were Mister Doctor Hislope," the lady said, stepping aside to let her in.

"He isn't here?"

"No, a farmer on the edge of town has a sick horse. I must go now. Can you stay until he comes back?"

"Sure."

"Hello, Donna," Marti greeted as she entered the bedroom. The curtains were open this time, but Donna was in the window seat as usual. She hugged a pink teddy bear.

"I wish he had killed me." Her words dropped with heavy thuds.

"No, you don't mean that. You'll be all right. I can't promise it'll go away, but you will take control of your life again."

Donna dropped her head on her knees and wept, deep, guttural sobs that made Marti wish Jesse were there. It went on like that for a long time, as if she had broken the dam and let the barred tears flow. Marti put her hands on Donna's shoulders, not feeling comfortable enough to hug her. Later, she called Jesse to let him know she would be later than usual. She was tempted to take him up on his offer to meet her there but suspected it would upset Donna if she knew.

"Call me when you're leaving," he said before hanging up.

She smiled, feeling that he at least cared about her still. "I will."

It was almost nine o'clock before Dr. Hislope arrived. Donna's renewed sobs reached them in the living room, and he rushed in to comfort her. Marti gathered her purse and said goodbye.

"If you'll wait a few minutes, I'll walk you out," he offered, but Marti knew by Donna's heaving chest it would be longer than that.

"Thanks, but I'll be all right. The moon's bright, and I'm parked just outside the door."

The crunch of the mango leaves beneath her feet obliterated her thoughts as she walked toward the car. When she reached for her keys, a voice scared her into dropping them.

"Marti, don't be afraid. It's me, Paul."

She stiffened, ready to run back inside. Would Dr. Hislope hear her screams over Donna's sobbing?

"What are you doing here?"

"How is she?"

"You're always so concerned about your victims, aren't you?" Her anger pushed adrenaline through her veins, making her less afraid.

"I didn't do that to her, to you, to anyone. But I've got to talk to you about something. This is going to sound crazy. Hell, I'm probably crazy for even thinking it."

Something in his voice made her listen. A confession, maybe? "What is it?"

"I noticed it the night someone broke into your house. I —" The sound of a truck approaching made Paul stop.

"It's Jesse," she said, not sure if she was relieved to see him or not.

"Damn."

"You'd better get out of here."

Paul turned into a silhouette in the darkness, then disappeared right before Jesse's headlights cut across the yard. She headed over to his truck, feeling as though she was betraying him by not alerting him to Paul's presence.

The old ways, coming back.

No, this was different. Her sixth sense told her that

she hadn't been in danger, but Jesse wouldn't believe that. He'd just kill Paul, and she had to admit, his waiting for her in the dark didn't look good.

"What are you doing out here alone? I was getting worried about you so I drove by."

"I was just leaving. Donna's crying up a storm, and I didn't want to wait for Dr. Hislope to calm her down so he could walk me out."

He hesitated for a moment, assessing the situation. "Next time wait for him or call me. Let's go home."

CHAPTER 16

He sat in the dusty, dark attic. Alone. Filling his lungs with stale air and the aroma of lingering ghosts. Ghosts that taunted him, calling him a failure, a weak, good-for-nothing pile of flesh. He thrashed around in the darkness, shoving boxes onto the floor. A box filled with old china dropped with a muffled shatter. Dust clouds filled the air as he pushed over a coat rack and toppled framed paintings that were stacked along the wall.

Spent, he dropped to the floor and coughed, and those coughs turned into sobs. He let himself cry for two seconds. Then he stopped and listened. Nothing.

Clutching at his head, he wished he could make the buzzing and the words go away. *Failure! Weak!* It wasn't his fault. If only the blood of his heart would have married him. If only his love would have seen that he was the only man for her. None of this would have happened.

Marti had looked so helpless, so female. Like that day long ago when his love had broken down on the side of the road and he'd given her a ride to the service station so many years ago. She had smiled nervously, the same way Marti had after admitting she'd run out of gas. Somehow, he'd felt he had another chance to win his heart's blood — and he wasn't going to let her get away that time, no matter how hard she resisted.

He'd nearly killed her in his rage. If he convinced her that he loved her, she would forgive him. This time he'd keep careful control over his fury, no matter how much she fought, how fiercely she rejected him. He ran his fingers through his short hair, tearing at his scalp, scratching until he drew blood. Pain, yes, pain would temper the rage.

Donna sure had not. She'd just lain there and let him pound into her. He pretended it was Marti, submissive, wanting him.

He shook his head. None of the past mattered now. Marti would be his soon. He had to find some way to make her understand how much he wanted her, and their baby. Their baby. He smiled. Yes, everything would be perfect ... once Jesse was out of the way.

When Marti returned home from her shift at Bad Boys, she felt huge and achy. Squatting down, she picked up a piece of paper lying in the driveway and trudged inside. The thought of driving to the Port Charlotte racetrack didn't thrill her, but Jesse had insisted, in light of Donna's recent attack. He'd already headed there, along with Caty and Helen, a few hours ago. They were willing to wait, but Priscilla wanted to go up, too; she and Marti planned to ride up together. Priscilla, however, had gotten sick at the end of her shift, worse than Marti's morning sickness, so Marti let her off the hook.

She changed and grabbed her oversized pillow for sitting comfort. Bumpus tilted his head at her as she made a groaning noise.

"Oh, I'll live, I suppose," she said to him. "Only a little while longer, and then I'm out of here." Bumpus made a whining noise. She started to stoop down to pet him but thought better of it. "Will you miss me, boy?" She rubbed his head. "Will your master miss me?" She let out a sigh. "He'll be happy to move on with his life. And so will I."

Bumpus didn't look as though he was buying those last words. Of course, she could be imagining it.

As she gathered her things and readied to leave, she remembered the piece of paper. She leaned over her pillow and read the scrawled writing:

Jesse, meet me behind the old Jenkins place before you go to the races. I want to settle this suspicion thing once and for all.

Paul.

Maybe Paul had left the note on Jesse's car, and he hadn't seen it before pulling away. She fingered the note, wondering what to do. If he'd seen it, he would have gone over to the abandoned house north of Helen's place. What if he had gotten into trouble?

After debating for a minute, she grabbed the note and headed out the door, feeling a great deal of trepidation about going to some abandoned place alone. Once she was heading over, her fears eased. Paul had wanted to talk to her about something, and she had a feeling it was important. He'd seemed scared. Maybe he decided it was safer to talk to Jesse about it instead.

It was bright and sunny, not at all foreboding as she drove down the dirt road and pulled into the gravel driveway overgrown with weeds. Jesse had pointed the place out to her once, telling her a story about how he and Billy had spent the night there on a dare when they were kids. She shivered at the thought of walking into the run-down wood house, much less sleeping there.

She saw Paul's slick black truck parked over to the side, but no sign of Jesse's truck. If the two had met here earlier, why was Paul still here?

She knew she should turn around and leave, but her hand put the car in park and turned off the engine. What if Jesse had gone crazy and Paul was lying here hurt? She opened the door, telling herself it was for Jesse as she stepped out. She couldn't bear to see him go to jail again. Especially if Paul hadn't attacked her.

A breeze made the leaves rustle and brushed through the tall grasses all around. A blue shutter, hanging from a corner on the house, scratched against the cracked wood.

"Paul?" she called out, though the wind took her words in the opposite direction.

Marti spotted a well-worn pathway leading around back. Obviously, kids still hung out here, probably dared each other to sleep there. As she walked around Paul's truck toward the path, she noticed the quickened pace of her heartbeat. Jesse would be furious if he knew. Remembering that look on Paul's face, she instinctively knew he wasn't a threat. Her shoes crunched softly on the rocky gravel beneath her feet as she walked around.

Her eyes scanned the area as she walked, her ears tuned to pick up anything beyond what the wind caressed. Everything looked serene ... until she saw the knife lying in the path.

Oh, crap.

The blade of the pocketknife reflected the sunlight filtering through the trees. She knelt to examine it, and her heart stopped when she saw "J J W" etched on the ivory handle. Her heart tightened, and without thinking, she picked it up to look for signs of blood, then dropped it when she saw faint smears. Dear God, what had Jesse done? Or had Paul done something?

Again, she searched the area behind the house, walking farther back. Her heartbeat pounded in her ears and her steps grew quicker. When she saw him lying by a tree, she fought the black spots that threatened to take her to unconsciousness. Her hand went to her mouth as she pushed through the high grass and choke vines to the body sprawled in the shadows.

Not Jesse. Relief, for a second. Not Jesse but Paul, with his neck twisted and blood surrounding a hole in his shirt. She pushed herself forward to grasp his wrist but didn't have to check for a pulse. His hand was cold and stiff, and she dropped it with a scream.

"Oh, my God."

Marti heard her own shock echoed in the voice behind her and spun to find Lyle Thomas standing on the pathway. Relief soared through her as she made her shaky way toward him. His gaze, locked on the body, quickly shifted to her, his hand going to the butt of the gun on his hip.

"Marti, stay where you are. Don't make me have to use this."

She came to a slow stop, bewilderment dazing her thoughts. "What are you talking about?"

"You're under arrest." He glanced at the body, so obviously dead. "For the murder of Paul Paton."

Numbness set in once Lyle escorted Marti to the

back rooms where Jesse had spent a morning not long ago. That ever-present smell of cleaner permeated the air, and the fluorescent lights made everything seem sterile. Lyle took her fingerprints and photo. He didn't say anything until he locked the jail door behind her.

"Think about who you want your one call to be to. I've got to process this paperwork, and then I'll be back." Before turning away, he paused, looking more like a hound dog than a deputy. "Marti, I hope this is all one big mistake. But I can't deny what I saw."

What he saw. She'd picked up the knife, dropped it, and then walked over to Paul's body. She'd touched the knife; put her fingerprints on it. Her thoughts had been on Jesse, not incriminating herself.

"Lyle, it *is* all a mistake."

"Remember, you don't have to say anything until you get an attorney."

"I don't care about an attorney. I didn't kill Paul. You've got to believe me." It all seemed so unreal, standing behind bars, pleading her innocence.

"I want to, Marti." He looked thoughtful. "Do you think Jesse saw that note?"

"No. He wouldn't have left it behind if he had."

She wouldn't believe Jesse had killed Paul. It was as unlikely as her killing him. Lyle nodded, then walked away.

"Lyle?"

He turned around.

"What were *you* doing out there, anyway?"

"Carl saw Paul writing the note to Jesse. Since he was going to be gone today, he'd asked me to keep an eye on the place, check to see if Jesse's truck was there. He didn't want any trouble."

"Does he know? About Paul, I mean."

"We've called him in, but he doesn't know why."

Chattaloo didn't have much of a crime rate, and Marti was the only one in the twenty jail cells that night. Company didn't have much appeal anyway, except for Jesse. He would come get her out of this, she knew. Win the race, rescue her from jail. No one could probably hear their phones with all the racket. Until then, all she could see was the horrid image of Paul. It made her stomach turn like worms in dirt ... an analogy she only knew because of Jesse teaching her how to fish.

Marti knew she hadn't drifted off, but a large amount of time had passed since she'd been arrested. Struggling to her feet, she paced for a few minutes, then called for Lyle. Except Carl walked through the open doorway, his face eerily free of emotion.

"Where's Lyle?" she asked, her voice quivering.

"He's gone to assist at the crime scene."

She backed away from the steel bars as Carl neared but kept her shoulders squared. "I didn't kill your son. And neither did Jesse."

"I think you were both in on it. But I think it was Jesse who killed him."

"He couldn't have done it. He left for the races at five this morning. That's probably why he didn't see Paul's note. The guy who let him in at the track can verify his arrival time. I want my phone call."

Carl's smile was flat, but his green eyes sparkled with evil. "Doesn't matter. Jesse got into an accident at the racetrack."

"I don't believe you," she said, although the blood rushed to her face.

Carl shrugged. "I guess I don't care what you believe."

He pulled out his gun and unlocked the door, nodding for her to walk ahead. She stepped out and followed his nod toward the phone on Lyle's desk.

She called Jesse's cell phone but got no answer. She started to call Helen's number, but Carl slammed his hand down on top of hers.

"That was your one call."

He wasn't kidding. He still held his gun at his side, finger at the ready as he escorted her back to her cage without another word. She didn't give him the satisfaction of revealing her fear. Jesse was a good driver. He wouldn't crash.

At nearly midnight, Carl roused Marti from a light slumber. "Helen is here."

Why wasn't Jesse there? Her chest squeezed tight in fear. "To bail me out?"

"No, to see you. Your bond hearing is tomorrow. The bail hearing won't be until next week. *If* you get bail. Until then, you're mine."

Her skin crawled at his words, at the strange glimmer in his eyes. She followed him to safety and warmth, to Helen. Carl led her to a series of phone-booth size cubbyholes with a telephone on each side.

Helen stood on the other side of the slate of thick glass, worry permeating her expression. That told Marti more than she wanted to know. She slid onto the vinyl chair between the partitions and picked up the phone. The moment Helen picked up her receiver, Marti asked, "Is Jesse all right?"

"Yes, he's going to be fine. It wasn't as bad as it looked."

All the hope and energy drained from Marti, pulling down her shoulders. "Then it's true? He was in an accident."

"Yes, but don't worry about him, Marti. You have enough right here to think about."

But she wasn't thinking about herself. "What happened? Where is he?"

"All I could understand was that he lost his brakes. He went off the track, hit the wall, and flipped the car. The doctor says he probably broke a rib or two and suffered a mild concussion. They're checking for internal injuries, and he'll be in for another day or two." Helen shook her head. "If they can keep him in there. Right now, he's drugged up, but when he hears about you being in here, he'll come tearing in to raise hell. I've been trying you all evening. Then I come home to find a message on my answering machine from Lyle. What in God's name happened?"

Marti paced, aching to be at Jesse's side. She relayed the gruesome events of that afternoon, ending with, "I know I shouldn't have gone there alone, but I was afraid for Jesse. I didn't kill him, Helen." Panic pitched her words in a higher tone.

"I know you didn't. Stay calm. Tomorrow is your bond hearing, and my boss is going to represent you. Bill Everhart plays bridge with the judge and his wife, so he pulled some aces and got your bail hearing moved up. We'll get you a reasonable bail and get you out of here."

"Does Jesse know?"

"He's pretty out of it right now. He did ask for you, but I only told him you were on your way. At the time, I was worried sick because you and Priscilla hadn't shown up at the track. Bill, my boss, will be in to talk to you about what to expect at your hearing." She glanced back at the door. "I'd better go. It's not really visiting hours, but I made Carl let me in for a few minutes. Are you going to be okay?"

Marti shook her head, then nodded. "Just get me out of here. And give Jesse ... my love." The words came out, and she swallowed hard.

Helen smiled knowingly. "I will."

Once she was gone, Carl pushed Marti back along the corridor toward her cell. The glint in his eyes was the only thing to indicate he was alive in there mentally.

"Carl, please let me out of here, just for a few hours. Jesse's in the hospital."

"I know."

"Let me see him. He needs me."

"You and your husband murdered my son and you want me to let you out so you can visit him?"

"We didn't kill Paul, and you know it."

He pushed her in and slammed the door shut. "I know nothing of the sort."

He left her alone to kick at the walls and hate him for keeping her when Jesse needed her.

She saw Jesse for the first time since his accident at the bail hearing Tuesday afternoon. His pallor told her what it cost him to sit there waiting through traffic violations. She saw him try to hide the grimace whenever he shifted. Helen had told her how he'd tried to break out of the hospital once he was cognizant enough to understand about Marti's arrest.

Even with Bill Everhart standing before the judge with pressed suit and perfect hair, it didn't look good. Carl was pushing for denial of bail altogether, repeating "risk of flight" over and over. He'd learned that she was leaving after the baby was born.

Judge Oldburn studied her, as though weighing her integrity. He set the bail at $150,000, and she felt the thud as her heart dropped to the wooden floor. So much for bridge-playing loyalties.

Helen maintained her determined stance: shoulders straight, mouth in a firm line. Marti wanted to cry but drew strength from her. Jesse seemed to draw strength from her, too, as he started to his feet to protest. Her softly spoken words made him sit down again. Caty whispered frantically, but Helen's words calmed her, too.

Lyle escorted Marti back to the jailhouse. Jesse was already waiting to see her when they pulled up. He glanced at her cuffs, but his eyes cloaked any emotion that threatened to show.

Twenty minutes later, Lyle escorted her to the visitors' room. "You have fifteen minutes." At her distressed expression, he added, "Gotta follow the rules."

Once alone, she rushed to the booth and leaned toward the glass.

"Jesse, I'm so sorry I couldn't be at the hospital. Are you all right? What happened?"

"Marti, how are you doing in here? God, it's good to see you."

They spoke simultaneously, stopped to let the other talk, then smiled.

Her lower lip trembled, wishing to comfort him, and wanting his strength. The last weeks of cold politeness slipped away. "I wish you could hold me," she whispered into the phone, holding back tears.

His gaze shifted away before meeting hers again. "Marti, I know the bail sounds like a lot, but we're going to get it. We only need to come up with ten percent;

we'll let a bail bondsman come up with the rest. Ma has money, I'll try to push through the loan for the baby's expenses..."

"No, I don't want you to do that. You won't be able to pay the hospital."

"Don't you think we're going to clear you and get our money back?"

"I don't know. It looks bad, and I've seen small town trials on television." She took a deep breath. "They want to nail you, too."

"They don't have anything on me." His expression changed to something she couldn't identify. "Did you think I'd killed Paul?"

"No. When I got to the Jenkins' place, I wasn't sure what I'd find. Then I saw the knife with your initials on it, and I got scared."

His mouth tightened. "How did the guy who killed Paul get that knife? My dad gave that to me years back, and I keep it in my truck. It's almost as if—"

"Someone was trying to frame you," Marti finished. "The note, your knife, and your past with Paul made it easy. But I found the note instead of you."

"Marti, I don't think I need to tell you how stupid that was, going there by yourself, especially when it was only Paul's truck there, so I won't tell you."

"Gee, thanks for not saying it." She took a quick breath. "It wasn't stupid if you'd seen him that night..." She trailed off, but Jesse's interest was too high for her to slide over that one.

"What night?"

She quickly found a lie to cover her mistake. "At the racetrack. I went down to get drinks, and he was there. He said he had to talk to me, and I could tell it was something important. Have you noticed how different he'd been since the night someone broke into my bedroom?"

"Probably scared thinking what might have happened if I'd gotten hold of him."

"I don't think it was Paul. It's a gut feeling, but I don't. Now he's dead, and what if I get convicted? What if I'm in jail when the baby comes? What if Carl is on duty and won't take me to the hospital? I could spend the rest of my life in some penitentiary." Her voice rose, gaining traces of hysteria.

"Calm down, doll. We'll get you out of this."

The word 'doll' instantly filled her with longing. And hope. He hadn't used it for a long time. She tightened her hold on the phone. "Tell me what happened at the race."

"We were toward the end of a long race, and my brakes wore out. When I realized it, I was right behind Alan and Josh. Now, I wouldn't have minded hitting Josh so much, but he was right up on somebody else's butt, and that would have hurt three of us. Hitting Alan was out of the question too, so my only other choice was to jerk it to the right and go into the wall. I hit it harder than I thought I would. The car flew up against the wall, tipped up on the front end, and real slow-like, dropped back on the other side."

She ran her fingers through her hair, the dangerous picture filling her mind. "But you're all right? It sounds like you shouldn't even be sitting here."

"I gotta be here. Just like the crash, no choice. But I'm okay. Really," he added to her disbelieving expression. "I broke some ribs, bruised my heel, a bump on the head, that's all."

"That's all? Broke *some* ribs? How many?"

"Three," he said with a shrug, trying to be cavalier about it, but his grimace at the action betrayed him. "Okay, it does hurt. But it isn't fatal."

She dropped her forehead against the glass, feeling overwhelmed.

"Hey," he said softly, tapping on the glass. "Stuff like this doesn't happen all that often, but it's part of the game."

He placed his hand on the glass, and she pressed her hand against his, aching to feel more than the cold glass. His expression was intense, and his gaze seemed to swallow her up. Their exchange didn't end when Lyle noisily opened the door behind her. After a few seconds, he cleared his throat. Jesse leaned back into his chair again.

"Sorry, you two, but time's up."

Using the table's edge, Marti pushed herself up. Jesse used the table for leverage, too. She wanted to cry. Then Jesse motioned for Lyle to pick up the phone. Lyle looked around nervously before doing so.

"When are you going to clear my wife, Lyle? You know this isn't right."

"First we've got to get a report from the medical examiner in Ft. Myers to get official cause of death. Things will happen fast after that."

Fast, Marti thought with a frown. Nothing happened fast in a small, Southern town.

Throughout the week, Marti got plenty of visitors. Each one brought a report on how much bail Helen and Jesse had collected so far. The list grew every day, and she was touched when she saw names of Bad Boy patrons who didn't even know her that well. By Friday, though, they were still five thousand nine hundred dollars short.

"I want you out of here by this weekend," Jesse said on the visitor's phone.

She leaned against the partition. "You're almost there. Maybe by Monday or Tuesday."

"No," he said harshly. "By this weekend. I can raise the whole amount by Sunday afternoon."

She knew she wasn't going to like it. "A race?"

"Yep. It's up in Georgia. The qualifying starts Saturday, and the race is Sunday. First place is eight thousand dollars."

"No, Jesse. You can't do it."

"I've got a ride."

"That's not what I mean. Look at you; you're still all banged up from the last race. What does your doctor say about this?"

"She says it's fine," he said through tight lips.

"You're lying, Jesse James West. You haven't even asked, have you?"

"You're right, I haven't. She's my doctor, not my mother."

Marti stood. "What *does* your mother say about it?"

"She knows I'm going to do what I have to."

Her emotions warred. He was risking his health for her.

"What do you mean you have a ride?"

"A friend of Harry's needs a driver. Chigger's an independent in the ASA; the minor leagues, remember? He registered for the race, but he's in the hospital. With pneumonia," he added at Marti's worried expression. "He's seen me race, so he asked Harry if I could race for him. I think I could win you the hell out of here. The deal is, I take what I need from the prize money, and he gets the rest."

"Does he know you just wrecked?"

"Yes, he knows. Harry and I are pulling the car to Georgia tonight."

She released a breath she didn't realize she was holding. "So, it's a done deal, then?"

"Yes. You going to give me hell about it?"

She sighed, leaning against the partition. "No. I learned a while back that it does no good." For either of them.

"Time's up."

Carl's presence behind Jesse startled her. He didn't intrude noisily like Lyle did.

Jesse turned to face him. "How long have you been standing there?"

"As long as I want. This is my jail, isn't it? I am the sheriff, am I not?"

"That's what they say."

Carl narrowed his eyes at Jesse, then turned and walked away. Jesse watched as Carl headed to Marti's side of the room and led her away. She had a funny feeling about this race, though she couldn't pinpoint why.

"I won't wish you good luck!" she shouted, her voice echoing in the empty rooms.

"Thanks," he called back. "I won't need it."

I love you! she wanted to shout, but caught herself short. No need to muddy the waters any more than they already were.

Things were not working out as he'd planned. Since he couldn't get Jesse out of the way by getting him jailed for Paul's murder, he'd have to resort to a more permanent way. He didn't want to kill Jesse. He dropped his head down on his desk. No, he had to do it. Just like he'd had to kill Paul.

Once Jesse was gone, Marti would be putty in his hands as he comforted her. It was too bad she was so in love with Jesse. That would make it harder, but he could overcome that, like he'd overcome everything else.

The question now was how to get rid of Jesse, who was stronger and smarter than Paul. He would definitely be harder to take down physically. Too bad the accident last Saturday wasn't fatal.

Yes, fatal. It happened all the time, racecar drivers losing control of their brakes or steering, whatever was convenient. Going round and round at over one hundred twenty miles per hour, and what if the steering cable snapped? And Jesse couldn't make the turn? He'd smash into the wall but good. He'd need to weaken the safety bars around the driver, too.

He took a deep breath, holding it in, letting it out as if it were cigarette smoke. It would be easy enough to find Chigger's car at the track. He'd go up tomorrow morning, wait until Jesse was through qualifying. Then he would tinker with the cable, enough to make it last through some of the race on Sunday morning. Wouldn't Jesse be pleased to die like his old man? By the same hand as his old man? Last time it didn't get him what he wanted. This time it would.

CHAPTER 17

Lyle Thomas stopped in at the Someplace Else Cafe for a quick dinner before returning to the station. When Carl had asked him to cover the weekend shift so he could spend some time alone, Lyle breathed a sigh of relief that the sheriff was finally grieving.

"Hey," Lyle mumbled to Nolen Rivers as he headed to his favorite booth in the corner. He settled in and scanned the nightly specials. The place was busy for a Saturday night. Sunday was usually the big night in Chattaloo, when all the families went out for supper after evening church services.

"Any leads on Paul's murder?" Nolen asked from the counter. "Newspapers ain't partin' with a word."

Lyle gave Nolen an official smile, tinged with smugness. "And neither am I."

Elwood Skoogs walked in and glanced at the busy counter, noting with chagrin that all the stools were taken. His short, squat frame and large belly made his arms look too small. They barely reached his thick waist. Lyle gave a thought to inviting him to join him, but having dinner with the Lee County medical examiner didn't bode well with his appetite. Elwood had the annoying habit of sharing his day's work over a meal.

Elwood made the decision for him. "Hey there, Lyle. Mind if I join you?"

Lyle waved for Elwood to take the seat across from him.

"Busy tonight, ain't it?" Elwood said absently, perusing the menu.

"What brings you 'round this end of town?"

"Wife has her women friends over playing some fancy card game tonight, so I'm in no hurry to get home. She was pretty mad at having to cut our vacation short. So, I visited a friend out this way until his wife gave me the old heave-ho. And I remember this place having good food and the prettiest waitress in town," he said as Rachel sauntered over to take his order.

"Why, thank you," she said, pink tinting her cheeks. She wrote their order on her pad as if she was signing an autograph, in big, loopy handwriting. Lyle thought she could easily be a movie star with those big, blue eyes and loopy blond hair that matched that writing of hers.

"Thank ya, boys," she said with a wink and departed with a swingy little step, moving in tune to the Alan Jackson song on the jukebox.

"Sounds like you people have quite a case this way, what with the sheriff's own son gettin' killed."

Lyle glanced around for nosy eavesdroppers, then whispered, "Well, not to be pushy, but we're anxious to get that autopsy report from you, I'll tell you that."

Elwood straightened. "I delivered that report yesterday, right to your office."

Lyle leaned forward. "What do you mean? I didn't hear about no report."

Elwood's bushy brows furrowed. "You didn't? That's mighty strange. No one was upfront, so I left it on the desk, but I called Carl to let him know. He said he'd take a look at it right away."

"What did it say?"

"Pretty strange, if you ask me. Paul had been dead for hours before Marti found him, figure it happened around seven that morning. It wasn't the knife that killed him, though. His heart wasn't pumping anymore when that blade plunged into him. Broken neck did him in, poor kid. Then the sick bastard, whoever did it, stabbed him."

Why hadn't Carl released Marti? Maybe he had some other evidence to tie her to the murder. "Maybe there's more to Marti's involvement than that."

"Naw. I saw her working the breakfast shift that morning at Bad Boys Diner. Paul was killed sometime during her shift, and the investigator has already confirmed that she was there the whole morning."

Lyle stood and dumped some wadded-up bills on the table. "I gotta let her out of jail. If I can't find that report, I'll need another copy."

"Sure. I'll stop by before heading home."

Lyle rushed back to the station and searched both his and Carl's desk, but turned up nothing. Why would Carl keep it from him? Maybe he hadn't read it yet. Yeah, that had to be it. After all, the man had just lost his son. His mind couldn't be completely on his job.

Lyle was still searching when Elwood walked in. "Did you find it?"

"No. I'm afraid I'm going to need a copy."

"No problem. Got nothing but time on my hands."

They drove over to the medical examiner's office

the next town over. While Elwood logged into the computer, Lyle wandered around out front, looking at the secretary's picture collection. Couple of fat kids, fat husband, fat dog. Skinny secretary. Hm, figure that. Then he saw the scrawled note on top of her in-basket:

Send Sheriff Paton another copy of coroner's report on Paul (son). He lost it. (What a dip.)

Lyle breathed a sigh of relief when he realized that Carl had just misplaced it. He probably hadn't even read it yet, maybe couldn't bring himself to do it. Well, he'd be proud that Lyle put everything right. It was nearly ten o'clock, but at least Marti would spend the night in her own bed.

Marti sat on the bottom bunk reading the magazine he'd given her earlier. She looked up when he stepped into the hallway.

"Well, little lady, looks like you're off the hook."

Her expression was a mixture of joy and disbelief. "You found the killer?"

"I wish. But you're cleared. I just got hold of the medical examiner's report, and Paul had been dead for hours before you found him."

She shivered. "He was cold and stiff." Then her expression changed to panic. "Lyle. I've got to get out of here and stop Jesse from racing!"

Lyle quickly processed her paperwork, feeling guilty for Carl's mistake in losing the report in the first place. Now she seemed frantic to get out and keep Jesse from doing further damage to his person. Lyle knew too well how painful broken ribs were.

Getting her belongings back, she pulled out her cell phone. It was dead.

"Why don't you use the phone here?" he offered.

"Thanks." Marti called Jesse's phone but obviously got his not-available recording. "Jesse, it's me, Marti. I've been cleared. Don't race. Please." She hung up. "Maybe I can catch him at his hotel room."

She tried that, to no avail, and then tried Helen's and Caty's numbers. No luck. He wished he could help her, but he couldn't leave the station. He'd tried the sheriff's house earlier, but there'd been no answer. She grabbed her bag of possessions and headed to the door.

"I've got to go to Georgia. If Jesse should call here for me, please tell him I'm out and not to race."

With that she was out the door, and Lyle realized he *could* help, even if in a small way. Marti was on her way back in.

"My car isn't here," she said.

He held up his police car keys. "I'll get you to your car in a big hurry."

He found a spot on the bleachers amidst what looked to be a noisy crowd of racing enthusiasts who got there early like he did to get a good seat. Everything had gone as planned. And Jesse was pole position, primed for a quick start. Damn, the kid was good. Too bad he had to die.

The accident should happen sometime after the tenth lap, maybe the twelfth. Hopefully he hadn't gotten overzealous and cut too much. Then he could get back and console the widow, who would still be in jail. He had once loved somebody else, many years ago. Marti would take her place.

"Jesse, are you sure you want to do this?" Harry asked. "You looked like hell yesterday after qualifying."

Jesse leaned against the hood of the car, willing the blood to his face so Harry would shut up. "I got the pole position, didn't I?"

"I didn't say you raced like hell, I said you looked like hell. And you don't look so great now. How do you expect to get by with a lousy grapefruit for breakfast?"

"I had toast. I always eat light on race days, you know that."

"It's different this time. Did you take your meds?"

"Of course not. I'll get by, Harry. It's painful right now, but it'll pass."

"Pass my ass. You were like this all day yesterday. I should have the infirmary black-flag you." At Jesse's hostile expression, Harry raised his arms. "Okay, you want to kill yourself, be my guest. I just got a bad feeling that your judgment isn't going to be so great out there today. I see the expression every time you climb in this car. But go right ahead and do your thing. I know you're going to anyway."

"Can't you see that I don't have any choice. I've got to get Marti out of jail, and this is the rest of the bail. I'll be okay."

Harry leaned against the car and slid his hands in his pockets. "You going to walk the track?"

"Not today. I've been here before."

"You always walk the track, Jesse. No matter how many times you been at a place, you always walk it."

"Harry, are you going to fight me all morning? 'Cause if you are, I'd rather you go hassle one of the other drivers."

Harry's expression became stern, almost fatherly. "I don't want to see you kill yourself out there. And I ain't leaving. One of us has got to have sense, and it ain't you. Just remember, you don't have to race. We can raise that money another way. I talked to Chigger yesterday, gave him an update. He says you won't be letting him down if you don't race."

Jesse turned away from Harry and stared hard at the red and yellow Thunderbird, wishing the pain would go away. Crawling in was the worst part. Once he was in, he was okay, after that moment where it hurt so bad, he thought he was going to pass out. Once his vision cleared again.

The excitement stirred through the crowd of drivers and mechanics as they readied their cars for the race. Almost time.

Marti fought exhaustion throughout the night, stopping only twice to buy a super-duper coffee and get gas. She should have asked Dean to drive up with her. Billy, Caty, and Helen were already there. Now that the sun was coming up, she felt more awake. A glance at the rearview mirror showed bugged-out eyes and disheveled hair. No time to pretty up.

She got off at the exit for the racetrack and immediately got stuck behind a stream of cars backed up for half a mile. She also knew she was running out of time. Once he was on the track, there would be no way to stop him, short of walking out on the racetrack and waving her arms. That wasn't out of the question.

When she neared the entrance, she realized how far away from the track the cars had to park. Too far for a pregnant woman to run. She raised an eyebrow as the idea popped into her head. Sure, she could pass for nine months. She felt big enough. Whipping the car to the shoulder, she sent rocks and dirt spinning as she raced alongside the waiting cars. They yelled and shook fists and fingers at her, but she was readying her speech for the attendants who were ready to turn her back.

A man wearing a bright orange vest leaned down as she rolled down the window. "Ma'am, I'm afraid—"

"I've got to get to one of the racers, my husband. I'm in labor. Is there a way I can get to the drivers' area fast?"

His expression changed as he peered in at her belly. "Sure, ma'am. See that road there. It'll take you 'round to the pits. The guys at the fence will let you in. I'll radio ahead."

"Thanks!" she yelled as he moved the gate so she could squeeze her car through.

She felt like a racecar driver herself, beeping at people who were about to cross the roadway, tearing around the corner. A garbled voice on a loudspeaker made her heart beat faster, made her foot press harder on the gas pedal. Almost there.

She pulled the car into a space and made her way to the gate. Gasping and in a panic, the guy at the pits entrance didn't dare doubt she was a woman in labor. Her pelvic bone ached with the pressure of the baby, and running wasn't helping.

"I'm looking for Jesse West. He's one of the racers. Can somebody tell me where he is?"

The skinny man shrugged, looking at her belly. "What's the matter, honey? You in labor?"

"Yes!" she shouted, drawing attention from nearby crewmembers. "I've got to find my husband!"

"Never heard of him. What car is he driving?"

"Uh, Skeeter's car. No, that's not it. Trigger's. Chigger's! He's racing Chigger's car."

"It's the red and yellow T-bird moving into position

now. You'd better hurry, young lady. We're about to start."

She ran past dozens of people, around empty trailers and revving racecars. Number 72 pulled into the inside lane on the track and stopped; other cars followed suit. The drivers had on their helmets.

"Harry!" she yelled when she saw the familiar face. "Is Jesse in the car already?"

"Marti, what the he — wait a minute. You're supposed to be in —"

"I know. I've got to stop him from racing."

"He's in the car, all right."

Before he could comment any more, she ran one more time. Two men started to caution her about going onto the track, but she paid no heed. Jesse was right there, across the track and grassy area.

She wasn't able to yell to him until she was nearly within touching distance of his car; she hardly had enough breath to compete with the roaring engines. He looked in her direction as she reached him and immediately yanked off his helmet and crawled out of the car.

"Marti, what in —"

She threw herself into his arms, leaning all her weight against him in exhaustion. His eyes widened, and he gave her a hug before pulling back in pain.

"What are you doing here? Are you all right?"

"I ... out ... report ... Jesse, don't race. Don't have to."

She leaned over, gasping for air. Harry ran to them, motioning for them to move off the track.

"I told the officials you weren't racing. Dan, one of the crew, is going to remove the car from the lineup."

Jesse was too busy holding her to object, and Marti didn't want him to leave for even a few minutes. He wasn't racing. Thank God he wasn't racing.

They walked back to the pits, and a few seconds later, number 72 roared into the pit crew area, turning sharply as it weaved through small groups of people. As Dan pulled up to them and started to turn toward the trailer, the car didn't turn.

It was coming right at them.

Jesse yanked her out of the way as the car kept coming while Dan frantically turned the wheel to the right. He slammed on the brakes and killed the engine.

"The steering gave out. I don't understand it." Dan climbed out and kicked at the tire. "We went over everything yesterday, and now the damn thing won't turn." He looked at them. "I wasn't trying to run you over, honest."

"I know," Jesse said, his arm tight around her. "I could see you pulling on the wheel. What do you think is wrong with it?"

He shrugged, staring at the car as though it could tell him. "It's the darndest thing." Then his eyes widened. "Jesse, the steering would have gone out during the race. You could've been—"

"Shh," Jesse said, covering Marti's ears and steering her away from Dan.

"And you think Paul wanted to tell you something? He wasn't just trying to finish the job?" Jesse leaned back against the swinging bench, releasing a long breath of indignation.

Marti realized it was time to tell Jesse about Paul's strange visit in Donna's front yard. She waited until the day after their return from Georgia, when the rain started pouring down. Bumpus emerged from his forage through the bushes and shook off a shower of droplets.

She knew Jesse would be angry at her for hiding it from him, but she'd justified her reason. With a spear of panic, she remembered how well she used to justify her actions in the past. With Jamie.

"This is different," she said aloud.

"What's different?"

"Paul was. He was scared, kind of. Urgent."

"Like he knew he was in danger?"

She shook her head. "I don't know. He said it was going to sound crazy. Something he noticed the night someone tried to kill me. Not looking-over-his-shoulder scared. Worried might be a better word."

Jesse stared at the rain dripping from the edge of the roof. "Maybe he was trying to cover his butt. But maybe he had an idea who it was."

"I'd like to think it was Paul, because then I'd be safe. But I don't feel safe. I look out the window at night and I can still *feel* someone out there. And Bumpus hasn't stopped barking."

Jesse looked at the dog. "Someone's been out there, haven't they?"

Bumpus gave a soft woof and glanced out to the woods. Maybe it was a coincidence that he'd seemed to understand Jesse's question. But it scared her to death all the same.

When Marti pulled into her driveway after a trip to the grocery store, she saw Caty's car parked out front. She and Jesse sat on the couch, the unobserved late evening news the only light on in the room. Something was wrong.

Caty stared blankly at something to the right of the television when Marti put her purse down and walked over to them.

"Dean's been picked up for questioning in Donna's rape," Jesse said blandly, as if he didn't quite believe it.

"Oh, no. Can't be." Marti sat down next to Caty. "How did they drag Dean into this?"

"He sent her flowers saying he was sorry about what happened. Her father reported it to the sheriff. Something about the way the note was worded," Caty said.

"Don't they know Dean's kind of strange by now?" Marti asked. "Strange in an innocent way." After a moment of silence, she added, "What? You don't think he raped her, do you?"

"He did send her flowers before, remember?" Caty turned to Jesse. "She came in the diner the week before her rape, telling us about her date with Paul and the flowers Dean had sent her and how he liked her, but she wouldn't deign to date him."

"Yeah, but don't you get why he sent her those flowers in the first place?" Marti asked.

Both Caty and Jesse stared at her.

"Billy told him to get you jealous, wake you up some. Dean told me his strategy when we were at the races that weekend, but I had to promise not to tell you."

"I am going to kick Billy's ass." Caty stood and paced in the blue glow from the television. "It doesn't matter anymore. Nothing matters."

"What are you talking about?"

When Caty didn't answer right away, Jesse clarified. "Dean was at the house when Carl picked him up. Caty was so shocked about the flowers and everything else, she couldn't answer him when he asked if she believed he was innocent. I guess he was pretty torn up about it."

"It doesn't matter," Caty said dully. "Everything's

screwed up anyway."

"Caty, I think it does matter. You love that boy, whether you want to admit it or not."

"As a friend, maybe."

"No, as more than a friend. He needs you right now."

Caty kept pacing. "He'll never forgive me for not believing in him."

"You don't know that, do you? Go down to the station and wait for him to come out. Sheriff's not going to find anything on him."

Caty looked at Jesse. "Why couldn't I have believed in him like she does? No, I had to show a glimmer of doubt. It was the flowers that made me wonder. And he turned away and never looked back. I hurt him bad." The resolve on her face crumbled, and a tear slid down her freckled cheek.

Jesse put his arms around her. "Do you think he could have raped Donna?" Caty shook her head. "Then let's go down to the station and pick the guy up. Marti and I'll follow you down there. We'll wait with you until Carl's through, then we'll leave you alone with him."

Caty swallowed. "You don't think he did it?"

Jesse shook his head.

"You always make fun of him and say he's weird."

He kissed her nose. "We give him a hard time because we know you like him. And he is a little odd, but he's not a rapist. Right now, I wouldn't trust anyone else with my sister."

She hugged him, then slipped her arm around Marti as they headed out the door. "Thanks, you two. I just hope Dean forgives me."

"He will if he loves you," Marti said. And she was sure he did. Just like Jesse had believed in her after her arrest. She looked at him, realizing how much having someone believe in you meant.

They only had to wait ten minutes before Carl came out with Dean in tow.

When Dean saw them standing there, he dismissed the sheriff and walked over, avoiding Caty's worried expression. "Did you come by to give me a ride home, or find out if they'd booked me?"

Jesse shook Dean's hand. "Hell, we know you're too stupid to do something awful like that."

Dean gave a grudging smile. "Thanks. I think. I sent her flowers, that's all. Never even took her out or anything. That jerk was trying to make me confess to something I didn't do. But he didn't have enough evidence to hold me, so I'm out." He glanced at Caty, then looked away.

Jesse put his arm around Marti's shoulder. "Well, my wife here is tired, so we're going to let Caty take you home. You don't mind, do you?"

Dean looked at his shoes, then back at Jesse. With a shrug, he said, "I guess not. That is, if she trusts that I'm not going to jump her."

Without any warning, Caty threw her arms around Dean, and he tentatively hugged her back. Jesse steered Marti to the truck. When they climbed in, Dean was holding on tight to Caty with his face buried in her curls. Jesse patted her hand as he turned the truck around.

"Ah, ain't love grand?"

"Grand," Marti repeated absently, still watching the couple now kissing on the sidewalk. *Grand if you can treat it right.*

Two weeks later, Marti and Jesse started Lamaze

class. The other six women in class laughed about how they couldn't even think of making love to their husbands, making Marti feel wanton for wanting Jesse so much. Sometimes she wished he would just throw her on the bed and make wild, passionate love to her and forget about all the other aspects of their relationship. There were times when she caught him looking at her, raw hunger sparking in his eyes. It caught her own desire on fire, but damn, all she could think about was how badly it had gone the last time they'd given in.

The baby moved almost all the time now. Jesse never seemed to get bored of feeling the baby move or hearing Marti tell him how many times he kicked or how he hiccoughed while she was taking measurements at a new client's house. He listened with rapt attention, his hand on her belly the whole time. It seemed that the baby was all they had between them anymore. That was the way it should be, she told herself. He had a racing career, she had California. But somehow those words didn't make the sense they used to.

She no longer worked at Bad Boys Diner. Jesse had insisted she quit when her ankles started filling up like water balloons. The heavier she got the more decorating clients she seemed to get. They didn't even mind standing on the couch and measuring the height to the top of the window themselves.

During their evening Lamaze class, Jesse was attentive and friendly, helping her to breathe properly and massaging her back. As the seven couples laughed at a joke, Marti longed to share that kind of intimate laughter with Jesse.

Back at home, she took a shower and slipped into Jesse's robe. His scent in the terry cloth made her close her eyes, thinking about the time they'd made love. Her face flushed when she realized that was exactly what it had been. Making love.

She caught that look again in the steamed mirror, the one she refused to admit was there most of the time: contentment. Foolish girl. For one thing, there was him. And for another, there was her.

Jesse hadn't asked her to stay since they had made love, not that she had any intention to stay. She could never be that good wife who was okay being second best. And she would never, ever ask Jesse to put racing second either.

No, he had Abbie, quietly waiting in the wings. She'd never mentioned the proposition or her observation to Marti again, but her boys kept her in their lives.

It shouldn't matter. It shouldn't hurt or annoy Marti. But it did.

She emerged from the steamy bathroom, tucking her wet hair behind her ears. With a roll of her eyes, she pulled it forward again. The canned laughter of a television sitcom drifted into the bedroom, and she walked to the doorway. Jesse was crouched over an upside-down Bumpus with his four legs up in the air as he patiently let his master clip his nails.

Wearing his faded blue jeans and nothing else, Jesse was a sight to behold. His muscles moved beneath his skin as he gently held each paw and clipped the nails with precision. Something stirred in her, making her feel warm and tingly inside.

For no apparent reason, Jesse turned around. Her face flushed even more, and she hoped it was too dark where she was standing for him to see it. She wanted to shrug, to make light of her standing there watching him; she wanted to turn around and go back in the bedroom, but she couldn't move. His gaze riveted her to immobility.

"What's wrong?" he asked, coming to his feet.

She instinctively put her hand on her belly, knowing it was the baby he was concerned about. At her movement, he walked over and put his hand next to hers.

"You all right?" he asked, concern making his eyes seem deeper, more like a moss green.

She felt as though some unseen force was squeezing her heart. She lifted her gaze to him, feeling that all of her heart was there for him to see and there wasn't a thing she could do about it. He would hate her for trying to complicate his life, but she had no intention of doing that to either one of them. The warmth from his hand emanated to envelop her.

She closed her eyes and whispered, "The baby's fine."

When he touched her cheek, she opened her eyes again. "Marti..."

She shook her head and walked into the bedroom, feeling embarrassed and angry at herself for the tears that threatened to spill over. She could not love him, no, no, no. Sure, she had felt *in* love with him, infatuated. But this feeling that overwhelmed her was more than lust or puppy love. It reached from her heart to every place inside her, even places she didn't know existed.

She wanted him to hold her, wanted to share evening walks down by the river, talks on the front porch swing, kisses anywhere and everywhere, even in the pits just before a race.

Idiot. Marti shivered, facing the bed, wrapping her arms around herself. She couldn't give up the value she'd found in herself. No matter that they were married, that they shared a baby together. Her fingers trembled as she put them over her mouth — *shared* a baby? Yes, she had thought that. Oh, God.

Jesse stood so close behind her that she could feel his body heat, feel his breath caressing her ear. He touched her shoulder so gently that she wondered how he could know she felt so fragile that even a regular touch would shatter her.

"Marti?" The question laced his voice like aged whiskey.

"Go away. I'm fine."

She heard his breath hitch, but he didn't go. Her heart was on a fine wire, balanced between wanting him to leave and wanting him to stay. She only knew one thing for sure: she wanted him.

He ran his fingers across her cheek and into her wet hair, turning her gently to face him. His thumb grazed her skin as he studied her eyes.

"Jesse," she said softly, her voice thick withheld-back tears. *Go away. It will never work.*

He didn't go away. He kissed her, firm, yet gentle. His mouth remained against hers, as though he were contemplating the sanity of the move. A second later he kissed her again, this time with more urgency. She relaxed her lips against his, opening them slightly. A hot tear slipped down her cheek, then another. She squeezed her eyes shut, wishing she could pretend things were different between them.

Jesse stopped kissing her, but his hand remained against her cheek. Still only an inch from her, his thumb stroked the wet skin where another tear had splashed against his hand.

"Talk to me."

She shook her head, looking down. Never in her life had she felt so caught up in a whirlwind of conflicting emotions and doubts. Maybe she could be happy here with Jesse and his family — her family now. But he had not asked her to stay, not from his heart. That had to be because he didn't feel the same way. Even if she agreed to stay, he might tell her that he'd changed his mind, and that would kill her. No, she had to keep her feelings from him, no matter what.

Jesse was sure he'd never seen a more beautiful woman, tears and all. He bracketed her face with his hands, wishing he could take away the pain that clouded her brown eyes. But she wouldn't answer him, wouldn't let him help her. God, but he wanted to take care of her, to protect her and cherish her. It went against everything he'd been telling himself he wanted — and didn't want — for the last few years, and especially the last few months. A woman would get in the way of his racing career, distract him, confuse him. Hell, she was already doing the last two.

He leaned back to get a better look at her, to put distance between them. Why did she look so darned sad? It was evident that she wasn't going to tell him. Maybe she didn't want to hurt his feelings by telling him how unhappy she was. She seemed content lately, other than being attacked in her sleep, of course. She didn't talk about her former husband or California anymore, and she didn't seem so out of place.

He pushed away the twinge in his heart, grasping on an answer. She must be thinking about them, though, impatient to have the baby and get the hell out of there.

"Marti, this will all be over soon." He touched her chin, smiling. "You'll have the baby and be able to go back home to California before you know it."

Her lower lip trembled, and another tear slid down her cheek. She turned away and hugged herself. Bumpus whined from the other room, and Jesse realized he was probably still waiting for the claw trimming to end. Marti moved away from his grasp and lay down on the bed, keeping her eyes closed. Her delicate hands were lying on top of her belly, rising and falling with each breath.

Jesse wanted to touch her, to somehow comfort her. Hopefully his words about going home soon had helped. He didn't let himself think about her not being in the house, sharing his bed. He couldn't let himself think about her staying either. She'd already told him she needed more than to be second best. Racing was more important than anything. He walked to the doorway, watching her. Wasn't it?

During the next week, Marti kept to herself. She ignored the almost constant pain that gripped her every time she thought of Jesse. He had been giving her odd looks since that night she had cried in front of him. She'd caught him twice just staring at her, his head tilted thoughtfully.

She wouldn't allow herself to think about the future, especially not after what he'd said about her being able to go home to California soon. He wanted her out, the sooner the better. Then he could go back to racing on the weekends.

Donna was a great distraction every evening, fraught with her own anxieties and shame. Marti sat in her chair next to the window seat. She could always tell her mood by whether the curtain was open or not. It was open.

"Did you kill Paul?" she asked Marti out of nowhere.
"Do you think I did?"
"I don't know."
"I didn't. He was already dead when I got there. Somebody had broken his neck, then — oh, sorry."

She shivered, then faced Marti. "It's all right. I wondered how he'd died. Nobody would tell me, and I didn't want to ask."

"Do you feel safer now that he's dead?" Marti fished for clues.

She shrugged. "Maybe. Maybe I'd like to have done it myself."

Marti proceeded cautiously, glad that Donna was finally opening up. "Do you feel angry enough to want to kill him?"

She clenched her fists. "Maybe to rip all his chest hair out, to gouge his eyes, to —"

"Did you say chest hair?"

Donna's eyes widened, and she wrapped her arms around her shoulders. "Yeah. I'd pushed that memory away, but yes. He had hair on his chest. I didn't see it, but when I tried to push him away, I felt it." She looked at her hands in disgust.

Chest hair. Marti vaguely remembered feeling something when she'd pushed away the man in her bedroom. She'd thought it was his shirt, but no ... it was a mat of hair.

She tried to remember if she'd seen Paul shirtless. Finally, she asked, "Do you know if Paul had chest hair?"

"Some, I guess."

Marti walked over to the desk where her sketch still sat on top of other papers and cards. "Is this what the scratch on your chest looked like?" Donna nodded without even looking. "Then it was the same man," she said on a breath.

Donna stared at the place where the ceiling met the two walls in the corner. "Paul tried to get fresh on our date, right there in his car outside his house. That's all he wanted, you know."

She swallowed hard, and hesitated, making Marti think she would go silent again. "I stomped home, through the patch of woods between our houses. I was almost home. He came out of nowhere. I figured it was Paul chasing after me, but I couldn't see his face in the dark. He shoved me to the ground, knocking the breath out of me. Then he dropped down on top of me …" Donna choked on her words.

Marti put her arms around the woman's shaking shoulders. "I know it's hard, but you need to talk about it. Let it out."

Donna nodded. "Maybe if I tell you, the nightmares will go away." She took a deep breath, staring at the corner again. "He was wearing a robe of some kind, and he threw it off. There was … nothing underneath. He pinned me down and … and … ."

She started crying again, and Marti soothed her.

"I didn't do anything. I mean, I tried to push him away, to scream. But once he'd pinned me, I stopped fighting. I didn't want to die. I feel like I should have done more, but I was so scared."

Marti thought of the woman whose place she'd taken. She had probably fought her attacker, and now she was dead. "That was the smartest thing you could have done."

"There's something else I need to tell you. He only said one thing to me, and his voice was weird, low, and dreamy sounding. He called me a different name. He said, 'Marti, the blood of my heart.' He called me 'Marti.'"

Those last words squeezed Marti's heart into a tiny ball of fear. It was definitely him.

"I didn't mean to frighten you," Donna said through her tears. "I thought you should know. I wanted to tell you before, but I couldn't. Why would he call me your name? And say those other words?"

"Maybe he was thinking about his attack on me." Marti's words seemed hollow as they left her mouth. The first Marti had seen her attacker as he stopped to help with her car problem. He probably worried that she would remember him. But why would he call her the blood of his heart? She shivered.

Then anger surged. "I don't want to keep living in fear of this animal. We need to either rule out Paul or find out whether he was the one. I can't stand this not knowing."

"What are you going to do?"

Marti stood. "I don't know."

But she did. She had to get hold of Paul's necklace and try to recreate the mark on her chest. Running to her car was physically out of the question, but she moved faster than she thought she could. As she passed Carl's house a few minutes later, she realized how easy it would be to get inside and find the necklace. Then she'd have her answer.

Still, she tried to find Jesse first. He wasn't at the house, Helen's, or at the garage, nor did he answer his phone. She didn't know where Abbie lived or even where else to check for him. Going to the sheriff was obviously out of the question, and she didn't want to drag

Helen or Caty into this.

The sight of Carl's car parked at the station gave her the adrenaline to drive directly to his house. She would find the proof. Even though Jesse would yell at her, he'd be happy to at least have an answer. Besides, Helen would do the same.

It was barely light when she drove past Carl's house, with the sunset's rays casting an eerie glow over everything. She pulled into an empty lot on the other side of the street, parking behind a large fig tree. Carl's colonial home sat on two lots, giving it room on either side. She walked casually up to the house, keeping herself hidden by the shadows of trees.

People in small towns were not given to locking their doors, unless there was a ruthless rapist in the vicinity. The sheriff wouldn't be afraid of such a thing. The front door was locked, but the back one was not. She slipped inside.

The rooms were dim and musty. The television played in some distant room, making her wonder if Carl was indeed at the station. She had to believe he was since his car wasn't out front, but she remained on alert and quiet just in case. With so many rooms to choose from, she realized she had no idea where to start.

She doubted Paul had been buried with his necklace, which meant Carl would have it somewhere, like in his bedroom or in Paul's room.

A quick check of the main level revealed no master bedroom, so she walked up the stairs and continued down the hallway. The second bedroom looked cluttered and dirty. Nothing like the rest of the house, which was immaculate in its appearance. Paul's room?

She found the chain and eagle pendant on top of a tall

chest of drawers. Tugging her collar down, she pressed the wings into her upper arm until it hurt. When she pulled it away, her body went cold. It was the same mark. Pocketing the necklace, she turned to leave.

Photos on the wall caught her eye. Old, framed photos of Carl in his uniform, Carl in what looked like a graduating class of police officers, Carl and Paul on a fishing boat. This had to be Carl's room, then.

Behind one of the photos, she saw the corner of another one tucked away. Even from the small piece, she could tell it was older. Pulling the frame down, she bent the prongs and removed the backing. The small photo behind it was of a younger Helen, obviously cut from a family photo.

Huh?

She started looking at some of the other photos, taking one down and peeling off the back. Another picture of Helen hid behind the boat photo, this one of her sprawled sexily on a couch. Behind that another one yet, this one taken without Helen's knowledge more recently.

The featured photo drifted to the floor. She needed to get out of here. Even though she'd only been in the house for about thirty minutes, it felt like hours had passed. She reached for it, but her gaze riveted on Carl and Paul: both men wore pendants. She put her nose to the photograph, trying to make out the shapes: eagles. Both had the same necklace. Her hand went to her throat. Paul's chest was lightly covered in hair, and Carl's ... covered with curly fuzz.

"Oh, my God."

The realization squeezed her heart, making it pound hard and tight in her chest. Carl. It had been Carl all along. She had to find Jesse and tell him the shocking truth.

A glint of light outside the window caught her eye. The sheriff's car sat out front. She blinked, hoping it was a mirage. No, not her imagination. How long had Carl been home? Where could she hide? In the closet of one of the unused rooms until he left again.

"Find what you were looking for?"

A cold fear blanketed her before she even looked up to see Carl standing in the doorway. Blocking her escape. Smiling.

CHAPTER 18

Carl's hair was disheveled. "Or did you ... come to see me?"

Marti's heart pounded so hard that it actually throbbed in her vision. Which way to go? Some reason for being there. To see him? To find something?

"I — I wanted some answers."

He should be angry to find her snooping in his house, trying to convict Paul even after his death. That would have been normal. Justified. But no, his eyes had a glassy sheen, as though he'd been doing drugs.

Carl moved closer. Without looking back, she tried to remember what was behind her. No escape, that she knew.

"Why don't you just ask me, Marti?" he said softly, enunciating each word carefully. "I would be glad to clarify anything for you."

"P — Paul. I wanted to know what happened." That seemed safest.

"You thought you could come here and prove somehow that I killed him? That I shoved him through the attic entrance and broke his neck?"

Ice shot through her veins, paralyzing her body. "You

killed him?" she stammered, wishing he had not confessed.

He took another step closer. "It looks like you already figured that out."

"No! I mean, I didn't know. I never thought you would k-kill your own son."

"It wasn't easy. He put up a fight, but he's a wimp, down to the core. His mother made him that way, coddled him and fussed until she left."

The crucial link between emotion and sanity was gone. She could see it in his eyes. The picture of Paul's broken body lying in the grass flashed in her mind, followed by the realization that the man standing before her had been in her room not long ago. He had tried to kill her.

"Jesse knows I'm here," she blurted out, trying desperately to hide the fear in her eyes. Too late. He already knew she was afraid.

"Sure, he does. Because that hothead would let his wife come into big, bad Carl's house all by her lonesome. And he's on his way over, right?"

Her nod faded at his knowing smile. Instead of the adrenaline she needed, her body felt weak. She watched him as a mouse might watch a snake, weighing her options, judging its next move.

Taking a deep breath, she relaxed her shoulders. "Well, I guess you're going to arrest me for trespassing. I wouldn't blame you. Let's go down to the station."

She started to walk by him. If she could make it to the door, she could run. The stairs would be too dangerous in her condition, but maybe she could make it to another room, lock the door, and scream for help out the window.

Just as she thought she was going to get by, he grabbed her wrist. With a swift movement, he pulled handcuffs from his belt and snapped one on her wrist. She wriggled, desperately trying to keep the other one away, but her strength was no match for his.

"You're not going to get away from me as easily as you did the last time. Pretending to die was clever, very clever. And then you got yourself released from jail before I wanted you out. But not this time, blood of my heart."

Those words sent chills through her body, but she kept her fear hidden. He touched her chin, and she jerked away from him. His finger remained poised in front of her, his expression hard. The cuffs were tight around her wrists, jangling every time she moved.

Stay calm. Something isn't right inside his head. He killed his son. He'll kill you, too.

Subtly, she sucked in a great big breath, and as he moved toward his dresser, she let out the beginning of a howling scream. His palm shot out and smashed her into the wall, crushing her nose. Blood started dripping down, trickling past her lips and over her chin. The sharp pain made her eyes lose focus for a second.

Carl reached into the top drawer, but she didn't see what he took out. The room spun as terror spun her brain in circles. Then darkness pulsed as she dropped to the floor. She tried to clutch at the walls, but her shackled wrists could hardly move.

No, not now! Don't faint now!

That was the last thought she had.

Marti woke with a start, staring into blackness. Lucidity eluded her for a few minutes as she struggled to wake from a nightmare. Her mouth felt full of cotton. Wait. It *was* full of cotton, or something, and no amount of pushing with her tongue would dislodge it. Because a gag tied around her head kept it in place. Afraid to move, she waited for her eyes to adjust to the darkness. Patches of dim light moved around in front of her, but she thought that might be her eyes playing tricks on her.

She turned over to touch Jesse, intent on waking him. With a screech of metal against metal, she was stopped abruptly. She jerked her hand again, but found it attached to something above her. Icy fear rushed over her, washing her with reality. She tried to kick, but shackles clamped around her legs, too. Her scream came out as a muffled noise.

The more she jerked and twisted, the more the handcuffs bit into her skin. She was cuffed to a bed in a dark, hot place. The baby kicked three times in succession, and she started to put her hand on her belly as she usually did. But her hand stopped far short. Could the baby feel her terror?

A creaking noise made her go still. A shaft of light shot up to the trusses several yards above her. She was in the attic. Another pinpoint of light in a dark reality. And no doubt, Carl was coming up some kind of creaky stairs or a ladder. Coming for her.

His silhouette loomed over her, reminding her vividly of the night he'd broken in to kill her. Was he going to kill her now? She didn't move, afraid to breathe. Sweat trickled down her sides. He stood there for several long seconds. She kept her eyes closed, wishing he'd go away so she could think.

Carl reached up and pulled a chain, sending harsh light from a bare bulb hanging above her. The fixture swung back and forth on its chain, casting wild shadows around her. She blinked painfully. He stood there with a stupid smile on his face. He was still wearing his uniform, unbuttoned down to his hairy navel. It seemed absurd that he should be wearing a sheriff's uniform when he was going to kill her in his attic. She wanted to tell him so but couldn't speak.

He glanced around with narrowed eyes, then stepped over an upturned cardboard box to pull a dusty rocking chair next to the bed. His pungent cologne and sweat mixed nauseatingly with the musty smell of the mattress beneath her. She swallowed, trying to push down the lump in her throat that felt like a tennis ball. He rocked back and forth in the chair, making the floorboards creak with every movement.

She was not going to plead, even if he did remove the blasted, foul-tasting cloth from her mouth. Somehow, she knew begging would incite him. Maybe the first Marti had found that out.

When he reached for her, she flinched. He didn't falter as he smoothed her damp hair back in the way a father might do for a sick child. His low, rumbling laugh shot fear through her.

"You're finally mine, Marti. I've wanted you for a long time, a long, long time. But you were always afraid of me." He pinched her chin between his fingers, his expression fierce now. "Why?"

She just stared behind him, wishing to God that Jesse would suddenly pop out of the opening and snare Carl in a killing throat hold. Jesse. The thought of him injected a small amount of hope in her. Carl glanced behind him as if she was really staring at someone. When he turned back to her, he held his finger threateningly near her nose, which still ached dully.

"Don't even think about screaming, blood of my heart."

That horrible endearment. He pulled at the cloth around her head until it finally came out of her mouth. She now recognized the taste as car wax. Her tongue felt like a withered prune.

"I am not yours," she stated simply, after moistening her mouth. "I'm Jesse's." Just saying his name gave her strength.

Carl's laughter sapped that strength as he gestured to her surroundings. "Looks like you're mine now." It was frightening the way his expressions changed so rapidly. His eyes grew hard again as they surveyed her body. "But now I don't want you. You're fat. You repulse me."

She flinched at the way he spit the words out. "Then why don't you let me go?"

That laughter again, fraught with evil. "Can't do that. You know too much. You and Jesse just kept snooping around. You couldn't let it rest, could you?"

His mention of Jesse made her suddenly afraid for him. Almost as scared as she was for the baby inside her. "You tried to kill me." He had actually killed Marti.

"Yes, I did." He said the words wistfully, tilting his head up. "But I didn't. And you know why? Because you are meant to be mine."

"Was Helen meant to be yours, too?" she ventured.

He turned to her, surprised. "Why do you say that?"

"You asked her to marry you, but she turned you down." Jesse had told her that after Bernie died, Carl had come around panting like a dog. Marti didn't mention the photo she'd found.

"Don't talk to me about Helen."

"You couldn't make her love you, could you?"

He leaned so close that she smelled the whiskey on his breath. "Are you calling me a failure?"

She shrunk back as far as the bed would allow. "No. You succeeded in killing your son, didn't you?"

He leaned back, placing his ankle on his other knee. "Yes, but that wasn't planned. He was going to squeal on his own father. He came in here accusing me of being the one who attacked you both times. Said if I didn't confess, he had enough evidence to interest the Ft. Myers police."

Marti remembered Paul's desperation that night outside Dr. Hislope's house. He'd known. That had been his crazy revelation, that his own father was the one.

Carl leaned forward, pointing at his chest. "He was going to turn his own father in. Can you believe the loyalty? Even before he knew I wasn't his real father." Marti's eyes widened, and he seemed pleased to surprise her. "I married his mother because she told me she was pregnant with my baby. But when Paul was born, I knew — *knew* — he wasn't mine. I made her tell me who she'd slept with. I forced the bitch to tell me."

She wanted to keep the conversation away from her and Jesse. "B-but you forgave her?"

He smiled, showing his perfect teeth. "No. I made her life hell until she ran away one night."

She shivered. "You killed Paul, then tried to set Jesse up for his murder."

"I wanted Jesse out of the way, but he left without seeing the note. You found it instead. You always did find yourself in the most interesting predicaments."

"How did you get his knife?"

"I saw it in his truck the night I arrested him for assaulting Paul." He shook his head. "I never wanted to hurt Jesse, I really didn't. He was just in the way."

Her body stiffened. "What do you mean, 'hurt Jesse'?"

"Sending him to jail for life didn't seem so bad, but when that didn't work out, I knew I had to get him out of the way. First, to get you. Second, to get him off my trail. He wouldn't give up, even all these months later. But you screwed that up, too, by getting out of jail early and stopping him from racing."

"The steering going out," she whispered. "And the weak spots they found on the car's frame later."

"That's right. But you see, it all worked out for the best. You're here, and he's alive. Unless he starts snooping around, that is."

That left her with the strange decision to either hope he did snoop or hope he didn't.

Carl stood. "I'm going to bring you something to eat. Don't want you thinking I'm a lousy host." His smile seemed almost normal then, not dark and sick. "Oh, and I took care of your car, too. Found it across the street. We wouldn't want to worry anyone, so I dumped it in a lake far from here.

"What are you going to do with me?" she asked, not sure she wanted to know.

He looked thoughtful for a moment. "I wasn't exactly planning to find you in my bedroom, you know. Such a gift. But you'll be the first to know when I figure it out." He tugged the gag back into place.

Jesse was frantic by ten o'clock that night. He didn't know whether to be angry or worried, but worried was quickly taking over. Sure, things hadn't been great between them, but she wouldn't stay out late just to make him crazy. She'd tried to call him, according to his phone, but hadn't left a message.

"Come on, Bumpus. Let's go for a ride."

He already knew she'd left Donna's earlier that day, but the woman was still too terrified to talk to Jesse personally. According to Dr. Hislope, Marti hadn't said where she was going. Phone calls confirmed she wasn't at the diner, his mother's, or at any of her current clients' houses.

The street Dr. Hislope lived on was unlit, save for a few lampposts outside some of the homes. Jesse glanced at Carl's old colonial as he drove past.

He was glad to see the sheriff home; Carl was the last person he wanted to report Marti's disappearance to. And it looked like the station was going to be a stop Jesse would soon be making.

The Hislope home was well-lit, but there was no sign of Marti's car. He knew that but wanted to see for himself. Then another drive through town. He even drove past the place where Marti had been attacked and far beyond. Nothing.

At eleven, he caught Lyle heading home for the night and filed a missing person's report. Behind Lyle's concerned face Jesse sensed pity that Marti may have hit the road.

"She didn't take off, Lyle, so stop looking at me like that."

Lyle let out a sigh. "I don't know what to hope for, Jesse. I mean, it'd be better if she did take off. Least she'd be okay. She was talking about leaving town before."

Jesse jabbed his finger at Lyle. "You'd better look for her like she's in danger and not like she's a woman who just decided to run off. Because I know Marti.

319

She wouldn't do that to me, not after everything we've been through. Something's happened to her." The thought of it grabbed his heart and squeezed tight. "Find her, Lyle. Those two are my whole world."

Marti watched Carl work feverishly to fill in the slanted walls with white insulation, putting up drywall, installing an air conditioner unit. To anyone else, it looked like a man fixing up his home. The implications of what he was doing terrified her. It looked ... permanent.

Her best guess was that it was Friday, two days after she'd come here. She had no way of telling what time it was. When the light bulb was off, she could see cracks of sunlight filtering through from the eaves if it was day. Carl seemed to take enjoyment in keeping the time from her.

Rock music from the group Queen pounded through the small area, sometimes hateful and full of power, sometimes oddly whimsical. He played their greatest hits CD on a portable player over and over again, hardly glancing at her at all. That part was good, but she wondered what thoughts rambled through a brain warping more every day. He had lucid moments when he seemed to realize what he'd done. He cried for the son who was not his, even for the baby inside her he was distressing.

There were more moments when his eyes were glazed, emerald crystals, hard and somewhere else. He looked at her, but she knew he was looking far beyond her. He would stare at her for half an hour at a stretch, just watching her, contemplating. Those were the times she tried to roll onto her side to relieve her stiff, aching back. She could only achieve a partial angle, and she felt like a pretzel twist, but it helped a little.

For the last day, he relentlessly worked on refurbishing the attic, closing in a small area with drywall, causing her to gag from the smell of paint. She breathed through the pillowcase while the paint dried, trying to filter the oxygen the baby was getting.

He left her alone for a while, then returned with a tray of food. He fed her well, pasta, fresh vegetables, and juice. He'd even bought super-strength multivitamins to replace her pre-natals.

"I read that you need your vitamins," he'd told her hours before. "I'm reading a book about pregnancy, so I'll know how to take care of you." He gave her a startlingly genuine smile.

She'd kept silent, fear pulsing through her. Now he set the tray down on a small table he'd brought up. It was a ritual, before he removed her gag to let her eat, he would grasp her chin and force her to look at him. Then he'd smile and remove the gag. This time he leaned over and unlocked one of her hands. She didn't comment on it, for fear he would realize he hadn't done that before and lock her back up again.

"Today, I have turkey sandwiches for us and carrot sticks. And this is for you, too." He held up a glass of some unidentifiable beige substance. "It's a protein drink. You're supposed to have one of these every day."

She wouldn't have eaten anything but for the baby who needed its nutrition. "What is it?"

"Milk, powdered skim milk, brewer's yeast, vanilla, a raw egg, half an eggshell, honey, and fruit juice." At her skeptical expression, he pulled a book out from beneath a legal pad. "Right here." He pointed to a paragraph on page twenty as though to prove his good intentions. It really was a book on pregnancy.

"Why are you doing this?" she asked, nodding toward the book. With a stiff hand, she took the glass he held out for her. He seemed to be waiting for her to drink before he answered, so with closed eyes and a grimace, she gulped it down. Trying not to think about eggshells and the raw egg, she finished the glass and handed it back to him.

He wiped some residue off her top lip. This was one of his semi-lucid days, she thought. He was there, yet acting as though their arrangement were perfectly normal.

"I want to take care of you, sweetheart. We're going to be a happy little family."

She cringed when he touched her belly. "H-happy family? You're going to keep me here after I have the baby?"

He leaned back in the rocker, putting his feet on the bed. "I'm going to keep you here forever, blood of my heart."

Her stomach turned, threatening to spew up the ghastly drink. "W-what about having the baby? I've got to go to a hospital." It was a hope that if he didn't kill her before she had the baby, he'd have to take her to a hospital when she went into labor.

Carl tapped the cover of the book. "I've got more of these to help. I don't want you going to some sterile, uncaring hospital. You're going to have that baby right here, with me helping you every step of the way. Lots of women opt to have their babies in their homes. So much more comfortable."

She tried to hold onto her own sanity. "What if there are complications? Those women have midwives to help."

"There won't be any complications, sweetheart. Look at you, healthy as a horse. I won't let anything happen to you, or that baby of ours."

Ours. The word stabbed at her. "It's not *your* baby, Carl. It's Jesse's."

Carl smiled wistfully. "Yeah, Jesse's a good name for the baby, if it's a boy. We'll name him Jesse. He'll be my son, my blood."

She shivered. This room was going to be her prison. For *forever*. No, Jesse would come for her, any time now. She had to keep hoping.

As though Carl read her thoughts, he pulled out the legal pad and handed it to her. "I think it's time you wrote a goodbye letter to your husband. Tell him you decided to leave early, that you won't be coming back."

She eyed the pad he'd thrust at her. "No."

He yanked her hair, jerking her head backward. "I will make your life hell if you don't."

"You won't hurt the baby, Carl. He's your blood," she lied.

"I won't hurt my son, but I will make you miserable. I'll turn the air off, feed you the most disgusting, albeit nutritious, food I can think of, make you lie there naked …"

As he spoke, her resistance hardened. Until she thought of something. Grimacing, she said, "Okay, I'll write the letter."

He smiled, handing her the pad and a pencil. "And don't think about putting anything in that shouldn't be there."

She nodded, but her mind was whirling. Carl dictated the letter to her, shoving her hand into action.

"Dear Jesse. I have decided to leave early because I'm very unhappy here with you. Go on. Write it. I want to start my new life in ... where were you going?"

"Oklahoma."

"Okay, in Oklahoma. I'm sorry I couldn't say goodbye in person. Signed you."

"What about the baby? I have to say something about him, since I'm legally kidnapping him."

He scratched his chin. "I guess you should."

She wrote:

You know how much I want this baby, enough that I got pregnant on purpose, deceived you, to have one. I'm so sorry to be taking him away from you. I promise to take good care of him.

She'd never told Jesse how the baby had grown on her, how feeling Eli — yes, she'd even started calling him by his name — inside her gave her both heartache and joy. So that sentence, too, would seem odd. "Can I tell him to say goodbye to his family for me? Since I won't be seeing them again? He would think it was weird if I didn't."

He gave it some thought. "All right, but nothing tricky."

She was taking chances, and she knew it. It was her only hope. She wrote, "Please say goodbye to Helen, Caty, Billy, and your dog, Caramel. I will miss them all."

Carl looked over what she had written, and she prayed he didn't know Bumpus's name. It was the closest she could come to spelling out Carl's name, and the wrong name might cause Jesse to look at it carefully. If he paid much attention after all the other words before it.

"Oh, no you don't," he said, shoving the paper back at

her.

Her heart caught in her throat. "W-what?"

"You didn't sign it."

She breathed out silently when he folded the paper and stuffed it into an envelope.

"Fill out his address. I'll head north a bit and mail the thing today."

Her hands trembled as she wrote Jesse's name. Would she ever see him again? Would he ever take her hand so casually and not know how warm it made her feel?

Carl leaned back in the rocker, a smug smile on his face. He made her uncomfortable under his silent stare, the way his gaze swept slowly over her, pausing over her distended belly. His eyes were glazing more, as though he wasn't seeing her but someone else.

"How are you going to explain having a baby all of a sudden, Carl?" she asked, wanting to break through to the small, sane part of his mind.

He cuffed her to the bed again. "Everybody knows I have a sister in Texas. She hasn't been out to visit in a long time, but the folks around here remember her as being wild. Well, she got herself into a little fix. Pregnant, by a married man. What a shame. But her big brother, Carl, will help her out. He'll raise the baby. No one will know about you, of course. But little Jesse here will become my son. Unfortunately, no one will know he really is of my blood." He grasped her chin hard. "It would have been so much easier last time, Helen."

A chill crawled down her body. "I am not Helen."

"You were once the blood of my heart, but you became the bitch of my heart. You knew how much I wanted you, loved you. But you wouldn't leave Bernie, not even when you were carrying my child." His voice became gruff. "You were blindly in love with him. And you never told him Jesse was mine. *My son!* Bernie believed he had fathered that boy, and I watched Jesse grow up hating me."

"I don't believe you," Marti whispered, realizing what he was saying.

"Helen, I knew that boy was mine the moment he was born. I was there, visiting the nursery. You never knew, but I held him a few hours after he was born. He was mine. And when you threw his first birthday party, I watched from outside the house, watched Bernie coddle and hug my son. But Jesse's eyes, his hair, they were mine. You couldn't deny it was my son." Carl's voice rose. "I won't let you deny that now."

She reeled from his words. Helen had told her she'd made mistakes, learned from them. *Before Jesse was born.* Marti conjured up Jesse's image for the thousandth time that hour and compared it to Carl's features. There were similarities.

Carl smiled, as if seeing her putting it together. "But we have a second chance, Helen. We have a new baby. This boy will grow up knowing who his father is. We can have that happy family together. You denied me twice, but you won't deny me now. I have wanted you for so long, lived for you, longed for you." He fisted his hand at his stomach. "Every time I saw Jesse, it killed me right here. But you ignored me, wouldn't even take my calls. Even after Bernie died, you wouldn't come to me. I did it for you, because I knew he couldn't make you happy like I could. But you still wouldn't come to me."

A shard of fear sliced through her. *Did it.* "Y-you killed Jesse's father?"

Carl shot to his feet, slapping her across the cheek as he rose. "*I'm* Jesse's father!"

The sharp sting brought tears to her eyes. "*I'm* not Helen! I'm Jesse's wife, and this is Jesse's baby!"

Carl turned away and started the CD again, cranking it louder than before. She continued to cry, for everything she'd just heard, for what it all meant. The words to the ballad, "All Dead, All Dead" pounded through her mind.

Hope drained away. Jesse thought she was gone and probably hated her. She wanted to die then, but there was Eli to think of. What kind of life would he have? How would Jesse have turned out under Carl's parentage?

She shook her head, trying not to think about that. Eli must live, that was all she knew. He might live a normal life, out with other people, going to school. Maybe Jesse would see him one day, and maybe he would know, somehow, that it was his son. Would Carl really name him Jesse? Would she still be up here in this attic, a prisoner of darkness? Or would she be insane by then? Probably, unless Carl let her see Eli a lot. Then she would have a reason to stay sane.

Over the next many hours, perhaps through a long night, she thought about what Carl was insinuating. What he believed. He and Helen had had an affair, and she got pregnant with Carl's child. Helen. The woman she believed in, the woman who had helped Marti believe in herself.

Marti grimaced as another cramp seized her insides. These were not the Braxton-Hicks contractions she had been feeling for the last week or so. This pain she attributed to something more emotional, more heartbreaking. She felt betrayed, let down. Helen, the woman she thought of as a mother, had cheated on the man she professed to love. How could Marti have been so stupid to start believing she could change?

The sound of the deadbolt turning pulled her from her agonized thoughts. Carl walked through the doorway he'd fashioned in front of the trap door entrance. He looked around with a smile at the eight-foot-by-eight-foot room, painted a cheery pink. His eyes were glazed again, far from lucid.

"I should be done with the bathroom tonight, Helen. Won't that make you happy?"

She glanced at the bedpan. Happiness was relative. "Yes, that will be nice," she said carefully.

Inciting Carl's anger was far too easy. And painful, as her cheek could attest many times. He now allowed her hands to remain free. The gag was gone, too, for a day's worth of hours now. With the room sealed and soundproofed, there was no need for it. She was biding her time until he finally unchained her legs and let her roam while he was gone. Then she would find a way out of this hellhole.

"You'll be able to wash yourself by tomorrow. Although I must admit, I enjoyed washing your hair ... and your body."

She tried to blank out those times when he gave her a sponge bath. Twice now, and he took his time, talking about how they would make love when she wasn't fat anymore. Thank God her size repulsed him. Memories of Jesse telling her how beautiful she was got her through those moments, through all of them.

It seemed like months since she'd seen him, and they hadn't been on good terms for a week before that. She estimated that it had probably been a day or so since he'd received that letter. He'd probably ripped it up, so furious at her for taking away his son that he'd missed her clues.

Her well of hope was drying up. Soon, everyone in Chattaloo would stop thinking about her. They'd forget about her. She pushed away the fear that threatened to seize her.

She glanced at the steel door, left ajar. Beyond that, the trap door was open, and below was the hallway that led to the staircase that Paul had been shoved down.

The cuffs jangled around her ankles as she moved them. She'd never get away from him. He teased her by leaving the door open, knowing she'd think about escaping. She rubbed her hard belly, trying to press away the fear about having the baby in the attic.

Sometime later, Carl emerged from the bathroom, a triumphant glaze on his expression. "After I clean it up, it'll be ready to use, sweetheart. Think about how you're going to show me gratitude." He gestured at the room. "All this for you." He hitched his jeans, grinning.

Her stomach churned at the thought. As he turned toward the steel door, he stopped suddenly. With the door open, he could hear anything downstairs. He walked to the tiny door he'd installed high up in the roof, climbing a stepstool to open it. Usually a heavenly spot of sunlight shone in for a while in the morning. It was nighttime now, no sun.

Sometimes he'd remark that someone was parked outside and go down to answer the door. Once she'd screamed her head off, testing the soundproofing. When he returned, he said nothing about her screams, so she knew it worked.

This time he said, "What the hell is he doing here?" The edge in his voice indicated the visitor was not welcome.

"Who is it?" she asked as she always did.

Usually he told her. This time he didn't. He walked out of the room, bolting the steel door behind him. She knew how long it took him to walk down and answer the door: a minimum of ten minutes, sometimes as long as an hour. When Lyle had stopped by, she'd counted twenty-five minutes. Long enough to try something.

Last time it took her fifteen minutes. She would have to be quicker this time. With her hands and weight, she scooted the bed closer to the tiny door, mentally counting out the seconds. With her large belly, it was dangerous to get to her feet on the uneven support of the bed, but she managed it with the help of a nearby wall. She opened the door and jumped, getting a glimpse of the street out front.

A jolt of hope shot through her at the sight of Jesse's truck parked by the road. She had to force herself to get the bed back before Carl might return. She was trembling as she maneuvered the bed back to its original spot, marked on the floor with a pencil.

As soon as she reached the mark, the door was unbolted, and Carl stepped inside. Her heart hammered, more from seeing Jesse's truck than getting the bed back in place in the nick of time.

She swallowed hard, trying to regain her composure. "Who was it?"

"Just someone looking for an address."

It was frightening how well Carl concealed the truth, both in his words and expression. If she hadn't seen

Jesse's truck, she would have believed him. When Carl locked the door behind him, she knew he was concerned. He went to the window and checked through the door again.

"They're gone." He knelt down beside her, grasping her arm. "Don't worry, Helen. I won't let anyone hurt you. I'll kill them first."

"I don't want you to kill anyone for me," she said, trying to reason with an unreasonable man. "Killing is bad."

The baby kicked her rib, causing her to flinch. Eli sat low inside her, pressing down on her pelvis. She could see Jesse's face light up in her mind, amazed every time the baby moved or kicked. Now she was able to put her hand on her belly, but she never indicated any movement to Carl. The last thing she wanted was his hand on her belly.

"I'll go make dinner," he said.

"I can help," she offered. "I'm a good cook."

He smiled. "That would be nice. I always dreamed about you and me cooking together, snuggling on the couch afterward."

Her heart squeezed inside her. "Let me help you. You're always doing all the work."

He pinched her cheek, causing her to flinch away in pain. "You must think I'm stupid." He looked around the attic. "Maybe one day, if you're really good to me, I'll get you a television. That's all of the world you'll ever see."

In an almost robotic way, he stood and walked toward the door. Hope drained away, filling her with terror and helplessness. As soon as he was gone, she scooted the bed over and peered out the tiny window.

It was darker now, as though the clouds had moved over the moon. Still, she could see that the road was empty.

Why had Jesse come to see Carl at his home?

Marti remained at the window, knowing Carl always took about thirty minutes to cook dinner. She rapped on the thick Plexiglas, wondering if anyone could hear. When the deadbolt clicked, she turned toward the door, ready to get caught. And punished.

CHAPTER 19

The door opened, and Marti's knees gave way as she sank down to the mattress. Jesse stood there, his expression a mixture of relief and fear as he rushed to her. She started crying, unable to talk for a few seconds.

"My God, Marti, are you all right? The baby?" He looked around. "The sick son of a bitch."

She clung to him for a second, then came to her senses. "Jesse, he'll be back up in a few minutes! Does anyone know you're here?"

"No. I came on a hunch when I realized what Caramel might mean after knowing something wasn't right with the Oklahoma thing." He looked down at the cuffs on her ankles. "I've got to get you out of here."

"You're not going anywhere with her," Carl's voice said in a deadly tone. He shut the door behind him.

Jesse rushed him, shoving him up against the wall. Chips of plaster rained down on the two. Dammit, she felt so helpless, chained to the bed. A sharp pain ripped through her stomach, and she grimaced, squeezing her eyes shut for a moment. When she opened them again, Jesse was looking at her. She shook her head, telling him not to worry.

Carl emitted a caterwaul as he twisted a distracted Jesse around and shoved him to the floor. Jesse moved right before Carl dropped down knees first, ready to crush him. They wrestled on the wooden floor until Carl pinned Jesse with his legs. He reached for a pipe wrench lying in the bathroom and swung it high in the air as Jesse struggled to free himself.

A severe cramp seized her. She managed to scream, "Carl, you can't kill your own son!"

Both men stopped and looked at her. Carl's fingers trembled, and Jesse grabbed the wrench and lurched upward, tumbling Carl onto the floor. He beat Carl until he was no longer fighting back.

Marti doubled over in pain, reaching for the handcuffs her hands had been in. "Here," she said breathlessly. "Put him in here."

Jesse dragged Carl to the bed and cuffed one hand to the rail. Then he searched his pockets for the keys to the cuffs around Marti's ankles. Carl's head lolled about before his glazed eyes settled onto Jesse, right in front of him.

"I'm your father," he uttered. "I just wanted another chance. You were never going to love me, but that baby would have."

Jesse gave him a disgusted look. "You are *not* my father, and I ought to kill you for saying it. I should kill you anyway." He slugged Carl in the jaw, silencing him.

When Jesse found the matching keys, he freed her ankles and helped her from the bed. Her legs were stiff from disuse. She groaned, leaning on him, her pain overwhelming.

"Marti, what's wrong? Is it Eli?"

She nodded. "I think ... I'm in labor."

"Okay, come on. Stay calm."

He helped her to the door, locking Carl into the prison he'd made for her. Getting her down the precarious ladder was the difficult part. Beads of sweat covered her body by the time they reached the floor. He eased her down on the couch and made two calls: one to the hospital, one to Lyle.

She was in too much pain to listen to either. Jesse rushed over and carried her down to his truck. He jumped in on the other side, threw the truck into gear, and tore down the road to the hospital.

"Hold on, doll," he said, squeezing her hand. "God, I thought I'd lost you." He looked at her for a moment, then leaned over and kissed her. "You're going to make it through."

She warmed at the words and their intensity. She wanted to tell him that she loved him in case she didn't make it, but something happened before she could get the words out: warm water gushed onto the seat, filling the cab with the faint odor of chlorine. "My water broke!" She looked at him, terrified. "I changed my mind! I don't want to have this baby. Not yet."

At four o'clock the next morning, Eli Bernard West came into the world with a healthy wail. Their two Lamaze classes had helped minimally, but Jesse had done everything possible to make it easy on her. Easy being a relative term.

"Jesse, would you like to cut the cord?" Dr. Diehl asked.

He looked hesitantly at Marti. "Will it hurt her?"

"She won't feel a thing." He handed Jesse the scissors, and he gently cut the cord. "Good job, son. Since the little fellow decided to come early, we're going to have to take him and run some routine tests. Now, don't worry, he looks perfectly healthy to me. You'll get to see him in a couple of hours."

"God, there's a lot of blood," Jesse murmured as the nurses started to clean Marti up. His hands were shaking.

"She's going to bleed for a while," one of them told him. "It's normal."

Marti felt overwhelmed as they wheeled her to her private room. Emotionally exhausted, happy, sad, she tried not to think about the last week of hell she had spent as Carl's prisoner. Jesse held her hand during the ride and sat next to her hospital bed once she was settled in.

She looked dazedly down at her belly, smaller now. "I need more of that sugar they were giving me intravenously. I'm so tired." Her voice sounded tiny and weak.

"You've been through hell in more ways than one." He brushed a strand of hair from her face. "Go to sleep."

She grabbed onto his hand. "I don't want to. Do you think the baby's okay?"

His green eyes studied her as he reached up and stroked her cheek. "Yeah, he's going to be fine. Marti, you gave me the greatest gift in the world. There's nothing I could do to show you how much that baby means to me, or that you stayed until you had him. The money doesn't even come close."

She'd forgotten about the money. "I don't want your money, Jesse. I've got some put aside, from decorating …" Her voice trailed off, and she fought tears.

He didn't say anything for a few minutes, but there was so much emotion in his eyes, so much she couldn't explore. She placed her hand on top of his, still resting against her cheek. *I love you, Jesse.* Exhaustion tugged her into sleep, leaving her words unspoken.

After Dr. Diehl stopped in to see how Marti was doing a few hours later, the nurse brought in Eli. Marti didn't even see the nurse, just the tiny person in her arms.

"He's fine," the nurse said. "Had a little trouble maintaining his body temperature and glucose for a few hours, but now he's perfectly fine. I'll be back later to check on you."

Marti's heart felt so tight that she could hardly breathe. Eli's eyes weren't open yet, but he reached blindly for her fingers, clutching them tight. She stared at him, feeling Jesse's warmth at her side, and his own awe of the tiny life in her arms.

"Hi, little guy," she whispered. He gurgled in response. *Oh God, how am I going to leave you and your daddy?* "You sure wanted to come out into this crazy world, didn't you? What was your hurry?" She kept her tone light, though her voice sounded strangled with the tears she was fighting. "Jesse, he's so perfect."

When she looked up at him, Jesse was watching her. He looked more tired than she felt, with his wrinkled shirt and tousled hair. In fact, pretty much the same as the first time she'd seen him, when she'd woken to find herself in another woman's body. How different things were now.

She handed Eli to him. Jesse's broad shoulders dwarfed the tiny being in his arms, but he cuddled the baby with supreme gentleness.

The door opened, and Helen crept in. Her smile glowed when she saw Marti and Jesse with the baby.

She gave Marti a hug. "How are you, hon? What a

traumatic thing to go through, the kidnapping and then going right into labor." Her kind smile faded when she looked at both of them. "What's the matter?"

Marti couldn't keep the chill of her heart from reaching her face. "I'm just tired, that's all," she lied. Helen had severely disappointed her and made Marti doubt herself. She had a feeling that tucked away in Jesse's heart were a lot of questions, waiting for the right moment to burst out.

He handed Helen her grandson. "Meet Eli Bernard West."

She cuddled him, closing her eyes. "I love that you named him after your father."

Jesse stiffened, his voice flat when he said, "Yes, my father."

When Helen met his eyes, hers were free of guilt or secret knowledge. "He would have been so pleased."

As hard as Marti tried to keep the thoughts at bay, she remembered Carl telling her that he'd arranged for Bernie's accident. She would tell them all that later, when Lyle came in to question her. For now, she could only hope that Jesse hadn't given any credence to the words that had made Carl hesitate before swinging that wrench at Jesse.

Marti drifted slowly from the trenches of sleep, aware of a voice speaking softly near her. At first, she irrationally thought Eli was already talking but dismissed that as she became more awake. She then recognized Jesse's voice and cracked opened one eye. He was leaning over the plastic crib Eli was sleeping in, speaking in a soft voice.

"What am I going to tell you about your mama, little man?"

As she fought to keep the tears at bay, her deep breath betrayed her wakefulness.

Jesse swung around to face her. "I didn't know you were awake."

"I just woke up," she said, swallowing hard. "Is he sleeping?"

"Yes."

He came to the side of the bed, and she longed for him to take her hand. He didn't. Instead those hands clenched the side of the table next to her bed.

"Did Lyle come in and talk to you this morning?"

"Yes. He said he was sorry he didn't see it. He knew something wasn't right with Carl, but he figured it was his way of mourning his son. I'll have to testify at the trial."

"So, you'll be back in town then?"

"Yes," she whispered.

He leaned down, bowing his head for a moment. Expelling a long breath, he looked at her again. "He didn't ... hurt you, did he?"

"No, he didn't hurt me. Or rape me. I was too 'fat.' Thank God for being pregnant," she said, trying to smile. "Carl was the one who killed Marti, and attacked me, and raped Donna." She told him how she'd put it together and ended up at Carl's. "He was going to keep me there forever and raise Eli as his nephew. That was when he was sane. Well, sort of sane."

The thought made her shiver and bury her head, trying not to cry as she had in front of Lyle earlier that morning. Jesse put his arms around her, and she melted into his touch. He held her for a few minutes. Finally, he moved away and steadied himself on the table.

"Marti, there's something I need to ask you. You

screamed that he couldn't kill his own son, and he stopped."

She nodded. "All I know is what he told me. He said he and Helen had an affair, and she got pregnant with you. I would have thought he was lying, but I'd found pictures of her in his bedroom." She took a deep breath. "His mind was warped; he thought I was Helen, and he was going to pretend Eli was you."

Jesse took her drink container and flung it into the corner, spraying water everywhere. She had never seen such betrayal in anyone's eyes, not even Jamie's. His body trembled as he struggled to stay in control. Thankfully she hadn't caused it. She maneuvered to the side of the bed and reached out to touch him. He jerked away, putting his hand out as a shield.

"Don't." He looked out the window. "His blood. My blood."

He stormed from the room, leaving her gripping the edge of the bed with all her strength. "You're nothing like him, Jesse," she called after him. "Blood or not!"

Jesse's insides were imploding, drawing into a tight knot. He didn't want to believe it. He would ask Helen, and if she said it was all an ugly lie, he'd believe her. His senses swirled around him, making him wonder about his own sanity. He had gone crazy worrying about Marti, and when he'd received that note, he believed she had left him at first. He shook his head, not wanting to relive those moments of pain. Almost losing her made him realize how much she meant to him. How the thought of her leaving had gutted him. With his baby, yes, but the thought of never seeing her again...

Helen looked up as Jesse stormed into the house. Caty's eyes widened as she flicked off the television.

Helen stood, her face taking on a panicked expression. "Is everything all right? Marti? The baby?"x

"They're fine. Caty, leave." At her shocked look, he took a quick breath and added, "Please."

She glanced at Helen, then slipped on some shoes and headed outside. A few moments later, her car started. Helen remained standing.

"Jesse, what is going on?"

He didn't want to be standing there asking his mother this. But he had to. "Did you have an affair with Carl before I was born?"

Her face paled, giving him as much of an answer as her words. "How —"

"He told Marti. As a matter of fact, Ma, he's still obsessed with you. Did you know that? He went fruitloop and believed Marti was you."

Her hand went to her mouth. "Oh, God."

"How could you do that to Pa?"

"It was only once."

"Once is enough."

"Let me explain, Jesse. I know it was wrong, but —"

Rage and hurt warred inside him. He turned, and, before he dumped it on her, stalked out. The sky was clouded over, and he wished for rain, for lightning, and thunder.

"Jesse, come back! Let me explain." She stood at the door. He couldn't bear to look at her another second.

Marti couldn't believe who she saw standing in the doorway of her room. Donna smiled tentatively, waiting for an invitation.

"My goodness, come in. You're out of the house," Marti said with a smile.

Donna nodded, sitting primly on the chair next to

Marti. "I'm ready, I think. It feels good to be out. And now I know I'm safe. The town is murmuring about your getting kidnapped and everything. It must have been terrifying."

"Not as much as childbirth," Marti kidded, not wanting to talk about the experience at Carl's house.

"I saw the baby. He's beautiful. Jesse must be so proud."

"He is. Eli looks a lot like him."

Marti was telling Donna about her daily routine at the hospital when she felt a presence at the door. Not Jesse. Helen stood there, looking even more hesitant than Donna. Her eyes were red and puffy.

Marti turned to Donna, but she was already on her feet, obviously taking note of the expressions on the other two women's faces. "I don't want to hog all your time, and my dad's waiting in the hall for me. Call me when you get out, and we'll have lunch. At a restaurant," she added triumphantly.

"Thank you for coming," Marti said as Donna retreated.

Helen shut the door behind Donna and took a seat. Marti had never seen Helen less than composed, and even under the circumstances, it left her feeling unsteady.

"Marti, I am so sorry that this happened to you. I'm sorry that Carl ..." She faltered, then continued. "Jesse came to see me a while ago. He didn't give me a chance to explain anything to him. You — you're a captive audience, so to speak. I don't know if I'll be able to explain it all to my son or whether he'll even care to hear it, but for some reason, I feel I should explain it to you, because I know that I've let you down."

Marti swallowed tears that were fighting to escape. "You don't have to explain anything to me."

"I do. Remember when we talked about fidelity and making mistakes. I told you about the time after Billy was born and Bernie was racing all the time. Carl became a friend during those lonely months, and that's all I wanted: a friend. But I made a mistake and let things get too far one night. We had sex, and that's all it was. Once.

"After that, I told him we couldn't be friends or anything else. I confessed to Bernie, and that wasn't easy. But I didn't deserve easy, and he didn't deserve to be lied to. It was hard, so hard to tell him, and he hated me for a week. But he forgave me and started spending more time at home. Carl kept pestering me, watching me. But I never saw him alone again, and I thought he let that die a long time ago."

Helen waited for some kind of reaction. Marti wasn't sure how she felt. She who had made mistakes and hadn't confessed them or learned from them. But there was something she had to know.

"Is Carl Jesse's father?"

Helen's eyes widened. "God, no. It was close to the time he and I, well, you know. I was worried. So, the doctor conspired with me and told Carl there was some concern about some disease going around. He took Carl's blood, and we ran the tests against Jesse's. There was no way they're related." Her expression lit with worry. "He thinks Carl's his father?"

Marti relayed the moments when Jesse rescued her from hell. As her words poured out, she felt a deep relief. And forgiveness.

Helen stood, wringing her hands. "I've got to talk to

Jesse, but right now he won't listen to me. It's a horrible feeling to know your son hates you."

"I don't think he hates you. He's just hurt and confused."

Helen looked at Marti. "I did let you down, didn't I?"

"I don't know why, but I feel almost as hurt as Jesse probably does. You gave me such faith in myself not to make the same mistakes I'd made before. If someone like you can fall, how can I expect to stay on the path?"

Helen's eyes glistened with tears. "Because you're better than I am. No, don't look so skeptical. I didn't think it could happen to me. I was this perfect wife. You don't have those delusions. You're walking in with eyes wide open, ready to protect what means the most to you. Your past doesn't disadvantage you. You know what to look for and what you can lose, because you already lost it once.

"Now you have a second chance to grab at love and happiness. Maybe you both can learn from my mistake. He needs you, Marti. And if you'll admit it, you need him."

"I think... I could be true to someone like Jesse, but it doesn't matter. I already told him, I can't be a runner up in his life. And I can't ask him to give up racing."

Helen touched Marti's hand, a soft smile on her face. "Whatever you decide, please don't leave until you say goodbye. You're like a daughter to me."

Marti's tears now flowed freely down her cheeks. "Thank you for explaining when you didn't have to."

Helen hugged her, then headed toward the bassinet. "Have to see the grandbaby," she whispered to the sleeping infant. "Eli Bernard West." She looked up toward the ceiling. "Do you see your grandson, my love?

They named him after you. I wish you were here to hold him. And me."

The evening breeze was humid and warm, but Marti wrapped Jesse's robe around her as she walked down to the tiny lake in the hospital courtyard. His cologne drifted from the terry cloth. The ducks were sleeping, tucked away in their hiding places, the lake deserted. She sat down on one of the concrete benches that surrounded the lake. Lights glistened on the water that shimmered as tiny fish moved beneath the surface.

"The nurse said I might find you out here."

Jesse's voice washed over her like the breeze itself, comforting and familiar. She turned to find him standing in the shadows where the pathway started to circle around the lake. He was wearing a black T-shirt and jeans, and his hands were jammed into his front pockets. His hair wafted in the breeze, but she couldn't see his eyes clearly from where he stood in the shadows.

"I needed to get away," she said. "To think. I'm getting out of here tomorrow."

"I know."

He walked closer. She looked up at him, trying to keep her heart from hammering inside her. What she wanted to do was stand up and press herself against him, hoping his arms would encircle her and comfort her as she knew they could. But he was already lost to her, removed in a way she couldn't define. He crouched down in front of her so that his face was even with hers.

"Are you all right?" she asked in almost a whisper.

He leaned forward then, putting his arms around her waist, and buried his face against her stomach. She leaned forward too, resting her cheek on his head, rubbing his back.

"Carl isn't your father," she said.

He didn't move for a few minutes, and she wondered if he'd heard her. Then he faced her again.

"I know. I talked to Ma a little while ago."

She reached out and placed her palm against his cheek, and he put his own hand on top of hers. He was her Jesse again, warm and real.

Her Jesse.

"Did you work things out with her then?"

"Yes." He looked away for a second, running his fingers through his hair. "I'm sorry I got so mad in front of you."

She smiled faintly. "Well, I kept telling you to show your anger."

"Yeah, you did. But you had the reason for my anger mixed up when Mark came down for that visit."

"I did?"

"Uh hm." He took both her hands in his. "I was mad at *you*, not at life's unfairness."

"Me?"

"More at myself, really. I was mad because I'd fallen so completely in love with you that even racing didn't seem that important anymore. That scared me, because I'd already come so close to losing my dream." He reached up and touched her cheek. "But I almost lost you, and that put everything into proper perspective."

Her chin was trembling when he took her hands and pulled her to her feet. She said, "I figured you were going to marry Abbie. I remember you saying something about her visit answering some question for you."

He smiled. "When I started falling in love with you, I kept denying it. I told myself I just wanted to have you stay because I wanted someone to help with the baby.

When Abbie offered me that, I realized I wanted you to stay for a lot more than just raising our son. Still, it drove me crazy. And so did you."

Her heart was in her throat. "Jesse, will you tell me again what your pa said about how you'd know if you truly loved someone?"

"Sorta a clenched gut, drop down to your knees, and die for her feeling, and you ain't in love 'til you feel it." He said the words slowly, and his fingers tightened around hers.

Her stomach clenched at the intensity of his gaze. She nodded, a smile across her lips. "Yeah, that about sums it up. Your pa was a smart man."

Jesse took her face in his hands. "Marti, I know I asked you to stay for the wrong reasons before. But now I want you to stay for the most important reason, the only one: I love you. This time I'm not asking you to stay, I'm telling you that you are staying. I'm not letting you go to California or Oklahoma or anywhere else. You are home, doll. Right here, forever. And you're not going to be second to anything."

"You're not thinking of giving up racing, I hope."

"No, but I realized I don't need to succeed at racing to be successful. Being successful, making it, means having what's most important to me." He pulled her closer. "That would be you. And Eli."

"Is that a proposal?"

"You can take it any way you want, as long as you take it. And me."

EPILOGUE

Eli hobbled unsteadily down the beach, intrigued by every shell and bit of seaweed. Marti and Jesse walked hand in hand behind him. She relished the feel of his fingers intertwined with hers as much as the warm splash of the waves around her ankles.

She took a deep breath. "Caterina seemed so dull to me a century ago. Well, it seems like a century. Now I see the wonder of it." She looked at Jesse. "And the romance."

He swept her up into his arms and twirled her around, kissing her all the while. "As long as you don't see the romance while you're thinking about the rich, blond guy."

"Jamie? You've got nothing to worry about, darling."

He raised an eyebrow. "Hm, I don't know. I'll probably never be able to buy an island."

She hugged him. "Yeah, but you can give me a ride in your fancy new racecar, and I get on television because they like to do those family interviews in the pits."

He touched her chin. "My two good luck charms cheering me on."

Eli's squeal of laughter made them turn. A baby girl,

about Eli's age, ran toward them with her hands poised for a hug. Eli, not knowing what else to do, sat on the spot.

"Kayla, what are you doing, sweetie?"

Marti looked up at the couple walking from a path that led from the jungle. Her heart stopped momentarily, and she felt dizzy. Jamie and Hallie both grinned when they saw that their little girl had found a friend. Three Shetland sheepdogs followed behind, interested only in chasing each other. Marti clutched at Jesse's arm to steady herself.

"Hi, welcome to Caterina," Jamie said, casually offering a hand. "I'm Jamie, and this is my wife, Hallie and our daughter, Kayla. We own this little place."

Jesse stiffened but shook Jamie's hand heartily. "I'm Jesse, and this is my wife, Marti." He planted a kiss on her temple. "I think Eli's found a girlfriend, huh, doll?" He pointed to the toddlers, probably drawing their attention away so she could gain her composure.

She had never seen Jamie so happy before. Seeing her old body was stranger yet, but she felt no ties to it anymore. The woman in it obviously took good care of it. Marti had never seen it looking so fit. Jesse noticed, too, and she nudged him.

"How do you like it here so far?" Jamie asked in his owner's voice.

"It's absolutely excellent!" Marti replied, and the look on his face revealed that he still remembered her old expression. Hallie's old expression. "What's wrong?"

Jamie put his smile back on. "Oh, nothing. I knew someone who used to say that all the time. Just like that, same inflection and everything." He shook his head, as if to throw off the memory. "Where are you two from?"

"Florida," Jesse answered, watching her carefully. Suspiciously. She could read his thoughts in his narrowed eyes: *What are you up to?*

Marti turned to Jamie. "I'm from California, originally. Oceanview."

Again, Jamie's expression looked haunted for a moment. Marti found herself wanting to tell him who she was. She could apologize for what she'd put him through, explain her messed-up-ness. What would his new wife think? Had she told him about her true identity? Hallie seemed just as interested in the 'coincidences' as Jamie.

"Well, maybe we'll see you later on," Jamie said, taking Hallie's hand. "Tonight's Jamaican Night at BooNooNoos. Great food, limbo, that sort of thing. My wife's one of the best limbo-ers around, and she'll be glad to show you a thing or two." He paused, giving her an interesting smile. "In fact, you're welcome to sit with us for dinner. It sounds like we have a few things in common."

"We'll do that." Marti pulled her gaze away from his speculation and glanced around. "Things have changed a lot since the last time I was here."

Jamie's eyebrows drew together. "You've been here before? I don't remember seeing you."

She took in the water and palm trees. "Feels like forever." She scooped Eli up in her arms, then spared an arm to link with Jesse's. "It was a time in my life where I made a lot of mistakes. Hurt people. Coming back is part of some healing I intend to do, so I can put my past behind me. Because life is all about second chances."

She gave them both a knowing smile. "We'll see you at dinner, Jamie. Hallie."

She turned and walked away from them, Jesse at her side. Her lips twisted in a huge grin.

"You are bad," Jesse said, though he was smiling, too.

"No, I'm good. I meant every word I said. The past is gone forever. I'm so glad they found their second chance, too. I lost the island, but I got the West. And the West is a lot better." She pinched his cheek. "Besides, Jamie isn't my type."

Thank you so much for reading *Stranger in the Mirror*. If you enjoyed it, please consider posting a review on Amazon.com, BookBub.com, and Goodreads.com.

Find links to more stories in the Love & Light collection and other series by Tina at www.WrittenMusings.com/TinaWainscott and www.TinaWainscott.com.

SNEAK PEEK

Jennie Carmichael rolled her wheelchair through the doorway of Sam's Private Eye and over to her desk by the window. Sam Magee's low, rumbly voice coming from his office was as familiar and welcoming as the scent of aged wood, the heat of the furnace, or coffee ... which, she noticed, was absent this morning.

Darn, he'd forgotten to pick some up again. The coffeepot looked cold and impotent in the corner. The mug she'd bought him for Christmas sat next to the empty pot, the hound dog face waiting patiently to be filled.

Speaking of hound dogs, she heard a jingling sound and turned to greet Romeo, the reason she'd picked that particular mug for Sam. Romeo's tail arced gracefully, and his dripping chocolate-brown layers of skin flopped this way and that as he ambled over for his rub. She always rubbed her cheek against the top of his head. He had the softest fur, but she really loved the way his eyes rolled in ecstasy.

Romeo's presence meant that Sam planned to be in the office for most of the day, and Jennie felt like rolling her eyes at that thought, too.

She shrugged out of her coat and then her sweater, hanging both on two low hooks Sam had put in just for her. She pulled the knit cap off her head, feeling several strands of her light brown hair crackling with static. Outside, snowflakes covered the city of Chicago, making her dread leaving and dealing with the snow.

She organized the papers on her desk as Romeo settled onto his dark green pillow with a contented sigh. She put copies to be made in one pile, reports to be transcribed in another. After firing up the computer, she put the tiny tape into the transcribing machine. She might have hated transcribing, but Sam was a good speaker and he had a voice she could listen to for hours.

"Sam's Private Eye," she answered cheerfully when the phone rang.

She put the call on hold and wheeled across the wood floor to the doorway nearby. Sam looked as if he'd been poured into that high-back chair. He had the old leather chair he'd picked up at an auction tilted all the way back, and his sock-clad feet were perched on the desk as he dictated another report.

That huge desk would have made most men look like elves, but not Sam. Not that he was a big guy in a burly sense; his strong shoulders tapered to a lean waist. He just had ... presence. His ash-blond hair was brushed back in waves, highlighting his broad forehead and blue eyes. Here, the aroma of leather and the citrus cologne he wore almost made up for the lack of coffee.

"Upon further surveillance, the subject twice stood and —" He clicked the little recorder off. "Morning, kiddo."

"Morning, bossman," she said, using the nickname

that had started out as a joke. "There's a Petula on the line for you." Petula of the long legs and blond hair and fake eyelashes. Like most of the women Jennie had seen Sam date. "She says it's, er, personal."

"Tell her I'm out of the country on a case," he said, then flashed her a mischievous smile that stretched his trimmed mustache. "A dangerous mission spying on Mexican drug lords in Africa trying to sell their wares to Swiss tourists. If I don't get nailed by the drug lords or the Swiss tourists, there're always the cannibals. They like white meat, I hear."

"Mm-hm," Jennie said with a nod, trying not to look so very pleased. "That didn't last very long."

"That woman's intelligence bled out with her hair color years ago."

Jennie felt a strange whirring in her heart when she said, "Well, maybe you should change your type."

"Ah," he said with a flick of his wrist. "I don't have time to woo and court a woman. This business is hard on a relationship."

"Long hours away, rushing out on a sudden call in the middle of dinner, canceled dates … "

He looked at her, tilting his head. "Yeah, just like that."

For a second, something clicked between them, something that smacked of a deep understanding. Was she imagining something more? Probably. She snapped out of her misleading thoughts. "Oh, I'd better tell Petula …" She gestured toward the phone and whirled around to give her the brush off.

Afterward, she mulled over what had probably been the gutsiest thing she'd ever said to him, that thing about changing his type. What made Sam's heart tick?

The blues, she decided when he turned up a particularly rhythmic piece, leaned his head back and started singing the chorus of "Drowning in a Sea of Love."

Ah, she knew that feeling well. She closed her eyes for a moment, savoring the richness of his voice. She could go on forever like this.

Her eyes popped open. She had thought that about her life before, about being able to walk and run and dance. Then twelve years ago, in one minute, it was all gone. Her whole life changed. Never again could she look at something as forever. For now, she was happy with her life, even if she was in a wheelchair. Even if she was hopelessly in love with her boss, a man she was totally wrong for.

Sam was a living-by-the-seat-of-his-pants guy; Jennie would only bog him down. Paralyzed from the waist down, she wasn't bound to be much in bed either. Mostly, his friendship wasn't worth risking by telling him how she really felt about him. He would never feel the same way about her, and her admission would put a strain on a friendship that meant everything to her.

Jennie wheeled back to Sam's office and peeked in the doorway. He was pacing behind the desk now, phone to his ear. "Mmhm. Mmhm. And what did you do?" he was saying.

"Sam, I'm going down to Shep's to make copies," she whispered, gesturing toward the door. She turned to head out. Thiers had died and he hadn't had a chance to buy a new one.

"Psst." Sam appeared in the doorway, phone scrunched between his ear and shoulder and gestured for her to wait. He slapped his palm to his forehead. "You slept with your wife? Aw, Harry, you just blew four weeks of surveillance. I don't care if it was the greatest sex you two ever had, don't you see? You knew she was sleeping around on you and you did the deed with her anyway. That constitutes forgiveness, and what that means, my friend, is you have no case. Her lawyer no doubt told her to hit you where your heart is, and I'm not talking about your stomach. ... *I* should have told you this before. I didn't think you'd *sleep* with her, for Pete's sake. You're the one who told me she was lower than a toenail."

He rolled his eyes at her as she tried to stifle a giggle. "Hold on a sec, Harry. Jennie, buy us some coffee from Shep, will you?" He handed her a couple dollar bills.

"Yes, bossman." She looked at the bills with a wry grin. That was his way of telling her that he'd forgotten coffee again. Mixed subtly into his expression was an apology.

"Thanks, kiddo. Listen, Harry, you don't have a leg to stand on, least of all your third leg. Forget the whole thing."

Jennie wheeled out into the hallway and knocked the door shut with her elbow. As she turned toward the elevator, she felt her wheels slide over something slick on the wood. Her chair slid backward toward the stairway that led down two more floors. She yelped, grabbing the railing to stop herself. Her back was to the staircase when she got the chair to stop turning. Glancing down the wood stairs, she let out a long breath and started the chair forward.

Instead, it went backward.

She lunged for the railing again, but she was already tipping over. The railing was out of reach.

The last thing she saw before she fell was Sam's horrified expression as he shot through the door and tried to grab her. She reached for him. Their fingers touched, slid without catching. Her stomach lurched as she fell, the steps jerking her chair forward and back.

"Sam!" she screamed out.

"Jennie, no!"

The world tilted, crushing her with pain and dizziness. Through some thick mist, she felt herself lurch down several more steps, landing on a flat, hard surface. Her body came to a jarring stop, but the dizziness kept swirling through her.

She heard voices filled with panic and exclamation. She smelled the coppery odor of blood, and heard Sam yell with a hoarse voice, "Someone, call an ambulance!"

Her heart thundered inside her, increasing the pain with each pulse of blood. She couldn't swallow at first. There was some kind of liquid in her mouth, warm and thick. When she forced herself to swallow it, she recognized the taste of blood. *I'm dying.*

Sam held her, smoothing back her hair with trembling fingers. "Jennie, don't leave me. Come on ... oh, God. Don't close your eyes. You're going to be fine."

Sam, I love you. She tried to voice her thoughts, but her mouth was filled with blood again. She wasn't even aware that her eyes were closing, but nothing could make them stay open. Even in the darkness, she could see Sam's face. She could still tell what was going on around her: Sam cradling her head, other voices in the stairway, Sam talking to her, the feel of blood trickling from her mouth down her chin and her neck.

She must look a wreck, she thought vaguely. Her impulse was to wipe away the blood. But nothing moved at her will. Panic gripped her. Not even a finger complied with her mental order to move. Was she completely paralyzed now?

"Jennie."

Sam's voice seemed so very far away, talking in soft, calming tones. She smiled, or at least thought she smiled. Yeah, she could listen to him forever. Then she realized she couldn't feel him anymore, couldn't hear the other noises. It was as if his voice had become a physical thing, a wave on which she rode, traveling through nothingness at a fast rate.

Then his voice faded, leaving her suspended and weightless. All of her fear, hopes, dreams, frustration—everything seemed to be sucked away from her, as if an unseen vacuum cleaner was pointed at her soul. She floated in some infinite darkness, feeling her life drawing to a peaceful end.

It seemed like an eternity, and at the same time only minutes from that fall down the stairs when Jennie opened her eyes. Time had no place here, nor did the physical. Her body was no more than an opaque mist. For the first time in many years she was free of constraints and limits. The silence was soft and comforting, rather than isolating. Yet, somehow, she knew she wasn't alone.

She felt as though she were in a fog bank suspended over a vast ocean. Through the gray mist a light as bright as the setting sun penetrated. Gentle rays of light emanated from the sun and shimmered through the mist like glowing fingers playing some giant, unseen piano. They became brighter and warmer as they moved closer, enveloping her in a feeling of warmth and peace like she had never known. She reached toward the light.

Then one word crept through the darkness, warming her even more than the light. *Sam.* She smiled, or at least thought she was smiling. Following that warmth was such a deep regret at not telling him how she felt about him, sorrow that she wasn't the kind of woman who could make him happy. *Take care of him* she asked the light. *I love him, you know.*

A soft, sweet voice emanated from the light. Not a voice in any physical sense but a wispy sound that seemed to penetrate her soul. *Some never get to fulfill their dreams the first time. A very chosen few get a second chance. You, Jennie, are one of those chosen. Soon you will be able to pursue those dreams the second time around.*

Another chance! To see Sam, to continue loving him, to nag him about getting coffee. This time she would tell him how she felt. Even if she wasn't the right woman for him — even if he could never love her that way, she wanted him to know her feelings toward him. Never again could she leave her life feeling this profound regret over her silence. This was one second chance she wasn't going to waste.

Then that blower started again. Only this time, it sucked her soul through the darkness. She was going back now. Everything happened at once. An incredible pain in her head, as if her brain had crystallized, then been dropped on a hard tile floor. Air filled her lungs so suddenly, she gasped with the force of it. Her heartbeat thudded through her, blood pulsing into every artery, every tiny vein. Her body was physical again. Gravity pulled her downward, pressing her against a hard surface below. She forced her eyes open, anxious to see what had become of her, knowing she would make the best of it.

The first thing Jennie saw, once her eyes focused in, was Sam's concerned face hovering over her. "Sam," she breathed, elated over the joy of smiling again — really smiling this time. Then she realized his finger was touching her neck, pressed gently against her pulse point. He looked startled as his gaze met hers. Slowly, he pulled his finger away. She was lying on the wooden floor, her body sprawled out like a ragdoll.

"You're alive again," he said in a low voice. "This is incredible. One minute you were gone — no pulse at all. Before I could even think about doing CPR, your pulse came back. All by itself," he finished softly.

"I did die, didn't I?" The light, the voice — it couldn't have been her imagination.

"How are you feeling?"

The throbbing pain in her head persisted, but she was more concerned about her hands and arms. She curled her fingers, breathing in relief as they obeyed her command. She wasn't completely paralyzed.

"I think I'm okay." Her voice sounded strange, lower, thicker.

"I should call an ambulance."

Sam's face wavered out of focus for a second, but she willed him back. Clearing her throat, she said, "But you already asked someone to do that." Her voice still sounded strange.

"No, I didn't, but I'm going to now." Something looked different about him. Maybe it was just his concern. "Stay put." He started to rise, but she grabbed his hand to stop him. Her whole world spun for a moment, and she squeezed his hand to steady herself.

"Just give me a minute," she whispered, letting the

nausea settle down again. She put her palm on the pounding area of her head and felt something sticky. That coppery smell assaulted her senses again. The blood on her hand sent the nausea into full tilt.

She took a deep breath. "Oh, geez. What happened to me?"

"That's what I was going to ask you. I heard a noise and opened the door to find you like this."

He headed back into his office and emerged a few seconds later pulling off his shirt. He cut one of his sleeves off with a pair of scissors. Gently, he pressed it to the gash on her forehead. When she put her hand there, her fingers touched his, reminding her of another moment when their hands had connected, then slipped from each other. He removed his hand, and she continued applying gentle pressure.

The pieces started coming together, shards of memories. "I fell down the stairs."

Sam's eyebrow twitched. "We're on the top floor."

"I know that, but ..." She turned behind her and was startled to see the staircase leading down. The one she'd fallen down. Well, she thought she remembered falling down the stairs. She looked down at her legs, sprawled out in front of her. She didn't recognize the gray wool pants she had on, or the long, black coat. Her feet were clad in nylons, and she squinted at what looked like red toenail polish. She'd been twelve years old the one and only time she'd ever put polish on her toes. Maybe she was seeing things.

Something else was missing. Her wheelchair. Before she could ask Sam about it, he said, "I think we've got some antiseptic in the office." A shadow darkened his eyes. "Jennie insisted we have a first aid kit." His voice had gone softer at those words, and he got up and went into the office.

Why was he using her name in the third person? She turned around to look for her chair. Without it, she felt as though a part of her was missing. Strange how she remembered falling backward down those stairs. Unless someone carried her up them and left her in front of Sam's door. No, that didn't make any sense. Neither did Sam's strange behavior. Maybe he was spooked by her coming back from the dead.

She noticed the rubber mat in front of their door. When had he put that there? She was sure there had been no mat when her wheel had slipped in the puddle.

She leaned toward her big toe to scratch an itch — and stopped. Her eyes widened. *Her toe had an itch.* Her *paralyzed* toe. A cold chill washed over her. She was sure it was all in her injured head. It had been a long time since she'd sent a message to her feet. She closed her eyes and concentrated. Her toe moved. Her eyes popped open. Then she saw her toe move. She couldn't believe it.

"I found some hydrogen — what's wrong?" Sam's voice intruded in her reverie.

Her voice was squeaky with her disbelief. "Sam, look! I can move my toe." Then another amazing thing happened. She moved her leg.

He didn't look quite as thunderstruck as she did, but he did have a measure of disbelief. He crouched down beside her. "I always knew you were on the edge, but I think that bump on your head pushed you over. Are you sure you're all right?"

She gave him a tremulous smile. "I might be better than all right."

He just looked at her for a moment. "What were you doing here, anyway?"

Her mouth dropped open at that one. "Sam. I was getting copies and coffee at Shep's, remember?"

His face paled then darkened with a shadow of agony. "Why the hell would you say something like that?"

He turned and walked back inside their office. What had she said? What was going on here? She could hear him on the phone a moment later. "Yes, we need an ambulance..."

Where was the man who had held her tenderly? Maybe she'd dreamed the whole thing. She lifted the piece of cloth from her head. Well, most of it. The bleeding seemed to have stopped. She reached for the bottle of peroxide Sam had left on the floor and poured some onto the cloth, then pressed it back to her forehead. She didn't want an ambulance; she wanted Sam to tell her why he was acting so strange.

What she needed was to find her chair. She grasped onto the railing behind her and pulled herself upward. Where could it be? It couldn't have just disappeared. After being virtually attached to it for twelve years, it seemed strange to be without it. That black, molded chair, or variations of it, was never out of her sight.

Her upper arms weren't as strong as they usually were. She struggled to hold herself upright, balancing herself while catching her breath. The sound of the elevator's doors sliding open brought her attention to Shep. Skinny, with gray hair and beard, he looked a bit like a goat, though Jennie had come to like him an awful lot over the years. He owned a small office supply store downstairs.

Shep's bushy eyebrows narrowed when he saw her

awkward position. "Ah, see you found Sam's all right." He glanced at the open door, then back at her. "Hope everything's okay. When you came running in my office looking for him, I thought you were in trouble or something. Are you all right, ma'am? You look shaky."

Her mouth dropped open. Shep didn't seem to recognize her. That warm sparkle didn't light his eyes, and he didn't call her by her nickname, Speed Racer. One of his words stuck in her brain. "Did you say I *ran* into your office?"

"Sure, don't you remember?" He shook his head then glanced at the stairway as if it had a life of its own. "Gave me the willies when you took the stairs three at a time. Didn't you hear me yell to be careful? What with the accident last month, none of us around here hardly uses them at all." Shep's face darkened with a palpable sadness, like the pallor on Sam's face.

Her mind couldn't sort the facts fast enough. She had bounded up the steps, *three at a time.* Maybe everybody was losing their mind, asbestos in the building or something. Her mind locked on the last bit.

"What accident?" Her fingers and arms trembled with the weight of holding herself up. Where was the upper-body strength she had worked on all these years?

Shep glanced in the open doorway again, then back. "Sam's assistant, Jennie. Speed Racer, I used to call her." His smile was filled with melancholy. "She was a real sweetie, nicest person you could ever know. Someone spilled some lubricant on the landing there, right in front of the office door. Still haven't figured out who done it, but I think it was one of the elevator service guys. Anyway, her wheelchair caught that spill just right — or wrong, you could say."

Jennie noticed Sam in her peripheral vision but kept her eyes on Shep. Her throat tightened, nearly cutting off her air. "What happened to her?" she whispered. *He's talking about me.*

"She fell down backward, hit her head. Poor thing, only twenty-six years old, and her life is over." His shook his head, lower lip pushed out.

Jennie wanted to hug him, to tell him she hadn't died. Instead, she fell to the floor amid a blizzard of black dots. No, they actually looked more like wiggly worms, all squirming this way and that. She was getting dizzier watching them.

"I've got her," Sam was saying as his arms went around her waist just before she hit the floor. "Shep, get her a glass of water, quick." He set her down on the floor gently, leaning her back against the railing she was blindly grasping for.

She was a real sweetie ... poor thing ... her life is over. The words floated through Jennie's mind, bits and pieces that refused to make sense to her. She had gotten a second chance, that's what the voice had told her. And she *was* there. But Shep said Jennie was dead. Neither he nor Sam seemed to know who she really was.

She thought of the wool pants she didn't recognize, the long black coat. Not her pants or her coat. Shep had seen her bound up the stairs. Not her legs. She opened her eyes, wiggly worms be damned, and glanced downward at the hands flattened against the floor to keep her upright. Long painted nails, strange rings on her fingers. Then further out at the legs sprawled awkwardly.

Holy angels in Heaven — she'd gotten a second chance in someone else's body. A body that was whole, a body that could walk, run ... dance!

Sam was trying to drape a wet, cold paper towel over her forehead when her head lurched upward.

"Get me a mirror." Her voice gave way at the last word.

His forehead crinkled. "Maybe you shouldn't look. It's kinda nasty. The ambulance should be here anytime, so just calm down."

"My face is kind of nasty?" Was she some monster?

Sam shook his head, a slight smile on his face. "No, the cut."

"Get me a mirror, or I'll get one myself."

He raised his hands. "Okay, I'll find a mirror. Vain woman," he muttered as he left.

"*Me*, vain?" She sputtered a laugh as he disappeared through the office door. "You've *got* to be kidding."

Jennie spotted a purse lying nearby, a large tapestry bag. Not her purse. Much too big and flamboyant for Jennie Carmichael. She fumbled through the contents until she found a Gucci wallet. She opened it to the driver's license. The woman in the photo had her hair pulled back, though several waves graced her forehead. Jennie's attention went to the name: Maxine Lizbon.

Sam reappeared with the mirror he used to obliquely see who came in the door.

Jennie threw her wallet back in her purse. "Nothing's missing," she said quickly, taking the mirror from Sam.

"Are you saying you think you were mugged?"

She looked at her reflection. Her throat constricted when she saw a stranger's face. No, not a stranger: Maxine Lisbon's face. There was no sign of Jennie there. The woman looking back had red hair, lots of it, curling past her shoulders. When she lifted her bangs, she saw the gash. She quickly let them go again, feeling woozy. Sam was right — it wasn't pretty. Instead, she concentrated on her general appearance.

Her eyes were the prettiest shade of green she had ever seen. Her skin was pale right then, making the streaks of blush stand out like a clown's. Her upper lip twitched, and she saw it move in the reflection. Even that little movement made her head ache, but she didn't care at the moment. Excitement shot through her veins, spreading a warmth through her entire body. She shoved the mirror back at Sam, not able to hide her smile.

"It doesn't look too bad." Her smile widened. She was Maxine now. Could she dare to hope this was real? With no wheelchair in sight, that meant — had to mean — she could walk. Shep returned with the glass of water, huffing and puffing next to her.

"Couldn't find a darned cup anywhere to save my life. Or yours."

She took a drink and handed it back to him. "Thanks. I think I feel better now." That was an understatement. She turned to Sam. "Could you help me up, please?"

"You should stay put until the ambulance comes."

"No, I'm fine."

Sam just stared at her for a moment, expelling a short breath. Finally, he extended a hand, and she grasped it, holding on for a second before pulling herself up. She had a whole new chance, a whole new body. Through Maxine, Jennie could now be the kind of woman Sam might fall in love with. She let her feet hold her weight for the first time in years. Her legs wavered, and she reached for Sam's strong shoulders. He steadied her with his hands, fingers tight around her waist.

"Did you hurt your legs?" he asked.

"No. I'm just a little ... weak, that's all."

Even though this body was used to walking, her mind wasn't accustomed to issuing those kinds of commands. She concentrated. Such a simple action, something she used to take for granted a long time ago. How did you walk? One foot in front of the other. Her legs wobbled, and she held tight to Sam as they walked inside the office.

"Shep, why don't you wait out front for the ambulance?" Sam asked.

"Is she going to be all right?"

Sam looked at her, lifting an appraising eyebrow. "As all right as she's ever been, I suspect."

Now what did that mean? Did he know? Could he somehow tell she was really in this body? No, he would have been celebrating this blessed event of walking with her. He would have looked at her in that familiar, warm way.

Shep set the glass of water on her desk and left to watch for the ambulance. Jennie made her slow way to the flowery couch Sam hated, the one his ex-wife had put in when she'd apparently used Sam's office as her first decorating assignment. He went into his office to put back the mirror he'd brought out for her. Romeo ambled cautiously over, his nose wiggling.

"Romeo!" She leaned down to rub her cheek against his head, but her head started spinning at the movement. Gripping the edge of the couch, she held her hand out to him instead. "Romeo, what's the matter?" Whoops. She knew what the matter was. He didn't know her.

Sam snapped his fingers as he reentered the front

area. "Romeo, go to your pillow." Romeo gave one more glance to Jennie, then swaggered over and dropped down on his pillow with a dog sigh, watching her.

Sam crouched down in front of her. "Maxine, did someone hit you out there? Mug you?" he asked, crouching "You said nothing was missing in your purse."

"No, I don't think so. I was just being paranoid, I guess." Well, she didn't think she'd been mugged. "I ... fell. Tripped or something." She tried to laugh it off, but Sam's expression was serious.

He stood and tilted her head back, his finger gently tracing the skin around her cut. "This didn't just happen. The blood around the cut is too dry. I'd say it happened about half an hour ago." His eyes met hers. "Try to remember what happened just before you came here to see me."

She didn't want him to think she'd lost her memory, but it was going to be hard to bluff through this one. Then she had a sobering realization. Whatever had happened to Maxine had killed her. Whether accidental or not, this gash had probably proved fatal. She decided to tell him the truth, or as close as possible.

"I'm not sure, to be honest with you. I can't remember what happened in the last hour."

"What about before that? Do you know who you are? Maybe there's something wrong with your legs."

"No, there's nothing wrong with my legs." She couldn't keep the smile away at that statement, but she tried to downplay it. After all, she'd bounded up the steps three at a time earlier, or at least Maxine had. Bounded up the stairs. What a wonderful thought! Her legs had to work pretty good for that. She lifted each leg, flexing her foot to demonstrate their ability. "See, they work just fine. And I know who I am. I'm Maxine Lizbon, and I'm thirty years old." She recited her address, the one from the license.

Sam gave her a wry grin, jumpstarting her heart all over again. "You must have hit your head hard; I've never heard you tell anyone your age."

"Huh?"

"But you don't remember how you got that gash?" he continued. "That's a serious injury."

"No. I can remember everything up until that point."

Sam tilted his head. "Why did you come to see me?"

Uh, except for that. She swallowed. "I-I don't know. Maybe it has something to do with this." She pointed to her forehead.

"In here," Shep's voice said. Two paramedics followed him into the office.

"I'm fine, really," she said.

The woman said, "Let us be the judge of that, okay?" She was short and stocky, and looked like she meant business.

Jennie tilted her head back and lifted her bangs.

"Yow," the woman said. "We'd better take you in."

"No," Jennie said, almost too quickly. She had an illogical fear that the doctors would see right through her, call her an imposter or body thief. "Can't you just stitch me up here?" At the doubt in their faces, she crossed her arms and added, "I'm not going to the hospital."

"Don't be difficult," Sam said. "I know you're really good at it, but not now. Maxine, are you listening to me?"

Jennie realized he was talking to her and not the

paramedic. "It's not that bad. I hate hospitals." She'd spent enough time in one after her accident.

"We can't stitch you up. All we can do is apply a butterfly stitch, which is more like a band-aid. Real stitches will close the wound much better, leave less of a scar."

"No hospitals. Just do what you can do here."

Sam shook his head, rolling his eyes upward. "You're just asking for trouble, woman." To the paramedic, he said, "Can't you forcibly take her to the hospital?"

"No, afraid not. All we can do is make her sign a release so if something happens, we're not liable." She turned back to Jennie. "Okay, we'll apply the butterfly, but if you have any dizziness or fainting spells, you must go to the hospital right away. Head injuries are serious business."

"Yes, ma'am," Jennie said solemnly.

After running a battery of tests, including looking deep into her eyes with their flashlight, the woman said, "I don't see any signs of concussion, but I really wish you'd let us take you in." When Jennie shook her head, the woman shrugged. "All right, it's your head. We've got to cleanse it first." The man with her handed her cleansing solution. When the woman pushed Maxine's hair back, she blinked. "That's strange."

"What?" both Jennie and Sam asked at the same time.

"I'd swear it looks better already. Like it's healing unnaturally fast."

Jennie smiled. "See, told you it's not that bad."

Jennie closed her eyes. Sam winced as he watched them do their ministrations on her head, which was why Jennie decided she couldn't keep her eyes open. Her fingers dug into the fabric of the sofa as the cleanser stung.

She focused her thoughts on her old life. She could tell Sam the truth, but would he believe her? He already seemed to think she was wacky, and her actions thus far hadn't done much to dispel that. Sam wasn't into the stuff that defied reason, like ghosts and UFO's. If she told him she was Jennie's soul come back in another body, she might lose him forever. That thought made her fingers curl over the arms of the sofa. She felt Sam's hand cover hers.

"It'll be over soon."

Jennie smiled. She couldn't risk losing Sam, not now. Even if he did believe her, he'd probably still look at her as the old Jennie anyway. Just because she looked different didn't mean his feelings would change. Besides, the old Jennie was dull. She had no life, no excitement. No, it was time to let Jennie die. As Maxine, she would be exciting, sexy, everything Sam wanted in a woman. They would start fresh, the two of them. She would make Sam fall in love with her this time, and nothing would get in the way of that.

"You're all set," the woman's voice said.

"You bet I am." Jennie's eyes popped open. "I mean, I feel better already. Thank you."

The paramedic shone the flashlight in her eyes again, and Jennie willed her pupils to dilate properly. "Well, you look just fine. Okay remember, any dizziness or fainting—"

"I'll go to the hospital right away," Jennie promised.

"And I would make an appointment with your doctor as soon as possible, as a precaution."

Jennie signed the release, with Sam shaking his head the whole time, and the medical team left. She was alone with Sam again. She'd been alone with Sam many times, but it felt different this time. The office was overly warm, and she pulled off her expensive London Fog coat and laid it on the couch.

"The heating and cooling system in this old building never did work right," he said, looking out at the snow flurries clinging to the window.

"Roasting in the winter, freezing in the summer."

He turned to look at her. "How did you know that?"

"I mean, I can tell. It's way too warm in here. The other part was a guess."

"Oh." He nodded slowly. "How are you feeling?"

"Okay. I'll live."

He looked so good, wearing his faded blue jeans and white cotton shirt. He'd cut the other sleeve off so they'd match, and the muscles in his arms ripples as he clenched and unclenched his fists.

"Do you remember anything more about the accident? Or why you came here?"

She shook her head, immediately regretting the action when Sam and the entire room swayed like a rolling ship. She gripped the arm of the couch again, subtly so he wouldn't notice.

"Are you all right?" he asked, noticing anyway. Of course, he would. That's what he did.

She forced a smile. "I'm fine." To prove it, she was going to walk to her desk and get the glass of water Shep had left there.

"What are you doing?" he asked when she braced the arm of the couch to get up.

"I want to stand for a minute." Oh, to feel the floor beneath her feet — the hard, flatness of it. She had left her cream pumps by the door, so her feet were bare but for stockings. Her toes wiggled. Slowly, she pushed herself upward, feeling all those wondrous muscles in her legs group for action. Lifting her arms out for balance, she straightened and stood there for a moment. Sam wouldn't understand the sheer joy at simply standing, but she could hardly hide it. This was all a precious gift beyond comprehension.

"Are you sure your balance is all right?" he asked, coming closer.

"Oh yes, I'm sure."

She eyed the water a good five feet away. She could do this. Her legs worked; it was her mind having a hard time accepting the simple motion. She took one step, then another, like a newborn learning to walk for the first time. Her legs started to wobble. Was there any way she could ask Sam to teach her to walk without sounding crazy? No, especially in light of her history of bounding the stairs three at a time. She took another step.

"I'm dizzy, that's all," she said, not lying entirely.

At each movement, the dull ache in her head thrummed louder.

Sam walked casually closer, arms at the ready. She had an errant thought about pretending to fall so he'd wrap those arms around her again but nixed it. Then her legs really gave way. She grabbed for the desk, but he got to her first. She wanted to melt against him, but he steered her back to the couch and deposited her there.

"Just as stubborn as ever," he muttered as he helped her lower herself to the couch. Kneeling in front of her, he lifted one of her legs and started running his fingers over it. Chills scurried down the length of her leg, an exquisite feeling all around. This seemed terribly forward of Sam, who was usually quite laid back and not the touchy-feely kind.

"Does this hurt?" he was saying as he pressed harder around her ankle.

"No." She watched his fingers circle her calf, thinking how erotic something so innocent could be. Even through clothing.

"How about this?"

"Nope. Er, exactly what are you doing?"

"I'm wondering if there's something wrong with your legs, and you're too damned stubborn to admit it. How about this?"

He was at her knee now, rubbing over the bony cap. A strange warmth spread through her when his fingers rubbed behind her knee.

"Maxine?"

"Mm? Oh. No, no pain there."

He went higher still, edging that warmth to more specific areas. What was going on with her body? Maxine's body? No one had ever touched her so intimately before. Tingling sensations traveled from the tips of his fingers to her most private area. She wriggled, embarrassed at feeling such a thing. Embarrassed, but intrigued, too. Mid-thigh, he glanced up at her. How could he look so entirely innocent and intent when she was going crazy inside?

"How about here?"

"No," she said, drawing out the word. "Sam?" He went higher, pressing his fingers into her thigh. The tingling increased, making her fidget even more. Yes, she wanted to get closer to him, but this was a little fast. Finally, she couldn't take it anymore. "Sam."

"What? Stop moving around. What about here?" His fingers prodded at the ridge between her upper thigh and her crotch.

She jerked so hard, that her bottom slipped off the couch, and she landed on the floor.

He put his hands on his thighs, still kneeling in front of her. "What is your problem?"

"I, well ... don't you think you're getting a little fresh?"

He rolled his eyes in that familiar way he had for all his loony clients. "Maxine, don't you think it's a bit late to be modest now?"

"What do you mean?"

"Hell, woman, we were married for five years."

Thank you for reading this sneak peek of *Woke Up Dead*. Find links to it and all of Tina's at www.WrittenMusings.com/TinaWainscott and www.TinaWainscott.com.

ABOUT THE AUTHOR

I hope you enjoyed *Stranger in the Mirror*! If you did, I'm happy to tell you that I have many other novels available for your pleasure in different subgenres of romance. I'm a *New York Times* and *USA Today* bestselling author of more than thirty novels published with St. Martin's Press, Harper Collins, Random House, Harlequin, and Written Musings.

I have always loved the combination of suspenseful chills and romantic thrills, especially with a bit of paranormal thrown in, so I decided to release my favorites in the Love & Light Collection. Although many of the stories have connections to other books in the series, all the novels are stand-alone stories — no cliffhangers!

Find the entire collection at
www.WrittenMusings.com/TinaWainscott
and www.TinaWainscott.com.

ACKNOWLEDGMENTS

Thank you to TJ for all your help with this book, and to Austin Walp for the awesome cover!

Made in the USA
Coppell, TX
09 July 2022